The Dating Game

Also by Susan Buchanan

Sign of the Times
The Christmas Spirit
Return of the Christmas Spirit
Just One Day – Winter

The Dating Game

Susan Buchanan

Copyright

First published in 2012 by Susan Buchanan

This novel is a work of fiction. Names and characters are the product of the author's imagination and any resemblance to actual persons, living or dead, is entirely coincidental

A CIP catalogue record of this title is available from the British Library
Paperback – 978-0-9931851-1-3

Dedication

For Dylan, Declan and Rhys

Lots of love

Aunt Sooz x

About the Author

Susan Buchanan lives in Scotland with her husband, their two young children and a crazy Labrador called Benji. She has been reading since the age of four and had to get an adult library card early as she had read the entire children's section by the age of ten. As a freelance book editor, she has books for breakfast, lunch and dinner and in her personal reading always has several books on the go at any one time.

If she's not reading, editing or writing, she's thinking about it. She loves romantic fiction, psychological thrillers, crime fiction and legal thrillers, but her favourite books feature books themselves.

In her past life she worked in International Sales as she speaks five languages. She has travelled to 51 countries and her travel knowledge tends to pop up in her writing. Collecting books on her travels, even in languages she doesn't speak, became a bit of a hobby.

Susan writes contemporary fiction, partly set in Scotland, usually featuring travel, food or Christmas. When not working, writing, or caring for her two delightful cherubs, Susan loves reading (obviously), the theatre, quiz shows and eating out – not necessarily in that order!

You can connect with Susan via her website www.susanbuchananauthor.com or on Facebook www.facebook.com/susan.buchanan.author and on Twitter @susan_buchanan or Instagram authorSusanBuchanan

Acknowledgements

Huge thanks to

Jaboof Design Studio for my amazing cover. This was a toughie, as I had very set ideas initially, and changed completely at the last minute – love what you came up with, Claire! – claire@jaboofdesignstudio.com

Susan Louineau, Melanie Hudson, Tracie Banister and Laura Cowan, for being fabulous beta readers. And last but not least, thanks to my Twitter family for their constant support.

Chapter One

'You are *not* setting me up with anyone ever again!' Gill said, clattering her wine glass on the table. 'It has been a disaster every time. I should have seen this one coming, too.'

'Oh come on, Gill, they've not been that bad,' said her best friend, Debbie.

'Yes, they have,' Gill said grimly. 'Let's just start with last night's fiasco, Graham, shall we?' She sighed then took a gulp of her Pinot Grigio, as if to give her strength for the tirade she was about to unleash. Lisa and Angela, completing the quartet of friends that evening, exchanged a glance. They knew they were about to get an ear-bashing.

'How did you describe Graham to me, Lisa?' When Lisa didn't reply, her answer stuck in her throat, Gill continued, smoothing a strand of her lustrous chestnut hair behind her ear.

'OK, let me remind you. You assured me I would get on well with Graham as we were almost the same age and he had no baggage. I think you said he was a workaholic like me, but also liked going to the gym, so pretty fit, in both senses of the word. Oh, and he liked reading and foreign films. Am I close?'

At silent assent from her friends, Gill went on. 'What

you didn't tell me was that he's five feet four, so three inches shorter than me, and in the heels I had on last night, make that seven, and that he has the personality of a gnat!' Drawing breath and getting back into her stride, Gill counted out on her fingers for emphasis. 'He talked about the gym all night. He didn't once ask anything about me, apart from if I had a gym membership as he looked me up and down. I now know more about pectorals, abdominals, protein shakes and the pros and cons of taking steroids than I ever thought possible.'

Gill tried to glare at her friends, but Lisa was looking at the ceiling, Angela at her shoes and Debbie had found the Guinness beer mat on the table fascinating.

'And, yes, he is divorced, but he'd only been married two minutes. What does that say about his attitude to commitment?' Not waiting for an answer, by now not expecting one either, Gill carried on. 'Then, there's his favourite book, or rather lack of. The last novel he read was *The Da Vinci Code* and before that a text prescribed for 'O' Grade English! How does that make him interested in books?'

A particularly keen reader herself, Gill couldn't fathom how anyone couldn't read a book a month at least.

'And his love of foreign films? He looked a bit of a perv, so yes, if they're Swedish and include the words, "Yes, baby, give it to me harder!"'

Debbie snorted with laughter. That set off Angela, and as Lisa started howling, tears running down her face, before long even Gill saw the funny side of it and her face visibly relaxed. Then she was laughing, protesting between gulps for air, 'It's not funny. How would you have liked it? I've barely been out for months, as you know. What a waste of a night. Here was me trying to talk to him about Aldo Giovanni and Fellini and all he knew about foreign film was Borat.' The giggles from Debbie, and the fact Angela ran to the loo at Olympic speed, attracted the attention of the vigilant barista.

'Everything all right, ladies?'

'No, I think we can quite categorically say, everything's all wrong,' Gill managed to squeak. 'But we'll be fine, thanks.'

As the barman shrugged and walked away, Lisa said, 'What about him?'

'What?' asked Gill. 'Brett?'

'Yes.'

'He's barely out of nappies.'

'No, he's not. He's about twenty-five.'

'Yes, and much as I would enjoy the stamina of a twenty-five-year-old, I would probably have as much in common with him as the workaholic, iron-pumping bore you set me up with last night. No, I think I'm much better off on my own.'

'You can't give up, you're only thirty-seven,' Debbie said.

'Yes, I can. I've had enough, really.'

'There must be another way,' agreed Lisa, as she readjusted her charm bracelet, which had snagged on the fine hairs of her arm.

'I don't think so. We did have one thing in common, Graham and me. Like me, he works a lot and didn't I get to hear about that, too. Riveting. I might be a workaholic, but at least I'm not a bore about it. Am I?' Gill searched her friends' eyes for confirmation when they didn't answer.

'No, no,' Lisa added hurriedly. 'You never talk about

your work.' The three friends dissolved into laughter again.

'I don't talk about it *all* the time,' said Gill.

'No of course you don't.' Lisa didn't even try to hide the sarcasm in her voice.

'Just ninety per cent of the time,' said Debbie.

'I'm not *that* bad,' said Gill.

'Yes, you are,' broke in Debbie, 'and that's why we need to find you a good bloke.'

'Well, that's not going to happen. Maybe I should just throw myself even more into my work.'

'Oh, that would be just great. Then you will have so much more free time,' deadpanned Lisa.

'Gill, you already work from seven in the morning until eight or nine at night, at least five days a week and you're always on your laptop at the weekend. There's got to be more to life. You're meant to work to live, not the other way round.'

'Really? Well, thank you, Miss Ross, for that illuminating insight, but I think I'll just try and find more people jobs. I'm obviously far better at that than I am at finding a partner.'

Chapter Two

Gill was fed up. Last night's conversation with the girls had left her unsettled. How come her friends ended up with guys they really loved and she didn't? Well, apart from Angela. She'd met a man, fallen in love, moved in with him, been with him seven years and had his baby. Then he moved out. He needed space. What a cliché. You would have thought he'd want to stay quite close to his ten-month-old son, but no, four hundred and sixty miles away in Brighton was close enough apparently. Naturally Angela had set the CSA on him, given that he'd only visited twice since he moved out and on one of those occasions he'd even had the audacity to ask for a loan, instead of actually paying his child's maintenance. At least she didn't have that complication in her life. Gill suppressed a shudder. Happy with most of her life, the one area which wasn't going to plan was the search for a partner to share it with.

As she sorted out a load of washing, Gill wondered where she was going wrong. Of course she was a bit of a workaholic, she knew that, but there were lots of driven individuals out there these days. She knew she wasn't alone in that. Surely she could find a like-minded workaholic like herself. They couldn't all be married already.

With a sigh, Gill tried to think back to the last date

she'd been on which had shown any promise. Not this year. Last year? Oh yes, Debbie's cousin's friend, who turned out to be married.

Colin was the last successful date she had been on, but their tastes were too different and he worked away a lot. Not just down the road either – Dubai to be precise. Good old Colin. Not the cheeky chappie she'd been led to believe, quite the opposite. *Wonder what he's doing these days. Maybe I could call him up? Nah, that's a bit sad.*

Yes, definitely sad, her relentless alter ego agreed.

Oh shut up, you!

Before Colin, there was Clive. Again that had looked hopeful. They'd gone to a Lightning Storm gig at King Tuts together, but it had all gone downhill when instead of being the sales director she'd assumed, he'd turned out to be a funeral director. He'd chosen to omit the word funeral when they first met. Ugh! The very thought made her stomach churn. But she could have got past that, maybe, but not the lying. She didn't do liars.

As Gill ironed her work trousers, she mulled over once again how best to meet men. Ironic when you thought about it. She met men every day, in her capacity as a recruitment consultant, and had fancied loads of them. But pursuing a relationship with one of them wouldn't be professional and she never mixed her personal and professional lives.

After Angela had split from her other half, she and Gill had even tried speed dating, just for a laugh. It had been a bit of fun, even if it had been a little forced. Gill preferred things to be straightforward and had felt a tad uncomfortable. By the end of the evening she'd been given two phone numbers, but hadn't called either. Was it really any worse, though, than letting your friends set you up with their colleagues, friends you didn't have in common, extended family members and well, pretty much, anything with a pulse? Probably not. But, as she'd sat there with her cards which held various pieces of information about the potential dates, it had felt all wrong. Clinical. Where was the romance? That's not to say there might not have been any, if she'd had the guts to call one of the interested parties. Anyway, it was all in the past. For now, Gill had decided she was a man-free zone. Give herself three months of steering clear of them, but not in a 'cross the road to avoid them' kind of way. No blind dates. No 'chance' encounters engineered by her friends. No making up the numbers at dinner parties. It was time to make a stand.

Gill stood waiting for the bus from Shawlands to the city centre. Her initiative from last month had been to become greener and of course, she couldn't hack the traffic over the Kingston Bridge every day. At least on the bus she could read, work or listen to her iPod, or even, as she often did, have a snooze.

Finally the familiar bendy bus pulled into the bus stop and after assisting an elderly lady in before her, good manners cost little, she boarded the bus, flashing her monthly pass at the driver.

Fortunately, she managed to find a seat. One of the many drawbacks of public transport, apart from potentially being subjected to verbal abuse, or sitting on seats the great unwashed had frequented before you, was not getting a seat. If you were lucky, you had a strap above your head to hold onto, which, thanks to the heels she was wearing, she could just about reach. That strap was the only safeguard of your survival if the driver chose to swing the bus around corners and catapult you through the window, or on top of other unwitting passengers. She also hated when the buses were jam-packed. Every sweaty male seemed to stand beside her, and nestled in some stranger's left armpit, holding her breath and wondering if she was the only one who knew what shower gel was wasn't her idea of a relaxing journey into the office.

Reaching a free seat, she barely had time to pop her black leather portfolio case onto her lap and push her umbrella between her knees to the floor below, before a grossly overweight man hefted himself into the seat next to her, firmly wedging her between him and the window. Why did it always happen to her? Could she not catch a break, just once? As she tried to exhale without touching him, he turned and smiled at her. Oh great, that was all she needed. Keeping her gaze blank, Gill studied the adverts. An advert proclaiming the arrival of Elaine C Smith in panto – again. Another for the PDSA. One for laser eye surgery. Teeth whitening. A nail bar. A common theme began to appear on these later posters. Self-improvement. *Obviously advertisers think we're just a nation of shallow creatures.* What was the next one? Happy Ever After – the dating agency for professional people. 'Short on time? High in qualifications? Half price joining fee – offer ends 30 September. Visit our website below.'

Interesting. Not that I'll be doing anything about it, but I wonder what they offer that online agencies don't? Probably just more of the same. Yet, she mentally stored the website so she could check it out later.

'Is that quarter to one already?' Gill asked her assistant, Janice.

'Seems to be. It *has* gone in quick.'

'You're not kidding. Listen, would you mind nipping over the road and getting us some lunch? My treat,' Gill added when she saw Janice look pointedly at the rain battering against the windowpanes.

'Sure, no problem. Can I borrow your brolly?'

'Yes, it's in the rack.'

Once Janice left the office, Gill typed Happy Ever After's website into her browser. Up popped a photo of a smiling man in his early fifties with twinkling eyes behind designer glasses. As the pages loaded, a very chic forty-something woman, in a red cocktail dress, diamonds adorning her fingers, earlobes and neck, joined him. Next a gorgeous guy, who Gill reckoned to be in his mid-thirties, came into view, sporting a tux and a cheeky grin, looking very debonair and akin to Daniel Craig's James Bond. Finally, a model-like girl, possibly in her twenties, in what resembled a debutante ball gown, holding a champagne flute, completed the set. The website was glossy with a sophisticated font.

After scrolling through each page in turn, Gill clicked on Contact: Caroline Morgan – co-founder, followed by the names of several executives. She was quietly impressed by the fact the founder appeared to meet every single one of her clients before passing them over to an associate for the day-to-day running. However, she choked at the cost. Eight hundred pounds joining fee! Oh, wait a minute, there had been a special offer on, hadn't there?

Gill was just about to act on impulse and ring them up, when Janice burst through the door, awkwardly juggling two lattes and paper bags brimful with muffins and baguettes. Quickly pressing the space bar, Gill activated her screensaver.

'It's torture out there. The town's mobbed.'

'Hmm,' murmured Gill, her thoughts elsewhere. She only really tuned in to Janice when she handed over her latte.

As they tucked into their sandwiches, Gill ran through in her mind what she'd read online. Happy Ever After's client base comprised almost a thousand current prospective dates, with an approximate fifty/fifty split between men and women. Their clientele were professional people too busy to find a date in the normal way. So they chose to join an elite club of potential mates. The matching service the agency provided guaranteed you would only be offered profiles of like-minded individuals. Their clients included company directors, lawyers, accountants, stockbrokers, doctors, bankers and wealthy investors, retired early and living off their investments. Some were simply too shy to find a date for themselves and required some help. After the registration fee, it cost thirty pounds a month. Well, that didn't sound too bad, but the initial joining fee, even if half price, would be hopefully enough to deter time-wasters and the wrong type of clientele. Maybe she'd give it a go. She'd keep it to herself for now. If her friends knew, they'd be all over her like a rash, at the thought of her even considering it. Gill knew they saw her as unlucky in love, the only one among them who wanted and hadn't had a serious relationship: no engagement, marriage or kids. They didn't count Barry. They regarded him as a blip.

With that thought, and after demolishing the last morsel of her lunch, Gill dabbed at the edge of her mouth with a tissue and said, 'Actually I might leave a bit earlier tonight. Miss the traffic that way. I'd get so much more done at home without interruptions.'

Janice's jaw dropped. 'You're leaving early?'

'Yes, think so, why?'

'It's just you haven't left early since dinosaurs last roamed the Earth.'

'Very funny. I just feel like being spontaneous for a change. My last appointment's at three. You OK to lock up later?'

'Sure.'

'Right, well, I best go and prepare for my one thirty then,' said Gill, picking up the candidate's CV and her latte as she crossed to meeting room one.

In reality, she wanted time to herself to figure out what should go in her dating profile. Even though she didn't know what would be expected of her, she began composing a physical description of herself in her head, then her likes and dislikes and most importantly, what she was looking for. What was she looking for? Friendship and perhaps something more? Someone to have a kiss and a cuddle with and in time, rampant sex? A deep and meaningful relationship?

The wall clock read ten past one. Before she could change her mind, Gill dialled the number she'd memorised from Happy Ever After's website. It rang six times and then the answering machine kicked in, informing her they were at lunch, but advising that if she would like to leave her details and a message, her call would be returned as soon as possible. After a moment's hesitation, whilst she pondered the lack of professionalism in not having anyone available during lunchtime, Gill stammered out a short, not terribly eloquent message and left her mobile number. She couldn't get off the phone quickly enough. She hoped she'd done the right thing. Oh well, it was too late now. She picked up the next candidate's CV, glancing briefly at her watch as she did so. Fifteen minutes. If he wasn't prompt, he could forget being put forward for interview. Punctuality was key in Gill's world, and there was no place in the current job market for tardiness.

'That's your candidate here,' Janice's voice burst into her thoughts.

'Thanks, Janice. Send him in, please.'

Thank goodness the day was over and the weather had cleared up. Now that Gill had made up her mind, she was determined to pay a visit to Happy Ever After's offices in Park Circus, which fortunately was within walking distance from the office. Thinking she may as well get some exercise, too, she set off at a brisk pace on the twenty-minute walk.

Smoothing down her chestnut curls with some fixing product and checking her reflection in the wing mirror of a handily positioned transit van, to satisfy herself she had nothing stuck between her teeth, Gill decided she was ready. Looking left and right, to ensure no one she knew was passing, Gill sped up the stairs of the Georgian townhouse which housed Happy Ever After dating agency.

She recognised the foyer from the website, all Italian cream marble. It would have appeared clinical if not for the array of potted plant, and strategically placed vases of flowers dotted around. Behind a balsa wood desk sat a perky, pretty receptionist.

'Good afternoon. Welcome to Happy Ever After, how can I help you?' The girl smiled at Gill.

'Hi, Millie,' said Gill, reading the receptionist's name badge on her jacket. 'I was hoping to see a consultant.'

'Do you have an appointment?'

'No, although I did leave a voicemail at lunchtime.'

'Oh, you must be Gill McFadden. I passed your message to Caroline Morgan, the director. She'll have you on her callback list, if she hasn't rung you already.'

'No, she hasn't,' said Gill, pulling her phone out of her bag. Missed call, one new message. As Gill listened to her message, she nodded at the girl, smiling. Ending the call, she said, 'That was Miss Morgan, asking me to contact her at my earliest convenience. I suppose that would be now.' Gill decided to push her luck.

'We-ll, we close at five thirty and a consultation does generally last between an hour and ninety minutes, but let me check,' the receptionist said, her nails tapping away on her Mac.

'She doesn't seem to have any appointments at the moment. Let me check if she can see you.' She disappeared through a door to her left.

Gill breathed a sigh of relief. It had taken a lot of guts to drag herself here. Now she was through the door, she just wanted to get it over with. She was dying to go to the toilet, but she didn't dare leave the reception area, in case this Miss Morgan did a runner. No doubt she wanted to miss the traffic, too.

The receptionist returned moments later. 'Miss Morgan can see you now.' She held the door open and invited Gill to precede her into a corridor with a thick burgundy pile carpet.

'It's the door at the end,' she added, when Gill looked at her, uncertain.

'On you go, she won't bite.' Gill wasn't so sure of that. The girl smiled at her reassuringly. Swallowing down her discomfort, and thrusting her shoulders back, she headed towards the door which read *Director*. Taking a few deep breaths for courage, she rapped firmly.

'Come in,' a voice called from inside.

No going back now. Turning the handle slowly, she opened the door, which gave into a bright and airy room, at the centre of which sat an enormous walnut desk. Seated behind the desk was a woman Gill bet hadn't needed to resort to a dating agency. Caroline looked as if she were of Swedish descent. Even sitting down, you could tell she wasn't much short of six feet tall and she glowed with health. Probably didn't even go to the gym, preferring outdoor activities: kayaking, mountain climbing, or extreme sports were the first three options that came into Gill's head. The vision rose from her chair to greet her. 'Caroline Morgan, nice to meet you.' She offered Gill a warm smile. Her accent did indeed have a trace of Nordic about it, even if her surname didn't.

Gill was aware that she was staring, not really sure what to do. She rarely became tongue-tied, but today proved an exception. Mumbling, she extended her hand until it met with Caroline Morgan's own. She couldn't help noticing the huge solitaire which adorned her left hand. She wasn't single then, either that, or it was for effect. If so, it worked.

Caroline gestured for her to take a seat and Gill sank into the leather swivel chair opposite her desk. Somehow she had imagined it would be all open-plan design, with squashy sofas.

'Thanks for dropping by. It was lucky I could see you. Some people lose their nerve if they have to come back.' Caroline smiled, her mouth upturning at the corners.

Gill stifled a laugh. *No kidding!*

'I thought I would start off by telling you a little bit about the agency, our history and why we are so good at what we do. Then I'd like to find out as much about you as possible, what you like, what you want from life, what you've done so far, that sort of thing. How does that sound?'

It sounded to Gill much as she did when she interviewed candidates, albeit she was asking them different questions.

'That sounds fine,' Gill managed.

Caroline then began to tell her about their services. 'We like to think we're a friendly agency. We realise how difficult it can be to meet someone nowadays, with similar tastes who hasn't already been snapped up. But, it can happen, and we can help.'

Caroline ran through what Gill could expect for her monthly membership fee and how many introductions she could expect. The average was between twenty to thirty-five per year. Gill was exhausted just listening to her.

'Now, I'd like to build up a profile of you, so just relax and try to be as honest as possible.' Caroline glanced at a sheet of paper in front of her and said, 'Are you sporty?'

After a momentary hesitation, Gill replied, 'Well, I'm a member at Pritchards Health Club.'

'So, you like going to the gym,' Caroline stated. 'Do you do cardio and weights, or do you do classes?'

Given that it had been three years since Gill last graced the gym with her presence, apart from the odd occasion when she went for a swim and a sauna with the girls at the weekend, Gill struggled with this. 'Classes. Body Pump.' She lowered her gaze, hoping Caroline didn't scrutinise her too closely. Anyone who looked at her would know that with her bingo wings, there was no way she went to Body Pump regularly. It was true that she had gone once, but it had almost killed her and she could barely get off the couch for two days. The only time she had been off sick in five years.

'Excellent,' Caroline said, making note. 'Anything else?'

The way she said it made Gill feel that one activity was too little, so fumbling around for something recent she had heard of, she offered up, 'Zumba. I love Zumba.'

'Wonderful.'

Well, Gill did love Zumba, or rather the idea of it. She had gone as far as signing up for a class once, but had had to work late that night and life had got in the way ever since.

'Musical interests?'

Clutching at straws, Gill blurted out, 'Well, I did play the recorder, but it was a long time ago.'

'No, no, no, I meant types of music you like to listen to, not instruments you play.'

Gill wasn't sure if Caroline was trying to hide a smirk about her recorder comment. Gill knew very little about modern music, and hadn't listened to the charts in years. The presenters on local and national popular radio stations annoyed her so much she preferred to listen to her own playlist on her iPod.

'Well, my tastes are pretty eclectic. I like most things, apart from house, hip hop and thrash metal.'

Caroline seemed content with her answer and moved on to the next point. Likes and dislikes in food. Did she watch TV? What kind of programmes? Did she go to the cinema? She did, but she reckoned the last time had been for a Harry Potter film. When had that been released? She loved the flicks, but rarely had the time to go. The problem, as ever, was her job. Being a recruitment consultant was terribly hard work, with exceptionally long hours, and the industry was very cut-throat and often unrewarding, but when she placed the right candidate with the right employer, she felt a warm glow, as if all was finally right with the world. The phone calls to express gratitude and the occasional bottle of wine from a well-placed candidate or client made it all worthwhile. She particularly loved when she placed someone who had been out of work for a while. The recession, which seemed to be stretching on and on with no respite in sight, put previously considered excellent candidates into the category of 'one of many'. The shock they felt when they realised they weren't as employable as before and more than likely would have to settle for a much lesser salary was almost palpable.

Gill snapped back to the present to find Caroline studying her. 'Are you all right?'

Damn, she'd been daydreaming again. Gill assured Caroline she was fine and they rattled through the rest of her likes and dislikes until Caroline had compiled a complete profile.

'Now, I also need a photo for your profile,' Caroline said easily.

Excellent. She hated having her picture taken, but of course, the agency needed a pic of her. She knew she couldn't decide now, and she seriously hoped Caroline wasn't about to suggest she take her mugshot there and then, as although she looked well-groomed and professional, unless she tossed her hair around, stood in front of a fan and unbuttoned a couple of buttons on her blouse, she wasn't going to ooze sex appeal.

'Can I e-mail that to you?' Gill asked hopefully.

'Of course. Last thing I need you to do is sign these

forms.' Caroline pushed a contract and a direct debit instruction across the desk to her, offering her a Mont Blanc pen to sign with. *Crikey, business must be good. Those pens cost a bomb.* She signed her name, with a mixture of dread and excitement.

'So by Thursday at the latest, I will have compiled your profile. I'll e-mail it across and if you're happy with it, we can proceed. Any changes you wish to make, let me know and we'll take care of it immediately. Once we receive your photo, we'll set about arranging your first introduction. How does that sound?'

Exciting. Handing over her credit card to Caroline so she could process the exorbitant joining fee, even with the fifty per cent off, Gill couldn't help but hope it would all be worth it.

As Caroline ushered her out of her office, reminding her to send the photo as soon as possible, Gill was already panicking over which photo to choose.

Chapter Three

Not used to leaving the office early, Gill had a lot of work to catch up on. Kicking off her heels, she switched on the kettle, opened the freezer and took out a low-calorie ready meal. She popped it in the microwave and turned it to full power, then methodically checked through her e-mails on her phone. Moving into the living room, she tidied up a little as she crossed to her laptop, which was resting on the low coffee table near the chocolate leather sofa she favoured. She barely used the sofa nearest the kitchen. She lived alone after all. Reaching down, she switched on her laptop at the mains, powered it up and watched it spring into life. It was all very well reading e-mails on a smartphone, but she wasn't getting any younger and her eyes often grew tired.

Gill walked through to the bathroom, located her contact lens solution and took out her lenses. She hated wearing them, but apart from constantly donning her glasses, the alternative was laser eye surgery. Although she knew others who had happily had it done, she just wasn't brave enough. Her brother's best friend, Adam, had changed from the typical boy next door to an insanely gorgeous guy after laser eye surgery. It was amazing how different he looked without glasses. And Adam had always had a crush on her. Gill had always liked him, even if not in a romantic sense. Boy had that changed. Pity that his new, sexier self also drew lots of attention from other women. Gill wasn't even on his radar any more.

Gill checked through her work e-mail, pulling up CVs for the candidates she would be meeting next day. A few new applications had come in for a high-profile role she was handling. The employer, a household name in the oil and gas industry, and one of her biggest clients, was being really finicky, constantly changing their mind about what they wanted. After saying they would consider candidates from outside the industry, they had summarily dismissed three of the four submissions Gill had sent them two weeks ago and hadn't returned any of her phone calls or e-mails since. She knew they were busy, but sometimes Gill wondered where these people got off. It was so unprofessional.

Although Gill herself didn't always have time to reply to every applicant, telling them they had been unsuccessful, or they weren't being considered, she did try her best, as she really felt for them. When possible, she advised when they had people with experience more closely matching the client's brief than theirs, but in these straitened times, she had more applicants than she knew what to do with. It took her all her time to view their CVs, or trawl through those which arrived via the various job sites, in response to their ads. And that was her working pretty much round the clock. She needed to think seriously about taking on someone else. The agency was doing well, but she could bring more business on board if she had more staff. Maybe she would get some of her life back, too. It had been embarrassing today, realising that she didn't really have any hobbies, as she had no time for them. Something had to change.

Chapter Four

As Gill lay in bed, she had difficulty dropping off. Should she tell the girls what she was doing? She couldn't decide. Debbie would be appalled. Lisa would say well done, and Angela? Well, Angela would probably demur and see how things panned out. She rarely judged. That was one of the things Gill loved about her friend.

Angela was a gentle soul really, so Gill found it difficult to understand how she could teach at St Swithun's. Unlike the grand and posh-sounding saint's name, the school was anything but. It was only one step down from the problem inner city schools in the US. The incongruity and irony of a school named St Swithun's in the east end of Glasgow wasn't lost on any of them.

Giving herself a mental shake, her thoughts returned to the dating agency. For now, she decided to keep it to herself, just until she received a few profiles and figured out how things were going to go. If she went on a date, then of course, she would have to let at least Debbie know. She didn't want to meet some potential nutter without letting anyone in on where she was going.

Gill found herself thinking about her failed relationships. She may as well start at the beginning. Barry. Everything before that was just messing around. But Barry she had loved – a lot as it turned out. *It's true what they say – you don't know what you have until it's gone.* They met at Strathclyde University on their first day of second year. Barry had previously studied metallurgy at Glasgow uni, but hated it, so had changed course and university in his second year. He decided electrical engineering was more him and they had both found common ground, since Gill was also studying engineering. They had chosen most of the same course modules, were in mostly the same tutorials and lectures and quickly became inseparable. It came as no surprise to any of their friends when Barry proposed on the day they sat their last finals' exam. Gill, in the heat of the moment, accepted. She wasn't sure now, if it had been with joy and relief at the exams finally being over, or if she genuinely had been happy at him asking her to marry him. She loved him, of that she was quite certain, but marriage? The big wedding followed less than a year later, with the prerequisite amount of lace and tulle, not Gill's thing at all and the last time she had had formal pictures taken.

Within a year the marriage was in tatters. They should have tried living together first. Even though they both worked hard and were very successful, Gill discovered that living with Barry was not quite the same as being with him. He was lazy, he never cooked, he wanted to order in all the time. He was more selfish than she had realised. It always had to be what he wanted to watch on TV; invariably sport. They didn't go out as much. The house had cost them too much and then the housing market dipped and they found themselves in negative equity, which only led to more arguments and ill feeling between them. They were both to blame. Gill sighed. They hadn't appreciated each other's good points enough and the bottom line was they had been too young. A year later, they were divorced. Thank goodness they hadn't had any kids. At least that was one less thing to sort out.

She still thought of Barry fondly sometimes. He lived in Brisbane now, had accepted a contract position not long after their divorce. She'd found out through a mutual acquaintance that he had married again and was father to four kids. Four! She didn't even have one. It wasn't a subject to which she'd really given much thought; difficult to think about having kids when she didn't have a partner. But who knew, maybe she would want them one day.

Of course there had been other guys after Barry, but nothing serious. Then there was Euan. They had met at a friend's birthday do. It was his smile which had captivated her. He was handsome, but nice, not like some guys who know they are gorgeous and play on it. He was a perfect gentleman. In fact she had been the one to coax him into bed. She wanted him and she wanted him to want her. Finally she had found her soulmate. They were great friends, shared so many likes and dislikes. They went for romantic weekend breaks in the country, avoided the party scene and instead toured the fine-dining circuit, both being avid foodies. They visited farmers' markets and went to food festivals. Euan was a pretty good cook, but then as a chef, he was bound to be.

Eventually after three years, they moved into a rented flat together. After what had happened with Barry, Gill hadn't wanted to move too quickly, or make such a large commitment, without a trial period first. It had proven to be an intelligent decision. Although they got on famously, shared the chores and rarely argued, Gill sensed a change in Euan not long after they started living together. An evasiveness, a restlessness. They stopped making love as frequently. His phone often went to voicemail when she called. She had just decided she needed to broach the problems in their relationship with him, when he came home earlier than usual from work one night. He looked shattered. He asked her to sit down and even though she knew what was coming next, she made him say the words. Why should she make it any easier for him? Her life was falling apart. She wasn't about to let him off the hook so easily.

He'd slept with someone at his friend's stag party two months previously. It wasn't anyone she knew, but they had seen each other a few times since. He wanted to see where it would go. He told Gill that she had to admit that the passion in their relationship had fizzled out long ago. Whose fault was that? she'd wondered. Although she was devastated, she forced herself not to cry. He said he would move out and give her a couple of months' rent to tide her over, until she could either get someone to share, or find somewhere else to live. She wouldn't give him the satisfaction of seeing how much he had hurt her. Once he had gone, she curled herself into a ball and howled until she cried herself to sleep.

Finally, there had been Timothy. Not Tim, but Timothy. He was so charming. She had been visiting friends in Poole and they had taken her to the yacht club. Most of the sailing crowd was very friendly, but Timothy was truly charming, without being effusive. He introduced his friends to her and asked them to relate anecdotes of their sailing exploits. To someone as uninitiated to the sailing scene as Gill, it sounded fun and glamorous. She'd ended up extending her stay by four days to spend more time with him. Her friends hadn't minded that in those extra days, she had spent more time with Timothy than them. They were delighted to see her so happy. Twice a month, either Gill or Timothy would make the journey by low-cost airline or train from the south coast to Glasgow or vice versa. Gill enjoyed the personal space she had, not living with Timothy, and they made the most of their time together.

Then Gill had to cancel one of their weekends. She had to work and there was no getting around it.

'But I've bought my ticket,' Timothy told her, 'and I want to see you.' Privately Gill thought those statements should have been made the other way around.

'I'm really sorry, but I can't get out of it,' said Gill, upset. But if Timothy had noticed her tone, he paid it no heed. He practically snarled at her that he would make other arrangements for the weekend then, and hung up.

He hadn't called her for two days. Two days when Gill had cried until she made herself ill and managed to do little at work, she was so distraught. Finally he rang, apologising, saying he was a fool and wanted to make it up to her. Could he come up the weekend after next? Happily she agreed and things reverted to normal.

One evening they were out for dinner in Glasgow and decided to go to a bar in Bath Street afterwards. It was jam-packed, eight deep to the bar. Timothy had gone to the toilet.

'Hello. What are you doing here all on your own?'

Gill initially didn't turn around, not realising the person was addressing her, until the voice called, 'Gill McFadden, are you ignoring me?'

Swivelling around on her stool, which she had scrambled to nab as soon as the previous occupant's derrière had vacated it, Gill found herself face to face with Toby Lewsley.

'Toby! My God, is that really you? I haven't seen you for years.'

'That's right. Fifteen to be exact.'

'Are we really that old?'

'Afraid so, but you look amazing.'

Never one to take compliments well, Gill blushed and said, 'Thanks,' as Toby grinned at her. It was the last grin she saw on his face, as a fist crashed into it and sent him sprawling to the end of the bar. Horrified, Gill turned to see who had attacked her old friend, only for her jaw to drop, as Timothy rubbed the knuckles of his right hand.

'Leave my girlfriend alone,' he spat at a terrified Toby. Timothy was a good six feet two, broad and muscular, to Toby's five feet seven slim frame. Toby didn't meet Gill's eye as he moved away from them, whilst Timothy grabbed her coat and said, 'We're leaving.'

Shell-shocked, Gill didn't know what to do. She wanted to check Toby was all right. A barman was already handing him some ice to put on his jaw. But she sensed it might work out worse for Toby if she tried to apologise for Timothy's behaviour. What the hell just happened? Timothy had never shown himself to be jealous or violent before. Timothy's actions were downright unspeakable. She was outraged, confused and more than a little scared. What could she do, though? Either she had a showdown, refused to get in a taxi with him, or they went back to her flat and she didn't mention it until the next day when they would both be sober. She chose the latter option and numbly followed him out of the bar. Once in the taxi, Timothy was sweetness itself, acting as if nothing had happened.

Gill wasn't sure how she got through the rest of the weekend, but she did. She could have won an Oscar for her performance. She knew what she had to do. After waving him off at the airport, she waited until she had confirmation his flight had landed and then she texted him, saying she didn't think they should see each other any more and that she had been appalled by his behaviour.

That was the start of a series of obscene, threatening calls, texts and eventually e-mails and letters. He had even turned up unexpectedly at her flat one night. Fortunately she wasn't alone. Debbie was with her, having a girly night in, eating chocolate buttons and watching animated films. Romcoms were out at that point, for obvious reasons. When they didn't answer the buzzer, which he pressed continually, Timothy started screaming at Gill from down below in the street. Unfortunately, one of the neighbours had come out to ask him what the hell was going on and Timothy had pushed past him into the stairwell, knocking him to the ground. He had bounded up the stairs two at a time and hammered on at the door, telling her to open up, he just wanted to talk. Gill was terrified, but didn't want to call the police, as she had loved him at one point. Then it became apparent he was trying to break down the door. Debbie was petrified, too, but already had her mobile out, dialling 999.

The door had partially given way and Debbie and Gill had locked themselves in Gill's bedroom, when with great relief, they heard the sirens. How they hoped they were coming to Gill's. The kicks suddenly stopped and they heard voices.

'This is the police. It's safe to come out now.'

Heart pounding, Gill helped Debbie unbarricade the bedroom door, in front of which they had dragged the chest of drawers. Then she opened the front door and came face to face with a young policeman, with his female partner. Debbie followed her and shaking, they both sat on the sofa and gave the police a statement. Gill also told them about the attack on Toby and the threatening calls and other nasty correspondence.

'Looks like we were just in time,' said the young policeman. 'You were lucky. We had an earlier call about the disturbance.'

After the police had taken all the details, Gill showed them out.

Gill was called upon in due course to give evidence in the assault on Toby and on Timothy's threatening behaviour towards her. He received a suspended sentence and the judge ordered him not to go within five hundred metres of Gill.

Some sweet dreams she was having, thought Gill. More like nightmares. She really could pick them. What was so wrong with her that she couldn't find someone who loved her and wanted to be with her and treat her well, without being jealous, or going off with someone else, as she wasn't enough for them? Exhausted by her depressing journey into her past, Gill finally drifted off to sleep.

Chapter Five

Next day, Gill was again gripped by indecision both over whether joining the dating agency was a good idea, and also if she should tell her friends or not. No matter, no time to think about it. Today was going to be a busy one. Her morning routine was one of military precision. Alarm went off at six o'clock, no snooze button for her, straight into the shower then, towelling her hair dry, she would traipse into the kitchen and open the cupboard which contained her Colombian roast coffee. If there was one thing Gill couldn't give up, it was coffee; her major, although not only, vice. But it had to be the real thing, none of that instant muck for her. Maybe she had been Italian in a past life. As she opened the packet and spooned three scoops into the cafetière, she was already running through the day's agenda in her head.

Coffee ready, she added a spoonful of sugar. OK, so she needed to lose some weight, but she was more concerned with the side effects of aspartame than whether sixteen calories in a spoonful of sugar was going to add pounds to her already slightly overweight frame.

She took a sip of her newly brewed coffee then returned to her bedroom to dress, grateful that she had sent her clothes to Full Steam Ahead to be ironed, as at least she didn't have that to deal with as well. Already keeping on top of housework proved hard enough. Her two bedroom flat in Shawlands, although roomy, was manageable, just. Turning her head upside down, Gill used her diffuser to help dry her naturally wavy hair. It was a curse having long hair in many respects, but she simply didn't suit short hair. Make-up applied in less than two minutes, she returned to her tiny kitchen and resumed her coffee.

Fetching a probiotic yoghurt from the fridge, she quickly drank it and then shoved the papers she needed for that day's meetings into her briefcase. A final glance around the room and she headed out to catch the bus.

It was another drizzly day, not uncommon in the west of Scotland. Opening up her brolly, she braced herself against the wind and rain. It was always a toss-up whether to put up an umbrella at all. Gill couldn't count the times she'd lost an umbrella to the fierce winds which swept the west coast, snapping spokes or turning the umbrella inside out.

Only three hundred metres to the bus stop, it was still far enough for Gill's trousers to be soaked by the time she reached it. At least it had a shelter. She smiled briefly at the occupants already waiting for the bus and sank into the furthest away corner of the bus shelter, trying to escape the elements. *Whose idea was it to be green?* she chided herself. *In Scotland? With weather like this?* She had a perfectly good Audi parked outside the flat. The bus was due at six fifty. Of course it turned up late, at two minutes past seven. She could already see the next bus behind it. There was nothing truer than the saying after all. Buses did all come at once. It never ceased to amaze her how buses could be late this early in the morning. There was still virtually no one around at that time. What held them up?

After twenty minutes, Gill arrived at the building she shared with a solicitor's, a dental surgery and a plastic surgeon. McFadden Technical Recruitment took up a quarter of the Victorian townhouse. She had taken out the lease a few months after her split from Timothy. The events surrounding it had made her re-evaluate her life and although she didn't yet have her work/life balance quite right, at least now she was doing something she loved and that she was good at. Plus being her own boss made a huge difference. Even if she worked long hours, it was *her* company that was benefiting and it gave her great satisfaction.

It was a standing joke with Donal Sullivan, the eldest partner of the law firm, Sullivan, Sullivan & Beattie, as to who would be the first to arrive at the office each morning. It was always either Donal or Gill. Most people arrived at a more reasonable time, usually after eight. Today the storm doors were still locked, so Gill guessed she had beaten him by a fraction. Right on cue, his Mercedes turned the corner as she put the key in the lock. She waved to him, and he raised his hand in greeting.

Gill unlocked her office and then after turning on all the lights, went through to the small kitchen area to switch on the kettle. Time for her second coffee of the day.

Gill's office was separate to the Reception area so clients didn't see her workspace, giving her complete freedom to do with it as she liked, including scrawling her thoughts across one of her two whiteboards. Instead she met with clients in one of the two well-proportioned meeting rooms.

The morning flew by, as Gill had a couple of meetings with new candidates and soon it was two o'clock.

Janice had popped in to give them tea and coffee a few times, and Gill had been grateful for the chocolate biscuits laid out on a side plate. Having missed lunch, she was starving.

When the meetings were over, Gill came and sat on the corner of Janice's desk. 'How's it been?'

'Busy but manageable.' Gill didn't doubt it. Janice could have managed an army unit, had she been asked.

'Good. I'm going across the road to see if they have any sandwiches left. Do you want anything?'

'I got you a sandwich when I was out.' Janice reached for a paper bag on the other side of her desk.

'Oh, thanks, you're an angel. What did you get?'

'Ploughman's.'

'You're a lifesaver.' Gill smiled, accepting the sandwich. 'If my three o'clock turns up early, can you tell them I'm tied up? I need some time to go through my e-mails.'

'No problem.' Janice then proceeded to run through the phone messages she had taken for Gill that morning.

With the list in her hand, Gill entered her office and closed the door. As she sat down, she took off her shoe and rubbed her foot, wishing she had broken in her new shoes properly before wearing them to work.

Clicking on her inbox, she sighed at the sheer number of e-mails sitting awaiting her attention. She clicked into her personal e-mail as she bit into her ploughman's. She scrolled down and hovered over one which read Profile, from Caroline Morgan. Opening the e-mail she read,

Dear Gill

Thanks for choosing Happy Ever After to help fulfil your relationship needs. Please find attached the pro-

file I have compiled for you. Should you wish to make any changes, please advise. On receipt of your confirmation, I will send your details to the first few candidates I have already matched you with, based on the answers you provided.

Please also find attached our list of Dos and Don'ts for Dating.

Regards
Caroline Morgan

Gill clicked on the first attachment.

Candidate Profile
Name: Gill McFadden
Age: 37
Lives: Glasgow
Occupation: Company Director
Qualifications: BEng
Height: 5' 7
Marital status: Single
Smoker: No
Interests: Socialising with friends, going to the cinema, eating out, Zumba, travelling and ice skating.
Further information: From Glasgow, I qualified as an engineer, but then moved into Recruitment Consultancy. I set up my own agency three years ago.
Looking to meet: Someone in their late thirties to late forties, who is open, honest, fun to be with and who can be relied upon. It would be good to meet someone who is open to trying new activities.

Gill read and reread it. Apart from the ice skating – where on earth had she dreamed that up? She hadn't been to an ice rink since she was in her late teens – the rest of the profile looked OK. Decisively, she pressed reply and told Caroline that the profile was fine and she could go ahead.

Sitting back on her swivel chair, she exhaled noisily, blew her hair out of her eyes and cast a glance across her desk, taking in the mountains of work amassed there. She needed some free time. This dating agency had been a good idea. She was sure of it. Feeling lighter, she picked up her mobile and texted Debbie. *What you up to tonight?*

She ate her ploughman's greedily as she waited for Debbie to reply. If her friend didn't reply within five minutes, it meant she was probably elbow deep in cow or de-worming a dog. Debbie had her own veterinary practice about ten miles outside the city, in the countryside.

When no immediate reply arrived, Gill turned her attention to the headings of the many e-mails cluttering up her inbox, trying to work out which were the most urgent.

Gill had published two ads on the local job-site search engines a few days ago and so far she had received two hundred and seventy-four applications. She had only had time to read through fifty of them.

Gill chose to leave the CVs until later, clicking instead on an e-mail from the sales director at a national heating company she recruited for. Jotting down on her notepad to call the candidates tomorrow morning regarding potential interview dates, she moved on.

Bryan Oliver, she hadn't heard of, but the subject, terms & conditions, made her think he could well be a new potential client and her assumption proved correct. Quickly she brought up his company's website and ascertained that they were in the aerospace industry. Glancing at her watch, she saw she didn't have enough time to go into detail with him before her three o'clock. She'd call him afterwards. A small company could never have enough new business. And on that note, she made another reminder to herself to investigate hiring another recruitment consultant.

She managed to answer a couple more e-mails before Janice buzzed her to tell her that her candidate had arrived.

The interview had gone well. She had spent the rest of the afternoon tackling some of her massive to-do list. It was with relief that Gill looked at her watch to find it was six o'clock. Time to go and meet Debbie.

'Hi, how are you?' Gill leant forward and kissed her friend on the cheek as she rose to meet her.

'Good thanks. Sorry I was so late in replying, but…'

'I know,' interrupted Gill, laughing, 'you had your hand up a cow's arse.'

'You'd be amazed how much less disgusting that is than some of the things I do.' Debbie smiled. 'Anyway, you'll be glad to know I've showered. Assisting at a calf's birth can be messy.'

'I bet you the cow thought that, too. Do you sedate them?'

'No. Natural birth for them generally. Animals are not wimps like us humans.'

'This from the woman who only had gas and air at Olivia's birth.'

'Well, I thought I would practise what I preach, although I have to admit later I really wished I'd gone for the epidural, but by then it was too late to change my mind. She was on the verge of popping out.'

Suppressing a shudder, Gill asked her friend what she

wanted to drink and attracted the barman's attention.

'Hi, can we have a large glass of Pinot Grigio and a vodka and coke, please?'

'Sure.' The barman smiled at her, leaving them to their conversation.

'Gill, do you honestly not notice the way people look at you? Sorry, the way men look at you?'

'What are you talking about?'

'Er, the admiring glance that barman gave you, or perhaps the sidelong glances he was giving you before he came over, and–' Debbie gestured towards the bar '–is still giving you.'

'You're imagining things,' Gill said dismissively.

Just then the barman returned with their drinks, his shy glance sweeping over Gill as he placed their drinks on the table. Gill blushed as he smiled at her.

'I told you,' said Debbie after he retreated behind the bar. 'He's surprised to see you twice in one week, since you haven't been here with us more than once a month recently.'

'He's just being nice,' Gill insisted. 'Anyway, he's not my type, too slim.'

'What, you want a big fatty do you?'

'No, but I mean he's not broad enough.'

'Gill, you don't have a type. You're just too picky.'

'Well, excuse me for having standards,' Gill retorted, marginally offended.

'Oh, don't go in a huff, you know what I mean.'

Not one to stay annoyed with Debbie for long, Gill said, 'I've got something to tell you.'

'Well, I know you can't be pregnant,' Debbie joked.

Gill looked at her sternly.

'Sorry…'

'I've joined a professional dating agency.'

Debbie's vodka and Coke sprayed out of her mouth and all over the sofa they were sitting on.

'You've what?' Debbie shrieked, then slunk down low in her seat, realising she had shouted out loud.

Keen not to draw any further attention to them, Gill whispered, 'You heard.'

'A dating agency? Really? No point asking why, of course, but, really?'

'Yep. I saw an ad on a bus.'

Debbie gawped at her friend as if she were deranged and had just admitted to joining a satanic cult. 'Oh, that's OK then. If it was advertised on a bus, it must be a reputable company,' she said in despair.

'Oh, c'mon,' Gill said impatiently. 'Of course, I checked it out.' Actually, all she had done was read the credentials and testimonials on their website, but on reflection she had seen something about them belonging to an association, like ABTA. No, ABIA. She gathered it must be similar to the ABTA scheme for the travel industry, but for dating agencies. She made a mental note to check it out and see exactly what it covered.

'Well, if they set you up with any dates, we're coming, too,' Debbie said firmly.

'What?' said Gill.

'You're not going on your own.' Debbie was emphatic.

'Oh right, I'll really be able to relax with you sitting at the next table,' Gill said sarcastically.

'Better than ending up chopped up into small pieces and left to be devoured by wolves in a wood. Seriously, Gill, if you're going on a date with someone we don't know, at least one of us has to be close by. Maybe next door?'

Gill mulled this over, saw the sense of it and said grudgingly, 'OK. But under no circumstances are you to come into the bar we're in. I'm not good at pretence, as you know.'

Debbie did know. Gill was a terrible liar.

'So, have you had any suitors yet?' Debbie asked.

This time it was Gill who almost spat out her drink. 'Suitors? What is this, the nineteenth century? It's not that long since I last had a date. I realise you're insisting on chaperoning me, but really, suitors? Next you'll be talking about him having to wait in the parlour for me when he comes to pick me up. And before you say it, no, he won't be coming to pick me up, just a turn of phrase. Of course we'll be meeting in a neutral environment.' Gill had been reading Happy Ever After's Dos and Don'ts.

Dos & Don'ts of Dating

DOs

Meet in a neutral place. Under no circumstances invite your date to pick you up from your home

Wear smart, but casual clothing

Be positive and friendly

Listen to your date and allow them the opportunity to talk

Exchange e-mail addresses or phone numbers if you want to see them again

Be honest – if you want to see them again, say so. If not, thank them for a nice time and say it was nice to meet them.

DON'TS

Accept a lift from your date until you know them well enough

Complain all the time

Talk about past relationships, apart from fleetingly

Insist – if they want to call you, or get in touch, they will

Give out your home or work address

'OK. So have you had any potential dates yet? Is your removal from the shelf imminent?' Debbie asked.

'Not yet,' Gill said. 'It's too early. I only confirmed my profile today. But the woman did say she had a few men in mind for me already, so maybe I'll hear something soon.'

'Well, I suppose as long as we're there to watch your back, I can't complain,' Debbie said.

'We?'

'You don't think I'm coming by myself, do you? Sitting around in a bar like a right saddo. The girls will need to come.'

'But I haven't told them yet,' wailed Gill, 'and I really wasn't intending to until I absolutely have to.'

'I think *absolutely have to* comes when you arrange your first date,' Debbie pointed out.

She left it at that and they had one more drink before Gill said she really had to go, as she had a lot to prepare for the next day.

'So, how exactly are you going to fit seeing someone into your hectic schedule anyway?' Debbie asked.

'I'm not seeing someone. That requires a lot more time and energy than a few simple dates.'

'Does it?' Debbie wasn't so sure. 'Once you're comfortable with someone, you don't have to go to the same lengths to prepare for going out with them.'

Gill admitted this was probably true. 'Anyway, I have it in hand. I'm going to recruit someone else for the agency.'

'You're going to hire someone so you have time for a relationship?'

'Well, not exactly, but without hiring someone else, I'll never have a social life, let's be honest. I've always too much on and Janice does her best, far more than a receptionist should do, but she's inundated, too.'

'Good on you. It's not before time. So, have you done anything about recruiting yet?

'Not yet, but I'm going home to write the ad tonight and then Janice can upload it to the site tomorrow. If I get as many applicants for our role as I have for these technical roles I've been advertising for recently, I'll be more than happy.'

'Good luck,' said Debbie as she left Gill at the bus stop. 'See you soon and text me when you get a profile. Promise?'

'I promise.' She hugged her friend and stepped into the bus shelter.

Chapter Six

Next morning, Gill arrived at the office even earlier than usual. She wanted to finish preparing the advert for the recruitment consultant. Although she had sketched the basics the night before, she hadn't quite perfected it.

Senior Recruitment Consultant
£25-£35K DOE + bonus

The company – McFadden Technical Recruitment is a small, but well-established recruitment agency based in Glasgow, addressing the requirements of a varied client base across Scotland and the UK. The company was founded in 2009 and is going through a period of accelerated growth, as we build our client base and continue to satisfy our clients' demands. We concentrate principally on Engineering and Sales & Marketing and have many clients in the Oil & Gas, HVAC, Environmental, Manufacturing and Industrial sectors.

The ideal candidate should have previously worked as a Senior Recruitment Consultant (SRC) and/or have specific experience in dealing with Technical/Oil & Gas clients. Your remit will include creating and delivering a business plan to ensure you build and maintain excellent business relationships on your own merits.

The rewards for the right candidate could be great and the possibility to make your mark and help influence the shaping of the agency's future is also within reach.

To apply, please send your CV and covering letter in the first instance to
admin@mcfaddentechrec.co.uk

Gill made a few minor adjustments and then turned her attention back to her e-mails. She would be out of the office most of the day, as she had meetings with clients in Clarkston and down in Ayrshire. Although most of her business came from the immediate Glasgow area, this was starting to change, due to word of mouth recommendations. She was pleased to see that she had already received a reply from Bryan Oliver. She had called him back after her final meeting yesterday, to discuss the agency's services and to go through the terms and conditions with him. He wanted to arrange a meeting as soon as possible to discuss filling three positions. This was excellent news. At £2,500 per client placing, that would be nice revenue, if she could get it. Checking her online diary, she saw that she had a space the following Tuesday, so quickly e-mailed him back to see if that would be convenient.

Not long after Janice arrived and they had talked through the schedule for the day, Gill left the office to head over to her first client meeting, which was at quarter past ten. She'd decided to ditch her attempt to go green by taking the bus. It simply wasn't possible with client meetings here, there, and everywhere.

The traffic had eased a little as the morning rush hour had passed, but there was still a steady flow of cars and Gill seemed to get stopped at every traffic light.

Typical. Taking advantage of being stationary at a junction where she knew the lights took an age to change, she checked her phone. There was an e-mail from Caroline Morgan entitled Profiles. Excited, she clicked and read Caroline's message,

Dear Gill. Here are the first three profiles. Let me know if you are interested in meeting any of them and I will contact them on your behalf. Regards, Caroline.

Gill tried to click into the first profile, but just then the lights turned green, and cursing under her breath, she eased the car into first gear. By the time she pulled into the client's car park, she had ten minutes to spare before her meeting. She took the chance to open the profiles. She could make out the photos, but the text was too small to read. Number one looked promising, though; broad-shouldered, sandy blond hair. Number two seemed old, really old. What age had she said was her upper limit? Late forties? This guy could easily be in his early sixties. Number three: she wasn't sure about number three. She'd have to blow up his photo when she could access her laptop, and of course, she'd need to read his profile.

Glancing at her watch, Gill saw she only had a few more minutes and she was a stickler for punctuality, so she rapidly tapped out a text to Debbie. *Three profiles received. Call later.*

The meeting overran. Gill knew today was going to be busy. With no time to check her messages, she jumped in the car and drove down to Mauchline in Ayrshire, to meet her next client. She was going to be late. Blasted average speed cameras.

A smiling Gill emerged two and a half hours later, starving but satisfied. Her appointment had gone even better than expected. The company manufactured chemicals for use in personal care products, such as shampoo, shower gel and hand wash. They had grown their business thirty per cent last year, amazing in these tough times, but she supposed their line of work was fairly recession-proof.

Beauty salons and hairdressers actually seemed to make more money during tough times, as people wanted to at least look good, when everything else was crumbling around them. Now her client hoped to expand by opening a plant in North Berwick on the east coast and intended to recruit staff both for the new plant and also for the existing one, as some of the key workers in the Ayrshire division would be relocated to North Berwick, so their expertise could be utilised.

Business couldn't be better. Gill was grateful for this, as she knew not every agency was in such an enviable position. It was very much a dog-eat-dog industry, but she truly believed you got what you put in. Gill was always decent towards people, and likewise clients and candidates tended to treat her with respect. To many agencies you were just a number. Even with the enormous number of applicants, she tried her best not to let that be the case with her agency. Algaeonics intended to hire another fifteen people initially. With the new Algaeonics contract won, Gill found herself hoping she received some replies to her SRC ad soon.

She stopped at a supermarket in Kilmarnock to grab a

sandwich and a cup of tea in the café, where she scrolled through her texts and e-mails. Seeing the number of unread e-mails, she wondered how she was going to get through them and prayed for divine intervention. She pressing speed dial for the office, quickly connecting with Janice, who ran through what had been happening. After advising Janice that she would be back in just over an hour, Gill hung up and resumed drinking her tea, shutting out the cacophony that was a crowded supermarket café. At least the schools had gone back now, as during the holidays she didn't dare enter supermarkets during the day. Gill loved kids and doted on her brother's two. Harry was four and George had just turned six and didn't he want to tell you all about it. Actually, he wanted to tell you about everything, just like his dad as a child. It was other people's kids, particularly in supermarkets, who drove Gill mad. She tried to ignore their tantrums or when they threw themselves on the floor, refusing to get back up. If they looked between two and three, Gill gave the parents some leeway. After all, even she had heard of the terrible twos. Although her brother, Christopher, did seem to have got off lightly in that regard with his pair, who were angels – well, most of the time. But if they were older than that, Gill often wanted to strangle the parents. She knew it must be hard being a parent, Debbie had told her often enough what a trial it could be, but there were limits to what she felt the general public should be subjected to, and shrieking which would shatter glass was well beyond that limit.

After returning her empty tray to a vacant spot on the catering trolley, Gill dialled Debbie, who answered on the second ring.

'Hi, it's me.'

'I know. I can see your number.'

'Right, anyway, did you get my text?'

'Yes, very exciting. So what do you think?'

'Well, I haven't been able to read any profiles yet, as I've only seen them on my phone, and you know how blind I am.'

Debbie knew. Gill was known for being clumsy, always falling over things and also for losing her contact lenses on nights out. She was as blind as a bat without her glasses or lenses in.

'Oh, right,' said Debbie. 'So, where are you?'

Gill explained to her friend about her morning and how the meetings had gone. 'I'm heading back to the office now. I was going to ask, I know we met up last night, but I was thinking I could print the profiles off and we could have a look at them together.'

'We-ell,' Debbie hesitated.

'Or do you need to pick Olivia up?'

'No, my mum's doing that, it's just I haven't seen much of Gerry this past week. He's been working a lot of overtime.'

'Oh right, don't worry then. I'll phone you when I've had a look at them.'

'No, let me see if I can work something out. I'll call you back.' Debbie hung up.

It took Gill less than forty-five minutes to get back into the west end of Glasgow, as traffic was still relatively light. Everyone was still in work. The rush hour would probably start within the next hour.

When she arrived at the office, the normally unruffled Janice appeared stressed out.

'You OK?' she asked with concern.

'Yes, it's just been bonkers in here today. The phones have been ringing off the hook. Three people have dropped in about the SRC role you advertised, bringing their CVs in person, and the e-mail is totally choked up. Plus the server went down after you called and I've only managed to get it up and running again now. All in all, today could have been better.'

Gill felt guilty, but didn't quite know how to respond to make things better. Perhaps in hiring this new recruitment consultant, Janice's workload would automatically reduce. She already did so much more than a receptionist and was an essential cog in the business. That's why Gill paid her more than the going rate for a receptionist role, and to ensure she didn't think of leaving.

'Do you have the CVs from the walk-ins?' Gill asked.

'Sure. Here.' Janice handed them to her.

'Thanks. I need half an hour without interruptions, unless it's life or death, OK?'

'No problem. You can count on me to hold them off.' She winked.

Laughing, Gill retreated into her office, where she booted up her computer and began working her way through the CVs Janice had handed her. She then made a start on the remaining mountain she still needed to address.

Apart from to read an e-mail sent by Debbie into her work account, saying in the subject simply, *All is cool. Spoke to Gerry. Meet me in Drummonds Kelvingrove at 7*, Gill barely glanced up all afternoon.

She was vaguely aware of Janice shouting goodnight just after five, and next time she glanced at her watch it was quarter past six. Hurriedly, she logged into her e-mail and brought up the profiles.

Number one – yes, he looked even better on the big

screen. Charlie Prentice. Broad shoulders always did it for her. Maybe he was a mechanic or a shipbuilder, something manual-labour related. On second thoughts, she doubted that, or he wouldn't be on a professional persons' dating site. More like Blue Collar Workers Are Us. *Not that there's anything wrong with blue collar workers On the contrary...* Gill thought back many years, to Paul, a production worker at the local factory which made ball bearings and other parts for the automotive industry. The sex had been fantastic. Gill hastily pulled herself back to the present, feeling a touch aroused at her reminiscing.

Candidate Profile
Name: Charlie Prentice
Age: 44
Lives: South side Glasgow
Occupation: Surveyor
Qualifications: BSc Hons Environmental Management and Planning
Height: 6' 1"
Marital status: Divorced
Children: One daughter, aged twelve
Smoker: No
Interests: Playing and watching rugby, swimming, socialising with friends, mountain climbing, dining out, cooking, travelling
Further information: Originally from Barra, I moved to Glasgow when I started university and ended up staying here.
Looking to meet: A woman who likes socialising and who is open to romance. She should be independent but enjoy being part of a couple.

Divorced? With a daughter. So he has some baggage, but don't we all? It was a plus that he didn't smoke. No wonder he had that build, if he played rugby, and the swimming would account for those gorgeous shoulders. Blond, shortish hair, blue eyes. Yes, there was a real possibility she'd feel some sort of spark, if she could meet him in the flesh. And he shared some of the same interests as her: travelling, dining out, and he could cook. That had to be a bonus. Just as long as he didn't expect her to cook for him, or any friendship would be over before it began. Domestic goddess she wasn't. And 'open to romance', should that be interpreted, as 'wants sex'? It was hard to know. You'd really have to give the guy the benefit of the doubt. She quite liked the Western Isles lilt, too. Charlie sounded promising.

Candidate Profile
Name: Ronald Fotheringham
Age: 49
Lives: Loch Lomondside
Occupation: Antiques Dealer
Qualifications: MA Art History, FDA Furniture Restoration, PhD Fine Art & Design
Height: 5' 9"
Marital status: Widower
Children: Three of adult age
Smoker: Occasional
Interests: Art history, restoration, fine dining, black and white movies, squash, tennis, reading the classics.
Further information: I have travelled extensively in search of various antiques on purchasing trips, including Asia, South America and Europe.

Looking to meet: A lady who wants to be treated to the finer things in life.

He sounded as old as he looked, and forty-nine? In his dreams. She wondered how long he had been trying to pass himself off as forty-nine. He did sound interesting, though, but a bit too fuddy-duddy. Her brain couldn't compute a squash- and tennis-playing antiques dealer. Instead she conjured up the geeky, bookish, effeminate, loner antiques dealer which the movies often portrayed. Ronald had snow-white hair and a tanned complexion, with sun spots. He was a no.

Candidate Profile
Name: Anton Sidorov
Age: 38
Lives: Stirling
Occupation: Research Scientist
Qualifications: Equivalent of MPhys in Theoretical Physics
Height: 6' 3'
Marital status: Single
Smoker: No
Interests: Golf, tennis, movies, reading, zorbing, potholing.
Further information: I come from Vladivostok and have been working as a research fellow in Scotland for five years.
Looking to meet: An intelligent, attractive lady who likes sport and trying new activities. She should enjoy the cinema and weekends away exploring new places.

Mmm. He actually looked quite nice, now she could zoom in on his picture. High cheekbones, in that inimitable Slavic style, piercing blue eyes and an indolent smile. Much slimmer than Charlie, but not unattractive. He had some interesting hobbies, too, and she could always use the joke on him, 'it's not rocket science' and see how it was received. The fact he was a research scientist didn't intimidate her, as of course she had an engineering degree. She could probably hold her own and would undoubtedly find his conversation quite stimulating. They shared a love of cinema. She wondered what type of movies he liked. Deciding that Anton definitely went in the 'possible' pile, Gill printed off the three profiles on her colour printer and popped them in her briefcase.

Good. She'd get a chance to go through these profiles with Debbie and gauge her friend's reaction to them. Gill didn't think she was terrible at picking potential partners, just unlucky.

After sending a few last minute e-mails, Gill freshened up in the toilet. Untucking her blouse, she applied some roll-on deodorant and, standing in just her bra and trousers to allow time for the deodorant to dry, turned her attention to her hair. Her hair didn't cope well in the heat, so she tugged a brush through it, and then applied leave-in conditioner, before spritzing her hair with fixing spray. A smattering of bronzer to give her a bit of colour, since she hadn't been on holiday yet, a slick of lip gloss and she was ready. Slipping on a fresh blouse, she donned a black fitted jacket, smoothed it down and returned to her office to collect her things.

Drummonds was just over half a mile from her office,

and as the weather was fine, Gill decided to walk. She arrived a few minutes before seven. As she entered the restaurant, a staff member, dressed in a crisp white blouse, black waistcoat and apron, greeted her.

'Good evening. Do you have a reservation?'

'Yes. It's under the name of Orr,' Gill replied.

The girl checked the reservation book, smiled and said, 'You're the first of your party to arrive. Would the table by the window be OK for you?'

'Yes, that's fine, thanks,' Gill said, and the waitress led her to a table which had an excellent view over Sauchiehall St.

Pulling out Gill's chair for her, the waitress asked if she would like a drink. Gill mulled this over for a few seconds then decided she could always leave the car where it was overnight, and get the bus in tomorrow.

'I'll have a small glass of Sancerre, please.' Best to pace herself.

The waitress swiftly brought the wine to the table, along with two menus. Gill explained that her friend had booked through a special deal they had on at the moment, so that was menu one, but they could also provide anything from the à la carte, which she left her, too.

Thanking her, Gill resumed her daydreaming and people-watching. Being seated by the window gave her an excellent vantage point, and since the restaurant was raised one floor from the street, no one could see in. There was nothing worse than being in a restaurant, at a window table, on the ground floor. You felt like a goldfish in a bowl and people were so rude, gawping at you.

Remembering she hadn't switched off her phone, Gill opened her bag to put it on silent. She had a new text message, from Christopher.

Missed you this weekend. The boys want to know if you will come for dinner on Thursday. Sarah's promised to make meatballs if you do. Please say yes.

Gill smiled. She'd missed lunch with her brother and his family on Sunday, as she was too busy, trying to catch up with work. She felt bad, as it was the only engagement that she usually kept without fail. She enjoyed this family time, a rare respite from the drudgery of work. Sarah was lovely, too. She couldn't have asked for a better sister-in-law. Pity they never had time to have a girls' night out together. Their schedules were simply too hectic.

The door opened and Debbie shed her short beige trench coat and handed it to the waitress then waved at Gill, who stood up to give her a brief hug.

Once seated, the waitress brought Debbie's vodka and both girls relaxed.

'Gerry dropped me off. I'll get a taxi home later. So, where are these profiles?' said Debbie excitedly. Originally against the dating agency idea, since it was now decided upon, she was embracing it wholeheartedly.

'Why don't we choose our food first, and then we can concentrate on my love life.' Gill enjoyed keeping the anticipation going for a few minutes longer.

'OK.' Debbie turned her attention to the menus.

After a few minutes they turned to each other and Gill said, 'I'm going to have the homemade pâté and then the chicken breast with Dingwall haggis, with whisky sauce. I can't see past that.'

Gill was known for her calorific tastes, so Debbie, a bit of a health freak, said, 'I think I'll have the salmon on herb and leek risotto.' She continued to read from the menu.

'And for mains, the sea bass fillet with scallops.'

'Sounds fabulous,' said Gill. 'You do realise, Mrs Orr, that there probably isn't a great difference in calories between your choice and mine tonight.'

'I'm having fish,' said Debbie, defending herself.

'Yes, but with risotto and creamy mash and garlic and herb butter? Tut.'

'Well, I work it all off, anyway. Don't tease me, or I may have dessert, too.' She picked up the menu again and said, 'In fact, puff candy meringue with honeycomb ice cream and hot butterscotch sauce sounds like it might round off the evening quite nicely.' Debbie smiled sweetly at her friend.

'Bitch,' Gill said sotto voce.

Debbie didn't get the opportunity to add anything else, as their starters arrived. They tucked in greedily, agreeing by unspoken consensus that their chat would have to wait, whilst they polished off their first course.

They laid their cutlery vertically across their plates, indicating they were finished.

'So, am I getting to see these profiles or what?' asked Debbie impatiently. 'C'mon, hurry up.' She tapped her fingers on the table, mimicking a drum roll.

'All right, all right,' said Gill, reaching for her bag. After some deliberation, she had decided to show Debbie the profiles in the order she had received them. Originally she'd thought it would be best to start with the worst and end with the best, but later decided it might be useful for them both to view the profiles in the same order. Gill wanted to assess Debbie's reactions to see how closely they matched her own.

'Do me a favour,' Debbie said. 'Cover up the photo

first. I want to get a feel for them, without the photo.'

'Oh, OK. I hadn't thought of that,' said Gill, feeling almost shallow for having greedily devoured their photos first. But then, she had been unable to read the profiles, as she had viewed them on her phone and with her poor eyesight, it simply hadn't been possible to pick out any words. That was her story anyway.

Gill handed over Charlie's profile, covering his photo with a coaster. Debbie slid the A4 sheet towards her and began reading the text.

"Forty-four. That's good. Surveyor. Probably drives a nice car and has a decent job – likely to be reliable.' She glanced at Gill approvingly. Lowering her eyes back to the page, she read on. 'Tall.' Debbie waved her hand in the air, giving that attribute a large tick. 'Divorced, though, *and* he has a daughter. Not a deal-breaker, but something to bear in mind?' She glanced up again at Gill, who remained silent, waiting for her friend to conclude her assessment, more interested in what Debbie would say when she saw his photo. 'Seems compatible with you, interest-wise. I say, unless he's pig-ugly, he's a yes.' With a questioning glint in her eye at Gill, trying to figure out how her friend felt about Charlie, Debbie withdrew the coaster to reveal his photo.

'Oh, hello! He's bloody gorgeous. What's he need to use a dating agency for?' Debbie said, flabbergasted.

'Ahem,' said Gill pointedly.

'Well, yes of course, you're gorgeous too, but I *would* kick you out of bed. I wouldn't kick him out of bed. In fact, I might tie him to the bed, so he couldn't escape,' confessed Debbie.

Gill laughed. 'He's not that good-looking.'

'Er, yes, he is,' said Debbie.

'Well, our tastes really must be different then. Personally I'd only tie him to the bed if he was Bradley Cooper, Matthew McConaughey or Hugh Dancy gorgeous.'

'He does look a bit like Bradley Cooper, but without the facial hair. Who's Hugh Dancy?'

'The boss and Isla Fisher's boyfriend in *Confessions of a Shopaholic.*'

'Ah. Yes, he is quite tasty.'

'So, if you had to rate Charlie on looks, what would you give him?'

Debbie debated this for a minute then said, 'Eight or nine.'

'OK. I think seven.'

'Yes, but your marks are always lower than mine. Seven is really high for you.'

'True,' Gill admitted. 'OK, here's the second candidate.' Again covering up the photo, she turned the sheet of paper containing Ronald's details towards Debbie.

'Forty-nine. Older man, eh?'

She doesn't know the half of it.

'He lives up in Loch Lomond. He might have a house overlooking the loch. Maybe even his own boat? Nice place to have lunch in the summer.'

Gill couldn't deny that. In her opinion, when the weather was good, there was no country on earth more beautiful than Scotland, with its diversity of scenery. The drive up Loch Lomondside was particularly rewarding. Pity that good weather came when least expected, without warning, and lasted all of two minutes.

'I'm more bothered by the fact that he smokes than by his three kids.'

Gill stopped her. 'OK, I'll think about that. Move on.' She had no intention of meeting Ronald, so didn't want Debbie to linger too long over his profile. She was more interested in knowing what she thought of Anton. She liked the name. Anton. It rolled off the lips nicely – very exotic-sounding, a bit like its owner's looks.

'Well,' said Debbie, summing up her thoughts on Ronald, 'apart from the square name, why not Ronnie, after all, he seems quite interesting. In fact, are you sure he's not a bit cultured for you?'

'What are you trying to say? I'm some sort of philistine?' Gill said indignantly.

'No, but you're hardly going to start spouting forth on art history, are you?'

Clearly not. Gill had been to the Uffizi in Florence once, under duress. She had made the mistake of not booking her ticket in advance and had queued for two hours to get in. After being blown away by the first five enormous floor-to-ceiling religious paintings, she was fed up and could no longer marvel at how amazing they were.

'I'm not quite so sure about him, but apart from being perhaps a little posh for you, I think he sounds OK,' finished Debbie. She removed the coaster which was covering the photo.

'Yikes! Forty-nine. There's no way he's forty-nine. He looks about sixty-five. Has he had Botox in reverse?'

'Yeah, I thought he might be lying about his age, too.'

'Lying? He should be prosecuted for fraud. That's a gross misrepresentation.'

Gill said nothing, as she was of a similar opinion herself.

'So, can I take it he's a no?'

'Yes.' Gill smiled at Debbie. 'Of course he's a no.'

'Right, let's see the last one.'

Quietly confident over Debbie's reaction to Anton, Gill repeated the process and showed Anton's profile without showing his photo.

'Oh. Nice name,' said Debbie. 'That was one of the names I had chosen if we had a boy, but Gerry was having none of it. Research scientist. That sounds impressive. Or has he souped up his title, so he sounds more impressive? Maybe he does data entry.'

Privately Gill had wondered the same thing, but she wasn't about to let Debbie know this. Nor did she want Debbie's judgment influenced negatively or positively by her comments, so she held back from berating Debbie for shattering her illusions.

'He's Russian. Sounds first generation and he's just older than you and no more. That could be nice.' Debbie winked at her friend conspiratorially. 'Vladivostok. Do you remember work wanted me to attend that conference in Russia years ago, in the middle of nowhere? I think the nearest hotel chain was four hundred kilometres from it, in Vladivostok. That's all I know about Vladivostok.'

Gill knew even less.

'Oh, he's tall, too. I wonder if he's 'Dolph Lundgren in *Rocky IV* playing the Russian boxer' tall, or if he's a tall, slim thing?'

'Who knows,' Gill said noncommittally.

'You share some interests and you could always try zorbing!' teased Debbie.

'Yeah, because I wouldn't feel sick doing that,' Gill said faintly. An ex-boyfriend had once bought her a zorbing session as a Christmas present and she had been secretly delighted when the company had gone bust, before she had the chance to use the voucher.

'I wonder how good his English is, though,' Debbie thought out loud.

'A lot of these boffins are used to speaking, reading and writing English.'

'Although it might be quite nice for him to be the strong, silent type, if his English is limited. Can't imagine you'd need to be able to talk to him much.' Debbie winked at Gill again.

'Will you stop that? You're making me nervous and it looks like you've got a twitch.'

Just then their main courses arrived. They smelled and looked amazing.

Realising just how hungry they both still were, they tucked in. Between mouthfuls, Debbie managed to add, 'He has my vote.' She'd uncovered the photo just after the waitress left and her eyes had gone out on stalks. 'I think I like him even better than Charlie.'

And there was the difference in their tastes. Gill did like Anton, but she thought Charlie was more suitable. Ronald was nobody under sixty's cup of tea.

'Each to their own,' Gill said.

They ate in silence for a few minutes then Debbie said, slapping her right hand against her forehead. 'I'm such an idiot. I completely forgot to tell you, the girls are meeting us later in Chrysalis.

'What?' said Gill. 'Have you told them?'

'No, but *you're* going to.' She grinned at her friend then shovelled another forkful of sea bass into her mouth.

Chapter Seven

'I can hardly move,' groaned Debbie.

'Sheer piggery. I told you, you shouldn't have had the meringue.'

'I know, but it sounded so good and tasted even better. Here's an extra five pounds towards the bill to cover my dessert.'

'Don't be silly. Put it away.'

'No, I always eat more than you.'

'I know, I'm used to it, but we're still splitting the bill fifty-fifty.'

'Well, I'm buying the drinks then.'

Knowing there was no use arguing with her friend, Gill closed her mouth.

'That's your taxi now,' the waitress said.

Scraping back their chairs, they thanked her and left the restaurant.

'That's four eighty,' said the driver, as he let them out on Bath Street. Debbie handed him five pounds fifty.

As it was midweek, the pub was pretty quiet. From Thursday onwards, it would be really busy, since live bands played there. They were usually quite good, too. Angela's cousin had performed there recently and the four girls had gone to cheer him on.

Debbie and Gill looked around to see if they could spot the other two. Debbie finally spied their friends in a corner by a large coat stand which seemed to be in danger of toppling over and landing on them. Gill saw Angela eyeing it warily. Lisa happened to glance up, noticed Debbie and Gill, and pointed them out to Angela as they approached the table.

'Hiya, how's it going?' asked Gill.

'Great. We're on our third cocktail already,' slurred Lisa. She didn't handle alcohol very well. But Lisa's motto was why put off until tomorrow what you could do today, and that usually meant enjoying herself. Who was to say she was wrong? Gill wondered, thinking of her workload. Plus Lisa always seemed to have some guy tagging along, when it suited her. Girls' nights out, however, were just that – no guys allowed. Lisa was never serious about guys. She had no intention, even at thirty-five of settling down. She was having far too good a time for that. She had numerous 'boyfriends' to call upon, as and when she wanted, and if they needed something more, she dropped them. She'd circumvented tradition. Men behaved like this all the time, why not women? she said. This way she had the run of her home. It wasn't very large anyway. As a beautician she didn't make a great deal of money, but she still owned a small, modern two bedroom flat in the suburbs, in Robroyston. She didn't want to have her peace shattered every evening with some guy rolling in from work, wanting dinner. Or even if he shared household tasks, she wouldn't be able to do just as she pleased. Lisa could always be counted on to liven things up, but she also liked her own company. She chose when to meet people. Tonight she was clearly in party mode, since she was on cocktails. Gill hugged her friend, who was, as always, immaculately turned out. Gill put it down partly to Lisa being a beauty therapist, but also just because she was Lisa. She liked to look good, but she wore too much make-up in Gill's opinion, and overdid it on the spray tan. That was mainly due to work and vanity. Lisa was obsessed with her work to almost the same extent as Gill, although Lisa could close the door on hers at five o'clock. She read every magazine aimed at beauty professionals that she could get her hands on. Gill kissed Angela on the cheek and sat down as Debbie asked the girls if they wanted another drink.

'No. We're fine, thanks. We've just got these,' said Angela.

Lisa looked at her and then at Debbie as if to say, "speak for yourself".

Going into work hungover wasn't quite as big a deal for Lisa as for Angela. You had to have your wits about you at all times dealing with thirty teenagers, particularly those at the secondary school in which she taught.

Debbie returned shortly afterwards with drinks for everyone, except Angela. She'd read Lisa's tacit instruction to bring her another cocktail.

'So, what's the occasion?' Lisa wanted to know.

Debbie looked at Gill and made an encouraging motion with her head. Gill could have killed her. She hadn't counted on telling the girls tonight. She hadn't even fully considered what their response would be to the dating agency, never mind the candidates' profiles secreted in her briefcase.

Sighing, she decided to just blurt it out, glancing around first to ensure no one was close enough to overhear. 'I've joined a dating agency.'

'What?' said Lisa, her jaw falling open in astonishment.

'You're joking!' said Angela.

'No, I'm serious,' said Gill.

'Oh, this is brilliant,' said Lisa, as she wiped the table with a napkin. 'So, are you on a website?'

'No, it doesn't work quite like that. It's a professional dating agency.'

'Ooh, a professional dating agency,' Lisa mocked.

'Stop taking the piss.' Gill snapped.

'But aren't you afraid that it will just be full of saddos and weirdos?' Angela asked.

'Far from,' Debbie said. 'Show them the profiles, Gill.'

'Profiles? Oh, let's see.' Lisa was more excited than a child on Christmas morning.

Resigning herself to Lisa's hilarity and fully expecting her to ridicule them, Gill bent down and removed them once again from her briefcase.

Rather than go through the long, drawn-out process she'd permitted with Debbie, she simply handed Lisa the three profiles and sent a silent signal to Debbie not to comment.

'Ooh, he's nice,' Lisa said, putting her index finger on Charlie's picture. 'I like him.'

Angela agreed. 'I like his hair and those shoulders,' she said, as she read the blurb on him. Lisa ignored the text completely, turning instead to the second photo. 'Oh my God. Who's this ancient guy?' Then answering her own question, she said, 'Ronald Fotheringham. Christ. Even his name sounds old and decrepit.'

'Is this a real date for you?' Angela asked, astonished.

'Yeah,' admitted Gill.

'Aren't you a bit concerned the agency isn't matching

you with like-minded people?' she asked.

'Well, to be fair, as you've all pointed out, Charlie is a bit of all right.'

'I suppose,' conceded Angela.

'Here's the last one,' said Debbie, handing it over.

'Anton. No, I don't like the look of him,' said Lisa. 'He's all cheekbones, but there's something about his eyes I don't like.'

'I disagree,' said Angela. 'I think he's gorgeous, soulful looking, tortured.'

'Yeah, 'cos tortured is a good thing,' said Lisa sarcastically.

'No, I think I know what Ang means,' said Gill. 'He looks like he has a story to him. I bet you he's deep.'

'Translate that as depressing,' said Lisa.

'The guy goes zorbing, for God's sake,' Ang said. 'He's hardly unadventurous, even by your standards.'

'Well, he doesn't do anything for me,' said Lisa, a tad snippily.

'He doesn't need to do anything for *you*,' Debbie and Angela said in unison. 'It's Gill he has to do something for.' Debbie grinned.

'Yes, Miss McFadden, what exactly would you like him to do?'

'I don't know,' spluttered Gill. 'I haven't even met him yet.'

'Ah, gotcha,' said Debbie, 'you said *yet*. That means you've decided to meet him.'

Thinking about it, Gill decided she had. Charlie too. 'I haven't told the agency yet if they can go ahead with any of these guys or not,' she said.

'Well, why not?' asked Lisa, rearranging herself on her

chair to make herself more comfortable.

''Cos I only received them today and I wanted to discuss them with you lot first.' It was only a tiny white lie. She had always intended discussing them with Debbie. 'I'll reply in the morning, giving them the green light with Charlie and Anton.'

'Oh, this is so exciting,' said Lisa.

'I hope they're nice blokes,' said Angela. 'You deserve one.'

'Well, I'm not intending to get hitched or anything,' Gill was keen to clarify. 'I'm just going to go on a few dates, see what happens, find out if we like each other.'

'Yeah, yeah,' Lisa said. 'We know you. Within six months, you'll be a couple, doing coupley things and hardly having time for us.'

'Oh, c'mon, you know that's not true,' said Gill.

Debbie coughed. 'Well, it kind of is. That's what you do, Gill. You get all loved-up and then get tunnel vision and we don't see as much of you.'

'But this is different,' said Gill, aggrieved that her friends thought she would ditch them when some bloke came on the scene.

'I know and we're happy for you, should it come to anything, of course, but just don't be all or nothing. Find a happy medium this time,' Angela said.

Gill knew her friends were right, but it would be easier in any case. She couldn't dedicate a lot of time to a guy anyway; she had so much to do running her company. That hadn't been a consideration last time around.

'Anyway,' Lisa shrieked, 'more importantly, what are you going to wear? You can come by the salon beforehand, or I can come to yours and make you your most be-ayootiful. Give you a complete makeover.'

'Thanks, so what you're telling me is I need an overhaul.' Gill was a little offended.

'No, of course not, but c'mon, this is what I'm good at. Emphasising your assets. You don't wear much make-up. I can do your colours for you properly and then apply make-up to suit. Nothing too heavy, I promise. Guide's Honour.'

Gill strongly doubted Lisa's Girl Guide credentials, but thought better of saying so.

'OK, I suppose, but it better be tasteful,' she warned. 'And I best not be any shade of orange.'

'You'll look great,' Lisa assured her.

The girls spent the rest of the evening discussing how dressy Gill should be and whether they had anything appropriate to lend her to wear.

Before long it was last orders. Getting into two taxis on Bath Street, they went their separate ways home.

Chapter Eight

Next day Gill was pretty hungover and she rose later than usual. Her head throbbed and she didn't want to take any painkillers before eating anything. When she got to work, she would beg Janice to run across the road to the café and get her a muffin. She was thankful that the car was in town. The walk to the bus stop had done her good and she needed the fresh air. She didn't even care that it was raining. She'd e-mailed Caroline Morgan from Happy Ever After last night around midnight from her phone, confirming she would meet Charlie and Anton. What was she like? Caroline Morgan would probably be dissolving in fits of mirth, seeing how desperate Gill was, replying to a dating agency e-mail at midnight. She probably realised it had been sent after a few drinks, whether for courage or celebration. In any case, this morning, Gill was more than a little mortified.

Janice arrived not long after Gill. 'You look rough. Good night?' she asked.

Janice didn't mince her words.

'Yes, but I'm feeling a touch delicate this morning,' admitted Gill woefully. 'Would you be an angel and get us some supplies from the café, please? I could murder a blueberry muffin and a latte.'

Although they had a perfectly good cafetière in the office, sometimes Gill just needed a professionally prepared latte.

'Coming right up. Can't have you going around like that all day. You'll scare people. Go and put some make-up on.' Janice dug into the piggy bank Gill kept for their café jaunts and upended eight pound coins into her palm. As Janice headed over to the café to fetch their elevenses, even if they'd be long gone by nine thirty, Gill pulled out her compact and examined her face. 'Ugh.' She didn't like what she saw. Never mind a caffeinated latte; she should probably be drinking five litres of water to rehydrate her skin. That's what Lisa would tell her. Lisa might drink like a fish, but she always had a pint glass of water beside her, which she alternated sipping with her cocktail/wine/spirit. Unzipping the make-up bag she kept in the office for emergencies, of which this was one, Gill slowly applied foundation then concealer to the enormous bags under her eyes and flicked her mascara wand briefly over her eyelashes. Janice was right. She didn't need to feel like crap and *look* like crap. Gill stood up and walked over to the oval mirror which stood at one end of her office. A slightly improved version of her stared back.

There, that was better. She had to laugh at Janice's forthrightness. Janice looked like a less well-dressed, more eccentric version of the crazy girl, Alice Springs Horton, in *The Vicar of Dibley*. Their tastes differed greatly, but all that mattered to Gill was having an efficient, reliable and honest receptionist, and Janice fitted the bill perfectly.

When Janice returned with their snacks, Gill thanked her and both of them returned to their desks.

When she'd finished her muffin, Gill felt considerably

more human. Turning her attentions once more to business, she shortlisted candidates to call for the recently advertised technical position, and started to sort through the CVs of those who had applied for the SRC role within her own firm. There were so many. She thought maybe a woman would be best, but then some MDs and CEOs only wanted to deal with a man. Unfair, she knew, but it happened. If she hired a man, then they would be able to address those gaps. Part of her was relieved at taking on an additional member of staff, but another part felt sad as, since the agency opened, it had always been only her and Janice. At least the eleven o'clock meeting had been worthwhile. The chap seemed just right for the technical role they'd been asked to fill. Plus the appointment hadn't overrun; a welcome bonus. By the end of the morning, Gill felt back to her old self, all traces of hangover gone. How much was down to positive mental attitude and how much to the two aspirin she had taken, she would never know.

By one o'clock, Gill's stomach was rumbling again. Stretching like a cat, shaking out the stiffness from her limbs, she decided she needed some fresh air. She'd go across to the café and get their lunch.

Janice was happy that Gill was going out, as the weather was blustery and miserable. They chatted briefly, catching up on the morning, then after taking Janice's order, Gill ran across the road to the café, which was thankfully less busy than usual due to the inclement weather.

Back at her desk, sandwich unwrapped, Gill took the opportunity to check her personal e-mails.

8:42 – Caroline Morgan – Thanks for your confirma-

tion. I have contacted the two gentlemen. If they are interested, they will be in touch directly by e-mail. Regards, CM.

Fair enough. Hopefully, she wouldn't have to wait too long. She felt a bit tense, now that it was all actually happening, and would rather hear back as soon as possible.

She knew it was too early to have already received a reply from Charlie or Anton, but just in case, she scrolled down. Damn, this was going to become more addictive than watching an item you'd bid for on eBay. There it was:

12:41 – Anton Sidorov

Excitedly, Gill clicked on the e-mail and started to read.

Dear Gill. I hope you are well. I am glad you would like to meet me. Your profile was very interesting and I hope this is OK to say, but you are also very pretty. Can you advise when you are free to meet? I am happy to let you choose the venue.

Regards, Anton.'

She read it a couple of times to see if she had missed anything, but no, it seemed pretty clear. He was leaving the ball in her court. She also thought it sweet of him to say she hoped it was OK to say she was pretty. Absolutely. She'd be more worried if he thought she was a total dog! Pretty was good.

She pulled out her mobile and texted Debbie. *Anton got in touch. He wants to meet and for me to choose when/where. What do you think?*

Not usually an indecisive person, Gill's inability to

choose decent men had sapped her confidence over anything to do with the opposite sex. Unless it was work-related, she behaved like a gibbering idiot in front of them. She was too transparent, always had been. She had never understood why it was inadvisable to divulge everything about yourself to someone, once you were both sure that you really liked each other. The need to keep a little something back would never occur to her. For that reason, she wasn't good at keeping men guessing and her friends despaired of her. This time she wanted it to be different.

Five minutes later she received a reply from Debbie. *Somewhere centrally located in town, either one night after work, for a quick drink, or Sat lunchtime. No food, just drinks.*

As Gill digested the contents of Debbie's text, ideas for venues swirled around her head. Chrysalis was out. Too noisy. They'd want somewhere they could talk. Tempo and Each To Their Own were out for the same reason. She discounted a few others, as either not being central enough, or being too noisy, before finally, punching the air. She had it! Chez Molinières. It was central, relatively quiet and upmarket, and it had the little private area off the main bar, too. The only problem was you couldn't be guaranteed a table. She wondered how to fix that. No matter. She'd come up with a solution before then. She checked her calendar and saw that the following week she had no late meetings on Monday. Today was Thursday. That was OK, wasn't it? That didn't look too keen. Four days. Not a weekend. That way he wouldn't know that her only plans this weekend were to visit her brother and his family, apart from doing housework and skimming through candidate CVs. Before she could change her mind, she typed, *Hi,*

Anton. Nice to hear from you. How about Monday at Chez Molinières, just off Buchanan St, in Glasgow, for a drink? 7pm?

She stopped herself from putting if that suited him. If it didn't, he could tell her. This way she would come across as more self-assured and she would be the one in control. She tempered that with, *I look forward to hearing from you, Gill.*

After pressing Send, she sat back in her chair, with a self-satisfied grin on her face. She'd done it. She'd taken a positive step. Reaching for her mobile, she texted Debbie the latest.

Chapter Nine

Once the news hit the grapevine, Gill's trio of friends was bursting to offer advice. She had the weekend to make herself beautiful, as Lisa put it, again answering Gill's warning glare with 'You know what I mean.'

By Friday evening, Gill was surprised not yet to have heard from Charlie Prentice. She felt slightly peeved that he wasn't keener. If that was his modus operandi, she was singularly unimpressed. *The woman should keep the man waiting, not the other way around.* She didn't care if that concept was old-fashioned. Putting Charlie to the back of her mind, she thought nervously about her upcoming date with Anton. She really hoped he matched up to his lovely name.

After yet another busy day, Gill closed up the office and headed home. The solicitor's office had locked up long before and Janice had also left Gill to it, a few hours earlier, to go to a murder mystery evening at the Warlock Hotel in Drymen for a friend's fiftieth.

Knowing that the evening ahead consisted solely of soaps on in the background as she sifted through CVs, Gill headed to the nearest supermarket.

A bottle of Chablis, moussaka, a chocolate pot dessert and a lottery ticket for the triple rollover meant Gill was suitably armed to cope with the evening.

Saturday passed all too quickly. At least Gill had more or less achieved what she set out to do work-wise the night before. Her day consisted of mind-numbing tasks: hoovering, dusting, laundry, changing the bedding, washing and cleaning out the car, paying bills, washing the kitchen floor. Such a shame there was no one to share these mundane tasks with, she always thought.

At least she had the evening free to pamper herself. A long, hot bath with the latest crime novel from her favourite Nordic novelist, some Merlot left over from her last girls' night in, a family bag of chocolate raisins and she was sorted.

Gill felt a little stiff after all the housework. She really needed to make time to exercise and damn, she still needed to wash the windows. Thank goodness her window cleaner did the outside, or she wouldn't be able to see out.

Pouring some lavender oil into the bath she had run, Gill picked up her paperback, fetched a towel from the laundry cupboard and lowered herself gingerly into the steaming hot bath. She did love a good hot bath. If she didn't exit the bath wrinkled like a prune and lobster red, she didn't glow with the same sense of satisfaction.

Sunday 1 September

'Aunt Gill, Aunt Gill,' shrieked Harry. 'Come and see me play the Wii. We've got a new wrestling game.' Harry pulled at her hand, dragging her towards his bedroom, where his brother was oblivious to their imminent arrival, absorbed in WWE.

As her nephew rattled off the names of the wrestlers who played in the tournament, Gill wondered where her babies had gone. George and Harry both used to love nothing better than snuggling up on the sofa with Gill, reading stories together, and acting out all the voices of the characters. Now she barely saw them when she went to visit, unless she entered their lair, where they often hosted friends in Wii tournaments. Since Gill hadn't possessed a computer until the age of thirteen, and it had been one which required cartridges or tapes or typing in three hours' worth of code herself, the ready-made gaming technology which her young nephews embraced so easily, bamboozled her.

Reluctantly, Gill followed Harry into his bedroom, strewn with toys, home to games without covers, and a floor covered in the detritus of cast-off instruction booklets, plastic cases and nunchucks. Was she alone in feeling really dim as her six-year-old nephew talked her through the moves he was making on his wrestling partner? It astonished her to discover they had a variety of names, much like the ballet terms of *arabesque, plié, demi-plié* and *pas de bras*. Instead, here she encountered flying clothesline, backhand chop, stinger splash and tilt-a-whirl crossbody. She was out of her depth and stared at her two beloved nephews blankly as they droned on in great detail. She sat down on the bed to watch George and Harry play each other and winced in pain. Reaching under herself, she discovered a figurine which turned out to be John Cena.

'Aunt Gill, come and play me. George is rubbish,' said Harry.

'I am not rubbish,' declared George indignantly. 'You're rubbish. Aunt Gill, tell him I'm not rubbish. I'm going to beat him in the next round, 'cos I'm going to have Big Show as my wrestler,' said George seriously.

Gill had no idea what they were talking about. She listened as her young nephews dumbfounded her with further wrestler-specific vocabulary, completely bemused.

'Lunch is ready,' Sarah called.

Relieved, Gill wrested the controls from a reluctant Harry and ushered both boys into the bathroom to wash their hands before lunch.

As Sarah passed the salad bowl to Gill, Christopher asked his sister what she had been up to.

'Working mainly, what about you two?'

'No, don't go changing the subject, sis. I'm worried about you. You're not relaxing enough.'

'Well, I've been out for drinks with the girls a couple of times this week.'

'That's a start,' said Sarah, glancing briefly at her husband.

'Gill, don't you think it's about time you started seeing someone again?' asked her brother gently.

'Don't push her, Chris,' his wife chided him.

'No, it's OK, Sarah. He's right. Actually, I have kind of been doing something about that.'

'You're seeing someone?' Christopher's eyes lit up. His attention was temporarily distracted as he retrieved the fortunately empty juice cup which George had sent crashing to the floor.

'Not exactly. I have a date tomorrow night.'

'Really!' her brother said and Gill didn't know if he was astonished or impressed. 'Who is he? How did you meet him? What does he do?' Her brother rat-a-tat-tatted the questions at her.

'Chris, let her answer,' Sarah said in exasperation, whilst smiling affectionately at her husband.

Gill cast Sarah a grateful glance. 'His name's Anton and he's a research scientist.' She chose to avoid answering how she met him, hoping Christopher wouldn't press her on it.

'Anton. That's a lovely name. Sounds sexy.' Sarah grinned wickedly.

'Yes, that's what I thought. He's Russian.'

'Ooh, exotic,' said Sarah.

'So, how did you meet him?' Christopher asked.

'Daddy, I feel sick,' interrupted George then promptly burst into tears.

'Hey, little man, come here,' Christopher told his son, then placed his forefingers on George's forehead when he sat on his lap. 'He is a bit hot, Sarah.'

'Let me see,' Sarah said. She then picked up her son and carried him out of the room.

Although sorry that her little nephew was unwell, Gill breathed a sigh of relief that she was no longer being quizzed on how she had met Anton.

Sarah returned twenty minutes later. 'He's OK now. Sleeping. He was sick.'

'Poor wee thing. Hope it's nothing serious,' Gill said anxiously.

'I'm sure it's just a twenty-four-hour thing. There's a lot of it going about at the moment. So, Gill, tell us more about your hot date!' Sarah said eagerly, settling herself back in her chair.

'Well,' began Gill, trying to offer something quickly, before Christopher could jump in again asking how they met. 'He's six feet three and lives in Stirling. He works at the university there and he's originally from Vladivostok.'

Sarah nodded her approval, keen to hear more. Gill tried to think what else she could tell them, given that she didn't know much more than that herself. But of course they didn't know that. Racking her brain, trying to remember what had been on the profile, she recalled a couple of his wacky hobbies – zorbing and potholing. When she relayed this to her sibling, he burst out laughing.

'Oh, Gill, I hope you really like this guy, 'cos I know what you're like. If he asks you to roll down a hill at breakneck speed in a large transparent sphere, you'll say, "*Sure, no problem.*"'

'Stop taking the mick, Chris.' His sister booted him under the table.

'No, you're right. So, where is he taking you?'

Ignoring the opportunity to come clean and admit that he wasn't taking her anywhere per se, they were by mutual agreement meeting in a bar in town, Gill replied, 'We're going to Chez Molinières.'

'Oh, is that the restaurant just off Buchanan Street?' Sarah asked.

'That's the one.'

'We went there for our Christmas night out a few years ago. It's very swish,' added Sarah. 'Full of city types.'

Gill gave a wry smile. She wondered if her sister-in-law considered her a city type, but she guessed she reserved that description for the male of the species, in their pinstriped suits, cufflinks and designer shirts.

'And the food's fantastic.'

Gill excused herself to go to the bathroom, escaping the possibility of Christopher asking her something she might not want to answer.

'Thanks for lunch, guys,' Gill said as she was leaving.

As she drove off from their three-bed detached townhouse on a new estate in the outskirts of Balloch, Gill beeped the horn and waved goodbye.

Chapter Ten

Monday 5 September

Gill appraised herself in the mirror. She hadn't looked this good since her brother's wedding and, of course, then she had been professionally made over, too. Lisa had tamed Gill's unruly locks, making them fuller, curlier and shinier. Her naturally wavy hair now looked effortlessly curly and tousled. Lisa had actually approved of Gill's choice of clothing, and had given her some jewellery to set off her outfit. Chocolate moleskin trousers, paired with a cream square-necked slinky top which fell to below her hips. She wore a gold watch, a gift from her parents, and gold earrings. Slipping on chocolate-and-gold-coloured sandals, with just a hint of a heel, she was ready.

It had been agreed that Lisa would drop Gill off, and then join the girls in the pub next door, in case Gill needed rescuing.

As Gill walked up the steps into Chez Molinières, laughter and the sound of several voices greeted her. It was Monday night. She'd picked this venue as she thought it would be quieter. It was five past seven. She'd tried to be on time, but Lisa wouldn't allow it.

'You have to make him wait. You can't arrive before him,' she said firmly, grabbing Gill by the wrist, as Gill once again tried to get out of the car. It simply wasn't in her DNA to turn up late for anything. Finally giving in, she waited a few minutes before sliding out of the car. She had been watching the entrance to see if he arrived whilst she waited. But she hadn't seen anyone go in who resembled him and he certainly wasn't hanging around in the entrance vestibule.

Bracing herself, Gill opened the door, holding it open to let an elderly gentleman pass her, and then she stepped inside. It was quite busy for a Monday, but as she entered she saw that most of the noise emanated from a group of about six men at the bar. Just then the waiter came to tell them their table was ready and she waited as they filed past her towards the restaurant, before she approached the bar. Gill glanced around as subtly as she could. Then she saw him. He was watching her. Smiling, he stood up and came towards her.

'Gill. Nice to meet you. Anton.' He kissed her on both cheeks.

Flushing slightly, Gill murmured hello and, at his invitation, sat down.

'What would you like to drink?' he asked her.

'A vodka and Coke, please.'

Anton smiled at her. 'One moment.'

She noticed he wasn't drinking vodka, but had some form of cocktail. Perhaps she would have one next.

Gill smothered a snort. *Next. What am I like? We've barely said hello and here's me thinking about a second drink.*

As he stood at the bar, she made the most of her chance to appraise him. He was tall, very tall. She thought perhaps he had underestimated his height. Often Europeans did when converting from metric to imperial. She reckoned him to be nearer six feet five. Short hair, blond, not a trace of grey, although she supposed he was only thirty-eight. Not quite as thin as his photo had suggested. It suited him. He was slim and wore beige trousers and a white open-necked shirt – very smart. She couldn't see any jewellery, only a watch. She liked that. Gill wasn't big on men who wore necklaces, chains or bracelets. He turned suddenly, smiling at her. Too late to avert her gaze, she returned his smile.

Placing their drinks on the table, Anton sat down opposite her, moving the cocktail menu out of the way so it no longer blocked their view of each other.

'So,' he said.

'So.'

'Feel strange?'

'A little.'

'Relax. Is this your first date with the agency?'

'Yes. Can you tell?'

'Can I be honest?'

Gill nodded.

'You seem a little terrified.'

Gill laughed. 'I probably am. I'm sure without cause.'

'We're just two people having a drink, getting to know each other,' he said softly.

She liked his voice, which was both soothing and sexy. It had to be said, foreign accents did add a certain je ne sais quoi to a potential date.

She began to relax as he asked her questions about herself. She wondered if it was his first date arranged by the agency. She thought not. He was too at ease, confident, but not arrogant, not smooth. His manners were impeccable. Before long, and after Gill had chosen from the cocktail menu, he unfolded his long legs from the chair he was sitting in and went to fetch them more drinks.

Once she relaxed, Gill made a joke about *her* drinking vodka and him being the Russian. He laughed and explained the reason he didn't drink vodka was because the vodka found in Scotland was nowhere near as good as that in Russia. She opted for a Cosmopolitan whilst Anton ordered another Poinsettia. He offered Gill a taste and it had seemed overcautious to refuse. It was lovely – a mix of champagne, Cointreau and cranberry juice. She found it a strange choice for a man, but she liked that he didn't conform.

The date was going well. She wondered if Anton thought so, too. She had heard horror stories, of girls on blind dates who thought it was going swimmingly, only to discover that their date had not actually gone to the toilet but instead legged it to the car park, leaving them stranded. She really hoped that wouldn't be the case with Anton.

Gill asked him about his work. He still travelled back and forth to Vladivostok, as well as St Petersburg, Minsk and Nizhny Novgorod, liaising with other institutes involved in the research programme of which he was a part. It sounded very interesting, although he couldn't go into detail, as a lot of the research was cutting edge and thus top secret. She told him she worked in Recruitment, but made a point of not giving him the name of her company, and he didn't press her. Nowadays, most information could be found on the internet anyway.

Gill studied his body language and tried equally to be conscious of her own.

Anton watched Gill as she bent over to pick up her bag, as

Greensleeves blasted from it. At least she didn't have one of those designer bags, he thought. Anton disliked women who were overly interested in labels, perhaps because he wasn't remotely interested in fashion.

As Anton surveyed Gill, he concluded she was pretty, not gorgeous, but very attractive; tall for a woman, which helped, given his own height. He'd put six feet three on his profile. Some women liked tall men, but few liked really tall men. It wouldn't be the first time he had been more than a foot taller than his date. At least that wasn't the case with Gill. He found her friendly, interesting and interested. Anton was far from a chatterbox, but could chat happily with someone when they had something interesting to say, and which held his attention. His low boredom threshold meant he was averse to small talk, so he was glad that Gill was intelligent enough to understand about his work. Surprisingly, it turned out she had studied Engineering. Not many women did that, he thought. Not in the UK. In Russia of course, it was much more common, along with many women becoming scientists.

Anton liked how Gill's hair fell in waves over her shoulders. He had a thing for women with long hair. *Don't all men?* he wondered. It was so feminine.

'I'm really sorry about that,' Gill apologised. 'I thought I'd put it on silent. I thought I was switching it off, but I must have hit Answer, when I was trying to take it out of my bag. It was a client,' Gill flushed. Not good form to take calls during a date. She hoped he didn't hold it against her.

'Don't worry about it, really.' Anton waved his hand in a gesture indicating it was already forgotten. 'Would you like another drink?' he asked, eyeing Gill's empty glass.

Gill looked at his half-full glass and was ready to say no, afraid he might think her a lush, when Anton suddenly picked up his glass and drained the remainder of its contents. Smiling at her, he said, 'So what would you like?'

For a moment she didn't know whether he was subtly referring to something else or if he was simply asking her again if she wanted another drink. Cute if he was going for the double entendre, and a little sexy. She blushed at the thought. They were on their third drink; surely a good sign.

Bravely she said, 'Whatever you're having.'

Surprised, but pleased she thought, Anton said, 'OK, leave it to me. I know just the thing.'

When he returned, he declared, 'Mango Siberian Sunrise,' and urged Gill to take a sip.

'Mmm. That's lovely. What's in it?'

'Russian Standard Original Vodka, lime juice, sugar and mango.'

'It's very refreshing,' Gill said.

They sat talking companionably, both seeming a little on edge, as if neither was exactly sure of how the other felt, discussing a multitude of topics. They were amazed at how much they had in common, including both being workaholics and chocoholics.

'Snickers for me.' Anton laughed.

'Flake,' said Gill. 'Can you excuse me a second? I'm just going to go to the Ladies'.'

'Of course,' Anton said.

Gill's absence would give him a few minutes to work on what to say and do at the end of the evening. He liked her, but he knew not to move things ahead too quickly. He didn't want to scare her off. He sensed she liked him, too.

But this was only her first date through the agency. She was bound to have many more. His instincts were divided. Try to secure a second date, let her know just how much he liked her, before anyone else muscled in, or take it slowly? He debated this whilst he awaited her return.

'Debbie, it's me,' said Gill. She had washed her hands and was standing to one side of the washbasins. Luckily there was no one else in the toilets at the time, so she was able to chat freely.

'How's it going? Need rescuing?'

'No, not at all. He's lovely, gorgeous too.'

'Excellent,' said Debbie, who then conveyed this to the others. 'Lisa and Angela have given the thumbs up to that.' Her voice was muffled for a second. 'What's that, Lisa?' Debbie's voice came back loud and clear. 'Oh, Lisa says it's about time too.'

'Tell her ha bloody ha.'

'So, are you going somewhere else after here?'

'I don't know. What should I do if he suggests it?'

'Well, what do you want to do? What do you want to happen?' Debbie asked her.

'I'm not going to sleep with him, if that's what you're asking.'

'I know you well enough to know you wouldn't do that on a first date, for various reasons, not least that I would kill you. I don't care how much you might be gagging for it, ahem, sorry, I mean, I don't care how long a drought you've had, you can wait beyond the first date. Or it will be the last date.'

'I know, I know, and to be honest, although I really like him, I haven't jumped ahead to that part in my head yet, anyway.'

'Well, just do what feels right. But make sure if you go on anywhere afterwards, that you let me know where it is. Personally, I wouldn't, and would wait to see if he asks for another date.'

'OK,' said Gill, doing her best to take in everything Debbie was saying, simultaneously trying to work out what to do, should the matter arise.

'Good luck, love.'

'Thanks. Call you tomorrow.' She hung up. After checking her face and hair briefly, Gill sped back upstairs, aware she had been gone a little longer than she'd intended and hoping he was still there.

He was, and a broad smile broke out across his face as he looked up at her.

'Will we finish these then go?' Anton asked. Gill's face fell a little, before she recovered enough to mask her feelings.

'I need to get the train back to Stirling. I couldn't drive here, as I wanted to be able to have a few drinks and relax.' Showing her his watch, he said, 'It's ten twenty already.'

'Is it?' Gill could scarcely believe it. They'd been yakking away for more than three hours.

'Yes. "Time flies when you're enjoying yourself," I believe the saying goes.' He smiled directly at her. He had very white teeth, one of which was a little crooked. It added even more to his charm.

'How are you getting home?' he asked.

'Oh, I'll grab a taxi.'

'Then I'll walk with you to the taxi rank, before I get my train.'

Gill almost said he didn't need to do that, but thought better of it, as it was a nice gesture on his part, and she needed to learn to accept behaviour like this graciously.

They finished their drinks and Anton helped Gill put on her jacket. Chivalrous – tick. She could get used to this. She hoped it wasn't all an act. But no, she pushed those thoughts from her mind. He seemed genuine enough. As they walked the few hundred metres towards Queen Street Station, Anton stopped suddenly and said, 'Can I ask you something?'

'Of course,' Gill said, wondering if he was going to ask if he could kiss her.

'Can we see each other again?'

Gill's heart leapt, then plummeted, then leapt again. 'I'd like that,' she said, smiling warmly at him.

'Excellent. I have one more question.'

Gill looked at him quizzically. Perhaps he would ask her to go to Stirling next time, as he had made the effort to come to Glasgow on this occasion.

'May I kiss you?'

Gill gazed up into his smiling face and nodded. Resting his hands lightly on Gill's arms, Anton bent down and kissed Gill very softly on the lips. His touch was so light, Gill initially wondered if he *had* kissed her. He kissed her twice more, each time gently and without opening his lips.

When they parted, he said, 'That was as nice as I thought it would be. We should get you a taxi.'

They walked the remaining few metres to the taxi rank. As they waited their turn in the taxi rank, Gill could still taste him on her lips; still feel the heat of him. Her body had responded effortlessly when he kissed her. She had wanted more. But it was nice that he had shown some self-restraint, she convinced herself.

'Are you free on Thursday?' Anton asked.

Gill knew she was, but made a show of checking the calendar on her phone. The girls had taught her something after all.

'Looks like it,' she said.

'Can I surprise you?'

She hoped he wasn't going to turn up naked, although on second thoughts, maybe that wasn't such a terrible idea.

'Can I trust you?' she asked, her lips curving into a smile.

'You can trust me.' His eyes twinkled.

'Then, it's a yes.'

'I'll be in touch then, about where to meet, but it will probably be around seven again. Is that OK?'

'That's fine.'

Just then the next available taxi pulled up. Anton opened the door for her. She climbed in, and once she had turned around, he pecked her on the cheek, before following that up with another little kiss on the lips.

'I had a really good time tonight. See you Thursday.'

'Me too, until Thursday.'

Anton backed out of the taxi, the door closed and the taxi rolled away along Duke Street, before turning towards the south side of the city.

Anton waved and watched the taxi disappear into the distance. Turning, he walked back into the station.

The next train was due in fifteen minutes. Anton sat on one of the benches, trying to block out the noise of the occasional drunk person stumbling past, shouting obscenities. The station was relatively busy and the vast semi-circular roof above him conducted the noise of his fellow passengers remarkably well. Taking out his iPod from his inside jacket pocket, he slipped the buds into his ears and selected Stravinsky's *Romance*. He was in the mood for something light and romantic. Who said romance was dead? Apparently women always wanted romance, but what about men? He wanted nothing more than to find someone he really liked and which could eventually develop into love, someone he could spend time with. He wasn't so naïve that he thought Gill could be the one to fulfil that role. They needed to get to know each other first. That could continue on Thursday. He would surprise her and see how it went. If they decided to have another date after that, then she could choose. The important thing was she had said yes to Thursday. He liked that. She hadn't made him wait, hadn't played hard to get, she'd simply checked her diary. He hated game playing. It was difficult enough dating someone, without all the mind games. Anton thought he was a pretty open person. He could also be very direct and occasionally a bit blunt. But he would never intentionally hurt anyone's feelings.

He removed his ear buds, as he heard the tannoy ring out. 'The train now arriving at platform one…'

That was his train. Anton took out his travel pass from his pocket, slipped his ticket through the machine and went through the barrier.

Luckily he managed to nab a seat with a table. As he stared out of the window, he remembered how Gill's hair had smelled of coconut. Her perfume was floral, but sensual. As the train drew out of the station, Anton's thoughts remained with Gill and would do so for the duration of his forty minutes journey back to Stirling.

Chapter Eleven

Tuesday 6 September

Next morning Gill overslept. She had slept remarkably well, but she must have forgotten to set the alarm on her phone. Picking up her mobile, she scowled at it, as if the obnoxious, beeping noise were its fault, instead of hers. Her e-mail alert pinged. Well, it would have to wait. She hated being late. Gill ran around like a mad thing, foregoing coffee in order to arrive at the office at the originally planned time. She had meetings this morning, both in and out of the office. She needed to impress the new client, too, she remembered. At least she had had the presence of mind to finalise her preparations for her meeting before she went out on her date last night.

Fortunately, traffic was light and she made up some of her lost time. When she arrived at the office, the first thing she did was switch on the kettle, even before she plugged in her laptop. She'd feel better after a caffeine hit.

Laptop on, coffee mug in hand, she checked through her personal e-mails before starting the morning's work. Charlie Prentice. Well, it was about time. Taking a sip of her coffee and swearing as it was too hot and burned the roof of her mouth, she clicked open the e-mail.

Hi, Gill. Sorry couldn't get in touch sooner. Away rock

climbing, only just got back. Had a long weekend. No reception to get e-mails. When would you like to meet up? Friday's out, I'm afraid, as I have a stag do. Apart from that any other night this week is OK for me. Charlie.

Well, he did have a reasonable enough excuse for not contacting her earlier. She would forgive him for that. But was he assuming that asking her on Tuesday, she would be free at such short notice? That was a tad presumptuous. Anyway, she was already going out on Thursday with Anton. Then chiding herself that she shouldn't be putting all her eggs in one basket so soon, she tried to think of when she could meet Charlie. If he was out on Friday at a stag do, it was unlikely he'd be in a fit state to go out Saturday lunchtime. She'd suggest Sunday afternoon.

Nice to hear from you, Charlie,' Gill began. *'I'm afraid I'm busy this week. What about Sunday lunchtime for a drink? Gill.*

There, short and to the point. Let's see if he would be happy to see her at the weekend.

Gill scrolled through the rest of her e-mails, responding to as many as she could, then came across one from Anton.

Gill, I just wanted to say that I really enjoyed meeting you, and our kiss…See you on Thursday, Anton.

Gill smiled to herself, remembering that fleeting kiss, which had held the promise of something more.

She'd almost reached the end of her e-mails, when she saw one from Caroline.

Gill, hope your date went well last night. I have two more profiles for you. Please see attached.

Gill clicked on the attachment.

Candidate Profile

Name: Gary Kelly
Age: 47
Lives: Renfrewshire
Occupation: Engineer (oil & gas)
Qualifications: BEng
Height: 5' 11'
Marital status: Divorced, no children
Smoker: N
Interests: Formula One, dining out, socialising, photography, reading the classics
Further information: Originally from Northamptonshire, I have lived in Scotland for ten years.
Looking to meet: A fun, sexy woman who likes to spoil and be spoiled by her partner. Also needs to be able to accept that, as an engineer on the rigs, I have odd shift patterns and be willing to work around that.

Gill read through his profile. He had short dark hair, was of medium build with, were those green eyes? He definitely had a twinkle in them, as if he knew exactly what you were thinking. He looked fun, quite sexy, in a Liam Neeson way. Very direct, too, about his work, and she didn't think he was rude in pointing out about his shifts, more practical. She knew that often these guys did two weeks on, two weeks off the rigs. *He must be working from Aberdeen.* The only surprise to her was that he lived so far down from there, in the central belt. Well, he certainly merited a second look. Formula One as his main hobby – she hoped he wasn't a petrolhead. She hated when men drove fast – it always appeared they were trying to make up for something else. Another engineer. With a wry smile,

Gill thought he could easily have been placed by her agency, although his name didn't ring a bell. She wondered who he worked for. Of course, if she were to go on a date with him, that subject was taboo until they knew each other better. Photography. That sounded more civilised. Unless he was photographing cars. Reading the classics. She wondered if he put that there to make himself appear intellectual. Anyway, Gary was a possibility.

Gill clicked the second file.

Candidate Profile
Name: Sean Hennessey
Age: 35
Lives: Glasgow
Occupation: Sound Technician
Qualifications: BA Technical and Production Arts (Management and Technology)
Height: 5' 9'
Marital status: Single
Smoker: Y
Interests: Listening to and playing music, films, rugby, hurling,
Further information: Originally from County Galway, I have lived in Glasgow since my time at the RSAMD. I love it here – brilliant city and good craic.
Looking to meet: A woman who I can romance…

Ah, a mere baby, thirty-five. How did she feel about a toy boy? Laughing out loud a little, she thought, *bring it on!* Thirty-five. He was bound to be quite energetic still, no seventeen-year-old, mind you, but hopefully he'd still have a healthy appetite for sex. Bloomin 'eck, what was she like, some sex-starved old maid? Well, actually, yes, but that wasn't the point. It was just the authentic Irishness of him. Gill loved Irish men and he was from County Galway. She'd been to Galway once and had loved the university city. Unfortunately she had caught a cold and ended up spending two days in bed in the tiny B&B. And she had been alone in that bed, the only comfort a chick-lit book by one of her favourite Irish authors, which she'd bought in the city before falling sick.

She'd taken a cheap flight to Ireland just after her break-up with Tim. A chance for her to get away and reflect upon the disaster that was her life and more specifically her love life. From that trip had sprung the seed of an idea to start up an agency of her own.

She'd been chatted up a few times in Galway, but she really hadn't been in the mood. It would be different if she went back now. She couldn't get enough of the Irish accent, and although she liked some northern Irish accents, she preferred southern accents. So Sean was a sound technician. Interesting. She wondered if he worked alongside any bands she knew. She scrutinised his photo. You could tell he'd made an attempt to scrub up – he had a shirt on and he'd obviously shaved, but his hair was still a little unkempt, which she found adorable. It surprised her that she'd received his profile. Usually men wanted younger women. Maybe that photo she'd put on her profile really had worked. She hoped he wasn't disappointed when he saw her in the flesh.

He liked hurling, such a quintessentially Irish hobby. She wasn't even sure exactly what it was, but she remembered it had come up on a quiz show recently. Was it played on ice, or was she mixing that up with curling? Now she came to think of it, she rather thought she was confusing the two. She'd need to check before they met so she didn't come across as stupid. Look at her, now potentially four dates.

Emboldened by her successful date with Anton, Gill pressed reply and typed,

Hi Caroline. Yes, my date with Anton went well, thanks. She almost put that they were meeting again, but Caroline hadn't asked and Gill suspected she might not set her up with the two new guys if she knew, so she left it at that.

Both Gary and Sean sound nice. Please can you go ahead and advise that it's OK to contact me. Regards, Gill.

'That's your first appointment here,' Janice called through to her.

Pleased with herself, Gill picked up her notes and went through to her meeting.

Chapter Twelve

Tuesday 6 September

When they'd arrived at Il Bistro Italiano, famous for its Italian 'tapas,' it wasn't very busy. Lisa had had the foresight to book a booth.

'Last time I was here the food was great, but it was really noisy. At least the booth shuts out some of the chatter and no one else can hear what we're talking about,' Lisa said.

The high ceiling gave the restaurant the acoustics of an auditorium.

Gill had finished at six and driven over to the Merchant City, parking just off Ingram Street.

'It's a pity Debbie couldn't make it,' said Angela.

'I know, but she's been out with me quite a lot the last week or so. I already gave her the verdict over the phone today. I'm not telling you what she said until I've heard what you lot think.'

'Well, you know you'll get a fair assessment from us,' Angela said.

'Yeah, we'll let you know if he's worth another date and what we think of these new ones,' said Lisa. 'And we'll be brutally honest.'

Gill didn't doubt it. She was sorry Debbie couldn't be

there with them to dissect her date and to discuss her progress with the others, but she needed to spend *some* time with her family. Fortunately, Angela's mum had her son, Matthew, overnight, so Angela had been let loose.

After a quick scan of the menu, they decided on a couple of sharing platters. Lisa ordered a mainly meaty one, Gill chose a completely vegetarian platter, and since they were all going to dig in to each other's anyway, Angela chose one of the two platters which contained fish.

'It's so good in here. I've never had room for dessert, but I've heard they're good, too,' Lisa said.

As the girls waited for their platters to arrive, Lisa and Angela quizzed Gill on her date with Anton. After the text he had sent the previous morning, she hadn't heard from him again, but then she hadn't expected to. Positively glowing, she relayed to her friends the events of Monday night. They agreed that it sounded promising and as she described his kiss, reactions were mixed.

'He sounds lovely,' said Angela. 'What a sweetheart.'

'Sounds a bit slow at coming forwards if you ask me,' said Lisa.

'I was hardly going to sleep with him on a first date, anyway,' Gill shot back defensively.

'Maybe he was just trying to tease Gill a little, make sure she was interested,' said Angela, sipping her wine.

'Hmm,' demurred Lisa as she twiddled a lock of her blonde curly mop, unconvinced.

'Well, at least he wasn't a git or a nerd,' said Angela, rolling her eyes in exasperation at Lisa's lack of enthusiasm. 'Think of all the losers Gill's seen over the years,' she said hotly.

Then realising what she'd said, she apologised to Gill.

'You know what I mean, hon, and you're not alone either,' she said wryly. They all knew she was thinking of her ex – Jason, Matthew's father. They rarely kept in touch now, and it pained Angela more than she let on, that he didn't have any desire to see their eight-year-old son. To make matters worse, Matthew was the spitting image of his father, with large almond eyes and a cheeky little grin.

'I know what you meant,' said Gill softly, 'and you're right, which is why Anton was so lovely *and* he's interesting and has a lovely voice.'

'You can't hang everything on one date with a guy and lay it on his voice!' cried Lisa.

'Have you not been listening?' Angela said. 'That's just what clinches the deal. The guy sounds like a winner to me.'

'Anyway,' said Gill, 'I'm seeing him again and that's that. And, Lisa, I haven't restricted my options. I've heard back from Charlie, too, and e-mailed him today to see if Sunday lunchtime would do. For a drink,' she added.

'Oh well, that's good. Two men on the go.' Lisa seemed reassured.

Angela also nodded her approval, draining her glass of wine and reaching for the bottle. Only Gill was driving.

'So, what was his excuse for not contacting you before now?' asked Lisa.

'He'd been rock climbing and had no mobile reception.'

'And where's he from again?' Angela asked.

'He's from the south side, too.'

'Oh, whereabouts?' asked Angela.

'The agency doesn't give you quite as specific information as that in the profile. It's meant to be to protect you. I suppose after the first time it's up to you to decide how much info to share, but the agency is very particular about not giving out home addresses.'

'Fair enough,' said Lisa.

'And that's not all,' said Gill, pausing to build up the suspense.

Just then the food arrived and the waitress described in great detail which of the twelve dishes was which.

Once she left, Lisa said, 'Did you get that?'

'Eh, no, but I think we can probably work out what most of them are,' said Gill, her mouth watering just looking at the array of plates in front of her.

They pawed over the food for a few minutes, Lisa dragging a meatball onto her plate, Gill popping an olive directly from the platter into her mouth, and Angela spearing a piece of sea bass.

'So, what else?' asked Lisa.

Dying to lead them on further, but knowing that Lisa was on the point of bursting, Gill said, 'I received two more profiles.'

'Really?' squealed Lisa. 'Let's see them.' She clicked her fingers in a fashion that Gill had always hated, but which was one of her quirks.

Gill duly fished out the profiles from her tote bag, and Lisa almost grabbed the pages in her desire to have a look at the new prospective dates.

'Gary? That's a bit of a boring name after Anton,' she said.

Frustrated and a little annoyed, Gill said, 'A minute ago you didn't think Anton was good enough.'

'I know, I know, anyway, never mind that. This guy's bloody gorgeous. Like an older Tom Ward.'

All the girls agreed that the forensic scientist in *Silent Witness*, one of their favourite programmes, was someone they would not kick out of bed. Lisa thought it was a crying shame he was married and had three children.

'Gary's definitely a yes,' said Lisa. 'Funny, he doesn't look the manual-labour type. Can't imagine him in a pair of overalls, can you?'

'Maybe he wears one of those yellow jackets over a shirt and tie,' said Angela.

'Stop ruining my fantasy. I want him in overalls,' growled Lisa.

'Eh, can I just point out that he's actually *my* date?' said Gill.

'Oh, so you *have* decided to meet him!' Angela seemed pleased.

'Well, yes, he's sex on legs, don't you think?'

Angela agreed she would meet him in a heartbeat.

'Why don't you join this dating agency, Ang?' asked Lisa.

'Eh, hello? I don't have time to go on dates and I certainly don't have the money to pay three hundred pounds joining fee and then fifty quid a month!'

'Fair point. We'll just need to find you someone going down the traditional route,' said Lisa. 'You can come out on the pull with me.'

'That'll be right,' said Angela. 'Last time I did that, you ditched me for some guy with an Aston Martin, at Hellenic.'

'Yes, well, the least said about that the better.'

Lisa didn't do verbal apologies. She expected her friends to know by her behaviour and expression that she was truly sorry. She had never done it before or again since.

It was an unspoken rule. You didn't dump your friends for a man. The guy could wait until next time you were free. There were exceptions to the rule, but those included at least another friend being there with you. The streets were too dangerous to walk on your own nowadays. There were a lot of nutters out there, overindulging in drink and drugs, and then acting out of character.

'Ahem, can we get back to Gary then?' asked Gill.

'Sure,' agreed both girls.

'I think he looks really sexy and he's been very open and direct about his shift work. Some people couldn't cope with that. What do you think about not seeing him for weeks on end, if you did start seeing each other? You need to think ahead,' said Angela, ever the pragmatist.

'Well, of course I'd miss him, even if this is a rather premature conversation to be having, but given how busy I am with work, I think I could handle it. Especially if he made up for it when he was here.' She grinned, and Lisa catching on, winked and said, 'I'm sure he'd love you to handle it, doll.'

They both burst out laughing as Angela muttered, 'You two are beyond help.'

After taking a sip of her drink, Angela, all efficiency, said, 'Right, so he's a yes. Who's the second one?'

'Right, here we have Sean Hennessy.'

Lisa and Angela squinted at the profile in front of them.

'Na, he's not for me,' said Lisa abruptly. 'One for the No pile.'

'I disagree,' Angela said. 'He has a certain something.'

'OK, convince me,' said Lisa.

Angela shot a sidelong glance at Gill, who smiled and

rolled her eyes. Useless reiterating to Lisa that it wasn't *her* Sean had to convince.

'OK,' said Angela playing along, 'He looks a bit like the lead singer from Snow Patrol.'

'Yes, but he also looks like he needs a good wash and a pair of ironed trousers.'

'Nonsense,' said Angela, in a tone that brooked no argument, 'Yes, maybe he's been wearing that shirt for a couple of days, but check out the sexy eyes, the creases at the corners of them, even though he's only thirty-five.' She checked the profile for this last part. 'He looks a lot of fun. I just wouldn't expect him to cook me lunch. His cooker probably hasn't been cleaned since he moved in.'

'Maybe his sheets will be the same then,' said Lisa.

'Lisa, why must you always lower the tone?' Gill asked.

'It's my contribution and what I do best, well, second best,' she said after a momentary pause, flashing her friends a wicked grin.

'So, you don't like him at all?' Gill said.

'I don't know the bloke obviously, but on paper he's not selling himself to me.'

'I didn't say he was an escort,' muttered Gill under her breath.

'Well, I think he deserves a chance. And he's Irish,' Angela spotted, glancing up at Gill. 'You love Irish accents. What more could you want?'

'My thoughts exactly, and even if he didn't merit a date on any other point, and I'm not saying that's what I think,' Gill added quickly, 'his very Irishness would be enough to put him through to the next round.'

'That's that settled then,' said Angela, high-fiving her friend.

'So, let me get this straight. You now have four blokes on the go at the same time?'

Gill moved slightly in her chair, feeling uncomfortable for the first time about the four potential dates.

'Well, when you put it like that…' she began.

'No, that's bloody brilliant,' said Lisa. 'Result!'

Chapter Thirteen

Wednesday 7 September

Wednesday was a flurry of activity. Gill was glad she hadn't drunk much the night before. At least she felt alert. She had fielded calls all day from candidates going for final interviews at Smythson Engineering. They were preparing to head to Leeds for the last leg of their three-month interview process. How drawn-out that had been. One of the directors had suffered a heart attack and the firm had needed to wait until he could return to work before making a final decision. Now they were down to a shortlist of eight.

Gill had been delighted to receive an e-mail from Charlie, saying he could meet her for a drink on Sunday, but he'd need to leave by four to pick up his daughter. Far from being miffed at this, his comment endeared him a little more to Gill. His commitment towards his daughter showed he obviously took his parental responsibilities seriously.

He'd suggested Cosmopolitan in the Merchant City. Did she know it? She did. She'd been for a few birthday drinks with a friend not long after it opened, prior to attending a concert at City Halls. It was an inviting place, cosy, but with an upmarket feel. The waiters were happy to mix you up any cocktail, even if it wasn't on the menu and without having to ask you what it contained. That was service – the difference between a good bar and a great bar. She loved the plush, roomy booths, essential to having a private chat. There was nothing worse than being on a blind date where everyone could overhear your conversation. After a slight delay Gill replied saying that was fine, and could they make it one o'clock? Her rationale was, that way if they liked each other, they could potentially spend three hours together, whilst still having the get-out clause of it only being for a drink, if it didn't go to plan.

Gill stood up and crossed off some items on her whiteboard and added a few others. She had made a mental list in the shower that morning of the candidates she wanted to see for her SRC position. She wanted to contact them today to check their availability for next Thursday and Friday for an initial interview. The sooner she hired some help, the better.

Pulling the well-thumbed stack of shortlisted CVs towards her, she leafed through them, making final notes as to each candidate's merits:

Leslie Crutherland – had worked for a large multinational recruitment firm, in their Technical Sales Recruitment division for five years. His client portfolio included ten blue-chip companies.

Angus Mackie – twenty-nine. Didn't have much of a background in recruitment, but had worked for a small competitor of McFadden Technical Recruitment for the last two years. Very occasionally Gill had lost business to him.

Roseann Lavelle – had worked for a multinational recruitment firm in Glasgow, Manchester, and Paris, where its European headquarters was located. She spoke fluent

French and Flemish, as well as having done a degree in Law.

Alexander Currie – not long out of university, but with good work experience and he had worked for three different recruitment firms, each time under placement. He might enjoy and be grateful to have a real full-time position, where he wasn't going to be let go at the end of six months. The freedom to grow in an agency such as Gill's could also be a carrot to be dangled in front of him.

Zoe Straker – twenty-three, had returned from doing a gap year travelling around Asia and assisting in orphanages, after completing her MSc in Global Human Resource Management at the University of Liverpool. She had some recruitment experience, having worked each summer at one of the main players in the Glasgow area. Perhaps she had just made tea and answered phones, but her CV read well.

Gill glanced down the rest of her shortlist. The irony of interviewing candidates both in her professional and her private life was not lost on her. She hoped she didn't grill her dates too much, and that she didn't go into 'interview mode'.

She sent off the template e-mails inviting the candidates for interview, amending the names as necessary, and had completed her fifth when an e-mail popped up.

Hi, Gill, the agency said you would like to meet up. Are you free this weekend? If so, thought we could go for lunch and a few drinks. Let me know, Sean x

Kisses already. He's hopeful. But then, this was the Irish guy; even his name sent tingles down her spine. Sean, sensual Sean, sensuous Sean. *Oh shut up, Gill.* And he wanted to have lunch with her. He was keen, or hoped they'd get on. She liked that – admired his optimism. Plus today was only Wednesday. Saturday and Sunday were three and four days away respectively. He had given her enough notice, except she was already seeing Charlie on Sunday.

Gill sent out the remainder of her interview e-mails and then turned her attention back to her personal e-mail.

Nice to hear from you, Sean. Could do Saturday lunch. Where would you like to go? Once she had sent it off into the ether, she allowed herself a little smile.

Now she had dates with three men in one week! It really was true what they said, whoever *they* were. Men *were* like buses.

Chapter Fourteen

Thursday 8 September

On this September evening, with the sun actually making its presence felt for once, Gill felt light of heart and hopeful. She couldn't wait to see Anton again. Admiring herself in the mirror, she was pleasantly surprised at what she saw. Finally her wardrobe was being put to good use. Apart from her business and casual clothes, much of her wardrobe went untouched for months on end. That was about to change. Although she'd rather wear black for its slimming purposes, she felt that all black gave off the wrong vibe, nor was it particularly summery. Feeling slightly guilty about her other upcoming dates, Gill sprayed herself with a subtle sprinkling of her favourite perfume, an unfussy floral fragrance, and left the office.

Anton had asked her to meet him outside a music shop in Buchanan Street.

Too far to walk in heels, Gill flagged down a taxi. As the traffic was fairly light, rush hour already past, she arrived quickly. She'd asked the driver to drop her at the corner of West Nile Street and Sauchiehall Street, the closest drop-off to their rendezvous point.

Anton stood on the steps leading up to the sandstone-coloured concert hall, appraising Gill, as she exited the taxi and headed towards him. He was more smartly dressed than last time, in navy trousers, a pale blue shirt and a navy blazer. Gill hadn't noticed him initially, intent on reaching her destination, but as she approached the corner, she had run her hand through her hair, and in that split second, her glance upwards connected with Anton's, who smiled at her.

Instantly Gill's face lit up and she walked towards him. 'I thought I was meeting you at the music shop. Were you watching out for me?'

'We are kind of meeting there. It's only a few metres away. And yes, I was looking out for you. The steps are a good lookout, but there's another reason I'm standing here.'

'And what's that?' asked Gill.

'We're going to a concert: Chopin, Beethoven and Fauré.'

'Really?' Gill was delighted. How thoughtful of him. She'd mentioned in passing on their date on Monday how much she loved classical music. He had certainly been paying attention. Definite brownie points.

'Is that OK?'

'That sounds wonderful,' Gill told him.

'Oh, I forgot something,' he said then turned towards her.

'What?' said Gill, but she had no time to say anything else, as Anton bent his head and kissed her softly on the lips.

'I forgot to say hello,' he said, pulling away from her. Gill wished he hadn't, that he had continued, but they were standing in the centre of the steps outside the concert hall for all to see. She wasn't sure she cared.

'Hi,' said Gill.

Anton slipped his large hand into hers and escorted her into the concert hall.

After collecting the tickets, they had a quick drink in the crowded bar and then headed for their seats.

He must have paid quite a bit of money for these tickets. Should I offer to pay for mine? They were among the best seats in the house.

Anton had thought of everything. Slipping a bottle of water into her hand, as they took their seats, he then produced a programme, which he discussed with Gill, as they waited for the performance to start.

'So, first we have Chopin's Piano Concerto No. 2 in F minor, followed by Fauré's *Pavane* and finally Beethoven's Piano Concerto No. 5 in E flat major, Op 73,' Anton said, reading from the programme.

Gill didn't know all of the various works, but she did generally like classical music and Beethoven in particular, even if she didn't know which key they were played in. Anton sounded very knowledgeable.

'So, who are your favourite composers?' Gill asked him.

'Well, of course I love some of my countrymen,' Anton said, sounding a little patriotic, thought Gill, suppressing a smile. 'But, my favourite non-Russians are Brahms, Beethoven and current day, Ennio Morricone.'

'Really? I *love* Ennio Morricone,' said Gill, 'especially *Gabriel's Oboe.*'

'Yes, that's my favourite piece too, but of course he did a lot of the music to many of the old westerns.'

'Yes, I vaguely remember that. They're not my thing, though.'

'Me neither. I'd rather watch *Il Postino* or *Chocolat.*'

'No way!' said Gill. She laughed and then apologized.

'I'm sorry, it's just I've never met a man who would admit to liking *Chocolat*. It's usually the girls who are swooning over Johnny Depp.'

'Yes, he has that effect on me, too,' Anton said, laughing heartily. It was rather sexy.

The lights intensified and rounds of applause broke out when the members of the orchestra made their way onto the stage, beaming at the audience as they settled into their seats, repositioning music stands so they were optimally placed.

Usually Gill would have been ogling the orchestra to see if any new musicians had joined since she had last attended one of their concerts, checking to see if there was any talent, in both senses of the word. Now, however, the thought only entered her mind with regards to her past visits, as Anton smiled at her and offered her the programme to read, whilst they awaited the arrival of the conductor. She glanced briefly through it, more because he had been kind enough to buy it, than for any real desire to familiarise herself with the composer's history. She was interested, but right now the man sitting beside her held more appeal. Gill risked a sidelong glance at him; he was gazing thoughtfully at the orchestra.

'Do you play?' she asked him.

'Not any more. I learned violin until I was ten, but then I fell in love with science and stopped.'

'A pity.'

'Yes, I often think so, especially when I come to an event like this. I love classical music, but I'm no longer confident enough to play. Do you?'

'No, I would have loved to play piano, though, or violin, or even the oboe. I wouldn't have cared, as long as I could have produced a sound like that. The nearest I got was a loan of my cousin's chanter.'

'Chanter?'

'Yes, it's the part of the bagpipe which you play the tune on.'

'Ah, I see. I can imagine it now. I went to the Edinburgh Military Tattoo once. It's quite something.'

'I've never been.' Gill laughed. 'How bizarre that you have and yet, I'm Scottish and I haven't.'

'It's always the way. No one ever visits what's on their doorstep.'

The audience started to clap as the renowned Russian conductor, Dmitri Budkovskiy, walked towards the stage, his coat-tails flapping behind him and his mass of unruly curls bouncing as he walked. Lukasz Karpinski, the young Polish pianist who had won the 2010 Best Undiscovered Talent of the Year award, for his prowess in playing Chopin's works, smiled shyly from beside the great maestro. Dmitri bowed to the crowd once he reached the podium, whilst Lukasz accommodated himself at the instantly recognisable Steinway piano. Glancing at Lukasz and waiting for his confirmation that he was ready, the great Budkovskiy turned to the orchestra. Some silent instruction passed between them, before he raised his baton and the lively sound of the violins introduced the first movement.

Gill relaxed into the music, which alternated between lively and gentle. Although she enjoyed classical music, she had no idea what *allegro* and all the other musical terms meant. She remembered quavers from music class in third year at school, but was more likely to be found eating their crisps namesake these days. After the initial introduction, the piano dominated the piece and Gill sat, eyes half-closed, letting the music wash over her. Anton's hand lay partially on her armrest, so close to hers that they were almost touching. Her eyes flickered open and she saw that he was looking at her. She smiled and his hand covered hers. It felt warm, nice. How was she meant to concentrate on the music now, though? Her heart beat faster, simply from being so close to him. She'd forgotten just how potent lust could be.

And she had always found classical music an aphrodisiac. Pity none of her former boyfriends had been into classical music – that would really have been a dream come true. She'd often fantasised about being with a pianist or a violinist. They showed such passion – she imagined they'd be the same in bed. It would probably have been much cooler to lust after the latest rock or pop star, but that had never done it for her. She loved that the male members of the orchestra were all clean-shaven and sporting tuxedos.

Anton started tracing circles on the outside of her hand. It was a delicious sensation. It felt forbidden, surrounded as they were by hundreds of people, but it was as intimate as kissing her. Gill was getting aroused and hoped that things might go further with Anton tonight. He was lovely, adorable, sexy and very well-mannered. What more could she hope for in a guy? And he loved classical music. Short of serenading her every day with his own violin, there wasn't really much he could do to top that.

At the interval, they grabbed a quick drink at the bar. Anton chose a glass of Pinot Grigio and Gill decided to make that two. There was no place for them to sit, so they claimed a section of the bar as their own, out of the way of new customers, and leaned against it. As they sipped their drinks, they talked about the weekend. Gill didn't want him to know she had another date, but neither did she wish to lie to him. She skirted around it by remaining vague, saying she would be out for lunch on Sunday, but would have a lazy day on Saturday.

'I'm going to have to work this weekend,' Anton said. 'I'm going to Minsk in a few weeks and I have so much preparation to do, you wouldn't believe. Sometimes I wish there were more than twenty-four hours in a day.'

'Or less work,' mused Gill, since his thoughts echoed her own. *Please let these candidates for the SRC position be suitable.* She couldn't bear it if they weren't. She had already been struggling to keep up, before she turned into a social butterfly, and now there was no way she could manage without help.

'That's an even better idea.' He smiled down at her. Gill was relatively tall for a woman in the west of Scotland, where the average height was five feet four, but Anton positively dwarfed her. She rather liked it. He placed his glass down on the bar and tenderly stroked her cheek.

'We need to work less,' he murmured. Gill, transfixed, could barely nod her response.

The bell rang out, indicating they should return to their seats for the second half of the concert. Fauré's *Pavane* had been wonderful, so beautiful, but Gill was really looking forward to Lukasz playing the Beethoven piece. As they shuffled towards their seats, trying to be polite and not overtake the elderly gentleman being assisted to his seat, whilst snails overtook him, Gill thought, *I could get used to this.*

Lukasz Karpinski was certainly the talent he was proclaimed to be. Although best known for having completed all of Chopin's works, Gill thought he did an amazing job of performing Beethoven's Piano Concerto No. 5. As soon as the violins and double bass played the first few notes, Gill realised she knew this piece, whether from a film, or a TV ad, she couldn't be sure, but she had heard it before. Its gentleness went some way to calming her ardour, as it really was a very relaxing piece of music, almost somnolent. Anton placed his hand in hers during the piece, and although he didn't trace circles this time, for which she was partly thankful, he left it there and she didn't remove it.

Gill couldn't recall the last time she had felt this at ease with someone. It was so effortless, but there was most definitely a frisson between them. And she rather hoped she'd be in a position to do something about that soon. But how? He lived in Stirling, so it wasn't feasible for him to invite her back to his. Would it be forward of her to ask him back? Would he assume sex to be on the cards? It might be, but that wasn't the point. She didn't want him to think she took having sex with someone lightly. That wasn't the case, but she really liked him and it had been such a long time. Anton, she knew, would be a considerate and probably very passionate lover. Daydreaming about what they would be like together, she didn't realise it, but she had begun gently caressing his fingers with the underside of her thumb, which caused Anton to throw her a quizzical smile. *Wow!* A thunderbolt of lust shot straight through her. There was such a thing as a time and a place, but her libido didn't know that. She'd wait to see if Anton made a move or gave any signals after the concert.

'That was fantastic,' Gill said as they made their way out of the auditorium.

'I'm glad you enjoyed it. Good idea then?'

'Great idea, thanks so much for bringing me.' Gill fell momentarily silent. Again she wondered if she should offer to pay for the ticket. Somehow she thought not.

As they walked down the front steps of the concert hall onto Buchanan Street, Gill didn't want the evening to end, but she knew Anton would have to catch the train to Stirling. Idly she wondered how much a taxi would cost to Stirling. Breaking into her thoughts, Anton said, 'Are you in a rush to get home, or do you have time for a quick drink, before I have to catch the train?'

Her hopes dashed of a passionate encounter with the gorgeous Russian just yet, Gill recovered herself and hiding her dismay, said, 'No, a drink would be lovely. Did you have somewhere in mind?'

As it was a weeknight, the hotel bar opposite the concert hall wasn't too busy and they managed to snap up a table farthest from the bar, which afforded them some privacy. Anton told Gill of his family, his two brothers, also scientifically minded, and his mother who was a teacher. His father had died when Anton was eleven. He spoke of his father with great reverence and Gill was touched. A man unafraid to talk openly of his emotions. She'd been limiting her options by seeing only British men. She should have broadened her horizons to include dating foreigners a long time ago.

As Gill listened intently to Anton, she couldn't help noticing his beautiful smile. And when she went to the bar for another round, she could feel his approving stare on her back.

All too soon, though, it was time to leave.

'Are you getting a taxi home again?'

'Yes, I'll get one from outside the station like last time.'

'Great, let's go.' He held open the door for her.

They meandered down Buchanan Street, as slowly as was possible, without Anton actually missing his train. Anton put his arm around Gill's waist and when he found no resistance from her, left it there. Gill revelled in the feeling of this gorgeous man beside her. She just wished he didn't have to go.

As they turned into West George Street, Anton stopped and gently turned her towards him,

'I wish I didn't have to go.'

Had he been reading her thoughts? Was he angling for an invitation to stay at hers? Should she invite him back? These questions buzzed around Gill's head until Anton said, 'But unfortunately I need to work. Hopefully, next time I will have more time. Maybe we could meet at the weekend and I could stay over in a hotel or something?'

Gill wondered if the 'or something' meant stay at hers. She hoped so. But he'd already said he was busy this weekend and so was she. Come to think of it, she was busy most of the week. What would she say if he asked her to meet up midweek? She already knew that she'd rather meet him than any of the others. She felt as if she'd already met The One, if such a thing existed, but she didn't want to rush it, and by the looks of things, neither did he.

Gill smiled and nodded, not trusting herself to speak, in case she voiced how she felt about him, and more importantly in case she let slip how much she wanted to jump his bones. He was the full package all right. She had a Bridget Jones moment where she fast-forwarded to their three beautiful children. She was distracted by Anton's voice and by him bending down to look into her eyes. He caught her off guard even further by brushing a strand of hair aside – his touch was electric – and then kissing her, initially as gently as before, but then more deeply. She felt her arousal return. Oh God, she didn't want him to leave. When was she going to see him? He was perfect and she wanted him – all of him – every last morsel.

'I'd like to see you again,' he said when he came up for air. Gill felt dizzy – that had been the perfect kiss. Gentle, but insistent.

'Me too,' she whispered, aware that by The Rules she should have kept her mouth shut and waited for him to continue.

'I'm going to be busy next week preparing for Minsk, but I'd really like to see you before I leave, as I'll be gone two weeks.'

'OK.' She didn't know what else to say. She wouldn't see him next week, then? She seriously thought about telling him to hell with work tomorrow, and inviting him back to hers. But she had gathered that he took his responsibilities seriously. He wouldn't intentionally let anyone down. A good trait, she thought, if he applies it to his relationships, and more importantly, to whatever's happening between us.

'Gill, you have no idea how much I'd like to be spending time with you next week, but I've been working on this particular project for three years and it's very important. You do understand, don't you?'

Of course she understood. She had an engineering background, plus she knew what it was like, from running her own business. Quite frankly, all she could think was how delicious it had sounded when he said her name. She had to get a grip and stop behaving like a teenager with her first crush.

'No problem. If you have to work, you have to work, right?' she said, hoping it came across sincerely.

'Thanks. I like you, Gill. I really like you.'

This time Gill followed The Rules, giving Anton a smile which reached all the way to her flashing emerald eyes, but said nothing.

As they stood waiting for a taxi to take Gill home, Anton kissed her as if he had no intention of ever stopping. When she finally had to pull away to enter the taxi, she knew she wasn't the only one who was aroused.

Anton remained in place as her taxi headed off towards the traffic lights at the corner of George Square. He waved once, and then headed into the station.

As Gill reclined in the taxi, en route to Shawlands, she felt like she'd won the lottery. Could she really be this lucky?

Chapter Fifteen

Friday 9 September

'Well, at least those interviews are sorted now.' Gill breathed a sigh of relief and sat down heavily on the edge of Janice's desk. 'Honestly, Janice, I know you'll be just as relieved as me to have someone else give us a hand, but seriously, roll on Thursday.'

Gill had received replies from each of the applicants successfully selected for initial interview for the SRC post. She had to keep reminding herself that the readily available ones should not go to the top of the queue, tempting though it was. Being in Recruitment herself meant she didn't automatically assume someone wasn't a worthy candidate if they didn't currently have a job. The number of redundancies lately and the highly competitive nature of the job market at the moment meant many candidates who shouldn't be available were, even in Recruitment.

Ten to five on a Friday and she actually felt she had things under control. Of course, she still had screeds of e-mails to get through, but that would always be the case. At least she could breathe now and hopefully soon also have some help.

She'd received an e-mail from Anton saying how much he'd enjoyed her company last night and reiterating his desire to spend some more time together soon. She'd like to spend a lot more time with him. She was meeting Lisa in town after work for a quick drink. The others had family commitments.

'Janice, why don't you just head off? You're going out tonight, aren't you?'

Janice had filled Gill in during the week about her cousin Siobhan's fortieth birthday party on the Friday. It was in Edinburgh city centre in some posh hotel. Gill felt sure Janice would want as much time as possible to get ready, before heading off into the capital. Even though Friday afternoon traffic was lighter than during the week, it would still take Janice a good hour and a half to get home. A forty-minute head start would help.

'Are you sure? There's still so much to do here.'

'I'm sure,' Gill said. 'You've put in more than enough hours here, especially the past few weeks. The least I can do is let you leave a little bit early to get ready for this party.'

'Thanks, Gill, I appreciate it.' Janice beamed at her as she quickly shut down her computer. She popped her tortoiseshell glasses into their case and then dropped the case into her bag. Picking up her keys from her desk, she wished Gill a good weekend and was gone.

Gill was trying to get finished up when her mobile alert indicated she had an e-mail waiting. Sean. 'Is the new Italian place on Ingram Street, Civitavecchia, OK for you, one o'clock?'

Sean either wasn't counting on kissing her, or was assuming they would both be garlic-breathed, so it wouldn't matter. She liked him instinctively. He hadn't overthought things. She replied saying she'd see him there at one.

Her phone beeped again. That was quick. He must have been sitting on his phone. Smiling, she checked his reply, but to her surprise, it was an e-mail from Gary.

Hi, Gill, was pleased you would like to meet me. Realise it's too short notice to meet over the weekend, but how's Tuesday for you?

Gill decided to wait a while before e-mailing back. She'd run it past Lisa first.

An hour later Gill walked into Flanagan's pub at the top end of Bath Street, near the Kings' Theatre, and glanced around for Lisa. It was very busy and men and women in business suits, thirsty after a hard week's work, filled the bar, laughing and joking. A bald fifty-something man leered at her, his ruddy, unattractive face blocking her view momentarily. She sidestepped him and walked deeper into the bar, trying to spot her friend.

Just as she had given up hope, she finally caught sight of Lisa, being chatted up by not one but two city boys. Whether she had sat at their table, or they at hers, wasn't clear, but one seat remained vacant. As Gill approached, Lisa stood up to kiss her hello.

'Hi, Gill, this is Danny,' she said, indicating the tall blond man wearing a pale grey pinstriped suit. He looked not dissimilar to Anton. Same height, hair cut the same way, but without the piercing blue eyes. Yes, not as handsome and no Slavic bone structure to set it off.

'Nice to meet you.' Gill extended her hand. His cool hand briefly grasped hers and he smiled at her.

'And this is Trevor.' Lisa indicated the shorter man with dark hair, starting to go grey at the sides, but interestingly not the temples. He seemed fit underneath the crisp white shirt he wore, tie undone, and navy suit jacket already discarded over the back of his chair. She wondered why he simply hadn't taken it off. It looked untidy, just hanging there, and gave him the air of a recalcitrant schoolboy.

Gill greeted him and sat down. She shot a searching glance at Lisa, who raised her eyebrows in an *'I know'* way, and Gill wondered if she was referring to how good-looking they were, or the fact that one of them was called Trevor. How boring was that? OK, a tad shallow of her perhaps, but Trevor? Trev to his friends, apparently. Within half an hour, Gill was bored. Yes, they were good-looking, particularly Danny, who made it quite clear he liked her, moving into Lisa's seat when she vacated it to go and use the Ladies'. Gill had never really been one for going to the toilets two at a time, so she remained with the two men. After a knowing glance between Trevor and Danny, Trevor asked what Gill would like to drink.

'Pinot Grigio, please. A small glass.'

'And what about your lovely mate?'

'Vodka and fresh orange, please.' Gill couldn't say exactly why Trevor and Danny irked her, but they did. Perhaps it was Trevor's cringeworthy 'lovely' and 'mate' indicating he had already forgotten Lisa's name, more intent on gazing upon her attributes. Or maybe it was simply that they were full of themselves. Whatever, she knew she had to disentangle herself and Lisa from them. Although you never knew with Lisa. Their tastes in men differed greatly. But they were supposed to be on a girls' night out, to have a catch-up and so she could tell Lisa all the gossip about Anton, not so they could be stuck with two arrogant, egotistical bores. If she had to listen to Trevor mention one more time the trades they'd done that day and how exciting it was, she'd scream. Didn't he realise that since the worldwide financial crash in 2007, a banker was persona non grata. It was rude in the first place to be spouting forth so much about themselves, barely asking anything about the girls in return, but to be a banker into the bargain. Was she meant to be impressed by this? Heaven forbid. Some people really could be dim.

Gill was vaguely aware of Danny droning on, as she nodded and said 'Hmm' every so often, willing Lisa to return and either tell from her expression that she wanted to leave, or give her the opportunity to find an excuse to get away from them so she could think.

Fortunately, Lisa returned from the Ladies', took in Gill's bored demeanour and said, 'We'll need to get going soon, Gill, if we're to make our table.'

Relieved, Gill said, 'Oh, is that the time?' Taking one final sip of her wine, she stood up and said, 'Nice to meet you both. Hope you have a nice night,' as the men stared, gobsmacked at their sudden departure.

Trevor asked Lisa for her phone number, to which Lisa replied, 'Tell you what, you give me yours. I like to always be in the driving seat' She winked at him. Trevor hesitated then hastily scribbled down his mobile number.

'It's often switched off, but you can leave a message.'

'Thanks. Right boys, we have to go and eat. Bye.' Lisa sauntered off, Gill at her side.

No sooner were they outside and able to hear again – the music inside had been very loud – than Lisa said, 'Married – both of them.'

'What? How do you know?'

'Well, first of all, Trevor hesitated. No single guy hesitates when I ask for his number.'

Seeing Gill's look at her, trying to coax some humility into her friend, Lisa said, 'Oh well, you know what I mean. I'm not one to hold back, Gill. Anyway, that bollocks he just mentioned about his phone being off a lot. I bet – in case it rings at an inopportune moment.'

'Maybe he's just sweet on you,' said Gill, wondering why she was defending one of a duo she had taken an almost instant dislike to.

'Nope – defo married.'

'And what about the other one?'

'Well, in his haste to give me his number, Trevor knocked over his friend's briefcase.'

'Yes?' said Gill.

'There was a baby's bib in it – hopefully clean, but if he's not married, he's definitely in a relationship and has at least one kid.'

'Crikey, you should work for Strathclyde Police.'

'No, I'm more an Interpol kind of a girl, me. Right, now that those prats have screwed up our venue for this evening, where do you want to go?'

They walked along Bath Street, until they reached the back of The Sauchiehall Centre and then went into The Dragonfly, which was diagonally opposite. Luckily, it was less crowded.

They decided a bottle of Sancerre was the order of the day, and as Lisa brought Gill up to speed on her week and how crazy work had been, Gill started to unwind and the alcohol began to take effect. She didn't like to get too drunk, but she did enjoy feeling nice and relaxed and having fewer inhibitions.

Lisa relayed the details of the facial which had turned

into a rush to hospital case, as the woman had neglected to tell the salon she was allergic to nuts. They had used almond oil in her facial, not realising it would provoke an anaphylactic reaction. They'd needed to administer her EpiPen, which thankfully she carried in her bag. Rather than be sympathetic, Lisa moaned about the woman's stupidity.

'Imagine knowing you have a nut allergy, carrying an EpiPen with you and not telling your beauty therapist you have allergies. I mean, we're lucky, 'cos she signed a disclaimer and she filled in our form which specifically asks clients to list any allergies, which she didn't. Otherwise, we could have been in trouble.'

Gill nodded. She felt sorry for the poor woman who had been rushed to hospital, when she had expected to be pampered, but she also saw Lisa's point.

'And then I had this old biddy who came in and told me that I had done her chin wax last week, and had missed a bit. Cheeky cow asked me to fix it for free. We already give pensioners thirty per cent off. This woman was like Grotbags! Do you remember Grotbags?'

Gill shook her head, then said, 'Oh yeah, vaguely. Wasn't she the witch in that kids' show with Rod Hull and Emu?'

'That's the one. Well, this woman had a hairy chin like that and warts on her face almost as large as Grotbags', too.'

Lisa was on a roll, and it was best to just let her rant when she was like this. She could be very self-absorbed, but once she got things off her chest, she then became the best listener in the world, and that was what Gill needed from her tonight.

'And then we had three cancellations. Man, does that

get my back up. Cancelling at the last minute on a Friday – our busiest day. I had just turned down two waxings and a spray tan as I couldn't fit them in, then the phone went three times in a row with cancellations. It makes me so angry. People have no respect or manners nowadays.'

Gill agreed, but it was just a part of life. You couldn't beat yourself up about it.

Lisa sat back, took a sip of her wine and said, 'Right, so what's happening with lover boy, the Russian Rascal?'

Taking a deep breath, Gill related what had happened the night before. She would probably have gone into slightly more detail with Debbie, but there were certain things she didn't linger over with Lisa.

'So, you've snogged him and there was a bit of hand-holding and that's it?' Lisa summarised, scrunching up her eyebrows.

'Well, yes, but he wants to see me again before he goes to Belarus.'

'What's he going to Belarus for?'

'Work – a course or project or something.'

'And you really like him?' Lisa said gently.

'Yes, I do.'

'But you're meeting Charlie tomorrow.' A hint of a smile played on Lisa's lips.

'Yes, do you think that's wrong?'

'No way. You hardly know Anton. You've not exactly declared undying love to each other – yet. Plus the guy has barely laid a finger on you. I get that he's being gentlemanly and he might even have given you the impression that next time he'd like to move things along, but the fact remains you've been out twice and you've only had a snog. You're nearly forty for God's sake. A woman has needs.'

'Are we talking about me or you here?' Gill asked, suppressing a laugh.

'Both of us and you know it. Anyway, it's a good thing you're going out with Charlie tomorrow. It will give you something to measure Anton against.'

'That's true.'

'And what else have you got planned then? Any other dates?'

Gill told Lisa about the dates she had on Saturday and Sunday with Sean and Charlie, and now possibly Tuesday with Gary.'

'Woo hoo! Would you look at you. You're the latest It girl. We'll see you in the society pages soon, most wined and dined woman in Glasgow,' Lisa joked.

'Well, it's just drinks, to see if we like each other, but who knows where it might lead. And you did say I should see as many different guys as possible.'

'I'm just winding you up. Of course you should. Plus, you're paying that agency through the nose for the privilege. And it's good to see you getting out and about. You've had more of a social life in the past few weeks than you've had in the past few years.'

Another truth. Yes, she really should make the most of it. She'd been very happy so far with the prospective dates the agency had sent her, apart from the antiques dealer, she reminded herself. And she couldn't fault their service.

'So, tell me about Gary and Sean.'

Gill gave her a potted history of the little she knew about them from their profiles.

'I haven't actually replied to Gary yet.'

'No time like the present,' said Lisa.

She waited whilst Gill dialled.

'What should I say?'

'Tell him Tuesday's fine and he should be prepared to take you somewhere fabulous.'

'No, Lise, really, what should I say?'

'I dunno – yes, Tuesday night's good. Did you have anywhere in mind?'

Gill dutifully typed out the message and pressed send.

'Done.'

They soon moved on to Lisa's plans for the weekend. She was working all day Saturday, of course, Saturday being another busy day for the salon. But she was heading out on Saturday night with her sister and one of her friends into Glasgow, clubbing, if Gill wanted to come. Knowing how much of her precious time would be taken up with the two dates she had lined up over the weekend, plus Tuesday's rendezvous with Gary, she thanked Lisa, but declined, saying she would have to work through most of Saturday morning, between e-mails and housework, just to stay on top of things. Gill told Lisa that she was hopefully close to finding a senior recruitment consultant and that that would not only take the pressure off her, but help her grow the business.

'It's not before time, Gill. That's three years you've been doing this single-handedly.'

'Yeah, I know, but I have Janice.'

'I know, and you'd be lost without her, but she's not a recruitment consultant, so there's a limit to what she can help you with.'

Lisa was right. If all went well, the next thing would be to get additional admin support, perhaps a student looking for work experience. Actually, that wasn't a bad idea. Why hadn't she thought of it before?

'Just a sec,' she said to Lisa. She opened her calendar and diarised to investigate hiring a student. 'So what are you doing on Sunday?'

'Well, whilst you are being fawned over by the lovely Charlie, I will no doubt be nursing a hangover. You know we don't do things by halves, our family. Amy wants to try and stay out until everything shuts. It always involves a taxi back, occasionally with one of us having to ask the driver to pull over so someone can be sick at the side of the motorway.'

'Nice...' said Gill.

'Yeah, but true. And then I think I'll spend Sunday in my pyjamas watching *Persuasion* and *Spooks*.'

'*Persuasion*? I wouldn't have thought that was your thing.'

'Not my thing? Are you mad? Rupert Penry-Jones is in it. Did you see him in *Silk*? Phwoar!'

Gill had watched *Persuasion* several times. She liked classical literature and several adaptations were very good indeed. And yes, if Colin Firth or Rupert Penry-Jones featured in them, so much the better. You could do far worse things with your weekend than lie on the sofa watching box set DVDs. But surely there were better things, too? Well, this weekend she hoped to find out.

Chapter Sixteen

Saturday 10 September

The forecast for the weekend was actually quite good. Gill got up early and spent the first half of Saturday morning paying bills, trying to work out what to wear, and catching up on housework. She really wished she had time to organise a cleaner. It would be so lovely to spend all of her weekend doing enjoyable things like reading, watching TV or even pottering a bit in the garden, maybe catching an occasional, and it was very occasional in the west of Scotland, ray of sunshine.

For her date, Gill plumped for a cream V-necked short-sleeved shirt showing just a hint of cleavage and paired that with rust-coloured linen three-quarter-length trousers. She married that with amber earrings which Christopher had bought her one Christmas. She pinned her hair up, with just a few loose tendrils falling around her face. She looked, she thought, very feminine. Too tall and slightly too heavy to be considered dainty, at least she looked pretty.

It was unseasonably warm for September. Last September it had rained almost every day. She had been quite glad to be heading off for a long weekend with the girls to Amsterdam. That reminded her, she really must organise the insurance for their upcoming trip to Barcelona, but first things first – she had a date to think about.

With such fine weather, Gill decided to make her way to Glasgow by bus. Going into town on a Saturday always proved a little chaotic. She just hoped there wasn't a football game on today. The season had started a few weeks ago and the city was always torture to be in when a few rowdy fans chose to spoil it for everyone.

Cars were backed up for several hundred metres and the traffic was slow-moving, but soon they got going again and edged over the Clyde and into the city.

Gill wanted to arrive at Civitavecchia with enough time to spruce herself up, make sure she looked fresh, and to ensure her hair hadn't fallen down more than it was meant to.

She hopped off the bus in Hope Street and ambled towards Buchanan Street, which was busy with Saturday shoppers. She ducked through into Royal Exchange Square, gazing up briefly at the old Stirling's Library. She hadn't been in it since its conversion to The Gallery of Modern Art.

Checking the traffic on Queen Street, she made her way across into Ingram Street, towards where the recently opened Italian restaurant stood. It had received excellent reviews and a national newspaper restaurant critic had given it nine out of ten. Gill was keen to try it, and just hoped she wouldn't be too nervous to enjoy her meal. In Anton's company she had felt relaxed. She hoped it would be the same with Sean.

She arrived fifteen minutes early. Should she go in, freshen up and sit down somewhere, and wait for him to turn up? Or clean up, come back out and go in again in twenty minutes? No, what if he saw her? Then she'd look ridiculous. But surely she'd recognise him. Deciding that the least idiotic option was to wait for him, she approached the door and went in.

She saw him straightaway, but his eyes weren't on the door. Either he expected her to see him, or he assumed she wouldn't be early. He was texting, concentrating on the buttons as he typed out a message. His head was slightly bent forwards, but she could still clearly see his face under his mop of black curls. He was handsome. The toilets were to the left-hand side. Sean was sitting to the right. Should she sneak to the toilet to check she was presentable and that her make-up hadn't sweated in the September sun? Or should she just approach him? She had no chance to deliberate further, as just then Sean looked up, his face creasing into a huge smile. He raised his right hand in greeting and dropped his phone into his pocket with his left.

Gill made her way to his table, her stomach churning like a washing machine.

'Hi, Gill, it's grand to meet you.' Sean kissed her on both cheeks.

'Very Mediterranean.' Gill smiled. 'Nice to meet you, too.'

'Ah well, I'm from Galway, so we're European all right. What would you like to drink?'

He was drinking Guinness.

'Could I have a glass of medium white wine, please?'

'Sure you can. Just you sit yourself down there, and I'll take care of it.'

Gill sat down as Sean went to the bar. She *loved* his accent. Irish accents always did it for her, but Sean's was particularly hitting the spot. He did look quite young. She knew he was only thirty-five, two years younger than her, but he barely seemed thirty. His photo hadn't done him justice at all. And he scrubbed up well, too; gone was the unkempt look from his photo. So, he had made an effort. Good. When he returned, he leant across her slightly to place her drink down and she breathed in the smell of his aftershave – not too noticeably she hoped. It wouldn't do for it to seem as if she were trying to drink him in. He scored a comfortable eight for presentation.

'So, Gill,' said Sean, as he sat opposite her. 'This is my first time, so can you be gentle with me?'

'Your first time?' Gill repeated, her tone a mixture of perplexed and horrified.

'Yes, meeting someone through the agency.' His eyes twinkled.

Gill tried not to burst out laughing and failed miserably.

'You didn't think…?'

'Just for a second…yes…I did,' she said, struggling to regain her composure.

'Well, I'm hardly Brad Pitt, but even I've managed to address that issue by now.'

'Anyway,' said Gill, eager to change the subject, feeling that joking or not, touching on the subject of Sean's virginity and when he lost it, was no way to start a date, 'who recommended the restaurant to you?'

'Oh, one of my friends, Gail. She started working here part-time in the evenings to get some extra cash, just after it opened. She says it's been booked solid since then. She obviously wasn't kidding.'

Gill's glance took in the restaurant part of Civitavecchia, where only two tables were unoccupied. Both had reserved signs and presumably one was theirs.

'I booked for half one. I thought we could have a drink and get to know each other a bit before eating. To tell the truth I was a bit nervous and wanted to make sure I wasn't going to be such a mess that I'd dribble spaghetti down my shirt.'

Gill laughed. Sean was very likeable and had an easy manner about him. She thought briefly of Anton.

They chatted a bit about work and then Gill quizzed him on music.

'Yeah, I came over to Scotland to study at the RSAMD, but I liked it here and so I stayed. I have a lot of friends here now.'

'You never thought about going back?'

'Sure I did, but I haven't yet and I've been here more than a decade now.'

'That is a long time,' Gill agreed. 'You'll have seen a lot of changes in Glasgow then.'

'Oh yeah, particularly new pubs opening up. Not so many closing down. Of course, there's the smoking ban, too.'

'That's right, you smoke, don't you?'

'Yeah, I know, it's a terrible habit, but I only do it to be sociable.'

This argument didn't convince Gill, but she let it go.

'So you're reduced to standing outside in the rain or under one of those huge heaters they have in beer gardens?'

'Pretty much. You can barely breathe when you walk out of a pub these days for the smog that smokers have created.'

'Excuse me, your table's ready. Would you like me to take your drinks over for you?' the waitress asked.

Saved by the bell. Gill grinned as she sat back whilst the waitress placed their glasses on a tray. They then followed her through the busy restaurant to a well-appointed table, away from the noisy bar, the kitchens and the toilets.

'That's better,' said Sean, once the waitress had provided them with menus and announced that today's specials were for antipasto: *Involtini di Speck con Mozzarella*; for pasta: *Spaghetti alle Vongole* – neither liked clams so that wasn't an option; and for main course, the special was *Porchetta*, Sardinian suckling pig. The waitress had explained that this was a special treat, usually only available if ordered twenty-four hours in advance, as it required a lot of preparation. But a party which had ordered it, and paid the fifty per cent deposit required, had just cancelled, so the *Porchetta* was being made available to all diners.

'I can never decide whether to have the specials, as that's likely to be the best they have, or whether it's just the restaurant offloading all the stuff they have left.'

Gill laughed. 'I know what you mean. I once tried wood pigeon as I was told it was to die for. It was nothing special.'

'Doesn't surprise me. OK, let's give this place the benefit of the doubt. It's had good reviews and every time a waiter walked past me with food earlier, I was like the Bisto kid with my nose in the air. Plus I'm starving. You?'

'Well, I had some cereal this morning, but yes, I could eat.'

'What do you fancy?' asked Sean, unfolding his napkin and laying it on his lap.

I think I'm going to have the *Involtini* to start,' Gill said.

'*Involtini*? Ah, the Wild Boar. Yeah, that looked good. I

might have the *Caprese* salad.'

Damn, now he'd chosen a salad and she was having a meat dish for starters, and she really wanted the *Porchetta* for mains, but how to do that without seeming like the pig she was about to order?

'Oh, and what's caught your eye for the main course?' Gill asked.

'I'm definitely having that suckling pig. That sounded like the dog's bollocks. I mean, it sounded really good.'

Deciding stuff it, she was hungry and she was also having the Porchetta, she told him of her choice.

'I like a girl who likes her food. Sorry, I mean, who's not afraid to order a normal meal, instead of just a salad.' Sean twirled his wine glass lightly in his hand.

Gill realised she didn't feel nervous with Sean. She was warming to him. It was too early to tell if there was a spark between them or not, but he was certainly entertaining company. She hadn't taken offence at his comment. She was slightly overweight, but not enough that she expected jibes about it. Besides, she did love food.

The waitress returned, just as they were deciding on the wine. In the end they opted for a bottle of a traditional red Sardinian wine, *Cannonau*. Gill had had it before and loved it, but Sean professed that it was his first time. This time Gill didn't blush.

As they waited for their starters, they chatted about music and who they liked and didn't like. Sean couldn't stand rap either, nor was he particularly enamoured of the acts which shook their booty, or botty as was so often the case, he said. He loved rock music and indie music from the nineties, some pop music and even some heavy metal. He didn't go to classical music concerts, but he did occasionally listen to it, depending on his mood.

Gill thought Sean was quite small for a rugby player. She didn't follow rugby but she'd seen some of these guys on TV and they were huge: six feet five, six feet seven. He was quite slim, too, fit-looking.

'So how often do you play rugby?'

'Not as much as I'd like. Once every two weeks or so. Depends when we can get enough guys together to play – there are always the fair-weather players who run for the hills at the least spot of rain.'

Gill smiled, so Sean continued. 'Yeah, I used to play a lot back home and was a member of Galwegians Rugby Club, which is a great place, great craic as well, but it's not the same playing here.'

'Could you not play for a club here, too?'

'I could, if work commitments didn't mean that sometimes I have to let the guys down, and I don't like doing that.'

Admirable. Reliable.

The waitress arrived with their wine and asked if they'd like to try it.

'No, just go ahead and pour it, please. I'm sure it'll be fine,' said Sean.

The waitress poured a glass for Gill first and then proceeded to fill up Sean's glass.

When she had finished and was about to place the bottle on the table, he said, 'Oh, it's half a glass you're giving us now then, is it?'

The waitress was a bit confused and moved as if to top up his glass, but Sean said, 'I'm just joking with you. It's fine.'

Once the waitress had gone, Sean said, 'Shall we toast then?'

'OK. What do you want to toast to?'

'To the lovely woman sitting in front of me.'

Gill could tell she had turned crimson, and he added hurriedly, 'And to meeting new friends.'

There was a slight pause, when Sean's gaze fixed on her for a second longer than was truly necessary, and then Gill jumped in with, 'So, you like hurling?'

'Oh, I love it. It's my favourite sport, even more than rugby. I'm really lucky. There's a club in Glasgow that I've played for since I moved here. We play matches a couple of times a month.'

'That's lucky. Correct me if I'm wrong – is it a mix of hockey and shinty?'

'Well, I suppose, but of course there are some rules which are different even to those two.'

Since Gill didn't know the rules of any of the three sports, she decided to leave it at that.

'So what would you normally be doing on a Saturday afternoon?' Sean asked just as a voice called, 'Sean! I can't believe it's you. How are you?'

'Dougal! I'm grand. Oh my God, I haven't seen you in ten years.'

'That's 'cos you haven't been home for ten years.'

Sean rose and greeted Dougal, slapping him on the back and hugging him. Suddenly, remembering where he was, he turned to Gill and said, 'Sorry, Gill, this is an old friend of mine from home, Dougal. Dougal, this is Gill.'

'I'm not that old,' said Dougal as he pumped Gill's hand up and down. His hands were like shovels and her own slender hand disappeared in Dougal's vast paw.

'So what are you two youngsters up to today then? A spot of lunch, is it?'

Gill guessed Dougal's age as early fifties.

'Yes, starters should be arriving any second,' Sean said.

'Well, I won't keep you from your lunch, but Sean, give me a call. Here's my business card. I'm in town all next week.'

After giving the card a cursory glance, Sean pocketed it. 'I will so. What are you up to in here then?'

'Oh, just meeting a few old friends. Didn't realise I'd be bumping into even older friends. I was looking for the toilet, but I don't think it's over here.'

'No, it's by the door, when you come in.'

'That's what I get for not paying attention. Too busy on my phone. Oh, here's your meal now. I best be going. Enjoy.'

Gill muttered a goodbye to Dougal as the waitress set their plates in front of them.

'That smells amazing,' said Sean, eyeing up Gill's plate then staring forlornly at his *Caprese* salad.

Gill stifled a laugh. Sean obviously regretted ordering the salad, which to be honest, also looked delicious.

'Would you like to swap?'

'Oh no, no, you're fine,' said Sean. His eyes conveyed a different message.

'OK, well, why don't we share the starters then?'

Sean's face lit up like a five-year-old who has been told he can stay up late.

'That would be grand. Would you like me to divide them up?'

'Sure.' *This could be interesting*, thought Gill, *on two counts*. First of all, would he divide them easily and allow her to choose first, or give her the larger portion? Secondly, would he make a hash of it?

But Sean more than capably split the *involtini* in two; it was really one huge *involtini*. Then he divided the tomatoes, mozzarella and even managed to position the basil carefully on top of each to form a trio. It looked almost identical to the original presentation.

'Well done,' said Gill. 'I'm impressed. If I had done it, half of the contents would have been on the floor and the rest would look as if a child had been smushing up its dinner.'

'That's a great word, *smush*.'

'Yes it is, isn't it?'

'I also like sploonging.'

'Sploonging?'

'Yes, it means soaking wet.'

'Is that an Irish word? I haven't heard that before.'

'No, it would appear that it's a word only used in my family, although I could swear blind that I remember other people using it when I was growing up, but there's no record of it anywhere.'

'Not even on Google?'

'No, on this occasion, I'm afraid to say, Google failed me.'

Gill laughed. He was so earnest. Sean really was fun to be around.

'More wine?' he asked as he raised the bottle.

'Not for me, thanks. I've still half a glass left.'

'OK so. Next time. Don't let me forget.' He winked at her.

They chatted easily over their starters, which they enjoyed, but both awaited the arrival of the porchetta with anticipation.

'I'm looking forward to this,' said Sean. 'I've heard

about it. I'm glad that party cancelled. Their loss is our gain and all that.'

Gill agreed. She was still hungry, or maybe her stomach was rumbling from nerves.

When the main course arrived, they both stared in awe. The head waiter carved it in front of them. It smelled absolutely amazing. Gill felt sure the smell of suckling pig would be clinging to her clothes by the time she left, but she didn't care. It completely assailed her senses.

The first few mouthfuls confirmed her suspicions – it was glorious. A hush fell over the table as they tucked into the porchetta, the only communication Sean rolling his eyes, indicating his enjoyment of the dish. Sean topped Gill's glass up once it was nearly empty, drained the remainder of the bottle into his own glass then signalled to the waiter to bring another bottle.

Once the waitress had cleared away their plates, Sean declared that he was as stuffed as the pig they had just eaten. Gill, who had left some, rather than feel uncomfortably bloated, also announced that she was full. When the waitress returned with dessert menus, they politely declined and asked for a break before coffee.

'So you go to Body Pump? Sean asked, as he set his wine glass back down on the table.

'Well...' Should she lie or tell the truth? Truth. 'I've been to Body Pump.'

'It wasn't your thing?' Sean leaned towards her conspiratorially.

'Not really, plus I couldn't move for three days because of the pain.'

'Yeah, that ties in with what people at work have said about it. I prefer my sports outdoors, although I have been to a gym. But it's usually full of vain ponces. I'm only talking about the guys here. Now the girls, that's something else.'

Gill was marginally taken aback by him referring to ogling other women so blatantly in front of her. She decided two could play that game. Although she wasn't remotely jealous, she did think it poor form to talk about other women whilst on a date, a first date at that, with someone else.

'Well, to be honest, the only enjoyable part about Body Pump was seeing the guys pump iron. It's quite a turn-on,' she said daringly.

Sean's eyes almost popped out of his head. He went to start a sentence but was so tongue-tied he came to a complete halt, before stammering, 'Er, right.'

Now it was Gill's turn to lean in towards him, 'I'm joking.'

His relief apparent, as he could in no way be described as a bodybuilder, even if he was fit, Sean smiled. 'Ah, you had me there.'

Gill raised her glass to him and, feeling bolder by the minute, said, 'So tell me Sean, what's *your* idea of romance?'

A cornered animal would have appeared less hunted. But he had put in his profile that he wanted to meet a woman he could romance, so Gill was putting him to the test.

'You want me to tell you now?'

'Well, I could wait until next Tuesday, but where's the fun in that?'

'OK, OK. Let me think, because there's not just one thing and it depends on who the woman is, and her likes and dislikes and what stage you are at in your relationship,' Sean floundered.

Gill laughed. 'I'm only playing with you.' Then realising what she had just said, by the colour Sean had turned, she amended that to, 'but if you already have an idea you want to share, that's fine by me.'

'OK, well, I like all the traditional stuff: Valentine's Day, Eiffel Tower, Venice, cuddly teddy bears, chocolates, flowers, but I also like to do things which are more surprising.'

Gill thought this could mean anything, good or bad, so she pressed him. 'For example?'

'Well, if I was in a relationship, I might buy my girlfriend a new dress or some expensive toiletries and have the bath ready when she got home from work, so she could relax. Then she could wear the new dress I'd just bought her when I took her to a newly opened restaurant.

'That does sound thoughtful,' said Gill. *And too good to be true.* So, as Sean was handsome, funny, romantic and charming, she couldn't figure out why he needed to use a dating agency. Why didn't he have a girlfriend? He clearly wanted one.

'What about you? What would be your ideal romantic date if you were in a relationship?'

Thinking Sean's idea was perfect, but not wanting to scare him off by telling him that too soon, Gill described her scenario. She outlined how they each took a day of the weekend to surprise the other, planning activities that they knew their partner would enjoy and that weren't always necessarily to the giver's taste. It was all about selflessness.

'Wow! My plan feels tame now in comparison.'

'Not at all – I just took it a step further.'

Sean ordered a third bottle of wine, before continuing.

Gill glanced at her glass. She didn't remember drinking much and they were on their third bottle. How had that happened?

Her reverie was broken by Sean hiccupping loudly. She studied him closely. Was he drunk? She felt fine. Had he drunk the majority of the two bottles of wine?

When the waitress arrived with the third bottle of wine, Gill took the liberty of ordering coffee for two.

As they talked about their favourite films, Sean became louder and louder, provoking startled and disapproving glances from the surrounding tables. The waitress returned and asked if they would prefer to have their coffee in the bar. Gill said that would be fine, but was mortified. She didn't know Sean well enough to tell him to keep his voice down, but neither did she want to be stared at by angry diners.

'Sean, let's go and have our coffee in the bar.'

'I'm perfectly happy here,' he slurred.

Oh Christ, he really is pissed. Gill didn't know what to do. 'Sean, they're really busy and could use our table.'

'Well, we booked the table. They didn't tell me it had to be given back by a particular time.' He was borderline belligerent now.

'Sean, the waitress is bringing our coffees out to the bar. Get a wriggle on,' she finally said.

'Oh, OK then,' he said sheepishly.

Relieved, Gill headed for the bar. Why hadn't she noticed how much he had been drinking? She turned at a noise behind her. Sean had crashed into two stools and knocked them over, then fallen over another and landed on a heap on the floor.

Brilliant. That's all I need. As she made her way back to assist him, a passing waiter helped him to his feet and asked him if he was all right.

'Why wouldn't I be?'

Could this *get* any worse? Gill wondered.

Realising that any warmth she had felt towards Sean had dissipated on witnessing the change in him, she sat on the edge of her bar stool and accepted the coffee the barista handed her. Sean ignored his, favouring the wine glass he held onto. He'd asked the waiter to bring the bottle of wine from their table.

What a pity. She'd had such a great time, up until Sean had become so drunk as to be no longer personable, and indeed an embarrassment. She couldn't wait to finish her coffee to make her excuses. Her thoughts were jarred, however, by Sean saying,

'So, where do you want to go from here, Gill?'

She wasn't sure if he meant it figuratively or literally, but had already made up her mind she was heading home in the next ten minutes.

'Actually, Sean, it's getting late and I have a lot of work to do. Do you mind if we just finish up here and get the bill?'

'Aw,' Sean said. For a minute he was transformed into a lost little boy and she felt a fleeting affection for him.

Who comes to a first date and gets plastered? Even if he was nervous, there was no need to drink that much. Look at the state of him now.

'I'll get the bill,' he said.

'Let's split it,' said Gill.

'No, my treat,' said Sean. She didn't insist. At least he was being chivalrous.

The bill paid, Sean said, 'It's a pity you have to go. We were just starting to get to know each other properly.'

'Yes, it is a pity,' said Gill, leaving the statement hanging, wondering if he would interpret that as she meant it.

He kissed her on the cheek and said, 'I'll call you next week. I might just stay here for a bit.'

'Right,' said Gill, striking him off on that count, too. No intention of walking her to a taxi or the bus station, left to make her own way home, whilst he sat at the bar and continued to drink wine. She was better off out of it. 'Nice to meet you, Sean. Goodbye.' Gill practically sprinted out of Civitavecchia and headed to the taxi rank. After that ordeal, she deserved the luxury of splashing out for a taxi home.

Chapter Seventeen

Sunday 11 September

'Oh God, Gill, I'm so sorry,' said Debbie, as she listened to her friend relay the previous day's events over the phone. Disgusted and disappointed, when the taxi had dropped her home she had decided *Persuasion* was called for. If it was good enough for Lisa, it was good enough for her. A little bit of Captain Wentworth to show her that not all men were selfish scum. No wonder she had love handles, she thought – giant chocolate buttons and almost enough glasses of red wine to rival the state Sean had been in earlier would not help her waistline, but just then she didn't care. What a contrast to her dates with Anton. She didn't know whether to look forward to her date with Charlie today, or dread it. Surely he wouldn't be a lush, too. But then, he was seeing his daughter later, so would be unlikely to drink much.

'It's just such a shame. He was lovely in every way and then he started slurring his words and got really loud. Everybody was staring at us. And then he fell over a stool.'

'You'll see the funny side one day,' Debbie assured her. 'Put it where it belongs, in the past, and move on. Treat it as a trial run for today's date with Charlie.'

'Yeah, I'll try,' said Gill, but she wasn't convinced.

By the time twelve thirty came around, Gill was calmer. She had put on some concealer to hide the dark shadows under her eyes, caused by a night of broken sleep. She was trying to remain positive about the dating experience, but was still understandably raw from yesterday's fiasco.

Unlike Saturday, the weather had changed for the worse. Rain streamed relentlessly down the windowpanes of her living room. To match her mood, Gill had donned a black halterneck dress, casual enough to get away with wearing for an afternoon date. Again she wore her hair up. She had just time to grab a cerise trench coat to add a splash of colour to her ensemble, and an umbrella, before the taxi beeped its horn.

Fifteen minutes later, Gill paid the driver and tried to open her umbrella from inside the taxi, so as not to get drenched. She strode into a relatively quiet Cosmopolitan.

Must be the weather keeping people away.

Charlie sat at the bar, facing the door. He smiled and raised his hand in greeting. He must have been watching out for her. He was very attractive, but in a totally different way from Anton or Sean. She reached him and he smiled at her.

'Good to meet you,' he said then kissed her on the cheek. 'What would you like to drink?'

His voice was like silk, smooth and sensuous. With that one sentence, she knew she could listen to him all day. Pity they only had a few hours. She checked to see what he was drinking. It appeared alcoholic – a pint.

'Can I have a medium white wine, please?'

He ordered and, reminiscent of her first date with Anton, Gill sized him up. She couldn't help compare them.

Both were tall, Charlie was six feet one, blond, with short hair and blue eyes, but there the similarities ended. Charlie oozed confidence. He seemed very relaxed; even his clothing was casual. Faded jeans and a rugby shirt clung perfectly to the contours of his body, and what contours! She remembered that he played rugby and, unlike Sean, it showed. She expected most people would describe him as powerfully built. And he wore those jeans so well…God, she really needed to have sex soon; she was becoming obsessed, but he was so sexy. She hadn't felt this instant lust with Sean yesterday. In fact, after the escapade with Sean, she had thought it might take some time before she experienced lust again. Now here she was, the very next day, almost panting over a guy she had just met. Guiltily, she thought of Anton. As Charlie turned to hand her drink to her, she put Anton to the back of her mind and listened intently to what Charlie was saying.

They moved to a corner table, which offered them more privacy.

Ten minutes in and Gill was really beginning to enjoy herself. They were laughing and flirting with each other. They seemed to like each other's sense of humour.

This dating lark's easy. You just glam up, turn up, be the best version of yourself and see what happens. Initially unsure whether she ought to ask him about his daughter, she couldn't help herself.

'So, you have a daughter?'

'Yes, Chloe. She's twelve. I'm trying to make the most of my time with her whilst she's still a kid. Next year, she'll turn into the female equivalent of Kevin the teenager. I'm not looking forward to that one bit.'

'What have you got planned for later with her?'

'Oh, we're going over to Braehead. She'll probably want to drag me around shopping for clothes, before we go to the ski slope, and then no doubt pizza will be on the menu.'

'Sounds fun.'

'Yeah, she's a good kid. Bright. Takes after her dad.' His eyes twinkled.

'Her humble and modest father.' Gill smiled.

'Everyone has their vices.'

She felt like asking what the others were, but resisted.

'So, you like going to the cinema?'

'Yes,' said Gill. 'I don't get to go as often as I would like, but I love it – the whole experience.'

'You mean paying fifteen quid for a Coke, popcorn and nachos?'

'Pretty much. I know, it's extortionate these days. Does that mean we're getting old, that we think that? I have a fear that I'll start talking about the price of butter soon.'

'Well, butter is damned expensive. Bring back that butter mountain, that's what I say,' said Charlie. His eyes glinted and the corners of his mouth turned up slightly.

'So what do you like to see when you do go to the cinema?' he asked.

'Romcoms, thrillers, period dramas. Most things apart from zombies, horror and sci-fi.'

'Damn, I love a good zombie flick.' Charlie smiled again, revealing very small white teeth, which seemed strange in such a large man. He certainly looked like he brushed thrice daily, either that or went in for teeth whitening. No, she thought he seemed too manly and not vain enough for that. They must be naturally like that.

'Have you seen *Shaun of the Dead*?' Charlie asked.

'Yes, but that's not really a zombie movie – that's a rom-zom com. I think that's the right order,' said Gill, scrunching up her forehead, trying to remember.

'OK, you got me. I don't like zombie movies. I'm more of an action movie, thrillers guy and I've even been known to watch the odd romcom. And I love animated movies.'

At Gill's raised eyebrow, Charlie shrugged and said, 'I know. It's not cool, but there's so much humour in those films which is intended only for adults, and I love how the filmmakers manage to make the characters look like the actors, as well.'

Gill knew what he meant. She also liked animated movies, but she didn't know that she'd specifically go to the cinema to see one.

'So what's your favourite movie then?' she asked him.

'Oh, that's easy. It has to be *Die Hard*, the first one.'

Gill hadn't seen it all the way through, and she'd never really been into Bruce Willis, although he had been kind of cute back in his *Moonlighting* days.

'How about you?'

'Again, difficult to choose, but probably *Dirty Dancing*.'

'Ah, Patrick Swayze in a cummerbund. Yes, gets the ladies every time.'

'Well, actually, it's what he looked like without the cummerbund which interested us most,' she said flirtatiously, '*and* the man could dance.'

'I can dance,' said Charlie. 'I do a mean Timewarp and know all the moves to The Slosh.'

Gill laughed. He seemed so sincere. He was very easy to talk to and great company. She wondered if they'd meet up again. She was trying not to check her watch, aware of how little time they had together today.

As Charlie drained his pint, Gill asked him if he'd like another.

'Lager shandy, please.'

As Gill ordered their drinks, it was Charlie's turn to appraise her. He liked her. She was fun, pretty, not stunning, but very attractive and those legs! He liked that she had worn a dress to show them off. Nice tits too. He could have some fun with those. Pity that he was meeting Chloe later. He would have liked to have taken this further. Maybe another time. He bet she would be great in bed. He could just tell.

'There you go, sir, one pint of lager shandy,' said Gill, as she sat the drink in front of him.

'Thanks.' Their hands touched briefly as Charlie went to lift his pint. A jolt ran straight through Gill. Charlie flinched slightly. Their eyes met and Gill was first to look away, although not before holding his gaze a fraction too long for her interest to be clear.

'So you studied Engineering at university?' Charlie said, after taking a sip of his pint.

'Yes, I really enjoyed it, but there weren't a great deal of jobs when I came out, so I moved into Recruitment. Recruiting people to do the very jobs I wanted to be doing.'

'That couldn't have been easy,' Charlie sympathised.

'Well, I thought of it like this – the people I was interviewing had years of experience. Graduates were the ones who had a hard time getting a position back then. Now we've come full circle.'

'How d'you mean?'

'Not only graduates have a really hard time finding something these days. Those with great qualifications are finding it much tougher, too.'

'That's depressing,' said Charlie. 'But I know exactly what you mean. I've been with my firm five years and we used to have seventeen staff. Since 2010, we've had eleven.'

'So, how did you get into surveying?' Gill asked, keen to steer them clear of any further talk of the recession.

'Oh I always loved architecture. I'm a big Charles Rennie Mackintosh fan, Alexander 'Greek' Thomson and all that crowd. Plus, I was good at techie drawing at school.' His smile was infectious.

Gill's phone beeped. 'Sorry, I thought I had turned this off.' She fished her phone out of her bag and saw that it was an e-mail alert from Sean. Hurriedly, she pressed the off button. 'Sorry, what were we saying?'

'We were talking about architecture.'

'Oh yes. So, have you been to the Hill House in Helensburgh?'

'Many times. I've been to all of Mackintosh's buildings in Glasgow and obviously Helensburgh.'

'I tend to just go to those that sell scones,' Gill joked.

'Well, the Willow Tearooms are lovely and the House for an Art Lover has re-opened. I hear they do good scones.'

'Actually, I went to the House for an Art Lover, for lunch, recently. The food was lovely.'

'Really? Must try it sometime.' Again his gaze held Gill's slightly too long. *Was that an invitation? If so, he'll have to be a bit less subtle.*

'So you like to travel?' she asked.

'Love it. I get away as often as I can.'

'So where have you been?'

'It's probably more a case of where haven't I been.'

'OK,' said Gill, wishing he would give her a bit more to work with. 'Where are your favourite places?'

'Well, in Europe, Tallinn in Estonia. It's like Prague, but much smaller, unspoilt. And in the US, California, for the heat and its diversity. Plus you have all those amazing vineyards up at Sonoma. Throw in Yellowstone and places like Carmel, Monterey and Santa Monica, and I have to wonder why I still live here.'

'Wow, you really have travelled!' Gill was impressed.

'I like to see new places, have new experiences. I bungee jumped off the Bloukrans Bridge in South Africa. It was amazing.'

'Bloukrans?'

'Yes, it's the highest bridge you can jump off there. I think it was, and maybe still is, the highest one in the world.'

'Rather you than me. I did one for charity years ago – never again.'

'Yeah, it's definitely a love it or hate it thing. So what about you, do you like to travel?' asked Charlie, glancing briefly at his watch.

Gill saw, but pretended not to. She hoped he wasn't bored. Probably just trying to keep track of time for the meeting with his daughter.

'I do, but I haven't been to half the places you have, I'm sure.'

'So where was the last place you went?'

'Amsterdam, with some friends, last year.'

'Great city, although I've spent more time in its airport than in the city itself,' Charlie admitted.

'Yes, I've been through Schiphol myself more than a few times.'

'And where are you off to next?'

'We're going to Barcelona in a few weeks for the *Mercè* festival.'

'Oh yes, I've heard of that. I've been to Barcelona twice, but never during the festival. It's supposed to be really good. Isn't it costing you a fortune, though? I heard they jack up the hotel and flight prices for it.'

'Yes, it certainly wasn't cheap, but hopefully it'll be worth it. It's my first time to Barcelona, so I can't wait to go.'

'It's a brilliant city – make sure you go off the beaten track, too, although not into the left-hand side of the *Ramblas* after dark.'

'Why's that then?'

'It's really seedy, strip joints, and worse.'

'Begs the question how you know,' Gill teased.

'Stag night gone wrong,' was all Charlie would say.

'So what about you, where are you jetting off to next?'

'I haven't booked anything, but I'd quite like to go to Bora Bora. But I think it's quite a romantic place, so not really somewhere I want to go with the lads.'

Again Gill had that sensation of an undercurrent between them. Bora Bora. He could bloomin' well take her to Bora Bora any day.

'So, when you planning on going?'

'In a couple of months perhaps. I'll need to see how things work out,' he said.

Gill wondered if that meant whether he had a woman to take with him or not. There were definitely worse things in life than being on a beach in French Polynesia with Charlie Prentice.

They had another couple of drinks. Charlie had switched to orange juice after his first few lager shandies. Gill gave him another tick for this – sensible, not going over the limit, especially when he'd be spending time with his daughter later.

When pressed, Charlie told Gill all about his passion for cooking and how he often prepared dishes from the places around the world that he had visited. She almost expected him to suggest he cook for her one night, but no invitation was forthcoming. Fair enough. They had just met. She told him how big a foodie she was, and of the restaurants she had frequented in Glasgow, Edinburgh and the west of Scotland in general. He keyed some of her recommendations into his phone.

There was a brief pause in the conversation and then Charlie said, 'Oh God, I'm going to be late. Gill, I'm so sorry. I've had a really nice time, but I've got to go. Chloe will be waiting.'

He pulled on a leather jacket, which had been hanging over his chair. It was the first time Gill had noticed it: brown, distressed leather. She couldn't help thinking of Tom Cruise in *Top Gun*, although Charlie was blond and a good six inches taller.

Gill stood up and donned her trench coat, belting it loosely at the waist. He walked slightly ahead of her and held the door open to let her pass through.

The rain bounced off the street. They hesitated briefly inside the entranceway.

'My car's just around the corner. How did you get here?' he asked.

'I took a taxi. Ah, there's one now,' she said, flagging it down.

'It was really nice to meet you, Gill. I enjoyed our chat,' Charlie said then kissed her briefly on both cheeks.

'You too.'

He smiled at her and then walked towards his car.

What? What! He hadn't mentioned seeing her again and when he had kissed her cheek, he had smelled divine, but he hadn't tried to kiss her properly. *What am I, his maiden aunt?* Deflated, she turned at the sound of the taxi horn beeping, reminding her of its presence.

Gill sat in the taxi, puzzling over what had just happened. *Why didn't he ask to see me again or for my number? We were having a really good time.*

Suddenly, she remembered the e-mail from Sean. Another waste of space. Yes, let's see what he had to say for himself. *This should be good.*

Hi, Gill. I don't know what to say, except I'm sorry. It was my first arranged date and I was very nervous. You were so lovely and I was really enjoying your company and I blew it. I'm not some alcoholic for the record, just someone who overindulged and really regrets it. Would you ever give me another chance? It'll be a dry date (for me) I promise. Sorry again, Sean.

Men! I'll never understand them – they're all idiots. She flung her phone back in her bag.

Chapter Eighteen

Sunday 11 September

Gill lay around for the rest of the day, moping and debating whether to ring Debbie or one of the others and relate the latest sorry episode with Charming Charlie as she had now nicknamed him, or of Shit-faced Sean's text. In the end, she grabbed some popcorn and watched *Notting Hill.* Her favourite scene was Julia Roberts in the book shop, saying to Hugh Grant, 'I'm just a girl, standing in front of a guy, asking him to love her.' *How bloody appropriate that is. But men are too stupid to notice, or maybe they just don't care.*

When she'd devoured a third of a bag of popcorn, she felt sick, so stopped. She tapped out a message to Debbie. *Shit-faced Sean has e-mailed me – here's the e-mail. What do you think?*

She lay back on the sofa cushions. This dating lark was exhausting, especially when it seemed to be going so well and then veered off in another direction altogether without explanation. Maybe she was better off single. Maybe she could just get a puppy if she wanted affection. But puppies needed care and attention. Pity she was allergic to cats. They freaked her out, too. There was something unnerving about their intelligence – she always felt they knew more than they let on.

Five minutes later, just when Gill had thrown the TV remote across the room in disgust, the phone rang. She hesitated, wondering if it was either of her failed dates, then realised they didn't have her number. It was Lisa.

'So, how did it go with the surveyor? Was he tasty?'

Slouching down into the sofa, curling her feet underneath her, Gill poured out the whole exasperating tale.

'Men are funny beasts,' said Lisa after a long pause. 'He'll be in touch. He was probably just distracted with his daughter.'

'Hmm,' said Gill, unconvinced. 'He said, "It was nice to meet you – goodbye." Sounds pretty bloody definitive to me.'

'Well, don't get worked up about it. If you aren't for him, you aren't for him and he's not for you. You're meeting another one on Tuesday, aren't you?'

'Don't remind me. At the moment I feel like swearing off men for life.'

'There's no point thinking like that. Who's up next?'

'Gary.'

'Which one's Gary again?'

'The engineer from Renfrewshire.'

'What was his photo like? You know I'm not that bothered about his job, unless he has two sports cars and a stately home off Loch Lomond.'

Lisa wasn't as shallow as she liked to make out, but Gill indulged her.

'He's the one that looked a bit like Liam Neeson.'

'Oh yeah, remember him now. Big nose.'

'It wasn't that big.'

'It was bloody huge.' Lisa was in her stride now.

'Lise, you're meant to be cheering me up,' Gill reminded her.

'I am? Oh, sure, I am. But you know what they say about big noses?'

'Well, here's hoping,' said Gill before Lisa could deliver the punchline.

'Aw, you're spoiling my fun,' wailed Lisa.

'Fat chance of that happening. So, who is the latest victim, anyway?'

'Charming, I'm sure.' Lisa feigned offence. 'Daryl. Met him last night. Fit. PT instructor in the army. Good stamina.'

'Lisa, enough with the detail,' Gill barked rather more abruptly than intended.

'Oh yeah, so, back to the matter in hand. This Gary guy, he's not the tallest out of the bunch, is he?'

'No, the others were six feet three and six feet one. He's five eleven.'

'Still, he's not short. Even in reasonable heels, you shouldn't tower over him. So, where are you meeting him?'

'He said he'd let me know. Tomorrow then, probably.'

'Good stuff. Right, love, I'm shattered, you can have too much of a good thing, you know.'

'Lisa, how many times do I need to tell you? You're meant to be cheering me up, not telling me how great the sex you had last night was, particularly when you know I haven't had sex this year.'

'Or last year,' mumbled Lisa.

'Yes, thanks for that.'

'Oh, I forgot to say, Debbie mentioned that your wee Irish guy got plastered.'

'Yes, and he's had the cheek to e-mail me begging forgiveness. I've just forwarded Debbie his e-mail to see what she thinks.'

'Oh read it to me,' begged Lisa.

'I can't. It's on my phone, and I'm talking to you on it.'

'Oh well, tell me the gist of it.'

After relaying to Lisa more or less what Sean had said, Lisa reached the conclusion that he should be given another chance.

'C'mon, anyone could have had a bit too much. It's happened to all of us.'

'Yes, well, not on a first date. That's meant to be when you make an impression. He certainly made an impression. Pity it was the wrong one.'

'Everyone deserves a second chance.'

'I'm fed up giving everyone second, third and fourth chances. I need to start putting myself first. Nobody else does.'

'Except us.'

'Naturally except you three.'

'And Christopher and Sarah.'

'Yes, yes and my parents – anyone who's related to me. They don't count.'

'Oh, that's lovely!'

'You know what I mean.'

'Yes, I do. Right, listen to me, chill, take it easy tomorrow so you're refreshed for Tuesday and consider giving Sean another chance. Sexy Irishman, accent, cute. Bit of a drinker. He's Irish, what do you expect?'

'Not like this, though, Lisa. It was downright embarrassing.'

'Well, he's obviously regretting it now and he must have liked you, otherwise he could have just not contacted you. He could simply have got the agency to set him up with someone else. That would have been a lot less embarrassing for him.'

Gill pondered this for a second. 'I suppose. I'll think about it, but I'm not promising anything. The last thing I need in my life is a perpetually drunken Irishman.'

'And here was me thinking they were the best kind,' said Lisa, and Gill knew she was laughing.

'Right, quit it, you. I have things to do, so I have to go.'

'What things?'

'Work things,' said Gill in exasperation.

'Boring. Right, talk to you when you have better chat. Bye.'

'Charming! Beat it, talk to you on Wednesday.' Gill replaced the receiver.

Monday disappeared as quickly as it had begun. Gill didn't stop all day. Debbie had replied mid-morning to say her phone had been dead and she hadn't seen Gill's message until now. *If you really liked him, give him another chance. If you weren't sure before he got plastered, don't.* Sage advice.

Gary e-mailed her at lunchtime, asking if he could meet her in the Veni, Vidi, Vici bar in Hope Street at seven o'clock. She knew it. It had been recently refurbished and boasted an adjoining award-winning restaurant which specialised in seafood. She hoped it didn't come out of the River Clyde. She didn't think a side order of shopping trolley would be particularly appetising. She replied to his e-mail, advising him that seven was fine.

On Tuesday morning, as she prepared her clothes for that

evening, laying them out in her suit carrier, she decided she *would* give Sean a second chance. Not caring that it was six thirty, and half hoping her e-mail alert would wake him, it was the least he deserved after all, she e-mailed him. *Sean, I had a good time up until the point when you fell down drunk. I believe in second chances, but not third. I'm free Thursday, Gill.*

She didn't care if she sounded judgmental. She had every right to be. He'd shown her up in public.

'So, how's it all going then?' Janice asked her. Prior to her second date with Anton, Gill had confided in Janice.

'You wouldn't believe me.'

'Try me.'

So Gill filled her in on all the details.

'Exciting times. My advice, enjoy it. Soon enough you'll find one guy to settle down with and then there'll be no variety.'

'Thanks, Janice.'

'Seriously, take it from one who knows.'

Dating was starting to cause Gill some wardrobe concerns, although she had become used to changing at work. She didn't really have enough dressy clothes that were suitable for first dates. Her wardrobe mainly consisted of work suits and co-ordinates. She'd found a sheer black top at the back of a drawer, which she wore over a black camisole. She pulled on a pair of turquoise Capri pants and she was ready.

The taxi drew up right on time outside her office. Seven minutes later, she stepped out onto the kerb in front of Veni, Vidi, Vici. She was beginning to get déjà vu. Get glammed up, take taxi, approach bar, find expectant male. Taking a deep breath and hoping that this date would run smoothly, she opened the door to the bar and went in. Inside it was quite dark, in contrast with the daylight in the street. Her eyes adjusted quickly, and glancing around, she didn't see anyone who could be Gary. A few lone males propped up the bar, but they easily looked twenty and seventy respectively, so surely she could rule them out? Either that or he bore no resemblance to his profile picture. She took one last look around to ensure he definitely wasn't there then approached the bar.

'Hi. Do you have any Sancerre?'

'Yep, small or large glass?'

'What's small, 125ml or 175ml?'

'It's Glasgow, 175ml,' joked the barman.

'OK, 175ml is fine.'

'Take a seat and I'll bring it over.'

Gill chose a seat which served as the perfect lookout for the entrance. She checked her watch. Five past seven. Hmm…late. She didn't like late. Maybe he had a valid reason, but it hadn't created a good first impression. She checked her phone to see if he had e-mailed her. Nope. But there was a message from Anton. She clicked on the e-mail and started devouring it.

Hi, Gill, I hope you are well. I am sorry I haven't been in touch since last week, but as I said, I knew I'd be really busy preparing for this trip. Are you free on Saturday? I'd love to take you to dinner. If so, I will also book a room for myself in Glasgow so I don't have to rush home this time. Anton.

Gill felt positively light-headed. She didn't know how to interpret his message, whether to take it at face value, or whether to read more into it. Was he hoping to sleep with her? They'd barely kissed, but wow, what a kiss. She knew what she wanted: to look fit and toned by the time she saw him again, but she couldn't exactly fit in ten sessions with a personal trainer between now and then. She didn't even have time for one. Distracted by Anton's message, willing it to reveal more of his thoughts and intentions, she didn't initially notice the man standing in front of her.

'Gill?' asked a tentative voice.

Raising her head, Gill saw a slightly less good-looking Liam Neeson. He looked almost the same age as Neeson, but Gill knew that he was about sixty, so either Neeson was good for his age, or Gary had had a difficult paper round.

'Gary.' She stood up to greet him, as she said his name.

He shook her hand. 'It's nice to meet you. I'm so sorry I'm late. The train was cancelled and by then it was too late to take the car.'

'No problem. You're here now.'

'Can I get you something to drink?' he asked, eyeing her still full glass.

'No, I just got one, thanks.'

'OK, give me a second and I'll be right back.'

As he stood at the bar, Gill observed him closely. There had been no spark. Maybe it was because he was late. She hated tardiness, and OK, he had a reason, but he should have allowed for that. She knew how unreasonable she sounded. *Give the poor man a chance. After all, he looks like Liam Neeson.*

Once Gary settled down with a drink and apologised again, they relaxed a little.

'So you're on the rigs?'

'Yes, two weeks on, two weeks off. I love it, but it plays havoc with my social life.'

'I can imagine. I actually interview engineers for the oil and gas industry.'

'Really? Oh, of course, you work in Recruitment.' Realisation dawned on Gary.

'Yes, I started my own agency three years ago.'

'That must be really rewarding.'

'Yes, it is, but bloomin' hard work!'

He smiled. 'Difficult to switch off?'

'Yes, it's why I'm trying to hire another recruitment consultant. Interviews are Thursday and Friday, so fingers crossed.'

'Hope it works out for you.'

'Me too.'

'So you like Zumba?'

Gill turned red.

'Ah, you've not been to Zumba, have you?'

When he smiled, laughter lines appeared around his eyes and he did look quite attractive. More open, friendly.

Gill reddened some more. 'Well, I was signed up for the classes…'

'But work got in the way?'

'Yes. It always does.' She could have kicked herself, no sooner the words were out of her mouth.

Ignoring her comment, Gary said, 'So, if you don't go to Zumba, what do you do to relax?'

She could hardly say 'watch Rupert Penry Jones in *Persuasion*', could she? He'd think she was a right perv and he'd be right.

'I go out with friends mainly, for dinner and drinks.'

'It's not a bad hobby,' he said, smiling at her. 'So where's your favourite restaurant?'

She rattled off a few, saying it was difficult to choose just one; it had to be one per cuisine. Gary laughed. He completely agreed, said he was no good at choosing just one of anything. He needed to split everything into categories. Only thing he knew for sure was that his favourite colour was blue.

Gill liked him, but there was something missing. She couldn't quite put her finger on it, but so far, there was just no chemistry, no desire to jump over the table and straddle him, and who wanted to settle for less than that? Perhaps his category divisions applied to women, too. Maybe he needed a blonde, a brunette and a redhead, or a doormat, an independent woman and someone who met him halfway. Gill turned her attention back to him as he told her how much he loved living in Scotland, even though he spent half of it working on the rigs. Originally he had worked in the central belt for a city firm, but the money on the rigs had been too good to turn down, when he'd been made redundant from his last firm.

'The money's good and it means I've pretty much paid off my mortgage, which is a bonus.'

'*Nice for you. God, why am I being such a bitch? He's a decent enough guy*. This wasn't like her.

She decided to see if they could get flirty. He was, after all, very good-looking, even if she hadn't felt any chemistry – yet. She lived in hope.

Directing the same question at him, as she had at Sean on Saturday, she said, 'So, Gary, you're quite the romantic. What's your idea of the most romantic date?'

Gary paled visibly and Gill realised she wasn't the only one who had lied on their profile questionnaire.

'Er, well, let me think for a second. So many possibilities. Yes, either the Eiffel Tower or Venice, or maybe the Empire State Building.'

Predictable, thought Gill, hating herself. This simply

wasn't working out. Thank God it was just a drink and not dinner. The restaurant looked lovely, too. She could see it from where she sat. Waiters passed occasionally with mouth-watering platters of food. She realised she was hungry. It hadn't occurred to her before, but she hadn't eaten since early that morning. Her stomach rumbled.

'Oh, someone's hungry.' Gary laughed.

Oh my God, this is torture. Excusing herself to go the Ladies', and accepting his offer of another drink, for fear of being obvious, Gill quickly walked to the toilet and dialled Angela.

'Ang, it's me. It's a nightmare. Help. Can you call me in fifteen minutes?'

Gill freshened up, although she didn't know why she was bothering to make the effort, and then returned to the bar.

When she sat down again, Gary started talking about how much he loved Formula One. Gill zoned out, waiting for Angela's call. When the phone finally rang, she was relieved.

'Oh, I'm so sorry; I thought I had turned it off. Excuse me a second.' Gill's bag had slipped under the table and, self-conscious about her arse being on display but being unable to do anything about it, she reached under the table to retrieve her bag. Too late. A ripping sound rent the air. A cool draught assailed Gill as she realised that she had snagged her Capri pants on something. As she struggled to free herself, a further rip sealed her fate. She had ripped the arse out of her trousers – seriously – from front to back. She sat back down hurriedly, pale as a ghost, and let the phone go to answer machine. Glancing round to ensure no one had witnessed her predicament, and satisfying herself that this was indeed the case, she turned to Gary and said, 'I'm really sorry, but I need to go. Can we get a taxi to my place and I'll explain on the way?'

Looking as if all his Christmases had come at once, Gary readily agreed.

'One more thing, can I borrow your jacket?'

Chapter Nineteen

Tuesday 13 September

Gill came downstairs and, looking rather sheepish, said to Gary, 'Thanks, I appreciate it. And thanks for not laughing.'

'Is it OK if I do now?' said Gary, stifling a laugh.

'I suppose.' Gill broke into a smile.

Gary couldn't help himself. The pent-up laughter he had been holding in since the restaurant, suddenly spilled out. 'I'm sorry, I didn't look or anything, but when you wrapped my jacket round your waist, and it trailed down your legs, that was possibly the funniest thing I've seen all year.'

'Yes, I see how that might have been funny. I just had to get out of there. Would you like a drink? One for the road?' she clarified, so he knew where the boundaries were.

'What do you have?'

'Beer, wine, vodka…'

'I'll take a beer, please.'

Gill fetched a glass of rosé and a bottled beer from the fridge. She handed the beer to Gary, who sat on the edge of the sofa.

He'd obviously realised nothing was going to happen tonight. She hadn't even felt worried about him now knowing where she lived, despite the agency's warnings. He just seemed so unthreatening. *That's what everyone always says about serial killers.*

Surprisingly, Gary drank his beer quickly, then said, 'I best be off.'

'Oh, let me at least call you a taxi, especially after the inconvenience I put you to. I'll pay for it, of course.'

'Don't be daft. It was entertaining if nothing else.'

'Glad to be of assistance.'

Ten minutes later the taxi arrived. Gary turned to Gill, looked her in the eye and said, 'I had a really good time tonight. I hope we can do it again soon.'

Gill mumbled something non-committal about how she had enjoyed herself, thanked him again and showed him out.

As soon as the door closed behind him, she pressed her full weight against it and sank slowly to the floor. After a few minutes, her thoughts turned to Anton. Anton. She jumped up. He'd e-mailed her. Pouring herself another glass of wine, she settled into her chair to reread and savour his message.

Missed calls – two new messages. She listened as she heard Angela asking her to call her back. Second new message: Angela again. *Gill, call me, you've got me worried. Want to ensure you haven't been chopped into little pieces and dumped in a wood somewhere.*

She phoned Angela straightaway.

'Hi, Ang, sorry, you'll never believe what just happened.'

Angela remained silent as Gill poured out the whole sorry tale.

'It wasn't funny!' she wailed, as Angela could barely

speak for laughing. Gill could hear her snorts and coughs from the other end of the phone, even though she was clearly holding the receiver away from her.

'So, not for you?' Angela asked, when she'd regained her composure.

'No spark.'

'And did he really look like Liam Neeson?'

'Sort of, yes, but there was no churning feeling in my stomach, no feeling weak at the knees, no *I'm going to orgasm by just looking at him* feeling.'

'Chance would be a fine thing.'

'Yes, indeed.'

'So what now?'

'Well, he said he had a really nice time and he hoped we could do it again soon. I dodged the question.'

'Gill!'

'I know, I know, but c'mon, it's been a tough night. I'd just ripped the arse out of my trousers in the middle of a bar in town, during a first date which wasn't going anywhere.'

'Look on the bright side.'

'There's a bright side?'

'You could have been totally into him and that could have happened. I'm sure you'd rather choose when to put your thong on display.'

'Yes, I suppose that's a blessing. Thank God I've got a night off from all this tomorrow. I'm wrecked.'

'So, who's next?'

'The drunken Irishman again.'

'Ah, so he gets another chance.'

'Well, I'm reserving judgment on that for now, but yes, I am meeting up with him again.'

'I heard he was cute.'

Gill demurred then answered, 'Yes, he was bloody adorable. Thirty-five. Probably hot as hell when not shit-faced. Let's see if the pleasure of my company will be riveting enough to keep him sober this time.'

'I'm sure it wasn't anything to do with you, or how good company you were. Like Lise said, he was just nervous.'

'If he felt nervous then, how's he going to feel this time, knowing he screwed it up last time? With that logic, he'd be better off not turning up at all.'

'But he is turning up and he obviously thinks you're worth the effort.'

'Hmm,' said Gill. 'We'll see.'

'So is there anything else new to report on the love front?' asked Angela. 'Any new profiles?'

'No, no new profiles, but I did get an e-mail from Anton when I was waiting for Gary to turn up.'

'You were waiting for him?' Angela said, confused.

'Yes, he was late. Train got cancelled.'

'Okaay,' said Angela, knowing what a stickler Gill was for punctuality. 'And this Gary, he's still alive, is he? You haven't hidden him under the floorboards?'

'Ha, you're not funny.'

'Beg to differ. Anyway, what's lover boy saying?'

'Anton?'

'Yes, Anton.' Gill could almost hear Angela rolling her eyes at having to spell it out to her.

'He wants to take me for dinner on Saturday night.'

'That's great then, isn't it? This is the one you've liked the most, right?'

'Yep. And, he might stay over.'

'With you?' Angela asked.

'No, at one of the hotels in town. That way he doesn't have to head back on the last train and we can stay out.'

'Or stay in.'

'Yes, or stay in,' repeated Gill.

'And how do you feel about that?'

'Ang, do you know how long it's been since I last had sex?'

'A while?'

'More than a while and there's only so much a vibrator can do.'

Angela burst out laughing. For a laugh, they'd all bought exactly the same toy at Lisa's sister's adult-themed party. They all swore by them, even those with partners.

'But how do you feel mentally? I mean you like him, but he's still a stranger really.'

'Yes, well, I suppose I'll only know on the night, and who knows, he might not intend for that to happen.'

'Gill.'

'Yes?'

'He's a man. Of course he expects that to happen, or at least wants that to happen.'

'He's not alone in that!'

'Right, well, as long as you're happy.'

'I am. I think. I won't do anything I'm not sure of. Anyway, I better go. I need to catch up with some work and e-mail him back, too.'

'Don't sit there overanalysing every word of a two-sentence e-mail for half an hour, will you?'

'Would I do that?'

'In a word? Yes. Don't.'

'OK, I won't. Talk to you soon. Hugs to Matthew.'

'I'll pass them on. Night.'

Gill hung up and ensconced herself once more on the sofa, where she checked her e-mails to reread Anton's earlier e-mail. To her surprise, she had one from Charlie.

Hi, Gill. Sorry I had to rush off on Sunday. Had lost track of time, as was really enjoying your company. Would like to see you again, if you fancy it. Are you free Friday night. Let me know, cheers, Charlie.

Wow, that was unexpected. She had given up on Charlie. So now, potentially, she was seeing Charlie on Friday and Anton on Saturday. Hmm. What to do? She had tomorrow night free to catch up, interviews on Thursday and Friday, but as long as they made it around eight o'clock, she would have time to nip home, shower and change. It was one thing meeting after work midweek and changing at the office, quite another on a Friday night, when everyone was glammed up.

She tapped into her phone, *I understand about Sunday. Don't worry about it. Could meet you eight o'clock on Friday. Let me know if that suits. Gill.*

Two minutes later her phone beeped. *Sounds like a plan. Do you like Thai food?*

She loved Thai food. She and the girls quite often went to a Thai restaurant up near the Mitchell Library for special occasions like birthdays. It wasn't the cheapest, but the food was amazing, worth every penny.

Love Thai food.

Great. Do you know Fountain of Siam? Do you want me to pick you up, or shall I meet you there?

Yes, I know it. I'll meet you inside at eight.

Look forward to it.

Maybe this dating game wasn't such a disaster after all.

Gary sat in the taxi and reflected upon the evening. He'd liked Gill. She was his kind of girl, but he didn't think he was necessarily her kind of guy. Had he bored her? She had seemed kind of distracted. Maybe she was annoyed with him for being late, but that was outside of his control. He sighed. Why was it that women who interested him weren't into him and vice versa? He didn't consider himself a bad catch. He even thought they might have had a lot in common, particularly with her having studied Engineering, but he knew that something had been missing. Neither could he fool himself that it was simply because of the abrupt way their official date had ended. He just hoped she'd give him another chance. He hadn't even tried to kiss her goodbye, because it was so apparent she wouldn't have been receptive to that. But he wasn't ready to give up just yet.

Chapter Twenty

Thursday 15 September

Gill was glad she had spent the evening at home on Wednesday. It had been a busy day and the rest of the week looked likely to be jam-packed, because of the interviews and her impending dates with Charlie and Anton.

She'd received an e-mail from Sean first thing on Wednesday morning,

Thanks for giving me another chance. We could go to the pictures, if you fancy it, and have coffee before or afterwards. Let me know if that's OK and if there's anything you'd like to see. Sean.

At least he would be less likely to get plastered at the cinema. Gill had checked the listings and e-mailed him back to say she quite fancied a new romcom which was on at the multiscreen in Renfrew Street. She didn't ask him if that suited. He had his penance to pay. The film started at seven and she suggested they have coffee afterwards.

Sounds great. See you inside, ground floor at ten to seven. Sean.

Gill had also received a message from Gary on Wednesday afternoon, asking if he could see her again and if so, was she free this weekend. She hadn't replied, as she couldn't make it this weekend, and she hadn't quite decided if she wanted to go out with him again. Her gut instinct said no, as there had been no connection, but he *had* come to her rescue when her trousers had ripped. Plus he looked like Liam Neeson. And it wouldn't do to put all her eggs in one basket just yet.

By the time Janice arrived at the office, Gill had already done two hours' work.

'Coffee, Janice? I'll get it. I need a break before I do these interviews. The first one's due in at half nine.'

'Love one, thanks. So, do you have a good feeling about this lot?' Janice asked, as she dragged off her dripping coat.

'Well, I really hope I can choose someone from this bunch. I don't want to do it all again. I'd like to start someone as soon as possible. Otherwise, you and I will both get committed.'

'You're not wrong there.'

Gill poured the coffee, handed a cup to Janice and then said, 'Would you prefer a man or a woman?'

Janice hesitated for a split second and then said, 'Never really thought about it. As long as they're hard-working, professional and have some personality, that's enough for me.'

'Right, good,' said Gill, thinking hard. She tried not to have preconceived notions before interviewing commenced, but sometimes it was difficult. Often those opinions changed anyway, as some candidates who seemed very promising on paper were dismal at interviews and vice versa.

'So who's first up then?'

Gill glanced at her list. 'Leslie Crutherland, and then at eleven, Angus Mackie. Then this afternoon, we have Carol

Leishman and Patrick O'Hara. Then four more tomorrow.'

'Fingers crossed, eh?'

'I'm keeping an open mind and everything crossed,' said Gill.

Leslie had an impeccable CV. Unfortunately, Gill found him pompous and overbearing. She couldn't imagine him working with her, never mind for her. In the interview he acted as if he was her boss, and constantly interrupted her with questions, whilst she was still speaking. No.

Angus she had met once before at an association dinner. Friendly and charming, and although he had only been in Recruitment for two years, he knew his stuff. He had in fact, even wrested a couple of pieces of business away from Gill. Maybe.

Carol Leishman, opinionated and very successful, but the woman's laugh could break windows. Since Gill and Janice would have to work in close proximity to her on a daily basis, Gill struck her off the list.

Charming Irishman Patrick O'Hara rounded off the day. But there was something missing. Gill didn't think he had the edge.

Gill sincerely hoped tomorrow's interviews were more productive. With an hour and a half per candidate, it had been a long and gruelling day.

Janice asked Gill if she wanted her to stay late to help, as she knew Gill would struggle to deal with everything she'd missed during the day.

'No, there's no point both of us being stuck here. And you've done more than enough holding the fort today. You go and have a nice night. I'm going out tomorrow and Saturday.'

'Well, don't overdo it. You don't want to turn up to

these dates looking the way you do at the moment.'

Fortunately, Gill was used to Janice's brand of honesty and didn't take offence. When Janice left, Gill sat down to do payroll, followed by taking care of various bills for the business. Thank God for internet banking. She'd never have time to go to the bank each week in person and Janice had enough to do. Remembering her thought about recruiting a student, Gill put together a small advert. Whoever she got in could carry out some basic admin tasks and help Janice. She then looked up the addresses of a few of the local colleges and universities and e-mailed the advert across to them. She felt elated that she was starting to put a small dent in her to-do list. She really hoped the interviews tomorrow yielded more results than today.

Gill didn't leave the office until ten o'clock, so she called a taxi, rather than take the bus, as she was exhausted.

Ready meal again, she thought, as she opened her front door and discarded her briefcase. She grabbed hold of the flesh at her stomach with both hands and decided she really needed to make some time to exercise. *Zumba's the answer. As soon as I hire this new SRC, I'm going to start a fitness regime.*

Taking a lasagne from the freezer, she scrutinised the instructions and put it in the microwave for the required six minutes. She kicked off her shoes then poured a glass of wine, promising herself it would be her only one tonight, as tomorrow would be another long day.

Gill sank onto the sofa and flicked on the TV. She channel-hopped for a few minutes before realising she hadn't had time to check her personal e-mails all day. Too tired to boot up her laptop, she logged on to her personal e-mail from her phone, and saw she had a new e-mail.

Hi, Gill, hope you are well. I enjoyed your company the other night. Were your trousers repairable? I get the impression things would never be boring with you around. I'd like to see you again. If you're interested, I'll be back on the twenty-seventh and could contact you then. Gary.

Gill's emotions were mixed. To be honest, she didn't know how she felt about anything at the moment. Too many things were happening at once. She couldn't work out if that was good or bad. At least some of it was social, as opposed to the constant work, work, work of before. She had difficulty keeping up with her social diary now. Gary seemed a nice bloke, but did she want to settle for *nice*? She eventually decided she was too overcome with tiredness to make any major decisions, so she put Gary on the back-burner and finished her lasagne.

Morning came all too quickly in Gill's opinion. She'd flaked out as soon as she hit the pillow last night. When her alarm trilled at six o'clock, she could have happily thrown it out of the window. She tried to snooze it for ten minutes, but next door's cat was miaowing to be allowed in, which put paid to her getting another ten minutes' sleep.

Gill felt sick at the sight of her office for the first time ever. She knew it was down to not being out of it long enough. She needed to perk up, not only for her interviews, but for her date with Charlie. At least today she would have time to go home, shower and come back into town.

'You look tired. What time did you leave here?' were the first words out of Janice's mouth when she came through the door.

'Morning. Ten.'

'Looks like it. I've heard those caffeine sticks are good.

Like roll-on deodorant, but for under your eyes.'

'I'll bear that in mind,' said Gill. 'Now, talking of caffeine, do you want a coffee? I need another.'

'What time have you been here since?'

'Quarter past seven.'

'Jesus. Well, let's hope you do find the right candidate. Otherwise you're going to be absolutely wrecked if this continues.'

'What do you mean I'm *going* to be wrecked?' joked Gill.

'Quite,' said Janice, as she switched on her computer.

Gill returned a few minutes later with the coffees. 'Right, I'm going to lock myself in my office and attack yesterday's e-mails before the first interviewee turns up.'

'No problem. I'll let you know when he gets here.'

'Thanks, Janice. Roll on the weekend, eh?'

'I think yours is going to be a wee bit more exciting than mine.'

'Well, I live in hope,' said Gill, retreating into her office.

After another gruelling interview session, Gill had come to the conclusion that her best bet lay with Thursday's candidates. She had her new SRC. She just hoped he agreed to the package she intended to put together for him, as quite frankly there wasn't a suitable runner-up. Angus Mackie would fit in just fine. Janice had liked the look and sound of him, too. He only needed to give a week's notice, which was a bonus, but not the reason she'd decided to hire him.

Five o'clock. Gill amended the draft proposal she'd been working on over the past few days, adding in details on salary and start date. She then printed it off, signed it and popped it in an envelope, ready for posting on the way home. Already she felt relief. Soon they would be three.

Chapter Twenty-one

Friday 16 September

Gill stepped out of the taxi and looked up at the lavishly decorated exterior of Fountain of Siam, complete with ornamental fountain. She hadn't been for a while, but she loved the food here. As she was entering the restaurant, a voice behind her called 'Gill!'

Turning, she saw Charlie waving at her, as he, too, got out of a taxi. He paid the driver and then walked towards Gill.

'Hi. You look fantastic,' he said as he drew level with her, taking in her little black dress and high heels.

'Thanks. You brush up pretty well, too.'

Gill felt a little overdressed as Charlie was wearing black jeans and a white short-sleeved linen shirt. He didn't even have a jacket with him.

'It's great to see you again.' He kissed her on the cheek.

'You too. Shall we?' Gill gestured towards the restaurant.

'Yes, after you,' Charlie held the door open.

'Table for Prentice, for two,' Charlie said to the maître d'.

The maître d' checked his computer and then, signalling to one of the waitresses, told her where to seat them.

The waitress led them to a table in the centre of the room. Charlie looked round, as if trying to see if they could be moved to another table, but the restaurant was packed.

The waitress pulled out Gill's chair for her and explained the specials. She then took their drinks order and left them with the menus.

'I haven't been in here for ages,' Charlie said.

'Me neither. We used to come here a lot. Me and the girls,' she clarified.

Charlie's momentary high alert relaxed. 'Ah.'

Everything on the menu sounded good to Gill. How to choose something which wasn't too garlicky? Maybe she should take her lead from Charlie. If he ordered a dish laden with garlic, then she'd feel she could do the same. Plus, he was so well travelled that he would probably choose something more authentic. She restrained herself from simply ordering red Thai curry, which she adored. Looking at the menu, she would be quite happy to order the starter sharing platter. Or maybe she'd have Thai satay. Chu chu beef looked a good option for the main course, but it had garlic in it. Gill scanned the menu to see what the options were that didn't contain garlic.

'Anything you like?' Charlie peered over the top of his menu.

'Too many things.' Gill smiled.

'It's good that you're easy to please.'

Gill wondered if he was thinking ahead to later. She didn't think she was particularly easy to please, as she had very high standards. She expected a lot of a potential partner, but then, she gave a lot, more than she ever received.

'What about you?'

'Well, what about the sharing platter to start?'

'I was thinking the same thing.'

'That's settled then. Any ideas for the main course?'

Since the starter probably contained garlic, Gill decided to have the chu chu beef: marinated beef, with garlic, spring onion, oyster sauce and straw mushroom, for her main course. Her mouth watered just thinking about it.

'Yes, I'm having the chu chu beef.'

'Oh, that's delicious. I had that last time I was here. I enjoyed it so much, I tried making it at home, but it didn't turn out quite the same. I'm going to quiz them about their secret ingredient,' Charlie told her.

'You're quite the cook.'

'I try, and I am pretty adventurous.'

From Charlie's tone Gill had the distinct impression he wasn't solely referring to his cooking.

'Indeed.' She wanted to move to safer ground. She had no idea how things were going to pan out with her and Charlie, but she wasn't ready yet for veiled sexual references.

'So, what have you rustled up this week then?' Gill fiddled with her napkin.

'Nothing terribly exciting. I made a really nice vegetarian lasagne. I'm not usually big on vegetarian dishes, but vegetarian lasagne, if made well, can be amazing.'

Gill agreed. It was one of the few vegetarian dishes she would eat. The thought of tofu, bean sprouts, and vegetarian meat loaf did nothing for her.

'Have you decided?' she asked him, as she closed the menu and placed it in front of her.

'I think I'm going to go for the weeping tiger.'

'Weeping tiger?' Gill scrunched up her face in disbelief.

'Yes, grilled sirloin steak on a sizzling platter.'

'Ah, OK.'

'I know I'm in a Thai restaurant, but that's what I'm in the mood for.'

'It's on the menu, no reason why you can't have it. Besides, the starter has plenty of Thai dishes in it.'

'True. Would you like some wine with dinner?'

'Red for me, please, since I'm having beef.'

'Me too. Cabernet Sauvignon OK for you?'

'Sounds good.'

Just then the waitress appeared with the drinks they had asked for.

'Are you ready to order?'

Gill sipped her drink and listened as Charlie talked impassionedly about food, the different dishes he knew how to cook, and those he would like to learn to.

'Cooking's easy. I haven't always been able to cook. Then when Jamie Oliver came on the scene, I tried a few of his recipes and I've never looked back. I've always loved food, so it made sense for me to learn how to make it.'

To Gill, who viewed cooking as a necessary evil and whose culinary prowess extended to chicken with a pour-over sauce, the concept of doing it for pleasure was alien. 'Yes, I suppose.'

Their starters arrived and they both used the chopsticks provided to drag the chicken in pandan leaf, tong tung and prawn satay from the platter to their plates.

Charlie laughed. 'Looks like we have the same priorities.'

'Sorry?'

'We've both taken the same three items first.'

Gill glanced at her plate, then at Charlie's. He was

right. She looked at the platter and saw that they had both left the relatively unadventurous spring rolls, fish cake and chicken satay until last.

'So, now that we've ascertained that we both like to eat the best things first, what else do you like?'

Charlie hesitated and then said, 'To be honest, anything tasty. I hate bland food and I particularly loathe floppy pasta.'

Gill knew what he meant. There were few things worse than being served pasta which wasn't al dente. It always managed to have the lack of flavour and unappetising consistency of a ready meal.

'So what have you been up to this week?' Charlie asked as he expertly used his chopsticks to lift his tong tung.

Neglecting to mention her other dates, Gill relayed to Charlie the events surrounding the interview process and how she had been doing a lot of work from home, to stay on top of things, whilst she looked for another recruitment consultant.

'It must be a relief to have finally found someone.'

'You have no idea.'

'Mmm, this tong tung is delicious.'

'The prawn satay's pretty good, too, but then I love satay.'

'I'm actually allergic to raw peanuts, but for whatever reason, I'm OK if they're cooked.'

Gill dabbed at her lips with her napkin. 'Bizarre.'

'I know, but it's just as well, as I love satay too much. I'd have to eat it, and then give myself an adrenalin shot to counteract it.'

'That sounds a tad extreme.'

'Well, don't you have a food you couldn't live without?'

Gill hesitated before saying, 'Chocolate.'

'Ah, yes I think a lot of women would give that answer.'

The waitress cleared away their plates.

'That was lovely.'

'Yes, I really enjoyed it, too. I've never had a bad meal in here.' Charlie stretched his right leg out. 'Sorry, I've got cramp in my foot.'

'God, I hate that.'

Unfortunately the waitress bringing their main courses didn't see Charlie's outstretched leg and tripped over it, sending the contents flying through the air. Gill could only watch in horror as their main courses rained down on Charlie, all the way down his pristine white shirt, with his steak catapulting into his stomach, making him flinch. It resembled a scene from a Carry On movie. Gill opened her mouth but nothing came out. In other circumstances it might have been comical, but Charlie looked so distraught, she really felt for him. The waitress clucked around and must have said sorry ten times. Charlie knew it was his own fault and didn't hold it against her. Instead he turned to Gill and said, 'Look, I'm really sorry, but I obviously can't sit here covered head to toe, or–' he looked down ruefully at his stomach '–at least, head to stomach in sauce. Do you mind if we get out of here?'

'Of course,' Gill said sympathetically.

The manager came over, apologising profusely. When Charlie advised they were going to leave, as he didn't feel comfortable sitting in a restaurant covered in food, the manager told them there would be no charge for their starters and handed them a voucher for a free meal for two.

'Thanks. Could you order us a taxi, please?'

Charlie went to the toilets to try to get the worst of the meal off his clothing. When he returned a few minutes later, his shirt still looked a mess, like one of the award-winning modern art pieces Gill had come across in her time and which she would never understand.

'Do you want to come back to mine? I could cook for you.'

A little voice inside Gill's head told her to be careful. She barely knew the man. Yet she felt touched that in the midst of his distress at having been liberally covered in Thai food, he was still thinking of a way to salvage their ruined date. That earned him a big tick in her book.

Deciding she was a big girl, who could handle herself, she said, 'Sure. I'd like that, if it's not too much trouble.'

'Not at all.'

'OK, let me just use the Ladies' before the taxi turns up.'

Once in the Ladies', Gill hurriedly battered out a text to Debbie. *Am about to go to Charlie's house. Waitress spilt food all over him at restaurant. He is going to cook for us. I'll be fine, but thought should let you know, Gill x.*

The taxi drew up in front of a block of sandstone flats near Queens Park. Charlie gave Gill his hand to steady her as she stepped out of the taxi. Unaccustomed to wearing such high heels, she was grateful for the small courtesy.

Charlie unlocked the outer door and said, 'After you.' Gill preceded him into the passageway and hesitated until Charlie said, 'Second floor.'

On the second floor, Gill came to a blue door with plant pots outside it. Opposite it was a red door with a Charles Rennie Mackintosh nameplate. Gill guessed that was Charlie's.

'The red door?'

'That obvious?'

'Mackintosh.'

'Ah.' Charlie opened the storm door, which led to a stained-glass inner door then showed Gill into a spacious hall.

'Go right in. The living room's on the right. I'll just get us some drinks. Wine OK?'

'Yes, white, if you have it.'

Gill entered Charlie's living room, which although definitely a man's domain, was pristine. Two brown Chesterfield sofas took pride of place, with an oak coffee table strategically positioned between them. Gill walked around the room, looking at the books in the mahogany bookcases. She picked up a couple, trying to work out what they told her about Charlie.

'Here you are,' Charlie handed her a glass. 'Semillon Chardonnay. It was the only white I had. I tend to drink mainly red.'

'That's fine, thanks.'

'Why don't you choose some music? My iPod's over there. Do you like seafood?'

'Yes, I like most things.' Gill smiled at him.

'Good. Make yourself at home and I'll be back shortly.'

Whilst Gill perused Charlie's playlist, Charlie changed his shirt, then busied himself in the kitchen. Luckily he'd been to the supermarket the day before and picked up a few ready meals. Seafood gratin, just enough for two. He'd serve that with some rocket. Turning on the oven, he removed the packaging and put it in the bin. Gill didn't need to know that he hadn't cooked it from scratch.

When he returned to the living room, Gill was standing at the window, with her mobile in her hand, tapping her foot to Blondie.

'Just waiting for the oven to heat up. How's the wine?'

'Fine, thanks. You have a nice home.'

'Thanks. I like to be comfortable,' Charlie said, ensconcing himself on the sofa.

'So what's for dinner?'

'It's a surprise.'

'A seafood-related surprise?'

'That's right.'

Gill sat on the sofa beside him. She was definitely attracted to him and felt at ease in his company. Did she want anything to happen? If so, then being in his home gave them the advantage of privacy. She knew she wouldn't sleep with him. Not yet anyway. She liked him, but not enough for that. It would, however, be fun getting to know him.

'Let me just check on the food.' Charlie nipped back to the kitchen, popped the seafood gratin in the oven and prepared the plates and cutlery for later.

What a stroke of luck, he thought. He'd been mortified and more than a little annoyed at the waitress spilling food over him, even if it was largely his fault. Yet things couldn't have turned out better. Gill was here in his home. He could tell she liked him. She looked a knockout in that dress – voluptuous and womanly – just the way he liked. If he had anything to do with it, after they'd eaten, she wouldn't be wearing it.

'That was delicious.' Gill's approval was clear from her

empty plate.

'Glad you liked it. More wine?'

'Please.'

Charlie topped up her glass, before removing the plates.

'Why don't you go back into the living room? I'll be through in a sec.'

'OK.'

Charlie found Gill seated on the sofa. Her dress had ridden up slightly, showing off more of her legs. Charlie had always been a leg and breast man. Gill passed on both counts. Flicking the dimmer switch down a little, Charlie changed the track on the iPod. Gill laughed when she discovered it was the *Dirty Dancing* soundtrack.

'I didn't expect you to have that.'

'I'm full of surprises.' Charlie faced her and held her gaze.

Gill knew he was going to kiss her. She found herself quite receptive to the idea. Rugged, sexy, Charlie oozed vitality and virility. What wasn't to like? And he could cook.

Charlie stroked her cheek and cupped her face with his hand. He waited to check the signal was definitely there and then lowered his lips to hers. Gill responded, her body waking up to this gorgeous man. Parts of her, long dormant, suddenly came to life. As their kiss deepened, she wound her arms around Charlie's neck and lost herself in the moment.

Great. Just as I hoped. He couldn't wait to run his hands over Gill's body, but held back a little, not wanting to frighten her off. But eventually, instinct took over and he tried to mould his body to hers, moving on the sofa so they were pressed against each other.

A dozen sensations flowed through Gill, all of them pleasurable. Anton entered her mind briefly, but as Charlie's ministrations continued, thoughts of Anton disappeared. She revelled in Charlie's touch, his kiss. His hands stroked her back, then slid downwards until he was caressing her bottom. His strokes were long and deliberate. Gill was so aroused. Her nipples hardened and he hadn't even touched her breasts. Yet. Charlie's hands moved from her back to her front and he started tracing the outline of her breast, making Gill gasp involuntarily. She had to stop this now. She wasn't ready. 'Charlie.'

'Mmm,' said Charlie as his left hand slipped to her thigh, trying to find a way under her dress.

'Charlie!'

'Yes?' He returned to Gill's mouth, looked into her eyes and kissed her again.

Oh dear God, she was so turned on, but no, she couldn't do this tonight.

'Charlie, I can't.'

'What?' Charlie drew up short. 'Is it the time of the month?'

'No, no, nothing like that. It's just, this is too quick for me.'

'OK, well, we can take it more slowly. You tell me what you're comfortable with.'

All of it, thought Gill. She was so mixed up. She wanted him, but at the same time, she wasn't sure. Her body said yes, but her brain said no.

She wrested herself out from under him. *How did I end up under him?*

'I'm sorry, Charlie, I've had a really nice night, but I think I better go.'

Charlie looked at her long and hard and then said, 'No problem. Let me call you a taxi.'

Charlie lived only a couple of miles from Gill, so she arrived home quickly. As she took off her make-up, she could still smell him, on her clothes, on her skin. He was an extremely attractive man, so what was holding her back? One word. Anton.

Chapter Twenty-two

Saturday 17 September

The bus pulled in on Hope Street and Gill got off then walked past the taxi rank and round into Buchanan Street, eager to get started on her shopping spree. Memories of last night still plagued her, but she had to put that aside for now and concentrate on her date with Anton. She'd arranged to meet Debbie for a quick bite of lunch. But first Frasers, then Debenhams. Gill wasn't good at shopping, so liked department stores as they covered all the bases.

As she walked, her thoughts turned inevitably to Anton. She'd replied saying Saturday was fine and she looked forward to their spending more time together. She had left it at that, still unsure what his exact expectations were, but hoping they matched hers. He had replied saying would Cecchinis' restaurant in Bath Street suit her, and could they meet there at seven? After a slight delay she had answered, '*Yes, see you then.*'

Anton's comeback had been '*Excellent, xx.*'

Promising...

She had no success in Frasers, so crossed a chaotic Argyle Street to the St Enoch Centre and went up the escalator into Debenhams. Not really knowing where to start, she went over to the personal-shopper area, on the off-chance they might have a free slot. Luckily they did. She told the girl, barely out of her teens, what kind of look she hoped to achieve. The assistant went back and forth with several outfits at a time, which Gill duly tried on, until finally she found the perfect one. A green silk wrap-over dress which accentuated her chest and small waist and covered those parts she'd rather keep hidden, and it came with a matching shrug. The assistant also suggested shoes, but Gill shook her head. The last thing she wanted was to be in agony all night from wearing new shoes that she hadn't had time to break in. What she really needed now was some lingerie. Although she liked to wear nice underwear anyway, what she owned couldn't exactly be termed new. No need to go all out for La Perla, but somewhere in between that and functional everyday underwear would do just fine.

Gill thanked the assistant, paid for her dress and strolled over to the lingerie section. She ran her fingers lightly over the fabrics to see how they felt. But what colour to choose? What style? A push-up bra was out. She was too well endowed for that. A balconette would have a similar effect. In the end, she chose a fuller cup black bra with cream trim and matching briefs. She tried them on for size and decided that short of losing two stone in the next few hours, she couldn't look any better. And the set was definitely feminine and sexy. She could actively imagine Anton removing them. Wow, if her thoughts continued in that direction, she'd be sizzling before lunch. Talking of lunch...Gill looked at her watch and saw she needed to meet Debbie in ten minutes. Flashing her credit card again, she paid and hotfooted it across to Princes Square.

'Hi, Debbie.' Gill sat down, dumping her bags on the seat next to her. 'Have you just come into town now?'

'No, I had to change a skirt in John Lewis, so I came in about an hour ago. What have you been buying?'

Gill showed her the contents of the bags. As Debbie lifted out the lingerie to have a better look, the waiter chose that moment to come and ask what they would like to drink. Hurriedly stuffing the garments back into the bag, both women tried not to laugh, as they ordered panini and glasses of rosé.

Debbie laughed then said, 'No use asking you what you've got in mind, Miss McFadden.'

'Well, it's not a foregone conclusion, but I just wanted to take precautions, be prepared.'

'You're going to need more precautions than sexy underwear,' Debbie joked, as she toyed with her cutlery. 'Condoms might come in handy, too, you know.'

'Yes, yes. I realise that. I'm sure if Anton has sex on his mind then he'll take care of that.'

'Gill, are you really not going to buy any yourself? Leave it all to him?'

'Well, it's embarrassing. Popping condoms into your shopping trolley along with your cornflakes and butter, the cashier giving you a knowing look. Or worse, going into a chemist and having the assistant know that you're thinking about having sex.'

'Since when were you so buttoned-up?'

'I'm not, it's just, it makes me feel awkward. Plus, remember, I haven't had sex for ages. And to be honest, it was almost always the bloke that bought them, in my relationships.'

'I still think you should buy some. How would you feel

if you really wanted to get jiggy and he hadn't brought any?'

'Horny and frustrated, I expect.'

'Exactly. Get yourself down to a chemist later, or even buy them in the Ladies' here.'

Gill looked at her friend in horror. 'I'm not buying them in the toilets, with all the ladies who lunch watching me!'

'OK, fair enough, chemist it is. Trust me, you'll regret it otherwise. Imagine if you have all that lovely lingerie and you can't take it further.'

As they tucked into their panini, they caught up with the week's events.

'You have been busy,' said Debbie, trying to stop a stray slice of pepper from falling out of her panini.

'Yes, but I'm so relieved to have finally hired someone, I can't tell you.'

'I can imagine. I bet all this dating is taking its toll on you, too.'

'You're not kidding. Not to mention on my bank balance.' Gill pointed towards the carrier bags.

They talked briefly of their trip to Barcelona the following weekend.

'Do you know, there's been so much going on that I haven't even had time to get excited about the trip,' Gill said.

'I know what you mean. The amount of call-outs I've done this week has been higher than usual. I've barely had a minute to myself,' said Debbie as she extracted her purse from her bag. 'Shall we get the bill?'

Debbie hugged Gill when they finally exited onto Buchanan Street. 'Good luck tonight. I'll be rooting for you.'

'Thanks. See you on Monday night. Enjoy the rest of

the weekend. Tell Gerry I said hi.'

'Will do. I want to hear all about it tomorrow, and be careful…in all senses.'

'I will.'

By late afternoon, ominous clouds covered the sky and Gill fretted that her outfit might get ruined if she had to wear it out in a heavy downpour. But she needn't have worried.

The sky cleared and the sun shone in the early September evening. Gill studied her reflection in the mirror and gave a twirl, trying to see how she looked from all angles. She slipped on a pair of strappy sandals and draped her shrug around her shoulders. She had applied a little more make-up than usual. It was the weekend after all, and a very important night – she hoped. One last check and she declared herself ready. She went to the window to see if her taxi was outside yet, and then heard her phone ring, signalling the taxi's arrival.

During the taxi ride Gill had butterflies in her stomach. What was wrong with her? She had never felt like this when meeting Anton, not even the first time. Was it the prospect of having sex, shedding her clothes in front of a stranger, after all this time? Was it perhaps the anticipation? She couldn't be sure, but what she did know was that she felt physically sick. Hopefully, she'd feel better once in the restaurant.

Anton had arrived in Glasgow at five thirty, nice and early, just in case his train was delayed. He wasn't taking any chances. He'd checked into his hotel and changed into black trousers and a pale blue shirt which looked good on him.

Cecchinis' had been a good choice, he thought – only a few streets away. Maybe they could have a drink afterwards and then, there was always the unspoken invitation. He felt pretty sure Gill liked him, perhaps a lot, maybe as much as he liked her. Yet he had no way of knowing if she also wanted them to take things further tonight. He couldn't wait to see her. He enjoyed her company and could listen to the tinkle of her laugh over and over. Her smile had captivated him and she was quite simply good company, as well as beautiful. He wanted very much to make love to her. He hadn't been with anyone, properly, in a long time. Of course, there had been the occasional one-night stand, but this was different. He *felt* different.

Applying some cedarwood cologne to his throat and jaw, he ran a comb through his hair and brushed his teeth. A gargle of mouthwash and he deemed himself ready. His hands shook slightly.

What have I to be nervous about?

Gill spotted Anton as soon as she entered Cecchinis'. He was sitting at the bar, facing the door, and when he saw her, he sat his glass down, just so, on the counter, and came towards her. Clearly pleased to see her, he looked her straight in the eye, put his hands on her arms and kissed her on both cheeks. She felt flustered and as if she were having a hot flush.

Is it hot in here? Perhaps it was just them. He smiled at the thought. 'It's so good to see you. Would you like a drink?' he asked her.

'Please. A glass of Pinot Grigio.'

'That's what I'm drinking. It's very nice. Why don't I get a bottle?'

Anton gave the waiter his order and turned back to Gill. 'You look beautiful in that dress.'

'Thanks.' Gill accepted the compliment graciously.

'So, how have you been?'

'Quite busy. I finally found a suitable recruitment consultant for my agency.'

'Did you advertise it with a specialist recruitment agency, or did you do it yourself? I know it might sound like a silly question, but your specialties are technical and engineering, correct?'

Gill was impressed he'd remembered. Attentive – tick. Two more brownie points. He smelled divine. A mixture of soap and a woody fragrance. Whatever aftershave he had on, she liked it.

'I actually did it myself. I advertised it on a couple of different job sites. It received a lot of attention and meant sifting through lots of CVs, but it was worth it.'

'You must be relieved. Finding the right people can be difficult. Even if you do it for other companies all the time, it's different when they're going to be working for you.'

'I couldn't agree more. Angus will definitely fit into our small team very well. He isn't all show, like a lot of recruitment consultants. They give the industry a bad name.'

'Excuse me, sir, your table's ready. Would you like to be seated now or would you like to remain at the bar for a while?'

Anton looked at Gill for confirmation then said, 'I think we can go to the table now, thank you.'

They chatted easily whilst they perused the menus. Gill immediately gave up on trying to find a non-garlic dish in an Italian restaurant. But if they were going to get more intimate later, she didn't want to have anything too heavy either. She chose a *caprese* salad to start and *spaghetti con gamberoni*. Prawns would be about the lightest thing she could have. Anton lowered his menu and said, 'Have you decided?'

Gill nodded, as she fought an impulse to play with the tablecloth. She did this whenever she was nervous. She ripped up beer mats, fidgeted, and toyed with tablecloths – basically anything except stay still.

'*Caprese* salad and spaghetti with prawns.'

'Good choices. I like both of those, but tonight I feel like roasted Mediterranean vegetables.'

'Yes, that does sound nice. Oh, they've included artichoke hearts, too. You don't usually get that, do you? It's usually just mixed peppers, aubergine, courgette and maybe tomatoes if you're lucky.'

'Well, you know what they say about artichokes…'

'No. What do they say?' A slight smile formed on Gill's lips. She knew full well artichokes were said to be an aphrodisiac, but she felt she and Anton should start the way they meant, or at least, the way she meant, to go on. Tonight was about teasing each other.

'Apparently in the sixteenth century, Catherine de Medici introduced them to France.' Anton then rattled off a quote she had made at court.

Gill must have looked a little stunned, crestfallen even, as Anton finally took pity on her and said, 'And, of course, they are meant to be a powerful aphrodisiac.'

Gill blushed to the roots of her hair. Her face was hot, probably not a pretty sight, and that wasn't the only area where she was warmer than usual. Anton rewarded her with a little grin. 'Would you like to know what I've chosen for my main course?'

Gill didn't know whether to be worried or not at what he might say next.

'Chicken *parmigiana*.'

With a sigh of relief, Gill took a moment to compose herself and by the time the waiter came back with his pad to take their order, she and Anton were completely at ease with each other.

She really does look amazing in that dress, thought Anton. The dress was so simple, yet so sexy. He liked the way her hair hung loosely down her back tonight. He didn't need an aphrodisiac. Making her blush, though, had been fun, not in a cruel way, but in a teasing fashion. Hopefully, there would be more of that to come later.

He reached for his wine glass and proposed a toast. 'To a wonderful evening.'

Gill raised her glass and they clinked them together.

As she took a sip, she drank in more than the wine. The man in front of her was a heady concoction all right. She hadn't felt this level of connection, sexual or otherwise for a long, long time, if ever.

Without realising what she was saying and the connotation it could have, she blurted out, 'So which hotel are you staying at?'

'The one next to the bus station.' Anton reeled off the good and bad points of the hotel, not least that beggars hung around the car park next to it.

When their starters arrived, they ate slowly, taking turns to relate anecdotes. Gill found out a lot more about Anton's research programme and she told him a little about her friends and Janice. For the next few hours, they laughed, ate, drank and talked a lot.

'That was delicious. I couldn't eat another bite.'

'Me neither.' Anton patted his completely flat stomach, 'I shouldn't have eaten that *zabaglione*. It just looked so good when that girl next to us had it.'

'I know, but I simply couldn't have eaten anything else. If I'm honest, I struggled to drink my coffee.'

'Do you think you could manage a drink, somewhere else?'

Gill hesitated before replying confidently, 'Sure, where were you thinking?'

'My hotel, if you have no objections.'

At first, Gill's words stuck in her throat, but then before she could spit out her answer, Anton clarified, 'They have a very nice bar, just off the lobby.'

'Yes, that sounds good.'

Anton paid the bill. They retrieved their coats and walked down towards the Buchan Hotel, on Renfrew Street.

'It's quite nice in here. I've never been before.'

'First time for me, too. Anton crossed his long legs and smiled at her.

They chatted about inconsequential things for a while, both realising that they were building up to something. The anticipation was almost tangible.

They were seated on a sofa together, side by side. But it was Saturday night and throngs of people crowded the bar. Anton rested his hand on Gill's thigh. 'Can I make a suggestion?'

'Fire away,' Gill replied, half-knowing what was coming.

'Would you like a little more privacy?' He looked directly into her eyes.

Gill didn't trust herself to speak.

Anton signalled to the waiter for the bill and ordered a bottle of wine to go.

They walked towards the lift in silence. Once inside, Gill took advantage of the fact they were alone to clarify matters.

'Anton, I want things to go further, but I need you to know, I'm not a hundred per cent sure I'm ready for *that*.'

Anton moved a lock of her hair and, kissing behind her ear, said, 'Gill, we won't do anything you don't want to.'

Feeling the pressure lifted considerably, Gill fell silent again as Anton kissed her again, this time on the lips.

The lift pinged their arrival at Anton's floor and they walked towards room 309.

Anton handed Gill the wine and the glasses, then took out his key card from his wallet and opened the door. Once inside, he took the wine from Gill and poured them both a glass. He sat on the sofa, which was at the far end of the room. Gill followed suit.

'*Slainté*.' Anton held aloft his glass then took a sip. Gill raised her glass to her lips. They looked at each other, wondering who was going to make the first move. Anton sat his glass down. He moved towards Gill and then his lips were on hers, the teasing they'd enjoyed earlier in the evening long gone.

Gill couldn't believe that they were really here, alone. Her nervousness evaporated and she kissed Anton back hungrily. The thought that her new silk dress would get crushed popped into her head and just as quickly disappeared again. Anton pulled her towards him and nuzzled her neck.

Gill slipped off her sandals whilst Anton struggled to

kick off his shoes. She stroked his back and then more daringly, untucked his shirt from his trousers, giving her access to his lean, flat stomach. She luxuriated in the feel of him. His chest sported a light sprinkling of hairs. He smelled wonderful and this time it wasn't his aftershave she could smell, but his masculinity. Impeded by Gill's dress, Anton resorted to caressing her nipples through the fine silk. He was so hard already. He groaned as Gill's hands slid upwards from his stomach, familiarising herself with the hard contours of his chest. They then travelled back down and rested on the waistband of his trousers, before Gill turned her attention to his belt. She unfastened the buckle and wrenched it free of the loops, tossing it to the floor. As she undid his zip, Anton whispered in her ear, 'Stand up.'

Gill obliged and Anton unzipped the back of her dress, kissing her neck as he did so, then her shoulder, then her back. Gill could scarcely breathe. It was so erotic. He eased her dress over her shoulders and let it slide to the floor, where Gill promptly stepped out of it. Hearing Anton's sharp intake of breath, she turned towards him.

Oh God, I need to have this woman right now. He thought he was going to come just looking at her. She was wearing incredibly sexy underwear. He was just wondering whether she'd bought it to wear for him, when he saw a tiny piece of the price label still affixed to one of the bra straps. He smiled and decided not to share that with her. It gave him enough of a glow that she'd gone to so much effort for him. As she stood before him in her bra and briefs, Anton feasted his eyes upon her: her beautiful ample breasts, curvaceous bottom and narrow waist. Where to start?

Gill pulling down his trousers, leaving him only in his

boxers, brought him back to the present. Anton's lips found hers and their hands roamed over each other, searching, anxious to explore. Somehow they made it to the bed and then Gill's bra landed on the floor, followed by Anton's boxers and finally Gill's briefs.

It was all too easy to get carried away, Gill thought. If Anton hadn't said, 'just a moment', whilst he withdrew a condom from his wallet, it wouldn't have occurred to Gill. She'd never had unprotected sex, but then she'd never felt such wild abandon. The sensations she had experienced with Anton were among the most exquisite of her life. The first time he came, he apologised that it had been so quick; he had just been very aroused. Gill looked forward to his idea of slow, as twenty-five minutes for quick made her have high hopes. Whilst he recovered, Anton took care of Gill's needs and soon she asked herself how she could have gone without making love for so long.

As they lay together afterwards, Gill stroked his chest, whilst she nestled in the crook of his arm. Every so often they kissed again until soon it was time for round two.

When Gill woke a few hours later, she watched Anton as he slept. His hair was mussed, definite 'I've just had sex hair,' and the sheet covered only the lower half of his body. The street lamp outside their window bathed Anton in a dim half-light.

Such a handsome man and she'd just made love to him – four times. No wonder he was sleeping so soundly. He must be exhausted. Each time had been better than the last. She got up and poured herself a glass of water, then crept back to bed and snuggled into Anton, who stirred momentarily, but soon became still again.

At eight thirty, the light entering through the gap in the curtains woke Anton. At first he struggled to remember where he was, but Gill's arm resting lightly on his chest soon oriented him. He turned to look at her. She looked so peaceful, content. He could make out the form of her body under the sheet and it brought back memories of the night before. Just then, Gill rolled over and opened her eyes, which widened in delight when she saw Anton.

'Morning,' she said sleepily.

Anton turned to face her and kissed her lightly on the lips. 'Hi.'

They looked at each other, smiled and then retreated under the covers together again.

When Anton and Gill left the hotel later that day, Gill felt self-conscious about being in evening dress.

'Don't worry. You look beautiful. I want to remember you just like this,' he said, pulling her towards him for one last kiss. 'I'll see you in a few weeks and of course I'll e-mail whilst I'm away.'

'You do that,' said Gill, as, reluctantly, she let go of him to get into her waiting taxi.

As the taxi pulled away from Anton, she sat back in the seat. *What a perfect night.*

Chapter Twenty-three

Sunday 18 September

'You look great, sis.' Christopher hugged her.

'Thanks,' Gill said, although she wasn't sure how that was possible, given that she hadn't slept much. She felt as if she were in a suspended state, a dream world. She handed her brother the flowers and bottle of wine she had brought, just as her nephews came tumbling towards her. 'Aunt Gill!' they screeched in unison, throwing themselves into her arms.

Laughing, Gill said, 'It's so nice to be wanted.'

'Did you bring us any sweets?' asked Harry.

'Harry,' his father said. 'What have I told you about asking for things? It's rude. Say sorry.'

'Sorry.' The small boy hung his head then two seconds later forgot all about it and chased his brother around the room.

Sarah came into the living room, taking off her apron. 'We made jam tarts this morning. The boys were in charge of the jam, so I thought it might be best to have something to cover up my new trousers.'

'Ah.' Gill had been surprised, as Sarah was usually very stylish and the image of her wearing an apron wasn't one generally associated with her.

'Garlic lemon chicken today, with roast potatoes and asparagus.'

Sarah was an excellent cook and Gill's stomach started to rumble. She had just had enough time to hightail it home, change and freshen up, before driving over to Christopher and Sarah's. She had arrived fifteen minutes behind schedule. Gill hated being late, but they didn't appear to have noticed.

As she perched on the edge of the sofa, feeling, and probably looking, rather pleased with herself, Sarah stared at her, then made sure the boys weren't listening, before she proclaimed, 'You've had sex!'

'What?' blurted out Gill.

Christopher's head snapped up. He looked first at his sister, then at his wife, then back at his sister.

Sarah repeated what she'd just said. Then she said, 'You have, haven't you? Oh, how exciting! Well, go on. Tell us all about it.'

'I think I'll just check on the potatoes.' Christopher excused himself, with a backward glance at the two women.

'So, give us the goss.' Sarah flounced down on the sofa beside Gill. 'I assume it involved the gorgeous Russian.'

'How...how did you know I'd had sex?' stammered Gill.

'Because you have a smile as wide as the little emoticon smiley-face chap, that's why.'

At this, Gill did smile.

'And you seem so content, not your usual flustered self.'

'Thanks, I think.'

'Sort of healthy and glowing.'

'Again, thanks.'

'You know what I mean,' Sarah said with a dismissive wave of her hand. 'So, c'mon, spill!'

Part of Gill was dying to tell someone, but she really thought it should be Debbie, plus some things she didn't feel she could share with Sarah. She was married to Gill's brother after all. Gill certainly wasn't going to give her the graphic details. She wanted to hug them to herself for a bit longer.

'I had a fantastic evening. Lovely dinner, great company and *that* was good, too.'

'How? Where?'

'He'd booked into a hotel in town. That way he wouldn't have to leave early to get the train back to Stirling.'

'Which hotel?'

Gill gave Sarah an account of the hotel and the events leading up to her finally sealing the deal with Anton, including the outfit she'd worn, although she didn't go into detail about her lingerie.

'So when are you seeing him again?'

'Well, he's going to be away in Belarus for the next few weeks, but after he gets back.' Sarah raised an eyebrow. 'He said he'd e-mail,' added Gill, waiting to see what was on Sarah's mind. 'What?' Gill finally asked.

'I just wondered when you found out he was going to be in Belarus for a few weeks.'

'A week ago, maybe ten days. Why?'

'Oh, nothing, just wondered.'

'Sarah, why?'

'No, seriously, it's fine. It's just that it wouldn't be the first time a guy has told a woman he can't see her for a few weeks, as he's going away, and that's the last she hears from him. But, in this case it's different, as he told you at least a week before you slept together.'

'*Hmm*,' Gill was thinking. She knew that couldn't be the case. They were so into each other.

'Anyway, Anton aside, have you had any other dates?'

As Gill filled Sarah in on her latest exploits, Christopher came back into the room.

Soon Sarah served up lunch and the boys traipsed in to sit at the dining table. Sarah had truly outdone herself this time.

After a delicious lunch, Gill spent a pleasant few hours playing games with her nephews. They had been banned from playing their computer that day, as they had spent too much time on it the day before. So, hide and seek, football out in the garden, and finally a couple of stories before bed, kept both Gill and her young nephews occupied until it was time for her to leave.

Christopher did, however, manage to waylay her on her way back in from the garden.

'Sis, is everything OK?'

'Couldn't be better.' Gill smiled at him.

'So, do you think this could be The One?'

'I hope so.'

'Just be careful. You know how you always fall head over heels.' He put his arm around her shoulder and gave her an awkward hug.

'I know, I will.'

'OK, I worry about you, that's all.'

'You don't need to. I'm a big girl.'

Christopher muttered something indistinct and went into the garden to call the boys in for their bath.

As Gill said goodbye, Sarah said, 'Good luck with Sean. It's not a bad idea to play the field a little for now.'

Closing the door, Gill was already counting the days until she could see Anton again.

Chapter Twenty-four

Monday 19 September

The driving rain battered against the office windows.

'How can you be so chirpy on a day like this?' Janice asked, curious. 'And it's Monday as well.'

'Just in a good mood, I guess,' Gill replied, then resumed humming the ditty she'd been subjecting Janice to all morning.

'Someone's been having their nookie by the sounds of it.' Janice had, as usual, hit the nail on the head.

'*Moi*?' Gill acted surprised.

'Yes, *toi*!'

'I'm just in a good mood because Angus has accepted our job offer.'

'Yes, that is great news, but you wouldn't be looking as if you were meeting George Clooney later, if that was all there was to it.'

Gill said nothing.

'Am I going to have to prise this out of you?' Janice rose from her seat, brandishing a stapler in a threatening manner.

'OK, OK. Yes, I had a great weekend and yes, things…progressed a fair bit with Anton.'

'Progressed, progressed?'

'Yes, progressed.'

'Look, I'm too old for this code nonsense. Did you shag him?'

'Janice!'

'Well, did you?'

'We slept together, if that's what you're asking.'

'Ha! Bet you there wasn't much sleep going on!'

Thinking back to Saturday night, Gill could only smile.

'I saw that! I'm right! Well, good for you. It wasn't before time.'

'Thanks, Janice.' Gill tried to be dry with her, but couldn't. She was too happy.

Everything was finally coming together. She had Anton, she had a new recruitment consultant, and she was off to the *Mercè* festival in Barcelona with the girls in a few days. Thank God – she really needed a holiday. Also, going away with the girls would take her mind off Anton in his absence. On second thoughts, who was she kidding?

'Janice, have you lost weight?'

'Not since Friday, no.'

'There's something different about you.'

'Do you think it could be the fact that my hair used to be brown and now it's blonde?'

'Bloody hell, Janice, so it is! It looks fantastic.'

'So fantastic, it has taken you three hours to notice.' Janice feigned offence.

'Never mind me. My head's in the clouds at the moment.'

'That's what happens when you're in love.'

Gill pulled up short. 'I never said I was in love.'

'You didn't need to. Look at you. You're positively gaga.'

'I am not!'

'Yes you are, but I suppose it beats gagging for it.'

'Janice! There are limits you know.'

'Yes, I've never really paid much attention to limits, me.'

'So, wait a minute, I tell you how great you look and then you offend me.' Gill tried and failed to appear outraged.

'Something like that.'

'Anyway, I'm not in love. I just like him.'

'A lot?'

Gill's silence lasted over a minute, before she said, 'OK, a lot.'

'I'm telling you, lady, you're in love.'

'Haven't you got some filing you could be doing?' Gill looked around hopefully.

'No, all up to date.'

'Right. Right. Oh, I just remembered I need to call Mr Farquharson.' And with that, Gill disappeared into her office, until Janice popped her head around to say she was heading home.

She couldn't be in love, could she? Surely it took longer than that? It had only been a few dates. Gill opened up her e-mail to see if she had by any chance received an e-mail from Anton. Nothing, but she knew not to expect anything. He was probably en route to Minsk by now. She did, however, have a message from Caroline Morgan. Caroline had dutifully checked in with Gill following each of her first dates to see how things had gone and to request feedback. Even after the Sean fiasco, Gill had simply said it was satisfactory. When Sean had contacted her again, she hadn't bothered updating Caroline to say they were seeing each other again. Gill gathered Sean would be quizzed, too. If he fancied telling Caroline, great, but Gill had too much else going on.

Chez Molinières was unusually busy for a Monday night. With such an excellent menu, the four girls had decided to make that their pit stop for their summit meeting, prior to their jaunt to Barcelona on Thursday.

The girls kissed and hugged. Lisa was her usual uncontrollably happy self, the bags under Debbie's eyes gave away how she was feeling, and Angela, well, Angela was just Angela – unflappable.

Lisa had printed off a list of trendy bars she wanted to go to, and the details for the wine and cava festival. Angela had similar printouts for the events for the Mercè festival and Debbie showed them restaurant recommendations from various people who had been there before.

But first off, they wanted the low-down on Gill's evening with Anton. As Gill narrated the events of Saturday night, Lisa and Angela sat riveted. Debbie had already heard this by phone from Gill, and listened distractedly. Lisa wanted to know every detail and she really did mean every. Angela sat, listened and nodded in the right places, then finally said, 'I'm happy for you, hon. This one seems like a keeper.'

Gill's face lit up. 'I know. I'm just so glad we're going away and I have something to take my mind off Anton for a few days. It would be no fun just sitting here, waiting for him to come back from Belarus.'

'Well, you're not exactly sitting around,' said Debbie. 'Don't you have a date with Sean tomorrow?

'Yes, we're going to the pics. Romcom. Men hate romcoms.'

'You're evil, do you know that?' Debbie tutted.

'He made a complete fool of me last time. It's only fair I get a little bit of revenge.'

'From what I heard he made a fool of himself,' Lisa said.

'Yes, well, that too, but he was so gassed, he probably doesn't remember.'

The girls ran through the itinerary for meeting up on Thursday. They were taking a no-frills flight from Prestwick directly to El Prat de Llobregat airport. The flight would land just before two, so the girls expected to be in the city around three thirty. Debbie had found out that the train ran directly from the airport into the city centre. The nearest stop to their hotel was Passeig de Gràcia, no more than a ten-minute walk.

They planned to meet in town and take the train down to Prestwick. That way no one needed to drive and besides, who knew what state they would be in, on the way back. The likelihood that they'd be sporting hangovers was strong – potent sangria and a wine and cava festival, too. It didn't take a rocket scientist…

The girls discussed what they wanted to see. Lisa wanted to go shopping.

'They have a huge shopping centre there, L'Illa. It has Zara and loads of other great shops. Of course I'm going.'

'I can probably get most of what I want in El Corte Inglés,' Debbie said.

'Well, I don't mind if you want to go and do a bit of cultural stuff, whilst I shop, but I definitely want to go to the Museu de la Xocolata,' Lisa said magnanimously.

'Mmm, me too,' Debbie said, as Angela nodded her agreement.

'OK, I think we've all decided to go to the museum. What else is a must-see for all of us?'

'I definitely want to see Casa Gaudí and Parc Güell,' Angela said straightaway.

'The forecast's good. I'm for the beach,' piped up Lisa, as she crossed her long legs one over the other, causing a middle-aged man at a nearby table to choke on his steak. 'Have you lot been waxed?' she asked.

Gill didn't go in for waxing. She simply shaved her underarms and legs. Waxing was too painful. Angela and Debbie looked at Lisa as if she had horns.

'I'll take that as a no, then. Get yourselves waxed before Thursday. You don't want to look like Germans on the beach, do you now?'

'To be truthful, I hadn't thought about the beach,' Angela said. 'I'm not that fussed.'

'Not that fussed? Not that fussed! When did we last see sun here?'

Debbie and Gill studied their shoes, as Angela said, 'Well, not everyone's a sun worshipper. You can go lie on the beach and I'll just do a city bus tour or something.'

After much discussion, the girls decided on what activities they would do together, and which they would do either in twos or on their own. They were so excited about the trip that they barely tasted the delicious food in front of them.

As they left the restaurant, Lisa wished Gill luck for her date with Sean. Debbie mouthed a *Call Me* and Angela gave Gill a wry smile.

At least she wouldn't have to make such an effort tomorrow. It was just the cinema.

Chapter Twenty-five

Tuesday 20 September

The prospect of watching a romcom on the big screen was a welcome one, Gill decided next morning. She'd got through a lot of work, and just as well, since she had to clear her desk before she set off for Barcelona. She'd already arranged a temp to help Janice during her absence. A few replies to the student advert had also come in, but those would have to await her return. Overall, it had been a good day.

In a strange sort of way, she was looking forward to seeing Sean, mainly because she wanted to see him squirm, to see how much he would apologise, the lengths he would go to for forgiveness. OK, maybe she was getting carried away, but she wanted to see how well he stomached going to a romcom. They wouldn't be able to talk in there and she'd limit their coffee time to an hour or so afterwards. He was cute and she had liked him. But seriously, she didn't see him being the big love of her life. She almost felt responsible for his well-being, ensuring his liver didn't give out on him. As a mate he promised to be fun, but Gill just felt any prospect of passion between them had been eradicated by his previous behaviour. And of course, her heart was finely tuned to Anton's now.

Gill dressed in jeans, heels and a floaty top, nothing too dressy this time. She was just going to sit in a dark cinema, after all. She left her hair down and doused herself with her favourite perfume.

At precisely ten to seven, she entered the cinema and looked around for Sean. His face lit up when he saw her.

'Hi.' He pecked her on the cheek. 'Love that top. It really suits you.'

'Thanks. So, how are you doing?'

'Yes, I'm good, busy at work, you know how it is.'

Gill did know. 'Should we go and get the tickets?' She pointed over to the ticket desk.

'No need. I've already taken care of it. Hope the leather seats are OK for you.'

'I'm sure they'll be fine.'

'Have you eaten anything?'

Gill had grabbed a toastie before she left. 'Well…'

'Say no more. We'll get some nachos and a couple of hot dogs.' With that, Sean led them to the bustling queue.

It seemed to take an age to serve them, but at least they had arrived early, and they entered the cinema laden with cheese nachos, a small drink each and no change from fifteen pounds. Sean had waved away Gill's offer of money.

The trailers yielded another romcom, an action movie predicting the end of the world, and the latest animated feature film. Gill sat back, careful not to get cheese sauce down her top, and relaxed. She was looking forward to this.

She could sense Sean glancing at her occasionally, but didn't turn towards him. Every so often, his hand strayed onto her armrest and she could feel the heat from his body. The film was pretty funny and there were a few parts at which they both laughed out loud. At one particular scene,

Gill thought she was going to wet herself. Turning towards Sean, she saw that he was doubled over, with tears running down his face.

'A lot better than I expected,' Sean admitted, as they rode the escalators back down to the ground floor.

'Thought you enjoyed it. And it a *girls'* film, too.'

'Well, it wasn't exactly a girls' film.' Sean started to lay his defence.

'So, you'd be happy to tell all your rugby mates, would you, that you enjoyed a romcom?'

'Maybe not.' He grinned and his eyes twinkled. 'But then they're all liars if they say they don't find them funny.'

Sean suggested they go to the bar in Buchan's Hotel, to grab a coffee.

'No,' said Gill a little vehemently. The last thing she wanted was for the bar staff to cast an enquiring glance at her, wondering where they'd seen her before. She could just imagine the twitching of the lips when they realised it was only three days since they'd seen her go upstairs with another man.

'I've heard bad reports about it,' Gill said, recovering quickly. 'Apparently their coffee is like dishwater.'

'Oh, OK then.'

'Why don't we go to Le Pays?' Gill suggested the hotel directly opposite the cinema.

They waited for the lights to change and then crossed the road to Le Pays.

'Do you fancy something to eat?' Sean inclined his head towards the restaurant section.

'No, I'm fine with coffee, thanks. Why, you hungry?'

'I'm always hungry.' Sean patted his non-existent stomach. He was very fit-looking, well, not just fit *looking*, fit, she reminded herself. He did do a lot of sport.

'Don't hold back on my account.'

'I might see if they have some olives or bruschetta, something light.'

When Sean returned from the bar, he wore a huge grin. 'Olives on the way. So, what have you been up to?'

Deciding dating half of Glasgow was probably not the best explanation of how her week had gone, Gill limited herself to, 'Pretty busy with work, but I met up with some friends last night at Chez Molinières.' Taking a sip of her coffee, then wishing she hadn't, as it had scalded her tongue, she said, 'We were meeting up because we're going to Barcelona on Thursday.'

'Barcelona. I've never been. That's where the big ugly church is, isn't it?'

'If you mean the Sagrada Família, Gaudí's unfinished masterpiece, then yes.' Gill smiled at him.

'It always seems to have loads of cats around it, when you see it up close on TV.'

'I hadn't noticed. Did you know they've decided to finish it?'

'What's the point of that? It's like someone trying to write the end of Dickens' unfinished novel. It's not Dickens.'

'I guess they thought it would be better for the city if such a huge building was actually finished.'

'Hmm.' Sean rubbed his chin, unconvinced. 'So why Barcelona?'

'Well, only one of us has been before, and the other three have always wanted to go, for various reasons. Plus the festival's on.'

'Festival?'

'Yeah, there's a traditional festival, the *Mercè*, with lots of events, open-air concerts, even ballet in the park.'

'I'd like the open-air concerts. Any room in your suitcase?' Sean shot her an imploring glance.

'Fraid not – girls only.'

Despite the disastrous finale to their last date, Gill realised that they got on well together. She didn't feel the need to try to be someone she wasn't. She hadn't particularly dolled up for tonight, and yet she felt confident in Sean's company.

As Gill sneaked a peek at Sean, whilst he watched a group of people coming in to the hotel, she thought how he looked like a more handsome version of the errant boyfriend from *Sliding Doors*. It wasn't just the accent. Sean made her feel as if they'd been friends for a long time, and he didn't bore her by talking constantly about sport, which he could have done, given his huge interest in it. It was, however, clear that music animated him and was the key influence in his life.

When Gill next looked at her watch, she couldn't believe it. It was already eleven thirty. They'd been here for nearly three hours.

'Sean, I didn't realise the time. I need to go. I have to be up early for work tomorrow, as it's my last day before I go on holiday.'

'Oh, of course, I understand. Are you getting a taxi home?'

'Yes.'

'Well, let me wait with you at the taxi rank. There's one at the bus station.'

'Thanks.' It was a far cry from last time when he had stayed on at the pub drinking. Dismissing this thought,

Gill focused on the lovely evening they had spent together.

They walked round to the back of the bus station, Sean steering Gill clear of the rowdies making a fuss outside the bus station entrance.

'You never know who's hanging about here. Bloody junkies.'

Gill couldn't agree more. She hated drugs, and although she knew some people had had very harrowing upbringings, she would never understand how any human being could do that to themselves. They scooted past as quickly as possible, trying not to attract attention.

The taxi rank was empty. A Tuesday night and not a taxi in sight.

'One'll be along soon,' Sean assured her.

It was a clear night and the stars lit up the sky. Unfortunately, that meant it was also pretty cold. With the heat of the day long gone, Gill shivered. She hadn't even brought a jacket, and the floaty top she was wearing did nothing to warm her. Self-consciously she folded her arms across her chest. She could feel her nipples standing out in the cold.

'Here, take my jacket. You must be freezing,'

'No, I couldn't possibly.'

'Seriously, I'm baking and this is a thick shirt I have on.'

'Oh, OK then. Thanks.' Gill accepted his light jacket and threw him a smile of gratitude. He was quite cute and he did have beautiful eyes, laughing eyes, most people would say. Cheeky, sexy, fun.

She started, but it was only Sean putting an arm around her.

'Sorry. I didn't mean to make you jump. I just thought

a bit of contact might heat you up.'

Well, that was certainly a new line. You had to give the guy his due for trying. Gill hid a smile and turned fully towards him.

'What sort of contact?' she said, playing along with him.

Emboldened by her question, Sean placed his hand lightly on her waist. 'Maybe, this sort of contact?'

'OK.' Gill waited to see what he would do next.

'Or perhaps like this?' He wrapped his arms loosely around her, pulling her towards him.

Now she really was startled. She hadn't expected to feel such a surge of lust. She had just been teasing him a little; she liked him, but really didn't think anything would happen, or surely there would have been signs earlier in the evening?

As they were the same height, Sean didn't have much to do to bring his lips to within inches of Gill's. He hesitated briefly and seeing no disapproval, brought his mouth to hers and kissed her. He kept kissing her and she responded, her eagerness all too evident.

'Get a room you two,' said a passing group of boys in white tracksuits.

Gill and Sean looked at each other, saying nothing. The sound of the diesel engine finally broke into their thoughts. When they didn't move, the surly taxi driver, shouted, 'Do you two want a taxi or not?'

'We'll take it.' Sean turned to Gill and said, 'Do you mind if we go past mine on the way? It's just there aren't many taxis at this time of night, as you can see.'

'No, that's fine. Where are you?'

'Top of Rose Street. Just off Sauchiehall Street, up the wee hill.'

'The one that's as steep as the hills you see in San Francisco on TV?' asked Gill, as she adjusted herself on the seat. Her jeans were digging into her.

'That's it. It was handy for the RSAMD. I bought it from the landlord when I moved here.'

Less than five minutes after leaving the bus station, the taxi drew to a stop in Rose Street.

'Gill, I had a great time tonight. You're very easy to get on with,' Sean whispered out of earshot of the driver. 'Would you like to come in for a coffee?'

At this Gill giggled. 'Sean, we've had three coffees. I'll be lucky to sleep a wink tonight!'

'Good point.' He opened the door of the taxi. 'Night-cap?'

'I can't. I have an early start. Truly – maybe another time?' Gill didn't mean to commit herself by saying this, but Sean immediately pounced.

'Good, because I'd like to see you again.'

'I'll be in touch when I get back from Barcelona,' she said, trying to read his expression.

'Are you getting out or what?' the driver barked.

'Give us a second,' Sean replied over his shoulder. Turning to Gill, he leant across her and said, 'Until next time,' then he bent his head to hers and kissed her.

As Sean closed the door, then waved, Gill touched her fingers to her lips where Sean's had met hers a moment before and wondered what the hell was going on with her.

Chapter Twenty-six

Wednesday 21 September

No time to dwell on the exploits of the night before. Wednesday was chaos. The temp had arrived, so, after a quick briefing, Gill asked her to shadow Janice for the day. The girl, Amanda, seemed quite bright, which was one less thing for Gill to stress about when she went to Barcelona.

Gill cleared her desk as much as possible. She hadn't scheduled any meetings for today. Arranging meetings for the day before a holiday was always a recipe for disaster. Long ago she'd realised she shouldn't overstretch herself, although realising this and doing something about it were sometimes two entirely different things.

Periodically she checked on the temp, receiving a nod of approval from Janice. That was all she needed to know. Breathing a sigh of relief, Gill attacked the rest of her tasks. Finally, she wrote a pending items list for Janice and e-mailed it across to her.

Only once she was home, had popped a 'fresh' meal from the supermarket chiller section in the microwave, and poured herself a glass of wine, did Gill finally have time to check her personal e-mails. There was another progress update request from Caroline Morgan, a couple of jokes from Christopher and an e-mail from Gary. Gary. When had they gone out? Screwing up her face, Gill tried to recall exactly when she had ripped her trousers. Shouldn't be too hard to remember that, you'd have thought, but she had difficulty with which day it had been. Ah, it was last Tuesday – a week before her second date with Sean. She hadn't really thought about Gary this week, but then there had been such a lot going on. She opened the e-mail and read,

Hi, Gill. Hope you are well. Am away on the rigs, but will be back next week. If you are game for meeting up again, how's next Saturday 28th looking? Gary.

To say that she was astounded was too strong, but very surprised, yes. But then, he had said he would like to see her again. With so many new friends at the moment, Gill was having difficulty keeping track.

Last Tuesday seemed a lifetime ago. So much had happened since then, not least that she'd slept with Anton. Plus, she'd been in a compromising position with Charlie and snogged Sean. Her head hurt with the logistics of it all. She'd pack for Barcelona and then answer him. But first, she really must phone her parents.

As Gill lay in bed waiting for sleep to overcome her, she replayed her last date with Anton, over and over in her head, every nuance, every detail, until finally she fell asleep.

Anton left the laboratory sometime after midnight. It had been a long day. He'd subsisted on sandwiches and coffee. At least the hotel wasn't far away, he thought. He couldn't wait to have a warm shower and then lie in a soft bed, where he could finally let his thoughts drift to Gill and what had happened between them. It had been every bit as good as he had anticipated. They had been so right together. He felt excited about the future. Concentrating on the road, windscreen wipers on full, he smiled to himself at the thought of her. The rain was becoming heavier, making it difficult to see. The newscaster on the radio warned of flooding and heavy rain and advised drivers to take extra care.

Headlights rushed towards him. He heard a scream, which startled him. The impact, the twist of metal, and the pain occurred simultaneously. As he started to lose consciousness, he realised the scream had been his own.

Chapter Twenty-seven

Thursday 22 September

Gill didn't manage to get back to Gary that night, since the grilling she received from her mother, who had made her feel bad for not phoning in the past few weeks, lasted more than an hour. Gill finally managed to get her mother off the phone by telling her she still needed to pack, but not before she promised to come down in a couple of months and spend a few days with them. 'Your father's not getting any younger you know.' The irony of this statement was lost on her mother, older than her husband by five years. And they were both fitter in many ways than Gill. In their early seventies, their days consisted of walks by the sea, squash for her father and tennis for her mother. Moving to Devon had rejuvenated them. Sometimes Gill wished she could move to Devon, although not next to her parents, no matter how much she loved them. She fancied somewhere tranquil, with a slower pace of life than in the city. Although no London, Glasgow was busy enough to need to escape from on occasion. For now, Barcelona would have to do.

Always first to arrive, Gill checked her e-mails at the station. Damn. She'd forgotten to reply to Gary. She typed fast. *'Gary, about to go to Barcelona. 28th should be fine.*

What did you have in mind? Gill.' Short and to the point.

As she waited, she noticed another e-mail arrive from Caroline Morgan.

Dear Gill. Please find attached two more profiles.

Realising she wouldn't be able to read them easily on her phone, she dug in her carry-on bag for her tablet, booted it up and logged into her e-mail again. There, better now.

Candidate Profile
Name – James McArthur
Age – 48
Lives – Edinburgh
Occupation – Company Director
Qualifications – MSc Marketing
Height – 5' 10'
Marital status – Divorced twice, four children
Smoker – Y
Interests: Stock market, cars, white-water rafting, good restaurants, wine, movies.
Further information: I set up my first company at twenty-five. I have dabbled with many industries since. I own several homes in France, Spain, the US, as well as pieds à terre in London and Morningside. I split my time between them when I can.
Looking to meet: A lady who enjoys travelling and who appreciates wine. Must love cinema.

Gill scanned the first profile. Company Director from Edinburgh, OK. Height fitted. Divorced twice – ouch! That was a big no-no. Once was unlucky, twice flagged up warning signs. At forty-eight, his kids could be anything from thirty downwards. Stock market – so, he found financial dealings and probably world affairs interesting – certainly more than she did. From the head and shoulders shot included, he appeared quite stocky. The image was very proper, almost as formal as a passport photo. The black suit did nothing to detract from his bulk. Gill also didn't like the way he bragged about setting up a company so young. It was very 'look at me', which Gill despised. Likewise, mentioning his homes around the world, screamed show-off.

Gill felt sure many women would be delighted to receive James' profile, and consider him a real catch, but she wasn't particularly interested in material wealth. As long as she had enough to live the life she currently led, she was happy. No, he wasn't for her. His eyes held no warmth. She'd like to say his smile didn't quite reach his eyes, but that slight twist of his lips couldn't even be classed a smile, more a grimace. It almost looked as if it pained him to smile.

White-water rafting – well, she'd always fancied that, a throwback to dreams of her adventurous youth, when she would have tried anything daring – hence the dreaded, never to be repeated, bungee jump. But she'd have to wait for another opportunity, as she certainly wasn't going with Mr Arrogant – Mr I Display My Wealth For All To See. He was into cars, too, probably had one for every day of the week. And Morningside, well that made sense. You couldn't be as wealthy as he was, and not boast a home in the most luxurious neighbourhood in Edinburgh. He didn't interest her at all. From his affluence to the severe military haircut, Gill simply wasn't taken with him.

She turned her attention to the second profile.

Candidate Profile
Name – Mark O'Hara
Age – 35
Lives – Prestwick
Occupation – Consultant
Qualifications – MBChB from University of Glasgow School of Medicine
Height – 5' 7"
Marital status – Single
Smoker – No
Interests: Motocross, rally driving, speedway, music, squash.
Further information: I recently took up a new post as Consultant Orthopaedic Surgeon. I come from a large family, all doctors. Also in a band, play guitar.
Looking to meet: Someone who wants to socialise and enjoy life.

Gill began to read, but not without first scrutinising his photo. He appeared to have strawberry blond hair. Ginger. Hmm. But he had a lovely smile, which did reach his eyes, unlike James'. He was a consultant – another high-flier then; quite short, though, at only five feet seven. A non-smoker. That deserved a tick. Another black mark for James – a smoker. Mark, too, seemed to like cars and bikes. He played squash. Gill had played once and, for three days afterwards, had felt as if she'd broken her wrist, unable to type, not even in a 'one finger at a time' fashion.

'What are you up to?' Lisa peered over her shoulder. 'Might have known you'd still be attached to a computer somehow. We're on holiday remember.' She plonked herself down on the bench next to Gill. 'So, who's that?'

'Another potential date. Mark. He's a doctor.'

'Ooh.' Lisa's eyes already displayed dollar signs.

'Don't even think it – he's only five feet seven.'

'And? We're all the same height…' She didn't get to finish her sentence, as Gill broke in, 'Lying down, I know.'

'He's cute, though, for a ginger.'

'Yes, he is,' Gill agreed, just as Angela and Debbie walked up to them.

'Hello, love.' Debbie embraced first Gill, then Lisa. 'Bumped into this one at the cash machine. So, how are we all doing?'

'What's that you've got there?' Angela strained to see, as she set her bag down on the bench.

'That's Mark,' Lisa said.

'Mark?' asked Angela and Debbie together.

'The agency sent me two more profiles,' said Gill.

'Really? Let's be having them.' Debbie's enthusiasm was catching, and all four friends huddled round Gill's tablet.

'Why don't we wait until we're on board? We really should get going.' Gill checked her watch. 'The train leaves in ten minutes and we still need to buy tickets.

'OK, get a wriggle on, girls,' Lisa said, shepherding them forward.

The packed train meant standing room only. No chance to discuss the profiles. By the time they reached Prestwick Airport, the girls were pretty hyper.

'I'm so glad we booked Speedy Boarding,' Lisa said, rummaging in her bag for her boarding pass. 'Look at the size of the other queue.'

'Yes, but we paid an extra forty pounds between us, just to board the plane earlier.' Angela's cynicism shone through.

'Well, it's done now. Let's just be glad we don't have to push in with all the rest of them.' Debbie jerked her thumb in the direction of the three hundred-odd passengers jostling each other behind the Wait Here line.

'That was much more civilised,' Debbie said, once they had all taken their seats.

A large woman, one of the last people to board the plane, tried to put her three carrier bags into the overhead compartment, but there simply wasn't space. She managed one and then asked Gill and Angela to move, so she could access the window seat. Angela stared at her. The woman had to be twenty stone plus. She really thought there was going to be room for her in the window seat, plus her two bags? How had she even sneaked the bags past the airline's checks? Angela and Gill slid out of their seats to let her pass, catching a whiff of body odour which would have knocked out a world heavyweight champion boxer. When they sat down again, Angela practically had to hug Gill to get away from the woman who now occupied one and a half seats.

'How long's the flight?' Angela whispered to Gill.

'Two and a half hours.'

'If nobody sits beside them–' Angela inclined her head to where Lisa and Debbie sat, undisturbed '–would you mind if I moved over there?'

Sympathising, Gill said, 'Of course not. I'm going to read anyway.'

'Great,' Angela's relief was almost palpable, if short-lived, as a woman came along with a young boy and asked Lisa to move up.

'I can let you past, but I want an aisle seat,' Lisa said.

The mother regarded Lisa with notable disdain. Muttering something indistinct to her son, the boy then wriggled past to the window seat. Seemingly content, the girls then paid no attention to him, until he started kicking the back of the seat in front of him, occupied by an elderly lady.

'Could you stop doing that?' Lisa glared at him.

The boy said nothing, but redoubled his efforts.

'Quit it!' Lisa said sharply. The boy started to cry. The stewardess appeared just then and Lisa stopped her, 'Excuse me, can you seat this boy elsewhere? He's kicking this lady's seat.'

'I'm afraid the flight's full,' the stewardess said apologetically.

'Well, can you seat him with his family? He's being a nuisance.'

'I'll see what I can do.' The stewardess then asked the boy where his mum was.

'What a flight,' Angela said, delighted that they had finally landed. 'I thought I was going to be sick. That woman reeked. I don't think she'd showered for a week.'

'I know. She should have been made to buy two plane seats and a can of deodorant,' Gill said, as she reached in her bag for her passport.

It was peak time at Prat de Llobregat airport and several flights had just deposited their passengers on the tarmac.

'Wow, feel that heat,' Lisa said, positively jubilant.

'I know, it's glorious.' Gill basked in the sun during the short walk from the plane steps to the terminal building.

Forty minutes later the girls entered the main section of the airport, in search of the tourist information centre. They wanted to know exactly where to get the train, as they found the signs difficult to follow.

'This airport's lovely,' Lisa said awestruck. 'Just look at these shops.' Knowing that shops had the same effect on Lisa as a siren calling a sailor, Gill grabbed her shoulders and turned her away from them.

'Train's not bad. Quite comfortable actually.' Angela reclined in her seat.

'Yes, just a bit busy.' Debbie hated crowds.

They alighted at Passeig de Gràcia and walked the ten minutes to the hotel on Carrer de la Boqueria, passing shoppers laden with bags from El Corte Inglés, as well as top designer names. Lisa appeared to be in heaven. Debbie regarded the cool Catalan women; always expertly coiffed, with make-up as flawless as if applied by a professional, sunglasses perched on their heads. Parents held the hands of their chattering children, as they tried to identify a café where they could have a drink.

'Is it much further?' Lisa moaned. 'My feet are killing me.'

'Well, maybe you should have worn something more practical than heels, for travelling?' Angela glared at her in exasperation. Although they were friends, those two rubbed each other up the wrong way most often.

'I think it's just down here.' Gill consulted the map and then said, 'Yes, see the sign?'

The girls looked up, and sure enough the sign for their hotel stood out fifty yards ahead.

The receptionist spoke good English and soon sorted them out with their keys. A porter showed them to their adjoining rooms. They were both family rooms. The Hotel Opera didn't appear to have simply double or twin rooms. Debbie and Angela took the first room, which comprised a single bed and bunk beds.

'We won't be in it much,' Angela said, taking in the small, but neat accommodation. A functional en suite was off to one side, but there was a serious lack of wardrobe space.

'Thank God I'm not sharing with Lisa. Five coat hangers?' Debbie said in disbelief.

Once unpacked, the girls went next door to hurry along Gill and Lisa.

Gill opened the door to them.

'Hey, your room's huge!' Angela took in the room, twice the size of their own, which boasted a balcony overlooking the street.

'Aren't they all the same?' Gill asked.

'No, ours is miniscule compared with this and we have bunk beds.'

'You're kidding.' Lisa burst out laughing.

'No, I'm not, and it has practically no wardrobe space.' Debbie pointed accusingly at the large walk-in wardrobe, next to the girls' en suite.

Gill felt bad, as Debbie and Angela obviously had a raw deal. 'Do either of you want to swap with me?'

Angela shook her head and Debbie said, 'It'll be fine. We'll be out and about all the time. We'll probably be too pissed when we get back to care, anyway.'

'I knew there had to be a reason to get pissed.' Lisa's face brightened.

As they were so hungry, having eaten nothing since a quick bite at the airport that morning, they decided to eat somewhere close by. Avoiding the main drag, with the aid of their map, they soon found Plaça Sant Josep Oriol and headed for Bar del Pi, which was thronged with people. All of the tables outside were taken, so they ventured inside to see if they could find a free table. On the verge of giving up, they spotted two couples coming downstairs and quickly nipped upstairs to nab their table. Bar del Pi was decorated in dark wood and not a lot of light entered, but it was an institution in Barcelona and much frequented by Catalans and tourists alike.

The excited chatter of Catalans and Spaniards assailed their ears as the four girls studied the menu which lay on the table. None of them spoke any Spanish, except for *gracias* and *por favor*. Fortunately there was also an English menu. To their dismay, they noticed that it didn't actually contain any proper meals, just tapas.

'Oh well, we'll just have to order lots.' Lisa's cheerfulness cut through the rumbling of Gill's stomach.

'What have *they* got?' Debbie pointed as discreetly as she could to a couple a few tables away. 'As the waiter walked past with it, I got a whiff and it smelled delicious.'

Lisa, ever the unsubtle member of the group, craned her neck to see. 'I think it's baby octopus.'

'Yuck, I'm not having that!' Debbie grimaced, as she hurriedly returned to perusing the menu.

They decided to copy their Spanish counterparts and share several tapas.

As they waited for their food to arrive, the girls planned the rest of their day. They agreed that they just wanted to wander around, get their bearings, nothing strenuous.

The waiter brought their wine and after Lisa tasted it, he poured them each a glass.

'This is the life,' said Angela.

'What, being inside, when it's glorious outside?' came Lisa's sarcastic retort.

'We're not all sun worshippers like you,' Angela replied curtly.

'Right you two – quit it,' Debbie said, intervening to keep the peace. 'We're on holiday. Yes, this is the life, Angela, and yes, it would have been better, Lisa, if we could have sat outside, but we've just got here, we're thirsty and we're starving, so drink up!'

'Hear, hear,' said Gill.

Soon afterwards, their first round of tapas arrived. Debbie, of course, steered clear of the baby octopus, so Lisa magnanimously said she would swap her chicken croquette in exchange for Debbie's octopus.

'Hey, don't look now, but five o'clock.' Debbie winked at Gill. Gill's back was to the room, so she had to make do with the others' description of the gorgeous Spanish man with the floppy black hair and gleaming white teeth who had just walked in, alone, and now stood at the bar. From their position upstairs, they could see him, without his realising he was being observed. Gill turned round, just as he glanced upwards. He saw her watching him and smiled. Mortified, she quickly looked away.

'He just caught me,' she hissed.

'He could catch me anytime.' Lisa, never one to be slow at these things, had no issue in expressing her obvious interest in him.

'Excellent, we've already spotted some talent.' Gill grinned.

'That's true. Anyway, cheers to an excellent time in Barcelona!'

Lisa's toast prompted them all to clink glasses again.

They requested a second round of tapas, this time plumping for *pan Catalan* – garlic bread rubbed with tomato; *montaditos* with *jamón* and *queso* – mini cheese and ham baguettes; *tortilla de patatas*, and *queso de cabra al horno* – grilled goats cheese with Seville orange and chilli marmalade.

Soon after their tapas dishes had been cleared away, Lisa said, 'Hey, there's a free table outside. I'm going to grab it.' She pushed her chair back and legged it outside.

They ordered another bottle of wine and sat in the sun, sipping wine and catching up. Gill was already beginning to feel a bit tipsy. The mixture of sun and wine always did that to her. She would have to pace herself. Thank goodness for the little shade the tree next to their table afforded them.

After an hour, they decided to move on, so they wandered back through the streets of the Gothic quarter and onto the Ramblas. They paid particular attention to their belongings, since Barcelona's reputation as a notorious hunting ground for pickpockets preceded it. Sauntering down the thoroughfare, they peered at the newsstands and watched the performing statues, as well as musicians from Russia and Peru. Soon they came across several open-air cafés, where virtually everyone appeared to be drinking huge *copas* of sangria.

'We've got to have one of those.' Lisa pointed to the mammoth goblet from which a tiny Japanese woman was drinking.

'Sounds like a plan,' Debbie agreed, and the others traipsed behind Lisa, who was already intent on sorting them out a table. It was busy, but a little flirting from Lisa, a toss of her long blonde hair and they had their table.

They ordered four *copas*, which arrived quickly, and were soon enjoying the delicious fruity alcoholic concoction, as they sat watching the motley crew which made up Barcelona's visitors and locals pass by.

'Hey, we never did vet those new dates Gill received,' Lisa said.

Gill carried her tablet with her, probably not a good move in Barcelona, she knew, with its theft problems, but she always carried her bag slung across her body. Even when seated, she wrapped one of the straps around the leg of her chair and sat with her bag between her feet. Her precautions might have seemed extreme, but apart from general pickpockets, teams of seasoned criminals from Colombia and other parts of Latin America came to Barcelona simply to steal from unsuspecting tourists who let down their guard.

The girls pored over the tablet and readily accepted that James didn't sound right for Gill, except for Lisa. 'Sounds a bit of a tosser, but so what, he's loaded. Think of all the places he could take you.'

Gill shook her head and they promptly stopped talking about James. Mark, however, was a different story. In the time it took the girls to finish their three quarters of a litre *copas* of sangria, everyone had given their opinion, and they had reached the conclusion that despite him being only five feet seven, Gill should meet him, as he was cute. Debbie even went as far as to say she liked ginger-haired men. The others stared at her in shock, until she said, "Paul Bettany in *Wimbledon*." Her friends conceded the point.

So, Gill sent a brief e-mail to Caroline, already buoyed up by a *copa* of sangria, saying she'd like to meet Mark, but regrettably didn't think she and James would be suited.

After two sangrias, plus all the wine they had necked at Bar del Pi, the girls were positively squiffy. In an attempt to sober up a little, they went for a walk down the *Ramblas*.

According to the map, Plaça Reial was just off Carrer Ferran, and Plaça Reial was the ultimate square in which to be seen. Carrer Ferran swarmed with Catalans, most likely returning from work. Debbie pointed a little way up and said, 'That's the *Ajuntament* or City Hall, where the action all kicks off tomorrow night. Maybe we can go for a walk up there later, before we head back to the hotel?'

More mumblings of agreement, before Lisa once again managed effortlessly to secure them a table at the absolutely heaving Plaça Reial.

'I'm hungry again.' Debbie's stomach emitted a low rumble of confirmation.

'I could eat again, too,' Gill said.

'Well, we did only have tapas,' Angela reminded them. 'No harm in getting a few more.'

The girls whiled away a few hours, drinking some of the lovely rosé wine which the restaurant recommended, and devouring *patatas bravas, aceitunas, albóndigas* and *croquetas de pollo*.

'Those chicken croquettes are to die for. Would it be really bad if I ordered some more?' Debbie asked.

'You're a pig!' Lisa said.

'They are pretty moreish, though,' Gill said, sticking up for her friend.

'Am I the only one that's still hungry?' Debbie wanted to know. 'I just love the food here. Juicy, fat olives, those spicy chips are fantastic, and as for those meatballs…'

'Stop it! You're making me hungry again,' Gill berated her.

They ordered another round of tapas and talked about their game plan for the next day.

A quick detour to check out Plaça Sant Jaume, venue of Friday night's festivities, then the girls threaded their way through backstreets, chock-full of people, until finally they arrived back at their hotel.

'That was a long road for a short cut,' said Angela, as they said goodnight to each other outside their rooms.

'What time we meeting tomorrow morning?' Debbie, ever the practical one, asked.

'Nine?' Gill suggested.

'Sounds good.'

As Gill brushed her teeth, she realised she hadn't thought of Anton all day. Now, however, she found herself wondering what he was up to tonight.

Chapter Twenty-eight

Friday 23 September

Their room rate didn't include breakfast. The friends were happy enough with this, as they quite fancied trying several of the little cafés close to the hotel.

Ambling onto the Ramblas, they headed up towards Plaça de Catalunya and stopped at a little café about fifty metres from the metro station. Tables set for breakfast greeted them and a few tourists were already sampling the continental breakfast. Marmalades, croissants, and fruit-filled pastries, as well as bowls of chocolate with *churros*, covered most surfaces. Diners held the obligatory *café sólo* or *café con leche* in their hands, as they chatted to their companions.

This time, Debbie secured them an outside table. They ordered their coffees and pastries and sat in the early morning sunshine, content. Today they would go to Parc Güell, quite a distance from the centre.

After breakfast they took the metro to Lesseps. When they exited the station, they didn't see any signs for Parc Güell.

Angela, ever astute, said, 'I reckon that's where everyone else is going. Look!' She pointed out a group of German tourists with a guide in tow. True enough, some of them were holding maps. As inconspicuously as possible, the girls fell in line behind the group.

Soon they turned left and saw a steep incline ahead of them, complete with escalators.

'That's bizarre.' Lisa said aloud what the others were thinking. 'Escalators outside? What happens if it rains? Would you not electrocute yourself?'

'It doesn't rain here much, I don't think,' Debbie said, 'I wish the same could be said of back home.'

'But it must rain sometimes,' Lisa said, quickly refuted Debbie's reasoning.

'Who knows? Anyway, hurry up, they're getting away from us.' Gill chivvied them along as the Germans strode ahead.

Eventually they saw signs indicating Parc Güell and Casa Gaudí. Once they entered the park, the path forked in different directions, so they decided to ditch the Germans. They passed Gaudí dragons and lizards, in the colourful and unmistakeable mosaic pattern. Soon they came to a café area, where they ordered soft drinks. It was baking hot. From up here, the entire city of Barcelona lay spread out below them, the Sagrada Família rising up majestically in the distance.

Drinks finished, they wended their way down the paths to the Casa Gaudí museum.

They listened to the audio tour and read the boards which depicted the history of Parc Güell.

Lisa, who was less interested in the cultural aspect, but quite liked the Hansel and Gretel appearance of the houses, appointed herself group photographer, snapping away in unison with the Japanese tourists.

They were almost ready to leave, but Debbie wanted a

photo of their little group first. Lisa went down below to take the shot of the other three, standing in the window of Casa Gaudí. On the other side of the main gate stood another colourful building, similar in style, which housed the souvenir shop. The girls bought Gaudí-themed souvenirs before leaving the park.

'Why don't we try walking back through the city?' Angela suggested. 'I'm sure it's not as far as we think.'

No one put up much complaint, so they meandered out of Parc Güell and down the road, back down the escalators, marvelling at just how many people were coming up.

'I'm glad we did this in the morning,' Debbie said.

'Me too,' Gill agreed. 'Can you imagine how hot it's going to be up there now?'

Angela checked her watch. 'That's half one, must be time to eat soon.'

'Well, why don't we just wander down until we see somewhere that catches our eye?' Debbie said, struggling with her bag, which kept falling off her shoulder.

'Good idea.' Lisa led the way.

The streets they took were empty. Any self-respecting Catalan was either indoors or still at work. Usually they ate lunch between two and four – already very late by British standards.

The girls happened upon some chairs set out in the street, but no sign of a bar or restaurant. Thinking they could at least sit there to study the map properly, they sat down. Their bums had barely touched the seats when a waiter materialised brandishing menus.

However, it was a bar, not a restaurant, and again, they didn't serve meals, only tapas. Deciding a small bite would do for now, the girls chose a mixture of *aceitunas, rollos de atún, patatas bravas* and *pan Catalan*. The wine wasn't as nice as the night before, but it was wet and it did the trick.

Once lunch was over and they were preparing to leave, Debbie had a brainwave. 'Why don't we go back down into the city, stopping at little squares on the way? We could have a drink in each of them, and then go back to the hotel and get changed for tonight.'

'Now, that is a great idea, Mrs Orr.' Lisa put her arm round Debbie's shoulder. 'So, which direction do we need to go in, to find the first square?'

They checked and identified one only a few streets away. They got lost a few times, ending up at a tiny church, then a row of old shops, but no square.

'That map's faulty.' Lisa fumed.

'No, I just think it doesn't have all the streets marked on it,' said Debbie.

'We really should try and buy a better map, when we get a chance,' Angela said, propping her sunglasses on top of her head and wiping her forehead. 'Jeez, it's warm, isn't it?'

'Thirty-one degrees according to that big clock we passed earlier,' Gill said.

Just then, Gill heard chatter coming from their left. Sure enough, rounding the next left turn, then a right turn, lay the square they sought. It was tiny – just one café, but it overflowed with Catalans, not a single tourist in sight.

The girls quickly grabbed a table, and deciding that it was time to really celebrate their holiday, they splurged on cava, instead of wine.

'Our heads will probably not thank us in the morning,' Angela warned, 'for mixing our drinks, but right now, I don't care.'

After two glasses each, they prepared to move on to the next square.

Again with Debbie in control of the map, they wove their way through the back streets of the Gràcia quarter and ended up, after a few failed attempts, in the Eixample district. They had to stand for a little outside the café, as no seats were available straightaway. They weren't the only ones either.

'This is a bit bizarre,' Lisa complained, 'queuing to get into a café.'

The others agreed, but Gill said she supposed it was no more unusual than waiting in line to gain entrance to a busy nightclub.

Thankfully the queue dissipated very quickly and soon they had a seat with a prime vantage point over the small square. School was clearly out for the weekend, as children in uniform walked past with their parents. A few small children played on scooters; one drove a little car across the square, squeals of excitement emanating from him, as his father pushed the car, making it go faster. Aside from the children's laughter, the overall atmosphere was one of tranquillity.

Two Spanish men, one dressed in a pink striped shirt and the other in a blue shirt sat down at the next table but one from them.

'Psst,' said Lisa. 'Check them out.' She waved her sunglasses indiscreetly in their direction. They were handsome, if a little on the short side.

'The Spanish speak so fast,' Debbie said.

'Well, it doesn't help that we can't speak Spanish,' said Angela.

'Or Catalan,' said Gill.

'Can you tell the difference?' Lisa was intrigued.

'What do *you* think?' Gill smiled at her.

The men must have felt their gazes on them, as one of them turned around and stared straight at Gill. The other, listening to what his friend leaned forward to say to him, then sat back and smiled at Debbie, who appeared flustered.

Lisa chose this moment to go to the toilet, making a point of going past their table, brushing lightly against Pink Shirt's chair, and continued towards the bar. She knew their eyes would be on her.

When Lisa sauntered back out, only to find an empty table where the two men had been sitting, her jaw dropped in disbelief. She looked over in bewilderment at her friends, who had dissolved into fits of laughter.

'What's so funny?'

Gill wiped the tears from her eyes, and then said, 'They're gay. Pink Shirt just kissed Blue Shirt full on the mouth, then as they left, Blue Shirt felt his arse!'

'You're kidding!' Lisa was gobsmacked. 'They didn't look gay.'

'Obviously Spanish gay men look different to Scottish gay men,' Angela choked.

'Your gaydar must be faulty, or out of range,' Debbie squealed.

'Very bloody funny. Well, plenty more fish in the sea. No biggie.'

Soon afterwards, they decided to head back. They needed to change before dinner, and they didn't want to miss a second of the evening's action. The parade of giant, dragons and *Capgrosses* – oversized heads – was due to set off from Plaça Sant Jaume at ten. It would then wend its way through the winding streets of the Gothic Quarter before finally returning to its starting point. Huge numbers usually attended and the girls had heard from previous festivalgoers that the squares were usually packed, sardine-style.

Surprisingly their hotel was only twenty minutes from the last square they had visited. Gill took a long shower and decided she needed another coffee, as she felt tired and a little tipsy. Food would help, too. Freshened up, the girls hit the city once more.

There wasn't a single seat to be found in Plaça Reial. The girls ventured down a few side streets and eventually found a little restaurant with tables outside.

Lisa's jaw dropped. 'Jeez, would you look at the prices! Six euros for a bottle of water!'

'Let me see.' Angela took the menu from Lisa. 'Dear God, this better be good, twenty euros for a platter of *jamón Serrano*, fifteen euros for a cheese platter, three euros per *pincho*.'

'What's a *pincho*?' Debbie asked.

'A *pincho* is like a tapa, but it's usually skewered on a spike or a toothpick,' Gill said knowledgeably.

'Have you been reading my guidebook again?' Angela asked.

'Can you tell?' Gill shot her friend a grin.

'In a word, yes.' Angela slapped Gill playfully on the back as she went to sit down.

'Anyway, that's bloomin' outrageous,' Debbie said.

'I know, but everywhere is full. We'd never get a table anywhere else.' Gill pointed out what they all already knew.

'Fair enough. OK, let's just have something small – I

don't like letting these greedy pigs rip us off.'

'Just you tell it how it is, Lisa,' Angela said, and they all laughed.

They ate their vastly overpriced tapas and drank the lovely, but terribly expensive wine, as Lisa grumbled you could buy it in the supermarket for five euros, and here it cost twenty euros a bottle. They were just about to pay the bill when Debbie gasped. Walking towards them were several *Gegants*. They looked like contestants from the eighties TV programme *It's A Knockout*.

'This is so cool.' Angela reached for her camera. Debbie clicked away with her phone camera, as Gill searched in her bag for hers. Only Lisa remained cucumber cool, sipping her wine and watching the proceedings.

'It's a bit like a fashion show,' Lisa said, as she refilled her glass from the bottle.

'Ah, I think I've worked it out,' Debbie said. 'The giants are going into the back of the building, so they can come out the front into the square.'

'I think you're right.' Angela held the map and tried to orient herself.

They watched as the Gegants filed past them. One stumbled and had to be righted by a passer-by.

When the waiter returned, they asked for the bill, which arrived quickly. Cheers arose from the square close by and the girls hurried so as not to miss anything.

Soon the crowds roared, as the first brightly coloured Gegant ventured forth from City Hall. The Gegant rotated and waved then started its parade through the streets, as the next in line emerged to another cheer. One by one the Gegants left the building, followed by the Capgrosses and finally a few, what looked like pantomime horses. The procession continued through the backstreets, onto Via Laietana and back to Plaça Sant Jaume, before the participants climbed the steps onto the stage.

'This is fantastic,' said Angela. 'Even better than I expected.'

Gill tried to take pictures, but night had fallen, and the photos were so indistinct as to be useless.

The king and queen of the Gegants began to dance together – no easy task, as each measured more than fifteen feet tall. It was almost eleven o'clock, but toddlers and children of all ages, accompanied by parents, were among the spectators. Three-year-olds hoisted on parents' shoulders frustratingly blocked the girls' view from time to time. The square was so packed with people, the girls found it difficult to move a fraction of an inch. After the king and queen, came the pantomime horses and what seemed like Morris dancers. It certainly rated as the most bizarre spectacle Gill had ever witnessed. She glanced over at Debbie, who grinned at her, as if to say, '*Isn't this mad*?'

The most dazzling display of fireworks, which lasted for around fifteen minutes and lit up the starry Barcelona night sky, heralded the grand finale of the event.

Everything moved in slow motion, whilst workmen removed the barriers to help the crowds leave the immediate area.

'That was amazing,' said Angela. 'I got some not bad photos.'

'Lucky you – mine are all dark and red eye,' Gill said.

'Don't worry. You can have copies of mine.'

'What's the plan now?' Debbie asked.

'Well, it's pretty late. I don't know about you, but I think I've probably had enough excitement for one day.

One more drink maybe, and then back to the hotel?' Gill said, still feeling the after-effects of daytime drinking, mixed with thirty-degree-plus temperatures.

'So I'm going clubbing myself then?' Lisa said.

You could never tell if Lisa was joking or not. The other three stared at her.

'Kidding! What about that place there? It's busy, but looks really nice,' Lisa suggested, indicating a restaurant full of Spaniards and a couple of tourists.

'Why not?' Debbie shrugged.

As the girls sipped the brandies they had ordered, they ran through the plan for the next day. One glass led to a second, at the waiter's insistence, but they drew a line at a third, recognising how tired and woozy they were.

When they left the restaurant, they took the more direct route back to the hotel, via the Ramblas. They didn't trust their judgment to find the hotel again, via a circuitous route, since their heads were a bit fuzzy and impaired by too much wine.

Chapter Twenty-nine

Saturday 24 September

After breakfasting on *churros* and coffee in El Corte Inglés, the girls split into two groups. Debbie chose to go with Lisa, to the l'Illa shopping centre, as well as window-shopping in Passeig de Gràcia, whilst Angela and Gill opted for the hop-on, hop-off bus tour, which included the Sagrada Família and the cathedral.

It was a good way for them to see the city and they agreed to meet the others back at the hotel late afternoon, when they would have lunch more in keeping with Spanish time.

'Ah, we're here a day and already we're operating on local time,' Angela joked, as she passed the bus tickets to Gill.

'I know, although I could have done with another hour in bed. That much alcohol mixed with the heat kills me.'

'I know what you mean.' Angela nodded sagely. 'Right, let's get this show on the road.'

The tour was in English and four other languages. The guide pointed out famous buildings and houses where writers and artists had lived, as the bus made its way down to the first stop, the cathedral.

'I always thought *the Sagrada Família* was the cathedral.' Gill scrunched up her eyebrows in puzzlement.

'Ah, you've obviously not read *all* of my guidebook.' Angela gave Gill a gentle smack on the arm with the map. 'The cathedral is the Saint Eulalia one, down near the port. It's Gothic and dates from the fourteenth century.'

'You must have a photographic memory,' Gill muttered.

The girls headed downstairs when the bus neared the first stop. Dozens of tourists busily snapped away with their cameras. Some ate sandwiches on benches outside, whilst others sat on the pavement. Gill paid the entrance fee for both of them, shooing away Angela's offer of money.

'Wow! This is really something.' Gill's jaw dropped as she took in the five aisles within the church, a chapel on either side.

They spent over an hour touring the cathedral, reading the history and studying the chapels, admiring the truncated transept and the high altar, which gave a fantastic view into the crypt.

'Ew! Crypts freak me out.' Gill shuddered, pulling her cardigan around her. 'Have you taken all the photos you want?'

Angela nodded.

'OK, let's get out of here.'

Once they were back outside in the sunshine, Gill said, 'Do you want to get back on the bus, or do you want to walk for a bit?'

Angela studied the map. 'Well, why don't we walk down to Barceloneta then pick the bus up further on? We really just want to have a tour around the city and get to Sagrada Família, don't we?'

'Yep. OK then.'

They strolled down towards the port area, which proved surprisingly crowded.

'Why is it so busy do you think?' Gill asked.

Angela pointed to the marquees ahead on Moll de la Fusta. 'Er, I think that might be the wine festival.'

'Ah,' said Gill.

On the promenade, rollerbladers zoomed past them, almost catching them in their slipstream. Mothers and nannies with children in pushchairs strolled by, whilst cyclists pedalled past on the cycle lanes. Despite having to dodge the various obstacles, they enjoyed a pleasant walk along towards the Ferris wheel at Barceloneta. It was very noisy there, but they were so thirsty, they simply had to stop and have a cold drink.

As they sat at a café, they noticed restaurants across the street, spilling over with customers, as more clients queued on the street.

'Must be good.' Gill thumbed in the direction of the restaurants.

'Yeah, I bet you the seafood down here is amazing.'

'No doubt. Maybe we could come here tomorrow after the wine festival?'

'Might be an idea.'

Finishing their drinks, they consulted the map for the nearest stop to pick up the hop-on, hop-off bus.

As they wandered round to check out the beach, knowing that Lisa would be interested for the next day, they wondered how the other pair was faring.

The wait to enter the Sagrada Família seemed interminable. But despite that, it was everything the girls had expected and more. It was enormous, majestic, and towering.

'No wonder they just call it Sagrada Família,' said

Angela, pointing to the plaque which read 'Basílica i Temple Expiatori de la Sagrada Família.'

'Yeah, bit of a mouthful,' Gill agreed. She listened whilst Angela told her how Gaudí had devoted his life to the project, and how it was only twenty-five per cent complete when he died in 1926.

'That's a bit of a bummer, isn't it?'

'Well, at least he left a legacy,' Angela said, as Gill handed over their tickets.

A quick *gracias* and they were in.

'This is amazing,' said Angela. Gill nodded mutely, taken aback by the sheer size of the church's interior. The beautiful stained glass sparkled, as if brand new.

Gill's neck began to ache from constantly craning upwards, but there was so much to see. The detail astounded her. Particularly impressive had been the main door to the church which was covered in a jumble of letters and words. The crucifixion, suspended over the crowd, had the same effect as being in a 3D movie.

'I can't believe the others missed this,' Angela breathed, rubbing her neck and then rolling her shoulders. 'It's just so…breathtaking.'

'I know. I think even Lise, philistine that she is, would have been impressed.'

They spent nearly two hours at the Sagrada Família, before Angela checked her watch and said, 'We better get going. By the time we get back round on the bus, the others will be waiting for us.'

Lisa and Debbie were exhausted; their feet killing them, Lisa's in particular, as she hadn't chosen appropriate shoes for their task.

'Lise, when will you learn that shopping is a sport and you have to be dressed for it?' Debbie despaired at her friend, as Lisa moaned once more and spying an empty seat in a pavement café, sat down heavily in it.

'I need a rest.'

'Yes, I can see that. Don't take your shoes off, you'll make it worse. Why don't you buy a pair of flip-flops?'

'I can't – all they have here are the thong type and I can't wear those. They rub.'

'You'd think you would have learned by now, Lise.'

'I know, I know. Thank God we'd finished shopping.'

'I am never finished shopping,' Debbie said.

'Well, at least we got what we came for.'

'S'pose, and I'm not sure my credit card could take much more, anyway.'

'Let's get a drink and see how much we've spent, if you can stomach it.'

'What, the damage or the alcohol?' Debbie said, tying back her hair, which had come loose. 'I'm just having a soft drink. I can't handle wine this early in the day, or I won't make it to tonight.'

'Spoilsport.' Lisa stuck out her tongue at her. 'I don't do drinking alone, you know that. It makes me feel like a mad alkie, even if I am on holiday. I'll just have an orange juice then. They probably have freshly squeezed, eh? It's Spain after all, Seville oranges.'

'Not sure if there are any orange trees in Barcelona, mind,' Debbie said, as she pushed her fringe back off her sweaty forehead.

'Whatever, I'm sure it'll be good. What do you want?' Lisa asked, as the waiter approached.

'I'll have the same – you're right, orange juice is bound

to be good here.'

As the two girls sipped their orange juices, they compared purchases and talked about how they would complement their existing wardrobes.

Soon it was time to return to the hotel to meet the other two, and slipping her feet back into her heels, Lisa hobbled off in the direction of the Ramblas, with Debbie close behind.

As Angela and Gill wandered along to the bus stop, they could see a queue ahead of them.

'There must be a bus due. What are they, every twenty minutes?'

'That's what the brochure said,' Angela said.

'I'm starving. How do you fancy…?' Gill screamed and Angela looked at her friend in alarm.

'He just stole my bag. Stop! Stop that man!' Gill sprinted along the street, but she hadn't a hope of catching him. Angela ran along behind her, as tourists jumped out of the way. She glanced around, trying to see if there were any policemen around. No. About fifty metres ahead, the thief was just about to round a corner and disappear from sight. Just then, in the midst of the multitude of tourists trying to stay out of the way, a leg shot out, tripping the thief and making him stumble. An arm followed the leg, trying to grasp the thief's arm. The stranger couldn't keep his hold on him, but in the thief's struggle to get away, he dropped Gill's bag. The man who had intercepted the robber picked up Gill's bag.

As Gill approached him, he turned to face her. 'Yours?'

'Yes,' she said, seriously out of breath. 'Thank you so much. My passport's in there. I don't know what I'd have done without it.'

'No problem. But I'd maybe keep my passport in the safe next time, just in case.'

'I will, don't worry. Can I give you a reward or something?' Gill scrabbled in her bag, trying to locate her purse. Angela nudged her. The man smiled at her, bemused.

'That won't be necessary. It's enough that you have your bag back. Enjoy the rest of your holiday,' and with that he was gone. It wasn't until later that Gill realised he was Scottish.

Her heart wouldn't stop pounding. She had barely felt that guy nicking her bag. They really were professionals here. Only at the last yank had she become aware of something amiss. Whilst she waited with Angela for the next bus back to the city, and as her friend tried to reassure her, Gill's thoughts wandered back to the man who had saved the day and her bag.

'Where have you two been?' Lisa stood hands on hips, evidently indignant at being made to wait. Debbie, unruffled, waited to hear the explanation. Her mouth dropped open as Angela told them what had occurred.

'You're OK, though?' Debbie asked, concern etched on her face. 'You're not hurt? Nothing's missing?'

'No, I'm fine. I just got a bit of a fright. Bastard! But we'll have to be really vigilant now, as I didn't think thieves were that blatant.'

'Right, said Debbie, 'we're not letting them ruin our holiday. If they do, they've won. So, let's put it behind us, be even more careful with our belongings, and let's go and enjoy ourselves. What do you fancy for lunch?'

Lisa suggested a restaurant that she and Debbie had passed earlier in Passeig de Gràcia, which served Catalan specialities.

Gill and Angela freshened up and they all set off, Lisa first donning flat shoes.

The restaurant was still busy, but after a ten-minute wait, a waiter led them to a table. They asked for his recommendation and when he mumbled something unintelligible back to them, they decided to take a chance. When the food finally arrived, it proved to have been worth the wait.

During lunch, Gill was itching to sneak a peek at her personal e-mails, to see if she had received any word from Anton, but she was standing firm for now. She had made a point of checking her work e-mail on Friday, and again for an hour that morning, just so Janice had answers on anything she needed. A few quick replies to some important clients and her e-mail had been closed down. She needed this holiday.

Around six thirty, the girls left the restaurant and took the metro to Barceloneta. Lisa talked them into it, saying she had walked enough for one day.

On leaving the station, they aimed for the marquees which Gill and Angela had spotted that morning, and joined the enormous queues to buy tickets for tapas and drinks.

'I didn't realise there would be food stalls, too,' Debbie said.

'Yes, I wish we hadn't just eaten,' said Lisa glumly.

'Don't worry, I'm sure we'll be able to fit in a few tapas later. We just need to stay until it shuts,' Angela said.

They bought two books of tapas tickets because they didn't want to have to queue later, and six books of tickets between them for drinks. Each book contained ten tickets. Stalls generally offered drinks worth two, three or four tickets, the number of tickets required directly correlating with the quality of the wine or cava.

The whole area was packed, with parents and their children, toddlers and even babies in buggies.

'The Spanish way of life is certainly different, all right.' Debbie nudged Gill. 'I wouldn't dream of taking Olivia to a wine festival.'

'Maybe you would if you lived in a climate like this,' Gill said, as she watched a group of children playing. 'The kids are all having fun, dipping their toes in the water next to the boats.'

As the girls searched for a good stall to start at, a gap opened up in one of the queues and they darted in there.

'Let's face it, none of us knows that much about wine. As long as it's not a sweet dessert wine, we'll be OK,' said Lisa.

The others recognised the truth in this and piled in behind her. Lisa also suggested they start with the cheaper wine first, as, if they started with the classy stuff, everything else would taste awful afterwards.

Taking on board her advice yet again, the girls accepted the glasses of white wine which the stallholder offered them. They took a sip then Angela said, 'Made with Xarel-lo grapes.'

Lisa took a large gulp. 'It's not bad this, for two tickets.'

Indeed it was quite pleasant. But they had another seventy stalls to get round. The girls worked their way through some cava from Penedès then moved on to *albariño* from Galicia and grenache from La Rioja. Whether wisely or not they were heading for a fifth glass, this time red, when Debbie, ever the voice of reason, said, 'I think we should use those food tokens now.' Agreeing that they needed some sustenance to mop up the intake of liquid over the last few hours, the girls queued at separate stands for food. They came back with a platter of aged cheeses; a few varieties of cooked ham, excluding the expensive *Iberico* ham; some *boles de picolat* – meatballs and olives in a rich spicy sauce, and a couple of polystyrene bowls of chicken and chorizo casserole. Struggling to balance all of these, luckily they found a table. True to Spanish style, the wine festival was not decked out with tables and chairs. Instead, it was like at a bar, where you stood to eat and drink. About ninety per cent of people didn't even have a table, and instead balanced their plates on their arms or shovelled forkfuls into their mouths, whilst hanging onto their plates, as passers-by bumped into them.

'This is delicious,' pronounced Angela, who had fallen on the chicken and chorizo casserole instantly. 'Debbie, you have to taste this, seriously, before I finish it,' Angela offered the bowl to her, interrupting Debbie spearing a piece of *jamón Serrano.*

'What?' Debbie stopped with the fork halfway to her mouth.

'Try this,' she said.

Debbie rested her fork on the plate again, dipped her spoon into the casserole and took some of the meat and liquid. 'Oh wow, that's incredible.'

'Told you,' said Angela, smiling.

The girls chatted and ate their tapas, whilst people-watching and commenting on the talent around the marina.

'Why are Spanish men so much fitter-looking than Scottish men?' Lisa asked.

'Fitter as in sportier, or as in better-looking?' Angela asked.

'Both.'

'I reckon it's just the tan, maybe the outdoor lifestyle. The weather's too miserable back home to be outdoors much,' Debbie said.

'Hear, hear,' said Gill. 'But to be honest, I don't really go in for dark or tanned men. I like them a bit…'

'Pasty?' Lisa offered.

'No.'

'Milk-bottle white?' suggested Angela.

'No!'

'I think what Gill is trying to say is she likes them pale and interesting, like Anton, for example. Isn't that right?' Debbie said.

Blushing at the mention of Anton and at the thought of what had happened between them, Gill managed to squeak, 'Yes, that's about it.'

'If we're going to chat about men, I definitely need another drink,' said Lisa. Who's coming with me?'

Angela followed Lisa in her quest to procure wine for the four of them. So far they had tried everything except red, so after a little deliberation, they opted for a light and fruity Tempranillo.

'Not bad that,' said Lisa, taking a sip as they made their way back. Pity we've only got one ticket left each. Not sure if I can be bothered queuing up again. Look at the number of people now.'

Angela turned towards the ticket booths. True enough, the lines were enormous. Droves of people still swarmed into the festival area, keen to sample the best of Spain's wine and cava.

As they rejoined the others, Lisa passed a glass to Gill. 'Here, get that down your neck.'

'It's not a shot, you know!' Angela said in frustration. 'You're meant to take your time with it.'

'Actually, I suppose you've got a point. We've only got enough tickets left for one drink each.'

'Exactly, so let's make the most of this one.'

After their final glass of wine, the girls felt surprisingly OK, tipsy, but not drunk. The tapas must have bolstered them. They decided to walk back to the hotel, and followed the hundreds of people flowing back in the direction of the Ramblas. Saturday night in Barcelona was party night. Usually young Catalans going clubbing didn't even venture out until midnight, but because of the Mercè and the wine festival, they were already out in force.

'We're not seriously going back to the hotel, are we? It's only ten o'clock,' wailed Lisa.

'No, but let's just head this way and find somewhere to go,' Gill suggested.

As the girls turned onto la Rambla de Santa Mònica, they realised the walk was a little further than they had originally thought.

Finally they reached Liceu metro and nipped into Plaça Reial to have a coffee. Fortunately, the majority of the population of Barcelona didn't fancy anything as tame as sitting in Plaça Reial, on the Saturday of the Mercè. Although it was still busy, Plaça Reial was rarely empty, they found seats and soon relaxed, sipping their *café con leche*. They watched the comings and goings for a while, relaxing in the balmy September evening. A light breeze had picked up and eventually the girls declared they'd had enough for one day and prepared to leave.

As they passed under the archway leading out of the *plaça*, an English voice halted them in their tracks.

'Excuse me. Are you ladies going clubbing?' a man of around Gill's age asked them.

'We weren't planning to,' said Gill.

'Do you know anywhere good to go?' asked his friend.

'As you've probably guessed, we aren't locals,' said Lisa.

'Oh, I could tell that straightaway. I love the Glasgow accent.'

Yorkshire. Clitheroe, Leeds, somewhere like that, Gill tried to place the accent.

They stood and chatted with the men for ten minutes or so, alcohol enabling them to speak to complete strangers, with few inhibitions.

'Right, got to run, boys,' said Lisa, noting a look from Debbie, and seeing that Gill was shivering a little. 'Nice to meet you.'

'But we were just getting to know you,' protested the one who had initially approached them.

'Well, weren't you the lucky ones then.' Lisa's cheek knew no bounds and, impertinent as ever, she leaned in and kissed him full on the lips.

'Something to remember me by,' she said, as she danced away to join the others.

Chapter Thirty

Sunday 25 September

'I can't believe how forward you are sometimes,' Gill told Lisa next day.

'What you talking about?' Lisa said distractedly.

'That guy last night.'

'Oh, him? Just a bit of fun. Made his night.'

'Lise, you should have been born a man.'

'Where would be the fun in that? Women have the upper hand.'

Shaking her head at her friend's attitude, Gill drained the last of her coffee. Lisa was dying to go to the beach, but the *Castellers* event was due to start at two o'clock in Plaça Sant Jaume. Four teams attempting to build the highest human pyramid – a definite must-see of the festival.

Since cafés tended to open later on Sundays, around eleven, the girls had opted for a lie-in. Just as well, as there were even fewer places open due to the festival. As the girls strolled along the Ramblas, it struck them how eerily quiet it seemed, all remnants of the party atmosphere from the night before long gone. The street cleaners had obviously sprung into action straightaway, as everything was spotless – typical Catalan efficiency.

The girls had the bright idea of hopping on the metro

and choosing a destination at random, far from the tourist trail. Arriving at Jaume I metro station, Angela said, 'What about Maresme Forum? Sounds Roman, 'forum'.'

The others willingly accepted her suggestion, happy to kill a few hours exploring another part of the city. Seven stations later the girls exited Maresme Forum into a relatively unassuming neighbourhood. Concrete apartment blocks towered above them. Gill and Debbie exchanged a look. Had they come to possibly the worst part of Barcelona? Compared to this place, the Ramblas had been a hive of activity. Gill wondered if it was like this every Sunday, or if the Catalans were sleeping off their hangovers. Who knew what time they had partied until?

After navigating a few streets, they came face to face with a main road. Opposite they saw a huge glass hotel, the Barcelona Princess, and, facing the hotel, an exhibition centre. On the corner stood a café, which was thankfully open. A couple of patrons already sat outside. Seeing the girls approach, a waiter fetched some more chairs. Since the girls hadn't eaten breakfast yet, they decided this was as good a place as any and promptly placed their order.

'This is nice, although I wish I had a paper to read,' said Angela. 'It's the kind of place you imagine coming to read and chill out.'

'I know what you mean,' said Debbie. 'There's so little going on.'

Lisa, who had been studying Angela's map since ordering breakfast, said, 'Do you think that's a beach over there?' She pointed to a path beside the Forum exhibition centre.

'What does the map say?' Angela asked her.

'Could be,' said Debbie, 'although I've lost my bearings since we came by metro.'

'Well, if that's the Barcelona Princess and that's the exhibition centre, then yes, I think that is a beach,' said Lisa, who peered at the map then drained her coffee. 'You coming to check it out, Debbie?'

'Give me ten minutes, so I don't get indigestion.' Even the placid Debbie could become impatient with Lisa sometimes. Everything always had to be done yesterday where Lisa was concerned.

Once the pair departed, Gill said, 'I know I promised myself I wouldn't look at my personal e-mails, but I think I've been very good so far. I have to check them.'

'Fair enough,' said Angela. 'I'll just read my book for a bit.'

After five minutes, Angela looked up. Gill had a strange expression on her face – a mixture of upset and furious.

'What's wrong?'

'Not a word from Anton. Nothing. I know he's busy, but I really thought he might have e-mailed. Especially after we…'

'I know, but as you said, he's busy and he told you he would be. He's back soon, though, isn't he?'

'Yes, another week or so.'

'Well, there you go. You've nothing to worry about.' When Gill turned to her, she said, 'Right?'

'Hmm.' Gill was unsure.

'Right?'

'Yes, I suppose. I'm just disappointed.'

'I know. So, anything exciting in your e-mail?'

Dragging herself away from thoughts of Anton, Gill said, 'Actually, yes. You won't bloody believe this, but that doctor has only gone and said he isn't interested in meeting me!'

'Whaaat?' Angela couldn't contain her surprise. 'You're joking?'

'I'm not! Jumped up wee…' Gill didn't finish the sentence as she couldn't find an expletive terrible enough to describe him.

'I'm sorry, Gill, but I suppose it happens sometimes. Remember, you turned down Ronald and James.'

'I know, but it's not the same when it happens to you, and although I agreed to meet him, I wasn't really that convinced. He was too short for a start.'

'Yes, it's his loss. Move on. Anyway, have you heard from sexy Sean, champing-at-the-bit Charlie or gormless Gary?'

Gill reddened. She'd told Angela of her evening with Charlie. She had been very turned-on that night, but something hadn't felt quite right. Going to Barcelona had come at the right time – getting away was exactly what she needed.

'Gary replied saying it was a surprise, but fairly formal. He asked if I could meet him at Central Station and we'll get a taxi from there.'

'Intriguing. Make sure you text one of us when you know where you're going.'

'I will. Anyway, I like a guy who puts a bit of thought into things.'

'Yep, he definitely gets a brownie point for that. Anything else?'

'No word from Charlie. Sean has asked if I want to go bowling with him. What am I, fifteen? I mean I know he's thirty-five and cute and kisses well, but bowling?'

'This is about Anton, isn't it? Why you stopped things going any further with Charlie and why you're hesitating with Sean?'

'I don't know,' Gill said slowly. 'Maybe.'

'Maybe you need to think about what you want.'

When Gill remained silent, Angela took the hint and returned to her book.

Ten minutes later, Debbie and Lisa returned.

'It is a beach. Are you ready?' Lisa resembled an overexcited puppy. 'What have you two been up to, anyway?'

Seeing Gill's warning glance, Angela said, 'Just waiting for you to come back. OK, let's hit this beach.'

'Great! I've got my bikini on under my shorts and a towel in my bag,' said Lisa.

Oh, here we go, thought Gill.

The girls wandered down and across a little bridge to the left of the Forum exhibition centre, which did indeed lead to a beach. And that's where all the young people in Barcelona seemed to be hiding. Some had clearly slept on it last night. How had the noise they were making not reached them at the café? Maybe the sound of the sea and the waves carried away their chatter. Small children played in the water, splashing each other. Some older children played an impromptu game of beach volleyball with their friends and siblings, as their parents stood watching them, cheering them on. Occasionally a dad would jump in for a moment of heroics.

The sun shone high in the cloudless blue sky. It was around noon and the strong rays of the sun made the girls sweat a little. They found somewhere to sit and Lisa, without preamble, stripped down to her bikini, daring her friends to do the same. Gill shook her head. She didn't feel body confident in a bikini and certainly not next to Lisa. Lisa's tiny thong and almost non-existent bikini top drew lots of attention from a group of men close by. One woman slapped her husband none too playfully on the jaw, seeing him openly ogling Lisa's breasts. It didn't help that Lisa rubbed sun tan lotion on herself slowly. Angela and Gill exchanged a look. They were used to her.

They'd been sunbathing for about an hour when two men approached Lisa. Since she didn't speak Spanish, chatting with them proved a bit difficult, but Lisa smiled openly at them. One spoke to her, whilst the other smiled at the others and said nothing. Initially it seemed that Lisa was quite into the guy chatting her up. A coquettish little laugh burst from her every now and then. Soon her body language changed, her spine stiffened, and her tone made the girls realise something was wrong. Lisa poked the man in the chest angrily. He held up his palms in an '*OK, OK*' fashion and, signalling to his friend, they left.

'What was all that about?' a bemused Gill asked.

'Those low lifes just offered me drugs.'

'Whaaat!' Debbie's shout could almost be heard from the other end of the beach.

'Seriously?' said Angela, dubiously. You never knew with Lisa.

'Straight up.'

'I thought one of them was interested in you and that's why they had come over.'

'They were both interested in me, but as a customer. Bloody drug dealers! They offered me hash, which I refused politely but firmly. Then they suggested I might like to try some ecstasy or cocaine. That's when I lost it.'

Angela suggested now might be a good time to head back into the city. They all agreed. The cheek of the men had left a bad taste. Their sojourn to the beach was over.

They'd expected it to be busy, but this was unbelievable. The girls managed to push their way into the square, but that was as close as they could get. It proved impossible to reach the front. Fortunately, given the nature of human pyramids, they didn't miss the action. Four teams pitted against each other. Five men at the bottom, then four would climb on them, then three on them, then two, then a small child would ascend and go right to the top. They all had their hearts in their mouths watching the latter.

'Oh my God, I can't look,' said Gill.

'That child must only be about eight,' Debbie said, appalled.

'They know what they're doing,' an unruffled Lisa said.

'It does look a bit scary,' Angela admitted.

The crowd held their breath each time a new member of the team climbed up. When it came to the children's turn, all eyes were on them. The child in question would scramble up as lithely as a cat.

Everyone applauded each member of the teams, with the children receiving the warmest applause. It was difficult for the girls even to clap their hands, as their elbows tended to dig into the person next to them. It proved very cramped indeed.

The ceremony for the winners took place, and then came the interesting job of emptying the square. Everyone shuffled forward, a fraction of an inch at a time.

'Where are we going?' Angela hollered over the noise.

'Don't know. Let's just get out of this square first and then we can make up our minds,' Gill replied.

'Which way now?' Lisa asked.

'Well, do you still want to go to Barceloneta beach?' Gill asked.

'No, I think I've had enough of the beach. What else is there to do?' Lisa asked, searching their faces expectantly.

'Well, I quite fancied going to the El Born part of town. It's meant to be an "eclectic mix of bohemian and trendy cafés, bars and restaurants,"' Angela recited from the guidebook.

'Cool. Everyone else happy to do that?' Lisa looked at the other two.

'Sure. Where is it?' asked Debbie, craning her neck to peer at the map.

'It's not really that far. We're already going in that direction,' said Angela.

The girls headed off into El Born, as Angela explained that both the Museu Picasso and Museu de la Xocolata were in this area.

'Great,' said Lisa. 'Count me in for the chocolate museum.'

Angela shook her head. 'We'll need to come back tomorrow for that. It's only open until three on Sundays and holidays.'

Checking her watch, Lisa said, 'Hmm, it's already half past three. OK, let's go and get a drink somewhere then.'

El Born turned out to be as diverse as the guidebook said. They chose a café and sat inside to escape the relentless sun. Even at three thirty, the rays were still very strong and the girls were suffering from a little too much exposure. Debbie thought she had the symptoms of prickly heat.

The staff couldn't have been nicer, and it was peaceful inside, as most people wanted an outside table. Gill took the opportunity to fill Debbie and Lisa in on her 'man situation'.

'This has been such a great holiday so far, well, apart from being mugged,' Gill amended quickly.

'It has, hasn't it?' Debbie said, taking her phone out of her bag. 'It's been so good, I keep forgetting to call my family! Back in five.' She walked over to the window to try to get a signal.

Giving a deep sigh, Gill continued, 'I just feel so relaxed. OK, I know I answered some e-mails on Friday and Saturday, but that just helped me keep on top of things, and apart from that, I haven't checked my e-mail at all.'

'Except for this morning to check on your lovers' movements.' Angela smiled at her.

'Well, yes, except for that. But, really, apart from the odd wee lapse, I haven't even thought about men. I've been having such a good time here.' As Gill said this, she realised it wasn't entirely true as Anton was never far from her thoughts. She couldn't wait to see him when he got back.

'We should do this more often,' Lisa broke in.

'Yes, but we can't all afford the time away or indeed the money, more often.' Angela's reply was honest, not sarcastic.

'I suppose I am lucky from that perspective. No ties,' Lisa mused.

'I am too, then.' Gill smiled at Lisa, wondering why that didn't always make her feel lucky.

'But you have the business, it's not the same.'

Actually, Lisa was right. In many ways the business was just like having a baby.

When Debbie returned from making her call, they drank a glass of cava each then decided they would head down to Barceloneta after all. According to the map, it wasn't very far away. Ten minutes later, they strolled along the promenade. It was six thirty and as they were hungry, the girls wandered round to one of the restaurants Angela and Gill had spotted the day before. The huge queue, which they had reluctantly joined, seemed to dissipate fast. The aroma wafting out of the restaurant and from the plates set in front of the outside diners had the girls almost drooling. Juicy steaks, cooked to perfection prawns, crab and oysters.

'Oh, I hadn't realised I was so hungry,' said Gill, stomach rumbling ominously.

'Me neither,' Lisa said, 'but if you think about it, it's been about six hours since we ate, maybe more.'

A smartly dressed waiter escorted them to an outside table. Fans whirred from the wooden canopy overhead. After perusing the menu, the girls asked for the waiter's recommendation. Shortly afterwards, plates bearing *esqueixada* covered the table, accompanied by the wine they had ordered.

'What is it exactly?' Gill asked.

'Raw salt cod with peppers and onions.' Angela nudged the plate slightly closer to Gill, who was eyeing it with distaste.

'Did we not mention to the waiter that we weren't sushi lovers?' Gill screwed up her face.

'Just try a bit,' Debbie coaxed her.

Gill cut off a piece, regarded it dubiously then finally popped it in her mouth. She chewed a few times and then said, 'It's actually not bad. A bit salty, but…'

'Eh, it's salt cod,' Lisa said.

'True.'

The next course consisted of a mixed platter of seafood, the freshest, most enormous prawns they had ever seen, oysters, massive mussels and crab claws. The girls soon scoffed it and were ashamed to admit they still had space.

'I quite fancied the stew, but I think that will have to wait until tomorrow. There's no way I've got room for it,' said Gill.

'I should think not, after we've just eaten that ginormous platter of seafood.' Debbie laughed. 'Maybe it's the sea air making you hungry.'

'Maybe. Why don't we have a wee rest and then see if we have room for dessert?'

They did as Gill suggested and chatted about what they expected over at Montjuic that night for the fireworks.

'I've heard the sound and light show is fantastic. They synchronise the movement of the water in the fountains to the light and the music. And there's apparently a recording of "Barcelona" by Montserrat Caballé and Freddy Mercury which gets blasted out in time to the fountains,' said Debbie.

'Nobody's mentioned that to me,' said Lisa, 'and Cara from the salon visited Montjuic a few months back for the light show.'

Gill's phone buzzed as they pored over the dessert menu half an hour later. She had already chosen *crema catalana*, since she'd been dying to try it for ages. Delving in her bag, she pulled out her phone and saw she had another e-mail message. Caroline Morgan. How bizarre – working on a Sunday. Maybe like Gill, she just worked every day of the week.

Hi, Gill. Sorry things didn't proceed with Mark; however, I have someone just about to complete registration who I think is right up your street. Will send details midweek, Caroline.

Gill read out the e-mail to the others, who professed

that to be a positive step, although Lisa said, 'How are you going to keep track of all these blokes?' She meant it as a joke, but Gill was beginning to wonder the same thing herself. She would need to do some serious thinking when she got back.

Stuffed with *crema catalana*, Gill suggested they walk back to the Ramblas, where they could take the metro out to Plaça de Espanya, where the Montjuic fountains were. They had plenty of time. The fireworks would start around ten o'clock, but they wanted to be there beforehand to get a good spot.

The metro was overrun with people coming and going in all directions. At least it was only a few stops to Plaça de Espanya. The cream and red Venetian towers impressed Gill the moment she stepped out of the station. The symmetrical fountains sprayed arcs of water into the air. At the end of the rows of fountains, steps led up to another strata which housed the main fountain and looming above that, lay the majestic Palau Nacional art gallery. As the girls shuffled along the pedestrianised walkway, it occurred to Gill that the view towards the art gallery, even in daytime, would be quite spectacular.

Several thousand people milled around, patiently waiting for the fireworks and light show. The majority appeared to be locals, although a good mix of tourists, cameras at the ready, were also present. The girls chose a position as close as they could to where they believed the main action would take place.

After forty minutes, even Gill's fuse was about to blow. 'I thought it would have started by now,' she moaned, leaning on Angela for support. Her legs ached, as did the others'. 'Wasn't the light show meant to begin twenty minutes ago?'

'Maybe it isn't on during the festival?' Angela said. They were on the verge of calling it a day, when music started up and lights came on in the National Gallery. The presenter said a few words and the crowd went crazy, the atmosphere suddenly charged. Cameras flashed and then the first of the fireworks shot up in the air.

Faster and faster, a dizzying variety of fireworks exploded into the Catalan sky. What a racket! Twenty-five minutes of non-stop noise, excitement, screams, shouts, squeals, bangs and electric ambiance. With the grand finale of the mortars, the presenter proclaimed the Mercè festival 2011 closed.

It took a good twenty minutes for the girls to make it into the metro and onto a train. By the time they finally emerged at Liceu, they were hot and sticky and gasping for a drink. A nightcap was called for at Bar del Pi.

They managed a brandy then headed for bed. Tomorrow would be the last day of their holiday and they intended to make the most of it.

Chapter Thirty-one

Monday 26 September

They didn't have to leave for the airport until around two thirty, so they thought they would have a nice breakfast somewhere, before going to the Museu de la Xocolata together. They'd pick up their luggage from the hotel afterwards then take the bus to the airport. They wandered up Passeig de Gràcia and found a little café which offered delicious pastries, including the famous Catalan favourite, *cabell d'àngel.* Despite the heat, they decided to have hot chocolate, the house speciality. It was thick and delicious and you could have stood a spoon up in it.

'This is very moreish, isn't it?' said Debbie. 'Do you think they have tins of it you can take back home?' she asked hopefully.

Angela shook her head. 'Sorry love, I think this is a made on the premises number.'

'It's gorgeous,' Lisa said, licking some off her spoon.

After a leisurely breakfast, they set off on the fifteen-minute walk to the chocolate museum.

The girls regressed to childhood for a few hours, as they made their own chocolate lollipops and chocolate bars. Gill chose milk chocolate with pine nuts; Debbie, white chocolate with lime peel; Lisa, dark chocolate with raisins; and Angela went for raspberries and orange peel with dark chocolate.

In addition to their own concoctions, the girls each bought chocolate gifts. As they walked back to the hotel, they discussed what a great experience it had been.

'Hope the chocolate doesn't melt by the time we get it home,' worried Lisa, a major chocoholic, as they left the hotel again.

'I'm sure it'll be fine. Anyway, just stick it in the fridge when you get home and it'll harden again,' Debbie suggested.

'There's a joke in there somewhere.' Lisa never missed an opportunity.

'Hysterical, Lise. Right, we best head up to the bus stop. Don't want to miss the bus now, do we?'

The others followed Debbie as she rolled her carry-on case behind her, up the Ramblas and onto Passeig de Gràcia.

Before long the bus took them to the airport and after a short wait, their flight took off, homeward bound.

As the plane soared into the air, Gill asked herself, *What now?*

Chapter Thirty-two

Tuesday 27 September

'Janice, can you tell Angus I'll call him back? I'm on the mobile,' Gill shouted through from her office.

'Sorry about that,' she said to the candidate she was talking to. 'Yes, so, hopefully I should hear back by Friday about final interviews. I'll call you to let you know.'

Gill sat her mobile down on her desk and, running her fingers through her hair, exhaled heavily. Her break to Barcelona seemed a lifetime ago already, and she was only halfway through the day. The phones had been ringing non-stop.

She checked her contact list for Angus' number then dialled from her office phone. After two rings she said, 'Angus, thanks for calling. How are you?' Gill listened to her new employee's questions, and when she had answered them all, said 'Enjoy the rest of your day off. See you tomorrow.'

Right, what do I need to attack next? Janice had left her a list of calls. Those took priority. Gill was relieved she had kept e-mails under control, as today had been pandemonium, and she still needed to work out Angus' schedule for the next few days.

Janice entered her office just after two and said, 'You

need to eat. You've been working flat out since you got in at seven.'

'I know, but there's still so much to sort out by tomorrow. I'll eat tonight.'

'No, you won't,' insisted Janice. 'I've bought you a chicken tikka wrap and I want to hear all about your trip.'

Resigned, Gill agreed. She probably ought to take a break away from the computer, anyway. Janice was right. Janice was always right. The thought made Gill smile.

As they ate their lunch, Janice asked Gill all about Barcelona. She was particularly envious of the festival, having heard great things about it. When she asked about men, Gill's response was unsatisfactory.

'You're a lot of good,' Janice joked. 'You go to a country full of hot men and you're too busy pining over one back here.'

'As one of my friends said, I like my men pale and interesting.'

'OK, so you're useless on that score. What about the grub? I love Spanish food – *paella, chorizo, jamón Serrano*.'

'Oh, Janice, the food was to die for. I'm sure I've put on at least a couple of pounds.' Gill looked ruefully at her stomach. The waistband of the trousers she had thrown on that morning definitely felt tighter than usual. Maybe it was time to go to Weightwatchers. Janice leant forward on the table, drinking in every detail Gill told her about the Spanish cuisine, the various tapas they had tried, and the amazing restaurants which they had dined at.

'I'm so jealous. Makes me want to go and book a short break.'

'So why don't you?' Gill eyed her evenly. 'Nothing to stop you.'

'Apart from not having the cash.'

'Can't you save up?'

'I suppose, but it means going without other stuff, like my weekly Chinese, or buying a new book or a pair of trousers.'

'Ah, well, when I really want something, I cut back on everything else, to make sure I can get it.'

Gill saw everything in black and white. Pity her love life wasn't as simple as that.

Brushing a stray piece of wrap from her blouse onto her napkin, Gill thanked Janice for making her take a break, but said she really needed to get back to it.

A wonderful surprise awaited Gill in her e-mail. She had been awarded three contracts she had been working on recently. Three. That was unheard of, in such a short space of time, and all for multiple candidate placements, too. It really gave her the lift she needed, post-holiday. And with Angus starting tomorrow, things were truly looking up.

Chapter Thirty-three

Wednesday 28 September

As usual Gill was first to arrive at the office. At least whenever she drove in to work, she tended to get a parking spot right outside. Today she felt organised and motivated. She'd gone home last night, called her mum and her brother to tell them about her trip, and then made pasta.

After five days in Spain, she couldn't face eating a ready meal. She was on a mission – new, healthy Gill. If possible, she wanted to try to cook at least four or five times a week, unless of course she ate out, which, when she thought about it, was fairly regularly at the moment. She had watched a bit of TV, showered and then gone to bed with a book. When had she last done that?

Angus arrived at ten to nine. Gill let him in, asked him to take a seat in the conference room and offered him coffee.

Gill chatted with him briefly and then got straight down to business.

'Angus, as you can see, from a recruitment consultancy perspective, I've been a one-man, or one-woman, band until now.' Gill smiled at him as she placed her mug on a coaster. 'For such a small enterprise, the agency has a lot of clients, and whilst I was away in Barcelona the last few days, we won three more, so we're going to be busy.' Gill shuffled the papers in front of her. Angus, seated to her right, reviewed those she passed to him.

'These are the accounts I want you to be responsible for initially. I've given you a mix of small and medium accounts for now. I'm not going to pass you any of our really big fish right away, but that will change in the next few months. There's a lot of potential with these accounts. I've also highlighted in red those that I think need your immediate focus. Plus I've made some notes which might help you with some of the trickier customers.'

Angus glanced up at her. 'Sounds good.' Looking through the list, he pointed to one or two names, indicating that he had dealt with them in the past.

Gill went on to explain that of the three brand new customers, she intended him to be the lead on one of them. They would meet the client together the following week, but she would already start copying him in on their correspondence.

'Your business cards should be here tomorrow. Janice ordered them on Friday. I've arranged a telephone extension for you and the desk next to Janice's will be for you to use when you're in the office. If this conference room isn't booked, and Janice can tell you that, or you can check the scheduler, feel free to come in and use it to get away from distractions. Working from a laptop does have its advantages.'

Angus agreed that being portable certainly helped. After Gill ran through further instructions, and advised him that she wanted him to sit with Janice for a part of that morning, so she could show him the systems they used, she asked him if he had any questions.

'No, that all seems clear. I did want to point out that I have some clients that you haven't mentioned. Now, perhaps you do already have relationships with them, but I made a list of my clients so that I could compare them against yours. There are bound to be a couple you haven't dealt with.'

Gill took the sheet of paper which Angus withdrew from his briefcase. It contained a list of some thirty names, most of them known to her, but also five new ones.

'OK, in addition to the existing clients I've transferred to you, I'd like you to see who you can convert from your list.' She made a few markings on his sheet and returned it to him. They left the conference room and Gill entrusted Angus to Janice's care. She had a good feeling about this young man. He was bright, articulate, showed initiative, and she thought they might all have a laugh together – essential in such a small workplace.

Gill spent a great part of the time Janice was training Angus on the systems, arranging appointments with the clients she intended to pass to him. It was very important to highlight the agency's professionalism. Yes, it would be time-consuming, but she wanted to make a proper, formal introduction to her clients, rather than a perfunctory e-mail or phone call to confirm the handover.

Around one o'clock, Janice came through to ask Gill what she wanted for lunch. Was that the time? Angus volunteered to nip across to the café to get lunch. Once he had gone, Janice and Gill exchanged a look of approval.

'How's the systems training going?' Gill asked.

'Fine, we're nearly finished. Just have invoicing to show him.'

Although the recruitment consultants wouldn't deal

with all aspects of admin, Gill felt it important they know every facet of the business. In a small company, everyone needed to be hands-on.

'Great. Amanda, after lunch, can you come in to my office for a second?'

Gill had received an e-mail from Janice, advising that Amanda's work ethic and enthusiasm were exemplary and that they'd got on like a house on fire. Janice had recommended they keep her on, if possible.

Knowing that two recruitment consultants would create more work, and having Janice's buy-in, Gill had done her sums and decided that the agency could afford it.

The four sat companionably in the conference room eating lunch together, with Janice or Amanda getting the phone whenever it rang.

Angus told them that he lived in the west end in a flat he had been in since his student days. As Amanda and he started talking about pubs and clubs, Gill assessed her new hire. At five feet seven or so, you couldn't call him tall; Angus had ginger hair, his face was dotted with freckles and his body language open. He had a belly laugh which made Gill smile. Some comment Amanda made set him off. It was a warm, rich laugh, and again, Gill had the sensation of having made the right decision. The platinum wedding ring he wore glinted in the sunlight, and Gill wondered why she hadn't realised he was married before now. Did he have kids? It didn't matter. She felt sure he would give her agency one hundred per cent and that was all that she cared about.

Amanda was delighted with the news that she was being kept on, subject to acceptance of the contract Gill would draw up for her. At one stage Gill feared Amanda might hug her, so she had been glad of the desk separating them.

Towards the end of the day, Gill spent a bit more time with Angus in the conference room, as they planned out the next few weeks. She had already received a couple of meeting confirmations. One client had been a tad bolshie, but she knew how to handle him. She'd go and meet him alone first, and arrange to have a meeting with both her and Angus a few days later. It had been a productive day and Gill couldn't help feeling excited that her agency was entering a new era.

A quick trip to the supermarket for some essentials on the way and Gill was home by seven thirty. She was determined to learn to cook. Pasta was the only thing she knew how to make and that was because often it just meant pouring a sauce over it. It was time to turn over a new leaf. Today she would prepare grilled chicken breast. Even she couldn't go wrong with that.

For a first attempt, Gill thought she had done pretty well. OK, some of the floury coating was probably thicker in some places than in others, but it didn't taste too bad and it was cooked properly.

Satisfied with her culinary efforts, she sat back, replete, and began checking her messages and e-mails. There were a few more replies to her meeting requests. She responded to these and then checked her personal e-mail, hoping to see a message from Anton. Nothing. Gill felt a twinge of unease. Wouldn't it be normal for a man to get in touch after sharing what they had? It hadn't just been sex, she'd felt sure of it. She couldn't believe that's all it had been to him. She'd give it a few more days. Yet she couldn't help feeling an overwhelming sadness at the sensation of something lost.

There was a message from Charlie. Charlie. She'd almost forgotten about him, with all that had been going on. But who could forget the few passionate moments they had shared?

Hi, Gill. Hope you enjoyed yourself in Barcelona. Keen to hear all about it. I've been thinking about you…a lot. Are you free on Saturday? Charlie x

Gill debated for about ten minutes, then deciding if Anton wasn't going to make more of an effort, she may as well go out with Charlie, she bashed out a reply.

Hi, Charlie, had a great time, thanks. Hope you are well. Unfortunately not free Saturday. What about the following Saturday? Gill. No kiss. In many ways it was lucky she was already meeting Gary on Saturday, as she felt less threatened by him, more sure that nothing would happen between them. She gave herself a shake. So why go out with him then? Because he's a nice guy, her inner voice told her.

Putting a ten-day hold on Charlie would give her more time to sort her head out.

In her heart, she knew she wouldn't sleep with Charlie, although it was certainly tempting. He'd be dynamite in bed. His skilled seduction of her that night had proven that. She had felt as if she were in a dream, and it had taken her a while to snap back to reality and put a stop to proceedings, before things got out of hand.

Charlie was sitting on the sofa, drinking a glass of wine and watching the news, when his phone buzzed. He read Gill's e-mail and almost gave a jump for joy. She hadn't got away from him just yet. He was a little annoyed that he couldn't see her this week. He'd have to make some arrangements for next weekend now, with regard to his daughter, who was meant to be staying with him. But nothing was going to get in the way of him spending time with Gill. Charlie quickly e-mailed back, saying that was fine, but could they meet around five o'clock, as he wanted to take her to a place about an hour's drive from the city.

Charlie cast his mind back to that night in his flat, when he had almost had her. He had been so hard and she had been so ready for him. But then something within her changed, the shutters came down and soon afterwards, she'd gone, leaving him with a raging erection and nothing he could do about it. He wanted to screw her so badly, wanted to taste her, kiss her breasts, feel himself inside her. Just thinking about it now made him really horny.

A voice disturbed his musings. 'Darling, would you like another glass of wine?'

Charlie looked up at his wife, who had just entered the living room. He stood up and walked over to her. 'No, but I know what I do want,' he said as he unzipped her dress.

Chapter Thirty-four

Thursday 29 September

'Everything's going well,' Gill told Christopher when he called that night. 'Work in particular. I made the temp permanent. She's a student, so isn't costing me that much right now, and I think, Angus, my new recruitment consultant, was sent from heaven.'

'That's praise indeed, sis. Particularly coming from you,' he joked.

'Thanks for that, Chris. I love you, too. So how are my beloved nephews? Misbehaving as usual?'

'Are you suggesting my adorable children are anything less than perfect?' Chris feigned outrage.

'Would I? Such angelic cherubs have never before graced this earth.'

'OK, don't overdo it. So what about the love life?'

Neglecting to mention Anton, Gill told Christopher she was going out with Gary on Saturday, and the following Saturday with Charlie.

'You *are* busy. Well, it's about time. You deserve someone great.'

'Thanks.' Gill knew that what Christopher really meant was that she deserved someone as amazing as Sarah. She thought Christopher and Sarah were really lucky to have found each other and even luckier to still be together.

What Gill couldn't tell him was that she had received another profile from the agency. She was glad he hadn't asked her how she had met Gary and Charlie, and the subject of the agency hadn't come up.

She replaced her phone in its cradle and picked up her mobile. She read Caroline Morgan's e-mail and then concentrated on the profile she'd received.

Candidate Profile
Name – Todd Grainger
Age – 39
Lives – East Kilbride
Occupation – Sales Director
Qualifications – MSc Marketing – University of Strathclyde
Height – 5' 11"
Marital status – Single
Children – None
Smoker – No
Interests: Golf, go-karting, books, music, films, dining out, keeping fit, comedy.
Further information: Originally from Edinburgh, now live in East Kilbride and have lived on the west coast for five years. In my spare time I'm a stand-up comedian and I like to go to comedy festivals and clubs. I'm scared of flying.
Looking to meet: Someone to share couple stuff with. Must have a sense of humour.

Gill stared at his photograph. It was always difficult to tell how attractive someone really was from a photo. Often the camera didn't do justice, but just as frequently the person didn't match up to their photo – especially if it had been taken five years previously. His jet black hair curled around his ears. His smile seemed a little unnatural, but not creepy. Difficult to determine eye colour – grey, green? She knew she liked pale and interesting, but Todd seemed almost cadaverlike. But he did look like he'd be a lot of fun, and what girl didn't want to be with a man who indicated a sense of humour as a requirement? Unless, of course, he was going to enforce his stand-up routine on her – that could be fatal, particularly if he wasn't any good. She noted that Todd liked books. At least they had that in common, since she didn't know one end of a fairway from the other.

Gill couldn't quite make out his build, but if he liked working out and played golf, surely he would be relatively fit. She thought briefly of Anton's body entwined with hers and then shook her head, as if to dislodge the memory. It still smarted that he hadn't been in touch. On impulse, she hit Reply and advised Caroline that she could go ahead and pass her details to Todd.

Chapter Thirty-five

Saturday 1 October

Gill donned the green silk dress she had bought for her date with Anton, as it was the only relatively formal item she owned which fitted her properly at the moment. Perhaps wearing it on a non-romantic date, how odd that sounded, would dispel visions of Anton unzipping it. Hair up or down? Down, she decided, the opposite of on her date with Anton. Would he ever get out of her head? She was annoyed with herself – so many men causing her grief. Only Gary had been sweet, no pressure. She wondered what his surprise was. She really needed something nice to happen to her, as she was feeling a bit low. Yesterday, she had felt on the verge of tears. No message from Anton. He'd be back in a few days, and still not a dicky-bird. To compound her misery, last night, just as she was leaving work, after a fruitful day, her phone had pinged to alert her to a new e-mail. Caroline Morgan.

Dear Gill, I'm sorry to say that Todd Grainger does not wish to proceed. I will be in touch again when we have someone more suitable. Regards. Caroline.

Gill could have thrown the mobile across the room. Was there a surer way to make you feel unattractive and of no interest to the opposite sex than being turned down before the person even met you, based solely on a photo and a profile? If so, she was yet to come across it. Angrily, and before she could stop to think rationally, she replied saying, *Caroline, in future, can you please only send me profiles of people that you have already verified are interested in meeting me? Regards, Gill.*

At that moment, she hadn't cared if she came across as abrupt, but perhaps her response had been a tad hasty.

Gary had arranged to meet her at the main entrance to Central Station at seven o'clock. Gill got off the bus in Hope Street, and walked around to the main entrance. At first she didn't see him. Eventually he spotted her. 'Gill, Gill,' he called, waving at her.

The man wearing a green tartan kilt, Bonnie Prince Charlie jacket and white wing-collar shirt approached her as Gill stared at him in astonishment.

'Well, what do you think?' He gave a little twirl and the pleats of his kilt fanned out as he spun.

'You look incredible,' she said, meaning it. He wore the kilt well. And Gill had always liked Bonnie Prince Charlie jackets. The question was, why was Gary wearing a kilt?

'Not as incredible as you.' Gary smiled at her as he took hold of her hands. 'That dress looks amazing on you.'

'Thanks,' said Gill. She noted he hadn't said '*That's an amazing dress*,' but had personalised it, paying her a bigger compliment.

'So, what's this surprise then?' Gill finally managed.

Gary smiled at her, eyes shining with excitement. 'We're going to One Devonshire. You'll find out soon enough.' He took her hand as they walked across the street to the taxi rank.

Gary wouldn't be drawn when Gill tried to quiz him en

route. She wondered if there was a ceilidh or maybe some other event on at the hotel. Sometimes One Devonshire held special events. The hotel was supposed to be a cut above. Whatever, it thrilled her that he had gone to such lengths to make their date special.

Once deposited outside the hotel, Gary led the way, nodding once at the member of staff they met on the way up the steps. Gill was busy lapping up the hotel's luxurious interior, when Gary turned a corner and they entered the Glenlivet room.

Immediately Gill's expression turned from one of anticipation to one of consternation. It was a wedding reception. *Oh my God!* She didn't know anyone, she hadn't been invited. How could Gary think this would be OK? She hesitated on the threshold, but soon had no choice but to enter the room, as a couple of girls were trying to squeeze past her.

Gary turned around to speak to her and realised she wasn't there. Confused, he glanced back towards the entrance and, seeing Gill's stricken face, rushed back over to her.

'Is everything OK? I thought it would be a nice surprise.'

'Gary, I know you meant well, but I don't know anyone here,' Gill whispered to him.

'Relax. They're a great bunch. They'll be more than happy to meet you and so they should be.' He smiled warmly at her. 'Here, let me get you a glass of champagne and then we can mingle.'

Gill nodded mutely. She stood to one side as Gary approached the table at the end of the room, where waiters poured champagne into flutes.

'Hi, you must be Gill. I'm Stephanie.' A woman who appeared to be in her early forties held out her hand to Gill.

'Nice to meet you,' Gill said for want of anything to say.

'You've made quite an impression on our Gary.' The woman touched Gill's shoulder gently.

'Have I?' Gill asked, dumbfounded. This was only their second date.

'Oh yes.' Stephanie's gaze was warm as she surveyed Gill.

'Ah, I see you've met Steph.' Gary held Gill's flute out to her.

'Yes, so how do you two know each other?'

Steph choked on her champagne. 'Sorry, I think Teresa is calling me. I'll see you both later.'

Wondering what all that was about, Gill turned to Gary, hoping for enlightenment, but he was waving to an elderly woman over in the far corner. When he turned back to her, he said, 'C'mon, let me show you around. Have you eaten?'

Gill hadn't, so Gary suggested they hit the buffet first. 'The food is amazing. It's all locally sourced. Have you ever eaten here before?'

Gill explained this was the first time she had ever set foot in the hotel. As they reached the buffet, she noticed several other people arrive.

'Evening guests,' Gary explained, 'seven for seven thirty.' Turning his attention back to the buffet, he said, 'I've been reliably informed the lemon sole tempura is out of this world.'

From the duck teriyaki, haggis balls, vegetable tartines and tempura that were on offer, as well as a vast selection of sandwiches, Gill avoided the sandwiches and the haggis balls and took one each of the others.

Gary piled his plate high then said, 'I can't believe I'm eating this. You ought to see the amount of food we put away at the meal.'

As they walked back from the buffet, and sat down at a table, Gary regaled Gill with the delights of the wedding meal. It did sound delicious. Part of Gill wished she'd been here then – the part that wasn't already uncomfortable about being at a wedding, uninvited and with people she didn't know. She didn't even know whose wedding it was. She was just about to ask, but she had already bitten into the vegetable tartine, and was busy chewing it – oh, it was lovely and fresh, light and fluffy.

Determined to ask before she took another bite, she was on the verge of interrupting Gary to ask him, when someone beat her to it. She turned around to the female voice which said, 'I thought you'd gone and left us,' as Gary rose to greet her. Wondering who could be causing Gary to smile in such a way, and feeling a tiny bit jealous, even though she wasn't sure why, Gill turned around and came face to face with the bride.

'Of course not, Suzanne.' Gary kissed her warmly on the cheek, then gave her a hug.

'This must be Gill.' The bride appraised her openly. 'Lovely to meet you. Sorry I didn't see you earlier, but it's been a bit of a day.'

'It's lovely to be here. Congratulations,' Gill said mechanically. What else could she say? She hadn't even known the bride's name until twenty seconds ago.

'Wife, are you leaving me already?' A handsome man in his mid-forties wrapped his arms around his new bride and kissed her neck.

'Stop getting fruity. There's a time and a place. I was just meeting Gill.' She gestured to Gill. 'Meet my husband, Billy. That still sounds strange.'

Gill let him kiss her on both cheeks, and then congratulated him. Only as he pulled away, did she feel a little stab of recognition. He looked very familiar. As he slapped Gary on the back and they engaged in conversation, Gill realised why she had thought she recognised him – he was Gary's double – a younger, heavier version. They must be brothers. Gary had invited her to his brother's wedding!

Breaking out in a cold sweat, Gill suddenly needed to get out of the room.

'Are you all right?' Suzanne asked her, concerned.

'I think I might just need a little air,' said Gill.

A worried Gary rose to help her and said, 'I'll come with you.'

'No!' It came out more vehemently than she intended. 'I mean, I'm going to the Ladies' first, to splash some water on my face. I won't be long.'

True to her word, Gill did go into the Ladies', although she didn't splash water on her face, as that would have ruined her make-up. Instead she took very deep breaths, trying to calm down. Why had Gary invited her to his brother's wedding? And even more importantly, why hadn't he told her that the groom was his brother?

Taking her mobile from her bag, she checked there was no one in the cubicles and then dialled Debbie's number. After five rings Debbie answered.

'Debbie. I don't know what to do. You'll never believe where my surprise date with Gary is.'

'Somewhere nice, I hope.'

'Yes, it is. One Devonshire actually, but that's not the point.'

'One Devonshire. I've been dying to go there.'

'Not under these circumstances you wouldn't be,' Gill said through gritted teeth.

'Why, what's wrong?' Debbie had clearly noted the edge in Gill's voice.

'He's only gone and invited me to his brother's wedding.'

'What? That's where you are now?' Debbie asked in disbelief.

'Correct. What do I do?'

Debbie said nothing for a minute. A tall, pretty girl came into the toilet. Gill smiled at her and moved to let her pass.

'Unless you want to cause a scene, do nothing. You don't want to create any animosity at a wedding. If I were you, I would try and enjoy myself, but make my excuses relatively early. Then I would either tell Gary you're upset, or that inviting you to his brother's wedding, particularly without telling you, isn't the done thing, even if he had the best of intentions. Remember, guys' minds work differently from ours.'

'You're telling me,' Gill muttered. 'What the hell was he thinking? And to cap it all, he still hasn't told me it's a family wedding.' Gill whispered the last part, aware that she was no longer alone in the toilets.

'What do you mean?'

'I worked it out, because the groom is the spitting image of him, but Gary hasn't actually told me.' Gill paced up and down the Ladies'.

'How odd. I wonder why not.'

'Exactly. Anyway, the whole thing stinks.'

'Do you think you can last the evening?' Debbie asked.

'I don't know. I just about had a panic attack in there.'

'Go back out there and see if you can handle it. If you can't, tell him you feel ill, make your excuses, then leave.'

'OK, thanks, Debbie. I knew I could count on your sound advice – as always. Have a nice night and say hi to Gerry for me.'

'Will do. Good luck.'

Gill hung up, faced her reflection in the mirror and said, 'You can do this,' just as the young girl exited the toilet and said, 'Great dress.'

Gill mumbled a thanks and left. That was all she needed, other guests to think she was loopy.

Returning to the table, she found Gary deep in conversation with Steph. The bride and groom had moved on to do their rounds.

'Ah, you're back,' Gary said, relief apparent on his face.

'Was the prospect of meeting our family too much for you?' Steph joked.

Gill looked carefully at Steph, then at Gary, who was looking daggers at Steph.

'Not at all, although Gary seems to have told you more about me than me about you.'

'Nothing much to tell. I'm the elder by ten minutes. Isn't that right, Gaz?'

Gaz had turned an impressive shade of beetroot.

'I, I, Gill, my sister is a right wind-up merchant. You'll have to forgive her.'

Steph, witnessing the colour Gill had turned, then sat back and laughed, 'I don't believe it. Gary, do you have no sense, at all?'

Gill sat back, unsure what to say, and played nervously with the edge of the slightly wine-stained linen tablecloth.

Gary looked at Steph and then at Gill, shamefaced.

'Oh my God, I'm right, aren't I? He didn't tell you about us. He didn't tell you it was his brother's wedding, and he didn't tell you he had a twin sister. Am I getting warm?'

Now it was Gill's turn to flush red.

Steph turned on her twin. 'Gary, you're a halfwit. Gill, come with me. We need to get you another drink.'

As Steph half-marched Gill to the bar, she put her arm gently on Gill's and said, 'Look, I'm sorry about my brother. He means well. He just doesn't think. Sometimes I think I got all the common sense and he got the big heart. I know it's a bit of a shock, but we're a good clan really, and you're here now, so why don't we get to know each other and just enjoy ourselves?'

With nothing to counter that with, Gill accepted the glass of wine Steph handed her, and when prompted, clinked glasses. 'To my eejit brother.'

'To your eejit brother!'

Back at the table, Gary didn't know where to look. Steph handed him the beer she'd brought him. Gary thanked her and said, 'Steph, can Gill and I have a minute, please?'

'Sure, but make sure it's just a minute. I don't want you scaring off my new friend.' Steph winked at Gill as she left the table.

'Gill, I'm really sorry. I should have told you it was my brother's wedding, but I wanted to take you somewhere really different and I thought if I told you, you'd think I'd asked you just so I had a date for it. And that absolutely wasn't the case. As you can see, I managed through the wedding itself, and the meal without a date.'

Part of Gill felt like saying '*bully for you*,' but she refrained from commenting and let Gary continue.

'I hoped that if you came here and enjoyed yourself, you might realise that we could have a good time together, that I wasn't just some nerd.'

'I didn't think you were…' Gill started to say, but Gary interrupted her, 'Sorry, but I wouldn't blame you if you did. I really like you, Gill, and I just wanted to have another chance at making a first impression.'

'Well, you certainly made an impression all right.' Gill was smiling.

'Friends?'

'Yes, friends.'

'Great. Oh, here she's coming back. What did you make of my twin?'

'She's a lot more forceful than you.'

'Nah, she just doesn't have my manners.'

'Right, you two sorted?' Steph asked. 'Great, so, Gill, tell us all about yourself,' she said, pulling up a chair. Gary rolled his eyes.

With the air cleared, Gill started to enjoy the wedding and the company she was in. Relatives and friends of Gary and Steph popped by their table, and either stood or sat, for fifteen or twenty minutes at a time, catching up. Gill calculated there must have been around sixty to seventy people there. Not a huge wedding, but she gathered it would be costing a fortune, for such opulent surroundings.

An hour later, with the tables cleared away, the ceilidh band started up to the strains of The Dashing White Sergeant. The bride and groom's unusual choice of first dance was welcomed by all, and soon, everyone was up on the dance floor. Gill, at first, protested, but Murray, one of Gary's friends, whom she had been talking to latterly, wouldn't take no for an answer. He taught her the steps as they danced and, after only a short time, she was twirling like an old hand. The Gay Gordons, an Eightsome Reel, a Military Two-step and a Strip the Willow later, and Gill was dying of thirst and perspiring in a most unladylike fashion. She excused herself to go to the toilet. Checking her face in the mirror, she saw her cheeks were flushed and her face aglow with happiness. Maybe tonight hadn't been such a disaster after all.

Chapter Thirty-six

Sunday 2 October

'Well, at least you had a good time in the end,' Debbie said.

'Yeah, it was quite a good night, and they were a nice crowd. The sad thing is I think Gary and I could be good friends. There's just no fizz.'

'How do you mean?'

'OK, let me spell it out. I'm not attracted to him, at all. He was wearing a kilt at the wedding, for God's sake. That in itself should have made me want to jump him!'

'So, are you seeing him again?'

'I don't know, Debbie. Not in that way. It doesn't seem fair. I don't mean to lead him on, but there simply isn't any chemistry. If I went out with him again, isn't that giving him hope?'

Debbie thought this over for a second. 'I suppose. God, why can't we ever fancy the nice guys?'

'Eh, you have Gerry.'

'Yes, but apart from Gerry. Look at Angela and you, with some of your past boyfriends.'

'I wish I knew,' Gill said glumly.

'So, what now?'

'I don't know. I'm seeing Charlie next Saturday. I haven't got back to Sean yet.'

'What, since he asked you to go bowling?'

'Yeah, I haven't replied to him yet.'

'Gill, I know we've said to keep them keen, but you are actually supposed to get back to them at some stage.'

'I know, but even with Sean, I don't know what to do.'

'OK, let's get to the bottom of this. Anton's the problem, isn't he?'

Gill said nothing.

'Gill, I can't see you down the phone, but I can sense you, and I know that Anton is the problem. Am I right?'

Eventually Gill whispered, 'Yes.'

'Still no contact?'

'No.'

'Well, what are you going to do about it?'

'There's nothing I can do about it. The guy shagged me and then never got back to me. End of.'

'You don't believe that.'

'I didn't believe that. Past tense.' Gill sighed and sat down heavily on the sofa.

'Is he back yet?'

'He got back yesterday.'

'Well, why don't you wait until this evening and then send him a text asking how his trip went?'

Gill chewed this over for a bit and then said, 'OK, I'll do that.'

'There could be a number of reasons why he hasn't e-mailed,' Debbie reassured her.

'I suppose. Thanks, Debbie. I'll drop Sean an e-mail, too. I'll go bowling.'

'That's my girl. Right, I'm being summoned to make the gravy. *Yes, Gerry, I'm coming*. God, that man, sometimes! Let me know how you get on.'

'I will. Enjoy your dinner.'

'We will. I made it. Good luck!' Debbie hung up.

Gill reclined on the sofa, unsure what to do. She couldn't go on like this. She wanted to know where she stood with Anton, although she feared she already knew. It hurt badly to realise she'd been so taken in. She'd truly believed he'd felt something for her. Her thoughts tortured her for two hours as she did mundane household tasks. At four o'clock, she caved and texted him. She tried to strike the right register, happy-go-lucky, but firm. *Hi, Anton. Hope your trip to Belarus went well. Would love to hear about it, Gill.*

She studied the message, read and reread every word. Did it convey what she was trying to say? Yes, she thought so. If he had half a brain, and in her experience men had exactly that, he would get the subtext – *why haven't you called me?*

As Gill flicked on the TV, more for company than anything else, she continued to ponder her predicament with Anton. Too late she realised that she had fallen in love with him, and his rejection hurt like hell.

Chapter Thirty-seven

Monday 3 October

A sleepless night left Gill out of sorts on Monday morning. Not even the unusually fine weather could buoy her flagging spirits. She had fully expected to hear from Anton by now. Surely he wouldn't ignore direct contact from her? Even if it were to say, *'Sorry, I'm not interested.'* That would be better than this constant limbo. Who was she kidding? She'd be devastated if he replied to her with those words.

In the office, Gill put on a brave face, not wanting to spoil everyone else's mood, with her frustration and anger. She *was* angry now. How dare he sleep with her, promise to e-mail her and then never get back to her? What a complete bastard! She'd fallen for the oldest trick in the book. Of course, men will say anything to get you into bed. She'd lowered her guard with Anton and he'd let her down in stellar fashion. She wouldn't cry. He wasn't worth it. She had a business to run. So, she'd pour her energies into her company.

At lunchtime, Gill took the plunge and texted Sean. *Hi, Sean. Sorry not been in touch. Bowling sounds good. When can you make it? Gill.*

'Angus, I'm going to the accountant's. Can you tell Janice I'll grab some lunch on the way and then work from home?'

'Sure, no problem. Anything else you need me to do this afternoon, when you're out?'

'No, just as we discussed, thanks.' Gill left the office, traipsed down the steps and got into her car.

Traffic was notably heavier this lunchtime. Gill hoped there were no roadworks. She wanted time to stop for lunch at the little delicatessen round the corner from her accountant.

As she sat in traffic, frustrated, her thoughts turned to Angus. That boy had been a real find. He was amiable and thorough – both qualities important to her in a colleague. As the traffic crawled forward, Gill smiled to herself, thinking at least that part of her life was going well. Suddenly the traffic broke away and Gill followed. Too late, she saw the car crossing the junction. Brakes screeching, gears crunching, Gill swerved and almost managed not to hit it – but still she clipped its rear. Shaking and furious at herself for not noticing the lights had changed to red, she climbed out of the car. The driver of the Astra she had pranged unfolded his legs and got out of his car. *At least he's OK.*

'Are you…?' Gill began then stopped. 'You!'

'Ah, it's the bag snatch girl.' The man smiled, despite not having yet checked the damage to his car.

'What are you doing here?' Gill managed after several failed attempts at speech.

'I live in Maryhill,' the man who had rescued her bag in Barcelona said.

'I can't believe it. Of all the people I could run into, no pun intended, I run into you.'

'Small world.'

Cars started honking all around them, bringing them

back to the fact that they were blocking one of Glasgow's busiest intersections.

'Tell you what, why don't we move the cars over there?' He pointed to some nearby parking spaces. 'Then we can assess the damage'

'OK, sounds good.' Afterwards she thought that was a bizarre thing for her to say, given she'd just ploughed into her rescuer's car. Really, what were the chances of meeting him again?

Gill drove her car over to one of the free spaces, locked it, then stood on the pavement waiting for Barcelona Man to park. She didn't even know his name. As he manoeuvred into the space, she saw that his colour-coordinated bumper had a slight dent in it. Even though it was only small, Gill knew it could be expensive to fix. Briefly she wondered if he would let her pay for the repairs rather than put it through her insurance, which would surely affect her premiums.

Barcelona Man got out of his car and said, 'Let's see what the damage is.'

He didn't seem the slightest bit fazed by the fact she'd crashed into his car. Gill found her voice. 'Sorry, I don't even know your name.'

'Liam,' he said, holding out his hand. 'Liam Gotobed.'

'You're kidding! Gotobed?'

'Yeah, yeah, I've heard it all before.'

Recovering herself, Gill said, 'Nice to meet you. I'm just sorry it's always under such awful circumstances.'

'But at least we did meet,' he said, holding her gaze.

There was such warmth in his look, it made Gill melt.

'Right, I don't think it'll take much to sort this. A mate of mine has a body repair shop in Bishopbriggs. I'm sure he could fix it pretty cheaply.'

'So we're OK not to go through the insurance?' Gill asked hopefully.

'I think so.' He walked around the car. 'I don't see any other damage, but I'll have it checked out. Sometimes being shunted can cause damage underneath, which you can't see straightaway.'

At Gill's worried face, he reassured her, 'But I really don't think that's the case here. Listen, were you going somewhere when you crashed into me?'

Gill winced at the reminder, and the corners of Liam's mouth twitched when he saw it,

'It's just I thought maybe you could buy me a coffee to make up for running into me?'

'Tell you what,' said Gill impulsively. 'Why don't I buy you lunch and that gets me off the hook for Barcelona, too?'

'Deal.'

'But I need to be done in an hour or so, as I was on my way to see my accountant.'

'Well, we can't have you being late for him.'

'Quite. Why don't we go to McSwains? That's if you like Scottish food.'

What a dumb question, Gill realised, no sooner had it left her mouth. What was it with her? Did she have *'I must behave like a moron around good-looking men'* syndrome?

'Sorry, what I meant was if you like Scottish fine dining.'

'I do. OK, let's go.'

It was only a few minutes to the restaurant and as they walked, Liam told Gill he had a day off, and had been on his way into town to do some much-needed clothes shopping – something he loathed.

When they arrived at the restaurant, Gill took charge – she was paying after all – and asked if they had a table for two, and confirmed that no, they hadn't booked. The waiter seemed doubtful, but just then the phone rang with a cancellation.

The waiter seated them near the window, overlooking Kelvingrove Park. It was a cosy spot and Gill blushed. She almost felt as if they were illicit lovers instead of two drivers post-accident.

Menus arrived swiftly. They refused the wine list, both opting for sparkling water instead. Although the small restaurant was busy, they had plenty of privacy. Not here a neighbouring table positioned so close to you that you felt as if either your stomach or your backside would surely knock over glasses or cutlery as you tried to squeeze past. The setting was intimate and Gill suddenly found herself at a loss for words. She looked at Liam, who was busy studying the menu. He raised his head and threw her an enquiring glance. With a tiny shake of her head, she buried herself in the menu. They both eschewed starters in favour of dessert.

'What do you fancy?' Gill asked.

A slight smile graced Liam's lips and then it was gone, as he replied, 'I think I'm going to have the breast of chicken with chorizo. You?'

'Yes, that sounded really nice, but I had chicken for dinner last night, so I'm going to have the sea bass.'

Running his finger down the menu, Liam found it, 'Ah yes, sea bass with sun-blushed tomatoes and feta. Sounds really nice, too, but I'm just not in a fishy mood.'

'I know what you mean. I have to be in the mood for some things.'

Liam's eyes glinted and Gill blushed again. How did he

do that to her?

'I'm just going to go and freshen up before lunch.'

'Good idea.' Liam followed her until they parted ways for the respective toilets.

When Gill returned, Liam was already back at the table. 'I've ordered, hope that was OK?'

'Sure. You already knew what I wanted.'

'Great. So tell me, what were you doing in Barcelona?'

Gill related how she'd gone to the Mercè festival with three friends for a long weekend. She explained that she and Angela had just come out of the Sagrada Família and were about to head back to the hotel, when the mugger stole her bag.

'They're just so brazen. That's what gets me,' said Liam.

'I know. I mean, I knew theft was notorious on the Ramblas and we were always very careful, but I didn't expect someone to try to steal my bag off my shoulder.'

'It's a shame, as Barcelona's a great city, but the police turn a blind eye. To them, it's just stupid tourists,' Liam said.

'Fair enough, some people have no sense, you know, coming out of a jewellery shop dangling their purchases, with their wallet or purse still in hand, Nikon around their neck. But even so, no one asks to be mugged.'

'Yeah, it's a pity.'

'So, what were *you* doing in Barcelona?' Gill asked.

'I was just passing through. I flew to Barcelona the week before and drove down to a few tile manufacturers. I'm a tiler by trade, but now I have five tile warehouses in the central belt. I've been trying to find new products for them. I was on the return leg of my trip, and had half a day to kill in Barcelona. I thought I'd see if the Sagrada Família lived up to expectation.'

'Well, I'm very glad you did, otherwise I would have had real problems: credit cards to cancel, loss of money, not to mention needing to get a new passport.'

Their meals arrived and they tucked in hungrily. Gill was pleased to see Liam had a good appetite and lovely manners. He spoke to her only between mouthfuls, asking her what she did for a living, what she'd liked best about Barcelona; did she need her bathroom tiled? The last was said with a sexy little smile.

He can tile my bathroom any day. Gotobed? More like Cometobed!

'So, tell me, Gotobed, really?' asked Gill.

Liam sighed and then trotted out the story, as he had clearly done many times before. 'My dad's English. Apparently it's one of the oldest surnames in England. There are only around two hundred or so of us in the UK.'

'But what a cool name!'

'You wouldn't think so if you'd had to have it all through high school, especially in Scotland.'

'Maybe not. So how old is your name then?'

'Well, we can trace it back to at least the fourteenth century, and it's rumoured that we might be linked to William Gawtobedde of Sussex in 1332.'

'Who was he?'

'I don't think he was anyone particularly famous. I think it's just they reckon that's where we came from, and then, of course, over the years, the spelling changed from Old English to what it is now.'

'That's really interesting.' Gill gazed at him, fascinated.

'Thanks.'

The dessert was to die for, but all too soon, it was time

to go, otherwise Gill would be late for her appointment.

'I really enjoyed lunch, thanks.' Liam helped Gill on with her jacket.

They walked back to their cars and taking out her keys, Gill said, 'We haven't exchanged details yet.'

'Neither we have.' Liam scrawled his name and phone number on a scrap of paper which he took out of his wallet. Tearing it in two, he asked Gill to write her number on it. Gill obliged and handed it back to him. Their hands touched briefly and a frisson shot through Gill.

'Listen, Gill, I'd like to see you again.'

Gill waited.

'Are you doing anything on Wednesday night?'

Gill thought for a moment and then said, 'Nothing special.'

'Do you like photography? Or rather, do you like free champagne and nibbles?'

Gill laughed. 'I have to confess to not knowing much about photography, shading, exposure and all that. But you've won me over with the champers.'

'Great. A friend of mine is having his first exhibition and I have tickets. Can I pick you up?'

'Where is it?'

'It's at the Lambkin Gallery in Byres Road.'

'OK, well, why don't I meet you there? What time?'

'It starts at seven, but if we're there for seven thirty, that's fine. We'll probably be among the first, but I want to support my friend, you know.'

'No problem. OK, I really need to go. See you on Wednesday.'

Gill went to shake his hand, but Liam kissed her cheek. 'I look forward to it.'

Chapter Thirty-eight

Tuesday 4 October

Beep, beep, beep. Oh no, it can't be morning already. Reluctantly Gill dragged herself out of bed and stood in the shower for a good twenty minutes. The feel of the pressurised jets on her skin was welcome to her weary bones. She really needed some exercise. First, work had been the problem, now her love life was taking up her time. At least she had addressed the work-life balance which had plagued her for several years. Thanking her guardian angel for sending her Angus, Gill got ready for work.

She'd received a reply from Sean yesterday, on leaving her accountant's, asking if Tuesday was too soon. Foolishly Gill confirmed Tuesday was fine. She had felt bad for not answering him for so long. He suggested the bowling alley at Springfield Quay and they agreed to meet there at seven.

That morning Gill had hastily flung a casual dress in a bag, along with some ballet pumps. That was her outfit taken care of.

She'd have to wear those awful bowling shoes, she thought, as she drove into town. Nobody could look good in those. At least her height gave her an advantage. She felt sorry for those less fortunate, who, without their four-inch stilettos, would be minute.

The introductions with Angus were going well. Three key accounts had received him warmly, and he had already begun to prove his worth. So far he'd coaxed five of his clients over to McFadden's Technical Recruitment, purely on relationship. Gill was pleased, and since she believed in giving credit where it was due, she'd told him so. Angus had glowed with pleasure. Evidently praise hadn't been doled out much at his last employer.

Back at the agency, Gill called Janice into her office. Janice left the door slightly ajar.

'Could you shut the door, please? It's a private matter.'

Janice raised an eyebrow in alarm. Gill smiled and assured her there was nothing to worry about. 'The exact opposite, actually,' she said as Janice took a seat.

'Janice, you've done a lot for me and this agency over the years, and now, I think, with Angus starting, that we'll be able to bring a lot more business to the firm. So, with that in mind, I'm raising your salary by two thousand pounds.'

'What!' Janice started in her chair. 'Really? Oh Gill, that's great! Thanks.'

Janice came round Gill's side of the desk and hugged her.

'Yes, yes, steady on. I'm only giving you a raise, because you're great. Keep it to yourself, mind.'

'Of course. My lips are sealed.' Janice made a zipping motion with her fingers.

A little later, Gill checked her watch. *Oh God, is that the time?* She went into the outer office where the others were packing up, except for Angus who was still tapping away on his computer.

'Night, girls. Have a nice evening,' Gill told them. As

soon as they had gone, she asked Angus, 'What are you doing?'

'Just replying to some e-mails, making some calls.'

'Right, well, it can wait until tomorrow. Go and enjoy your evening.'

When Angus started to protest, Gill gave him a look that brooked no argument.

After Angus left, Gill answered a few more e-mails then paid some bills online. A quick change in the toilets and she was ready to go bowling – or at least, as ready as she was ever going to be.

The noise that greeted Gill as she entered the bowling alley made her want to cover her ears. She wasn't sure if it was the din of the pins being knocked down, or the screaming youngsters. Gill wasn't often in the company of children, except her nephews, and she sometimes found it difficult to tolerate 'other people's children'. She soon spotted Sean, putting coins into a slot machine.

'Winning?'

Sean jumped. 'Jeez, you gave me the fright of my life!' His hand covered his heart, feigning heart failure.

'Jumpy, aren't we?'

'Clearly. So, are you ready? Nice dress,' he said with a smile on his face.

'Thanks,' said Gill, wondering why he was smirking.

Sean took down his pint from where he had left it on top of the machine. 'I've booked it for seven fifteen. Would you like a drink?'

'Yes, but I suppose I better change first. Now, where do I get those hideous shoes?'

Sean grinned, pointed to the left, and said, 'This way, ma'am.'

As Gill changed into the red, white and blue monstrosities, Sean paid for their two games of bowling. *Twice the embarrassment.*

Gill just knew she was going to be dreadful at this game. She hadn't bowled for years, and couldn't have been classed as good then.

'What kind of wine do you have?' Sean asked, once they reached the bar.

'We have red and white,' said the sullen barmaid.

Her colleague chipped in, 'Remember we also have that new white zinfandel.'

Before 'Her Happiness' could relay this to Gill, Gill cut in, 'White zinfandel will do fine, thanks.'

'I'll have a Stella,' Sean added.

As they walked away from the bar, towards lane twelve, Sean voiced what Gill was thinking, 'She was a right barrel of laughs.'

'I guess some people just love their job.'

'Well, I wouldn't like to see her on a bad day,' said Sean as he put his glass on the counter. 'Right, have you played before?'

'A long time ago.'

'OK.' Sean sat himself in the low seat, poised to process their details.

'What do you want to be known as?'

'Er, how about Gill?'

'Yep, that works. Me, I'm always Seanster.'

'Seanster?'

'Yeah, blokes can't just have their own name.'

'Oh really?'

'Yep, it's not cool.'

'So it's far cooler for a thirty-something man to have a nickname?'

'Got it in one. Right, do you remember what to do?'

'I think so. The balls are all different weights, aren't they?'

'Yes, depending on how strong you are, I would suggest a ten or a twelve. You're tall, so maybe a twelve, but then if you haven't played in a while…'

'I'll go with a twelve.' Gill stopped short Sean's ramblings.

'Great, well, ladies first.'

Horrified, Gill said, 'Oh, I thought you'd be first.'

'Ladies always go before gentlemen.'

Gill muttered something under her breath about not seeing any gentlemen; otherwise she wouldn't be in this godforsaken place. Lifting the green twelve ball, she put three fingers into it and walked towards the line. On the way she watched what she assumed was the father of the family in the next lane, to see if she could pick up any tips. He was no help; he bowled with flair, even doing that little knee flick that professional bowlers do. There was no way she was going to attempt that.

Gill tried to swing the ball, but it was heavier than she had anticipated. Damn, she should have used the ten, but the holes in the ten seemed really small, and she didn't think her fingers would have fitted inside. Eventually, she swung her arm back, then forward, and released the ball. It trundled miserably off to the side and into the gutter.

Gill watched in embarrassment as it very slowly reached the end.

'Daddy, I did better than that lady. She didn't get any pins.' The boy in the next lane pointed at Gill in glee.

'Shh,' the father said and then smiled a *'Sorry'* at Gill.

Gill returned to where Sean was standing and tried to

put a brave face on it. 'I'm just warming up, trying to lull you into a false sense of security,' she joked, as she sat down.

'Er, you might be doing that,' said Sean, 'but it's still you to go,' he indicated the scoreboard which registered a bit fat zero.

Of course, Gill had forgotten that each turn consisted of two shots. Reddening again, she said, 'I knew that, I was just...resting.'

'Yeah, yeah.' Sean laughed then took a sip of his beer. 'Go on. Show us what you're made of.'

That's what Gill was afraid of. She wasn't made of very much where ten-pin bowling was concerned. She picked up the twelve ball, but when she went to throw it, her fingers didn't come out easily. The ball fell clumsily out of her hand, narrowly missing her feet, as she jumped back, and then it rolled onto the family's lane.

'No, no, no!' Gill looked on panic-stricken and the mother glared at her in frustration as Gill's ball headed slowly towards the pins, ready to muck up the family's scores.

'I'm really sorry,' Gill said.

The mother shook her head as if to say it didn't matter, but her body language said something else entirely.

The father said, 'Don't worry. I'll go and get them to reset the score.'

Meanwhile Sean hid behind the screen, his shoulders shaking with laughter.

'It's not funny!' Gill said, fighting a desire to slap him.

'Oh, I'm sorry.' Tears ran down Sean's face. 'But it is funny, really funny.'

'Anyway, your turn now.'

Sean bowled a spare and then managed to knock down the final pin, resulting in a third go.

In the next few shots, Gill at least managed to stay in her own lane and even hit a couple of pins, with first a score of one and then three.

'That's not bad,' said Sean magnanimously.

'Oh, shut up!' said Gill, good-naturedly. Finally over her embarrassment, she was now quite enjoying herself.

'Have you eaten?' Sean asked.

'No, why?'

'I thought I might get us some fries whilst we're bowling.'

'OK, sure.'

'Do you want anything else to drink?'

'Eh?' Gill glanced at her three-quarters full glass of wine and then at Sean's empty glass.

'No, I'm fine, I've barely touched my wine,' she said pointedly. But her barb was lost on Sean, who headed to the bar.

Sean won a hundred and eighty-four to sixty-seven, but at least Gill had improved. The fries were actually quite good, but Gill realised she needed a soft drink to go with them.

'I'm just nipping to the toilet. I'm going to get myself a Coke on the way back. Do you want one?'

'No, I don't drink the stuff, but I'll have another Stella, thanks.'

Gill tried not to frown and just enjoy their evening, but the niggling thought wouldn't go away. Last time Sean had drunk too much in her company, he'd become a complete arse and embarrassed her.

In the next game, Gill was actually doing quite well.

On her fifth frame, she already had ninety-five points, a vast improvement on last time. She seemed to be getting the hang of it.

Deciding she'd be a little bit more daring, Gill thought she'd try the fancy footwork the father in the next lane favoured. Maybe it wasn't that difficult after all. Concentrating hard, Gill swung and– *bloody hell, what's happening?* –her right foot crossed the line, milliseconds before she let go of the bowling ball; she slipped on the waxed surface and both legs shot up in the air. The ball trundled happily toward the pins and unbelievably Gill scored a strike. Not that she was particularly caring about that. She was more concerned at having just flashed her knickers for everyone to see. Hurriedly she adjusted her dress so that it covered her. She made a mental note never to wear a dress when bowling again. Thank God she wasn't wearing a G-string. She tried to pick herself up off the greased lane, but kept slipping. Eventually, between sliding on her bum in the direction of the booth and Sean coming to her aid, a tad late in her opinion, Gill was able to stand up.

'Are you all right?' Sean asked; face half concerned, half amused.

'Not really, no.' Gill could already feel a bruise forming where she had fallen on her tail bone. She ran her hands gently over it. 'Ow!'

'Have you hurt yourself?'

'Mainly just my pride, but I hit my lower back when I fell.'

'Sit down a second.'

Gill tried, but it was too painful. 'I can't. It hurts.'

Seeing Gill's strained face, Sean eventually said, 'OK,

game abandoned, let's get you home.'

As they stood waiting for the taxi, Sean said, 'Who knew ten-pin bowling was an extreme sport?'

Gill threw him a warning glance, which he ignored. Sean, not noticing, continued, 'I mean, short of wrapping you in cotton wool, there couldn't really be a safer sport than ten-pin bowling. It's not a contact sport, or rather, it's not meant to be.'

Sean rambled on in this vein as they waited for the taxi to arrive. Gill was ready to throw a wobbler. She wished he would just shut the hell up.

The taxi drew up and Gill, assisted by Sean, got in.

'Well, Gill, I hope you feel better soon. Sorry the night had to end like this. Put some ice on it and get some rest,' Sean said, as he pecked her on the cheek, then patted the driver's door, to let him know he could go.

'Oh, and Gill,' Sean called to her just as the taxi started to pull away, 'Nice pants!'

Gill sat thinking, *What? Is that it?* Wasn't he going to come and make sure she was OK, prepare her an ice pack? No, Sean might be cute and Irish, with a lovely lilting accent, but his heavy drinking and lack of sensitivity had finished him off as far as she was concerned. Boyfriend material he was not.

Chapter Thirty-nine

Wednesday 5 October

Next morning Gill sported a huge bruise, the size of the palm of her hand, on her left thigh. Her tail bone was a peculiar colour, starting to go purple and was particularly tender. Bloody ten-pin bowling! Never again. Bloody Sean! Ditto.

As she eased on her dress, wincing at the pain, Gill smiled, remembering her impromptu date with Liam that night. At least she couldn't injure herself in an art gallery, she thought, unless one of the exhibits fell on her. She shouldn't tempt fate. Knowing how clumsy she was, anything might happen. Actually, she was kind of hoping anything might happen, or rather something. She chuckled to herself, as she checked her phone once again for news of Anton. Nothing. Nothing from Sean either. Screw Sean. He was history. She, Gill McFadden, was going to stop taking shit from men.

She couldn't have asked for a better day at the office, which was a relief, as the paracetamol from lunchtime hadn't kicked in yet. Her mobile beeped and she picked it up. It was just a text from a client confirming their meeting. Still nothing from Sean, asking her if she was OK, but what had she expected? He was a fun guy to spend some time with, but not one you could rely on. A bit like some of the others she had met recently. Her thoughts turned to Anton. Just as quickly she dismissed them. No good came of going there. Gill made a few notes, then went out and asked Angus if he could join her in the conference room in fifteen minutes.

By early evening, when she packed her staff off home, Gill was feeling better. Another few painkillers had helped. Since the exhibition was in a gallery, Gill felt it appropriate to dress up. She shrugged out of her shift dress, freshened up and wiggled with difficulty into her clean dress, cursing at the pain as she zipped it up. She thought about how much use she was getting out of this green silk sheath, which she'd originally bought to go out with Anton. Thank goodness for twenty-four-hour dry cleaning.

As Gill changed her jewellery and brushed her hair, she realised how much she was looking forward to her date with Liam. It also dawned on her, that unlike her recent dates, she didn't know very much about him. No profile. She was almost flying blind. But he'd rescued her in Barcelona and hadn't chewed a piece off her yesterday when she'd hit his car, so he must be one of the good guys, she reasoned.

Gill called a taxi and ten minutes later arrived at the Lambkin Gallery. Standing uncertainly on the pavement, Gill glanced around for any sign of Liam. It was seven thirty five. She was getting better at being late. She'd certainly learned some things from this dating caper. Just then, Liam's frame appeared in the doorway and he came down the steps.

'Hi.' He smiled, kissed Gill on the cheek and said, 'Shall we?'

Gill nodded and let him escort her upstairs into the gallery, the palm of his hand resting lightly on her lower back as he ushered her into the exhibition.

As they entered the room, Gill saw perhaps ten people in addition to the serving staff.

'These are great,' said Gill truthfully. 'I mean, I know nothing about photography, but I know what I like and these are pretty amazing.'

'They are, aren't they?' said a voice behind them.

Gill turned around and came face to face with a small man, about five feet four, with ginger hair and the most freckles she had ever seen on one person. She looked at him enquiringly and, just as Liam went to intervene, the man said, 'Julian Summers. Pleased to meet you. Thanks for attending my exhibition.'

'Ah,' said Gill, understanding. 'Very nice to meet you, I'm Gill. Liam invited me.' She turned to Liam for affirmation.

'And I'm very glad he did, too. Liam, how are you, my friend?' Julian clasped Liam's arm with one hand and shook his hand with the other.

'Very good, Julian. The exhibition's amazing.'

'Thank you. It's been a long time putting it together. Walk with me and I'll explain my thoughts, then I will leave you to yours.' He smiled charmingly at them both.

Gill and Liam followed him to the opposite end of the gallery.

'We begin with my Asian section, photos taken in Hanoi, Phnom Penh and Ho Chi Min City, before moving on to Cambodia. This one is the Mekong River in Laos;

what a beautiful country. This is Muang Ngoi Neua. Anyway, I digress. I wanted to point out simply that we have structured the exhibition by continent, and where there are too many exhibits for one continent, we have subdivided it by region. So, for example, Russia and the Urals, the Nordic countries, and Southern Europe are classed separately.'

Julian turned on hearing his name, and waving to the caller, he rested his arm on Gill's and said, 'Please excuse me. I hope you have a lovely evening. Liam, make sure this young lady gets a drink.' He gestured to the waiters circulating with canapés and glasses of champagne.

'Will do. I'm sure tonight will be a huge success – enjoy it.' Liam clasped Julian's hand briefly, before he headed off to catch up with the lady smiling expectantly at him.

'He seems nice,' said Gill.

'Yes, he is,' Liam said distractedly, as he tried to attract a waiter's attention. Two glasses of champagne soon found their way into Liam and Gill's hands and, raising his glass, Liam toasted, 'To Julian's success.' Gill raised her glass and uttered the same words. She had just lowered her glass to take a sip, when Liam raised his again, as an afterthought and said cheekily, 'And to bumping into people – literally, in your case!'

'I'll drink to that,' said Gill, feeling a warm glow that she couldn't attribute to the champagne.

They walked around the gallery, Liam adding a bit of history which the placards below the photos didn't tell. It became clear that Julian and Liam were good friends. He knew when Julian had shot many of the photographs. Gill felt as if she understood a lot more about the photographer, from the commentary she received from her date.

Once they had toured the entire exhibition, stopping only once or twice, to sample the canapés, Liam asked Gill which was her favourite exhibit.

'I think the black and white photograph of the little girl in the strawberry field in Korea, with her face covered in strawberry juice.'

'Yes, I liked that one, too.'

'What about you?'

'Funnily enough, another one of a child. The little Cuban girl sitting in the window of her apartment, drinking from a bottle of water, as she watches the children in the school playground below her.'

'Yes, that's an incredible photo. He really does have a way of capturing the moment, doesn't he?'

'Yes, but then I wonder how many shots he has to rattle off, before he gets the one he wants.'

'True. Thank goodness for digital, eh?'

'Yeah. It must have cost photographers a fortune, back when they had to develop almost every photograph.'

'I know. I can remember having to put in my twenty-four- and thirty-six-exposure films. Now you can get everything straightaway.'

'It's certainly convenient, but not all of those photos in the exhibition were taken digitally. In fact probably only about half.'

'Oh?' Gill raised a questioning eyebrow.

'Yes, some, due to when they were taken, were shot with a 35mm SLR and others simply because, as Julian tells me, he doesn't get the same level of satisfaction when shooting with a digital. With a traditional camera, more skill's involved, you *have* to create the picture; adjust the shutter speed, you have more control, whereas with a digital it can be done pretty much automatically. Julian swears his best photos are those taken with a medium-format camera, when the conditions, subject and moment are right.'

'I didn't realise that. So, do you know all this just from talking to Julian, or do you dabble in photography yourself?'

'I dabble. I'm nowhere near as good as Julian, but I've entered a few photos in *National Geographic* and won a couple of prizes.'

'Wow, that's amazing!'

'Thanks.' Liam grinned. He glanced around the gallery, which now held around two hundred people. 'There's the press.' He pointed out a short, tubby man with greying hair, to Gill.

'How do you know?'

'Press pass around his neck. They reckon Julian's the next big thing, so they wouldn't want to miss this.'

Gill watched as the man stopped a waitress and piled a selection of canapés onto a plate, before swilling back some champagne.

'Would you like to go somewhere else? We've probably seen all there is to see here, and I've done my good friend bit, too.' His smile revealed small, even, almost perfectly white teeth.

'Sure.' Gill was delighted. She'd had a lovely time; Liam was charming and great company.

'How about coffee at My Place?'

Gill, taken aback, didn't know how to respond.

Liam laughed. 'Sorry, I couldn't resist. I've wanted to say that, ever since it opened two months ago. It's a new coffee shop on Great Western Road.'

'Ah.' Gill regained her composure.

'Is that a yes?'

'Yes.'

'I wish I hadn't explained now. I'd have loved to hear your response to what you thought I meant.' With a wicked grin, he clasped her hand and headed towards Julian, who was explaining to a minor celebrity, the significance of the photograph of the fruit-pickers in Poland.

At a suitable moment, Liam jumped in, 'Julian. That's us off. Great exhibition. Even better than I'd hoped, and busy.' Liam opened his arms in a gesture which included the whole room.

'Yes, I'm really pleased. I've already had some interest in five of the photographs. Three are already sold – deposits taken.'

'That's brilliant, Jules.'

'So, where are you two fine people off to now?'

'My Place.'

Julian raised an eyebrow then looked approvingly at Gill. 'This man moves fast.'

As Gill made to correct him, Julian stopped her. 'I'm joking. I introduced Liam to My Place. I practically live there. Have the double shot caramel latte, if you dare.' He winked at Gill.

'I'll keep that in mind.'

They said their goodbyes and collected their coats.

'Do you want to walk or take a taxi?' Liam asked.

'Let's walk. If my feet get too sore, we can take a taxi then.'

'Done.'

They walked along Byres Road, and up towards the Botanic Gardens. Gill noticed Liam was only a couple of inches taller than her, so around six feet, considering the heels she had on. As she openly appraised him, it struck her that recently she'd taken a liking to men with blond hair. She'd never really thought about it before she started this dating agency lark. Liam's hair was longer than Anton's – kind of fluffy. There she went again, drawing comparisons. Would this ever stop? Wrenching herself back to the present, Gill listened to Liam's voice. Its timbre was surprisingly deeper than Anton's, whose English, although notably foreign, was quite melodic to listen to.

Five minutes later, they reached My Place. Gill loved it immediately. Bookcases lined the walls and patrons relaxed in plush sofas and overstuffed armchairs, sipping coffee and reading or chatting with friends. The décor gave it a lovely, homely feel.

Interestingly, it appeared to be table service, unlike the majority of trendy coffee shops. Liam secured them a table and said, 'Are you hungry?'

'Well, I could eat,' she admitted.

'Good. I was hoping you'd say that, because I'm starving.'

They pored over the menu together, with Gill deciding on a brie and cranberry wrap and Liam on a steak baguette. They also ordered a glass of wine for Gill and a Guinness for Liam.

'So,' Gill asked, when their drinks had been set in front of them and she'd taken a sip, 'how's your car?'

'Fine, thanks. My friend checked it over, and as I suspected, it's only superficial damage. A hundred and fifty pounds for the bumper, even though it's colour-coordinated, which I thought wasn't bad.'

Gill agreed. She'd been envisaging about eight hundred pounds for a respray and repairs.

'Is a cheque OK?' she asked.

'Are you good for it? It won't bounce?' Liam teased her.

'I think you'll be fine. Should I make it out to you or your company?'

'Just me. The car's mine, not the company's. We use vans at the firm.'

Gill had brought her cheque book so she could settle her debt this evening, never one to be beholden to others. When she reached for her bag, Liam stopped her. 'Leave it for now. I want us to enjoy our evening. I'm not here because you owe me money,' he said, pointedly.

Gill reddened and Liam smiled. 'You're even prettier when you blush, did you know that?'

Not knowing how to answer that, Gill said nothing.

'I like you, Gill.' Liam lowered his voice.

'I like you, too,' Gill was quick to reply.

'No, I *like* you.'

Now Gill really did turn red. Inside she was pleased, but she was unaccustomed to men being so forthright, particularly Glaswegian men, who were renowned for their reticence in discussing their feelings.

Liam stared at Gill intently, but not in a way that made her feel uncomfortable; just long enough for her to realise he meant what he said.

Then, without warning, he changed the subject back to Julian. He talked of the importance of this debut exhibition, the kudos it could bring his friend, and more importantly the visibility it would give him in the photographic world.

'That's really good, isn't it, that he's already sold several photographs on the opening night?' said Gill.

'Yes, that's not as common as you'd think. Many buyers wait until the last minute to see if they can pick up a bargain, but with those pieces that he's sold, he clearly has buyers who think waiting's too risky.'

The conversation halted when their food arrived. Silence reigned for a few moments as they tucked into their meal with gusto.

Gill realised just how hungry she was. It was nine thirty and except for a few blinis and a vol au vent, she had eaten nothing since lunchtime.

'So, why did you choose Maryhill?' Gill asked, after dabbing her mouth with her napkin.

'Actually, it kind of chose me. It was my brother's flat and he went off to America to work. In the beginning I rented it from him. Then he made the decision to stay there, so I bought it from him so he could afford the deposit for a condo in North Carolina.'

'Sounds great. Do you visit him?'

'I've been a few times. Not as much as I'd like, but it's difficult when you have a business to run.'

Too true, thought Gill. 'So why tiling?'

'I was always good with my hands–' he looked meaningfully at Gill then grinned '–and since I didn't have any qualifications, I decided to go for a trade. Tiling appealed more than others. I quite enjoy it, actually.'

'That's the main thing. So, do you still tile now? You said you have a few warehouses.'

'Yes, I only really do it for close friends and family, now and again. Even then, sometimes, I get one of my guys to do it. I'm just too busy.'

Gill knew what that felt like all right.

They continued to chat easily and Gill told Liam about her agency, her parents who lived in Devon, and her brother in Balloch.

'Oh, I used to go up to Balloch all the time.'

'Really?'

'Yes, a friend of mine had a speedboat and we used to go up most weekends. We'd head up the A82 in the morning, spend the afternoon on the boat and then pitch a tent and have a barbecue in the evening.'

'Sounds great.'

'It was. Unfortunately, my friend sold the boat – he got divorced.' Liam gave a rueful smile.

Gill took advantage of the opening. 'So, have *you* ever been married?'

'No, not married, but I did live with my partner for several years.'

'Right.'

Liam didn't elaborate, so Gill moved on. He'd tell her when he was good and ready. He'd said he liked her and that would do for now. This time she would be more careful. She liked him, too, but she wasn't letting her guard down, not just yet.

Chapter Forty

Saturday 8 October

It really seemed like October now. Not that the summer had been great, but with the considerable drop in temperature, light summer jackets and sandals had been rapidly replaced by boots and coats. The lashing wind and rain were a common sight north of the border.

Gill had been glad of the two nights at home following her first proper date with Liam on Wednesday. It had been a chance to catch up on bad telly, and she'd even managed to sit down for a few hours and read a book. At the agency, the pressure was definitely off both her and Janice, with the additions to their team.

When Gill and Liam had left My Place the other night, he had kissed her. It had been nice, but not earth-shattering. She was sure it would improve as they got to know each other.

Liam had said he would be busy over the weekend, but wanted to know if they could meet up on Tuesday. He promised to cook a meal for her and, touched, Gill had accepted.

She had also taken the last few days to finalise a few things which needed doing – sorting out Sean and letting Gary down gently. Sean still hadn't contacted her to see if she was all right, after her fall at the bowling alley, so she'd sent him a message, which said simply, *Hi, Sean. I've had a good time with you, but I don't think it's going anywhere. Hope you meet someone lovely, Gill.*

It was only *just* stretching the truth.

With Gary, it proved a bit more difficult. He had contacted her to ask if she wanted to go out for dinner. As he was a good guy, he'd done nothing wrong apart from foolishly invite her to his brother's wedding without telling her, she had called him. The conversation wasn't an easy one. Yet Gill had been very direct, told him she did like him and enjoyed his company, but simply didn't feel a spark and, after a few evenings together, didn't think she would. He wanted to remain friends, but Gill knew this would just be prolonging the agony. So, resolutely, she told him she didn't think men and women, who'd had a romantic interest in each other, could be just friends. She wished him all the best and told him to say hi to his twin. He took it well, in the end.

With a sigh of relief, Gill turned her thoughts to Charlie. She wondered where this mystery place was, an hour from the city – it could be Edinburgh. It was only an hour and there was so much to do there, but who would choose to drive to Edinburgh? Or maybe he would take her to a country inn down in Ayrshire? She let her mind wander in this vein to distract her from further thoughts of Anton. No matter how hard she tried to lock him away in a little box in her mind, images of him came to her unbidden, when she least expected it. Memories of his touch, the smell of him, the feel of his skin on hers invaded her mind daily. Debbie had asked if Anton had contacted her. It hurt to tell her friend no, but after a few well-meant placatory remarks,

Debbie left it at that, as she knew it would only upset Gill more. Gill hadn't shared with any of her friends just how devastated she had been, nor how she had cried herself to sleep on several occasions, unable to believe that she had been so deceived. She found herself torn between anger at his deception, and incredulity since his behaviour and feelings for her had appeared so genuine. His silence had shown her the truth: he wasn't interested. Dating Charlie and now Liam, at least gave her, in theory, reasons to take her mind off Anton, but it wasn't always so straightforward.

Both Gill and her friends had been busy since their return from Barcelona, so they hadn't had a chance to meet up. They were, however, all up to speed with the bizarre turn of events in Gill running into Liam. Debbie thought it was fate. Angela said he had seemed nice, and Lisa said she wished she'd seen him in Barcelona, and that Gill shouldn't look a gift horse in the mouth – there weren't too many knights in shining armour out there.

Gill caught the bus into Glasgow around eleven. She wanted to buy some new trousers and a top for her date with Charlie. There was no way she was wearing a dress, not after what happened last time. She didn't trust herself and she certainly didn't trust him. She had also made a mental note not to drink too much.

Traipsing around town turned out to be a miserable task, umbrella almost blown away by the near gale-force wind. Just as well she wasn't wearing a dress and sandals tonight. She'd be a soggy mess. Finally she selected charcoal grey trousers with a side zip, which were very flattering and she hoped flattening! A rose silk top, with a tiny artificial rose just above her left breast, went very well with the trousers. Good, one more thing taken care of.

Charlie had arranged to collect her next to Buchanan Street Bus Station. He was being coy about where they were going, so again, since she liked surprises, Gill went along with it. It couldn't be any worse than going to Gary's brother's wedding, without knowing about it in advance, could it?

By four thirty, Gill was showered, dressed and made up. Studying her reflection in the mirror, she decided the trousers had been a good buy. They detracted from her generous hips and the flattering side zip held in her stomach. Five minutes later her taxi arrived and she set off for town.

Even though it was rush hour, and busy with Saturday shoppers and football-goers, she arrived in town within twenty minutes. When the taxi dropped her off above the rank at Buchanan Street Bus Station, Charlie was already sitting waiting for her in a silver BMW 5 series. He tooted the horn so she knew it was him and, smiling, Gill approached the car. Charlie got out and greeted her with a kiss on the lips.

'Ready?'

'As I'll ever be.'

'I've missed you,' he murmured into her hair, before he released her.

How to respond to that? Gill wondered. She settled for a non-committal, 'Yes, it's been a while.'

Charlie *had* missed her and tonight he would pull out all the stops to get what he wanted.

As they drove along the M8 and across the Erskine Bridge, Gill couldn't help but be impressed. A bit of thought had gone into this. Charlie asked her about Barcelona and she filled him in on her trip, although she intentionally left out the part about getting mugged.

As they headed up towards Balloch, Gill had an inkling of their destination. There weren't so many exceptional, well-known places in this area. Of course, Charlie didn't know that her brother lived up this way.

They pulled into a viewpoint at Luss, and Gill was pretty sure she had guessed tonight's venue correctly. With the rain recently stopped, a magnificent rainbow hung over Loch Lomond and made for a breathtaking sight. The mist dissipated, enhancing the vista of the famous loch. It was still cool, however, and as they chatted and walked a little way along from the viewpoint, Charlie put his arm around Gill, ostensibly to keep her warm. When they turned back towards the car, Charlie stopped suddenly and Gill turned to him with a questioning look. His eyes raked over her face, and then putting his hands on her waist, he kissed her.

Wow! If there was one thing Charlie excelled at, it was kissing. Gill felt dizzy. The kiss was so languorous, so soft and so incredibly sexy. She felt quite hot, as they came up for air, and her heart was beating like a drum.

'I've needed to do that since you got in the car.'

Gill simply smiled at him.

'Hungry?' he asked.

She was hungry, but she didn't know if for food or something else. Charlie had that effect on her. For all her best intentions, this man had an incredible aptitude for turning her on.

Gill nodded, and he put his hand in hers as they walked back to the car. Neither said anything.

They drove along the road, until they, as Gill had suspected, took the turning for Cameron House.

As the car swept into the grounds, a seaplane landed on the loch nearby, no doubt bringing some wealthy clients to the hotel. Charlie parked and then they walked together into the Michelin starred restaurant.

The maître d' and a waiter showed them to their table, then offered to take their coats.

Once they were seated and presented with menus, Gill commented, 'Very swish.'

'I thought you might like it. Have you been before?'

'No, I've been to Cameron House, but not this restaurant.'

'Yes, they have several. I love it here. I've stayed here quite a lot over the years. We used to come for golf breaks.'

'My brother lives just down the road.'

'Really? We should pop in on the way back.'

Noting Gill's alarm, Charlie grinned and said, 'Just kidding. The last thing I want to do right now is meet your brother and have him grill me about my intentions towards his sister.'

Gill laughed. 'Chris isn't like that. He's very laid-back.'

'That's good to know, for when I do meet him,' said Charlie.

He was very sure of himself, Gill thought. But then, thinking back to that kiss, no wonder.

Charlie asked Gill if she'd like to choose the wine. Gill accepted the wine list he held out to her, and after being bamboozled by the sheer number of wines the restaurant stocked, and feeling quite faint at some of the prices of the more exclusive ones, she chose a Mâcon Villages. She then turned her attention to the menu and her mouth watered at the array of choices. She opted for the Orkney scallop with wild mushroom, truffle sauce and Bellota ham, whilst Charlie went for langoustine ravioli and braised endive with orange, for starters.

'It all looks delicious,' said Gill, trying hard not to openly salivate. Heavenly smells assailed her senses, as waiters brought food to tables around them.

For mains, Gill decided upon the halibut, and after initially being unable to make up his mind between the roe deer and the sea bass, Charlie opted for the roe deer.

The waiter took their order, and minutes later their bottle of white was opened for them, with the remainder being left to chill in a silver ice bucket.

The food was truly superb. The scallops, so soft and tender, just a tiny bit chargrilled to add that extra depth of flavour, were divine. The halibut, faultless – a meaty fish, in Gill's experience, unless cooked to perfection, it could become chewy and bland, but it was excellent. The wine flowed and Gill forgot her resolution to keep her alcohol intake in check. She was quite simply having a wonderful time, with an incredibly sexy man who had brought her to Cameron House for dinner.

When the meal was over, Gill tried to split the bill with him, as it was pretty hefty. Charlie would have none of it. 'My treat.'

'Then thanks.' Gill smiled warmly at him. 'It was lovely.'

'I'm glad you enjoyed it. How about a short walk to work off our meal?'

Gill readily agreed, and after Charlie had settled the bill, they set off for a walk around the grounds. Every so often Charlie would stop, supposedly to admire the view, but he always found an opportunity to kiss Gill, hold her to him, or brush against her. It was quite thrilling and Gill found herself becoming turned on.

As they headed back towards the car park, Charlie kissed behind Gill's ear and said, 'We don't have to go back, you know.'

Gill stared at him. Being outside had made the alcohol she had drunk treble in effect. Her head was starting to spin, whether from the booze or the company, she couldn't quite make up her mind.

'How do you mean?'

'I booked a suite, just in case you wanted to stay.'

'You what?' Gill tried for indignant, but it didn't quite come out that way, as she was privately a little impressed.

'No pressure. I just took the precaution in case we were having so nice a time, we didn't want to drive back tonight. What do you think?'

What did she think? She wasn't sure – although a lie-down sounded like a great idea at the moment. She really shouldn't have drunk so much wine.

Charlie sensed her hesitation and pounced. 'Tell you what, why don't we take a look? It can't do any harm just to see what it's like. And if you still want to go home tonight, I'll drive you. I've only had two glasses of wine. With the amount of food we've eaten, over the space of a few hours, I'm fine to drive.'

Realising the truth in this, Gill thought, why not? She'd never stayed at Cameron House before. Why not see what the rooms were like? It would be a shame to pass up the chance.

'OK, let's see what it's like, but no pressure?'

'None at all.' Charlie returned to his car and removed an overnight bag. 'Just some essentials.'

They made their way into the hotel, Charlie asked for the key, and after swiping his credit card they headed for the lift.

Charlie let Gill enter the room first. It was incredible. *It must be costing him a fortune.*

Gill took in the sumptuous suite, the four-poster bed, the free-standing bathtub which she glimpsed in the en suite. She copied Charlie when he hung up his jacket, then stood at the window, admiring the view.

'It's stunning,' she said.

'Not as stunning as you,' Charlie said.

Gill jumped. She had thought he was still on the other side of the room. Just being this close to him drove her wild with desire. He smiled at her, gazed into her eyes and kissed her. His hands caressed her back as he pulled her gently towards him. Gill kissed him back. It was difficult to tell who was more aroused. Soon her hands were untucking Charlie's shirt and she stroked his back as he moaned against her. His fingers crept underneath her top, roaming over her stomach until they reached what he sought. He stimulated her nipples through her bra until she gasped. He stopped momentarily whilst he undid the zip on her trousers. Gill giggled and gasped again, as initially he was searching for the zip of her trousers at the front, but merely succeeded in touching a rather heightened part of her. She let her hands travel over his chest, as he continued his ministrations lower down. Finally, she could wait no longer. She unzipped his trousers. Soon they were sprawled across the bed, both of them wearing just their underwear. Gill was thankful to be wearing her second-best lingerie set tonight. She hadn't expected this to be the outcome. But right now she wanted nothing more than to feel Charlie inside her. She felt as if every molecule in her body was on fire. They continued their foreplay until Charlie asked Gill if she was ready for him. As he bit the wrapper off the condom, Gill tingled with anticipation.

There was a knock at the door. Startled, Gill looked at Charlie. He shook his head. The knock came again, more insistent. Irritated, Charlie simply said to Gill, 'They'll realise they have the wrong room and go away in a second. Now, where were we?'

Then whoever was outside began hammering on the door. This dampened their ardour considerably.

'All right, I'm coming,' said Charlie, muttering under his breath, as he threw on his trousers, 'I wish.'

He reached the door and opened it, his expression thunderous. 'Yes?' he barked, ready to annihilate whoever was interrupting him.

'Hello, darling, interrupting something, am I? asked his wife, as she pushed past him into the room.

Chapter Forty-one

Saturday 8 October

'Gill, what on earth are you doing here? Is everything all right?' Her brother's face was full of concern as he led his sobbing sister into the house.

'I'm sorry. I'm just such an idiot.'

'Come in.' Christopher steered her into the living room, where Sarah stared open-mouthed at Gill's unkempt state.

Gill was trembling with shock.

'Sarah, can you make her some sweet tea, please?' Christopher said.

'What's happened? What are you doing up here? How did you get here? I didn't see your car,' her brother asked her as he put his arm around her shoulder then cradled her to his chest when she continued to sob.

'I g-g-got a taxi, f-f-from Cameron House.'

'Cameron House? What were you doing there?'

And then the whole sorry tale unfolded. Gill told him how she had been out with Charlie a few times, how they had gone to Cameron House for dinner and had a lovely time, and that the meal was amazing. She had to stop herself from extolling the virtues of the wonderful food, even in the state she was in and with everything that had happened.

When Sarah returned with the tea, Gill launched into how Charlie had booked a suite, just in case they felt like staying up by the lochside. Christopher's face turned puce with rage.

'I don't really feel very comfortable telling you the next bit, but basically we were just about to…'

'Get jiggy?' Sarah asked helpfully.

'Yes, but then there was a knock at the door.'

'Who was it?' asked Sarah, curious.

'His w-w-wife.'

'I'll kill him,' said Christopher, already reaching for his jacket.

'Chris, no. I think his wife might do that. I can't believe I didn't know he was married. He told me he was divorced.'

'So what happened when his wife turned up?' asked Sarah.

'She burst into the room, pushed past Charlie and when she saw me, turned to him and said, "I knew it. I knew you'd been up to your old tricks – shagging about again."'

'What did you do?' asked Christopher.

'Well, to start with I couldn't do anything. I just froze. It was like time had stopped. I physically couldn't move. I couldn't believe what was happening. And then I turned to Charlie and said, "You're not divorced?" He couldn't even look me in the eye and then his wife shouted at him again, "Oh, is that what you told her?" Then she turned back to me and said, "Cover yourself up, for God's sake." So I did, whilst she yelled at him that she had suspected him of cheating again for some time, so today when he left, she followed him. She wanted to catch him in the act. Then I left them to it. She was screaming blue murder. I went down to reception and the receptionist was really nice, and asked me if I needed a taxi.' Gill paused and then said, 'Charlie didn't even say anything to me before I left.'

'What a complete bastard!' said Sarah.

'If I get my hands on him.' Christopher was shaking with anger.

'Are you all right, though?' Sarah asked. 'You know…'

'We didn't, if that's what you're asking, but we very nearly did.'

The tea and talking about it helped, and Gill soon calmed down. She had sobered up very quickly. Not long after, she went to bed in the spare room and slept a fitful sleep, dreaming of men who were forever letting her down.

Sunday 6 October

Next morning, things seemed a bit brighter. After a hot shower and a loan of some clothes from Sarah, Gill tried to put things in perspective. But she'd made one key decision. First thing, she e-mailed Caroline Morgan and told her she didn't want her to send her any more dates and informed her she was cancelling her subscription. She gave her no further details, although she hesitated over whether to tell her that Charlie was married. Eventually she decided his wife had probably put him off the idea of cheating, at least for the moment.

With the dawn of a new day, Gill felt better. Her little nephews squealed with delight when their parents told them Aunt Gill had come for a sleepover. They bounded into her room, jumped on her bed and relayed to her the exploits of their favourite wrestlers – their main topic of conversation. It warmed her heart to see how excited they were to see her. At least their devotion was real. Pity she couldn't invoke that in a man. She ruminated on the fact that the only men she could depend on in her life were her father, her brother and two under-sevens.

She spent a lovely day with her nephews and it did her good. When lunch was served around three, they all piled into the kitchen laughing and exhausted. After a quick wash, they sat down and tucked into the Sunday roast which Sarah had prepared. She had even made dessert from scratch to cheer Gill up.

'You're welcome to stay here tonight again if you want,' Christopher said.

'Thanks, but I need to get back. I have things to organise for work tomorrow.' She also didn't want to invade their home any more than she needed to. Plus her nephews had been just the tonic she needed. She felt miles better already.

Gill had texted Debbie and asked her if she would mind convening an emergency girls' meeting on Monday night. She needed to talk with her friends, figure out what she was doing wrong where men were concerned. The agency had been her last hope – more like loss of hope.

Back home, Gill checked her phone, just in case Chancer Charlie had deigned to get in touch, but nothing. What was it with men treating her badly and then never getting in contact? Maybe she would have been better off with someone like Gary, someone who didn't set her pulse racing, but who was dependable, even if a little misguided sometimes.

Chapter Forty-two

Monday 7 October

Mercifully Gill's day had flown by – a busy one, but busy in a good way, two more new clients won, and Amanda was really beginning to settle in.

By six thirty, Gill was already in Chez Molinières waiting for the girls. Brett, the Aussie barman, smiled at her as he served her the mojito she'd asked for.

See? Not all men are bastards.

Angela arrived first, hugged Gill and gave her a sympathetic smile. Some of what had occurred between Gill and Charlie had obviously already made it through the grapevine.

Shortly afterwards, the other two arrived. They ordered dinner and then the girls sat back to listen to Gill's tale of woe.

When she finished, the girls, as one, stared at her dumbstruck. For the first time in Gill's memory, she witnessed Lisa speechless.

'What a complete bastard!' said Angela, saying what everyone else was thinking.

Lisa finally broke her silence by saying, 'It sounds like something that would happen in a film.'

Gill shrugged. 'No, that's just my life.'

'Poor you. Have you heard from him since?' Debbie asked.

'Nope, but then I didn't really expect to. What was he going to say? *"I'm sorry my wife caught me about to shag you."*'

The girls murmured their agreement. Then Lisa, typical glass half-full girl, lifted everyone's spirits, 'Fuck him. He doesn't deserve you. So, how are you getting on with Barcelona Man? What was his name again?'

'Liam. Fine. I'm seeing him on Wednesday.'

'Where are you off to this time?' Angela asked.

'He's going to cook for me.'

'Impressive,' Debbie said, and Lisa nodded her approval.

'Well, I haven't tasted it yet, mind–' Gill laughed '–but it's a nice gesture.'

'Do you know what he's making?' Lisa asked.

'No, it's a surprise.'

'Oh, you like surprises,' Debbie said.

'Actually, I'm kind of going off them, given how my last few have turned out.'

The other three fell silent at this then Debbie said, 'I'm sure that's not going to happen this time. I have a good feeling about this guy.'

'I had a good feeling about the others, too,' groaned Gill.

By the time they all went their separate ways a few hours later, and a little before the staff turfed them out, Gill felt considerably better.

As she sat in the taxi, Gill hummed an Abba song which she had heard as they left the restaurant. Surely that was a good omen.

Tuesday 8 October

Since dinner was at Liam's house, Gill didn't want to be too overdressed. In the end, she wore a long rose-coloured skirt, a white open-necked blouse and minimal jewellery; just a watch and a necklet with a glass rose. She'd picked up a bottle of wine and a cheese selection, on the way home. She was more nervous than she had expected. Perhaps because everything had gone so wrong on her dates recently, but her stomach was in knots.

So they could both relax and have a drink together, Gill opted to take a taxi. At seven thirty exactly, Gill arrived at Liam's flat in Maryhill. She pressed the buzzer and tried to shield herself from the driving rain as she waited. Liam answered the intercom with a cheery, 'Come on up.'

Gill ascended the two flights of stairs, noting with surprise that the inside of the close was carpeted with a rich red weave. Plants adorned either side of the staircase and the walls were tiled in a cobalt blue and white, Spanish mosaic style. Liam and his neighbours clearly liked to take care of their hallway.

When she reached the top of the second flight of stairs, Liam was leaning against the door frame, waiting for her.

'Hey.' He leaned forward and kissed her on the cheek.

'Hi. Something smells good,' Gill said, as they walked together into the flat.

'It's nearly ready. Hope you're hungry.'

Gill had to stop herself from telling him that she was always hungry.

'These are for you.' She handed him the two bottles of wine. 'I wasn't sure which you'd prefer, so I got one of each.'

'You shouldn't have bothered, but thanks. Montepulciano d'Abruzzo and Marlborough Sauvignon Blanc. Hmm, difficult to decide. Depends what mood I'm in. But either will go well with tonight's meal.'

'So what are we having?' Gill asked, as she climbed onto the bar stool Liam offered her, so they could talk whilst he finished preparing dinner.

'We're having king prawn cocktail – I made the sauce myself – it's very light, just in case you find cocktail sauce sickening. Then we're having chicken cacciatore, or hunter's chicken, which is the smell you picked up on when you came in.'

'It smells lovely. I wish I could cook like that,' said Gill. She could have kicked herself straight after she said it. She didn't need Liam to know she was useless in the kitchen.

'Don't you cook, then?'

Coming clean, Gill said, 'Well, let's just say no one's beating down my door to have me host my own cookery programme.'

Liam smiled. 'I'm sure you're not as bad as you think.'

'Oh no, I am.'

'Well, what can you make?'

Gill thought for a bit and then said, 'Chicken breast wrapped in Parma ham, filled with Roulé cheese.'

'There, that sounds good. What's wrong with that?'

'Glad you like it, because if you're ever at mine, that's what you'll be eating, whether it's for breakfast, lunch or dinner! I mean, obviously it wouldn't be for breakfast. Not that you would be at mine for breakfast.' Gill was digging herself into a deeper hole.

Liam decided to rescue her again, 'Don't worry, I know what you meant. Anyway, what would you like to drink? I have Chablis, White Zinfandel or Shiraz, or you can have some of the Montepulciano d'Abruzzo you brought, if you'd prefer that.'

'Erm, I think the Chablis, since we're having prawns to start.'

'And may I just say, Madam, I think that's an excellent choice.' He poured them each a glass. 'Cheers.'

They spent a wonderful evening together. The prawns were perfectly cooked and the sauce, as promised, was very light, not the usual mass-produced muck often served in restaurants. The chicken cacciatore tasted delicious, and the roast potatoes and parsnips which Liam had teamed it up with were cooked to perfection. The honey glaze made the parsnips very moreish.

'I'm stuffed,' said Gill, groaning slightly. 'Your chicken cacciatore was so good I couldn't leave any of it.'

'Now that's a good sign. Do you think you can roll yourself through to the living room and we can have a little break before our cheese course?'

'Yes, I think I can just about manage that.'

They sat facing each other on Liam's sofa, reclined at opposite ends, with their bare feet tucked up under them, as they got to know each other a bit better. With Liam, Gill didn't feel under any pressure. She liked him and he liked her, but she didn't have the impression he was waiting for an opportunity to pounce on her. They were just taking things nice and slow, exactly what she needed.

After an hour or so of enjoyable conversation and playing around with Liam's iPod, choosing different tracks they both enjoyed, and discussing genres of music and when were the best eras, Liam said, 'Coffee? Biscuits and cheese?'

'I'm still full, but I could manage a coffee.'

'Well, if I brought the biscuits and cheese through for me, and you chose to nibble one or two, would that be OK?'

Gill laughed. 'Yes, I suppose. C'mon. I'll help you.'

They both returned to the kitchen where Liam prepared the coffee and looked out a cheeseboard and cheese knives.

'That's a really nice selection: lovely ripe, smelly brie; Wensleydale – I always have to say that in a Wallace voice, I can't help it – creamy Stilton and Jarlsberg. I love them all,' Liam said.

'Me too. Here, let me.' Gill took the tray containing the cheeseboard, knives, butter and grapes – he was going all out – and carried it through to the living room, leaving Liam to bring the coffee.

'I can't believe you have a real coffee pot. I don't know anyone who has one, not even my parents, but I love it.'

'Yes, it's sterling silver. It was my parents'. It's very decadent, I know, but I love it. On a Sunday, I get the papers, make myself some real coffee and have it through here. That's my chill-out thing. Or sometimes I'll sit at the dining table in the kitchen and spread the papers out there.'

'Sounds relaxing.'

'It is. So, what do you get up to at the weekends?'

Gill paused for a second. 'Well, apart from a regular lunch date with my brother and his family on Sunday afternoons, whatever, really. Out with friends, chilling out at home or unfortunately doing housework, as the weekend's the only time I get to do it.'

'I know what you mean, but I'm lucky. I have a woman who comes in three hours a week and does the majority for me. She even irons my shirts, which is great.'

'Yes, I keep meaning to try to arrange something, but then I tell myself, it's only me. Surely I should be able to keep it tidy? Sorry–' Gill broke off, realising that she might have just made out Liam was lazy and incompetent '–I just meant...'

'It's OK. No offence taken.'

Gill did eventually succumb to eating one or two crackers and cheese, for which she blamed Liam entirely. They were sitting on the floor, sifting through his DVD collection. Liam poured more coffee into Gill's cup. As he did so, his hand grazed hers. With a jolt, Gill looked at him. That was the moment. She knew he was going to kiss her and she wanted him to. They'd had a lovely evening. When he cradled her face in his hands, and his lips met hers, Gill responded and opened herself up to the kiss, which lasted an incredibly long time.

'I can't believe I've managed to hold back all night without doing that.' Liam laughed.

'I know. It's ridiculous. I was beginning to wonder if something was wrong with me,' Gill joked, then put her hands on her hips in a mock-indignant stance – rather difficult since she was sitting down.

'No, there's absolutely–' Liam kissed her neck '–nothing–' then her collar bone '–wrong with you.' His lips returned to hers, and they kissed and they kissed some more.

He really is a very good kisser. It hadn't set her on fire, as it had with Charlie and Anton. It was different, but very good. Interestingly, she didn't want to sleep with him – not yet. She knew she shouldn't sleep with him. Something intrinsic made her want to spend as much time as possible simply kissing this man, without going any further. *Kissing is very underrated.*

An hour later, Gill left in a taxi, with a permanent smile fixed on her face.

As Liam watched her get safely into the taxi, he congratulated himself on an excellent evening. The meal had gone down well and the wine had flowed, although he noticed Gill stopped him topping up her glass a few times. The *pièce de resistance* had to be kissing Gill. Her lips were the softest he'd ever kissed, full and with only a hint of lipstick. There was an air of vulnerability about her. An occasional comment or change of subject had made him notice she was holding back about certain things. It seemed obvious to Liam that someone had hurt her, perhaps fairly recently. He didn't want to be her rebound guy, but what he did know was that he wanted Gill McFadden in his life. He was a patient man and good people were hard to find, he'd discovered. Gill was a good person. He had an instinct about these things and he wasn't going to let her go.

Chapter Forty-three

October

Leaves fell hard and fast from the trees as autumn took hold. The wind, wild and relentless, buffeted Gill as she waited for a bus into town. She was meeting Liam at the cinema. They were off to see a thriller – a mutual choice. It had been two weeks since the meal at his flat, and they had been out a further four times.

She still hadn't slept with him, and although they had fooled around with each other, they were in no hurry. It was freeing to not be constantly thinking about how to juggle her various dates, but know that she had someone who liked her, a lot, whom she could spend time with as part of a couple. They had no set routine, rather they just arranged at the end of each date when they would see each other again; it was rarely more than a few days. Gill had stifled a laugh when Liam had suggested ten-pin bowling. Not about to enlighten him with regard to Sean, she agreed. This time, however, she made sure she wore jeans and stayed well back from the line.

One night, Gill had joined Liam for coffee in town, where he had been meeting some friends earlier in the day. A few had hung around, apparently because they had lost track of time. But, as Liam told her, they were vetting her suitability. She liked that his friends looked out for him.

Liam had been to her house for dinner. She had bought posh ready meals and champagne, and made a real effort with the table, the lighting – candles of course – and the mood music. Since she couldn't cook, she'd wanted to add a sense of occasion with the drinks, hence the bubbly. They'd also gone for Thai food to a restaurant in Argyle St, which was new to Gill. It didn't quite match up to Fountain of Siam, but it was decent. Plus, it lacked the melodrama of her last visit to a Thai restaurant.

Gill rounded the corner to the cinema and saw Liam lounging against the pillar waiting for her.

'Hi.' He kissed her full on the mouth. 'Missed you.'

'I missed you, too.' Gill gave him a full-beam smile. 'Got the tickets?'

'Yep.' Liam patted his pocket. 'Let's go and get some nachos.'

The film was pretty good, although a couple of times, Gill hid her face at a scary part, whilst Liam laughed at her and cuddled into her. 'You've nothing to be afraid of. I'm here.'

'I know it's just a film,' she said, 'but it seems so real. You could imagine that happening.'

Liam clasped her hand in his and they watched the rest of the film, Gill occasionally resting her head on his shoulder.

'So, what do you want to do? It's still relatively early. We could go for a drink or a snack, if you like?'

'We could,' agreed Gill.

'Or we could go back to mine,' offered Liam.

'We could do that, too. Do you have any food in?'

'Yep, I could rustle us up an omelette, pasta, or even

some cheese toasties.'

Gill laughed. 'Do you know, I haven't had a cheese toastie for ages. You've just put me in the mood for it. C'mon.'

They headed over to the car park diagonally opposite the cinema and retrieved Liam's car.

Back in Maryhill, Liam busied himself making them cheese and tomato toasties. 'Do you want Marmite on yours?'

'Ugh, no! Marmite's evil.' Gill pulled a face.

'I love it, it's delicious.' Liam dipped a teaspoon in the Marmite jar and then licked it clean.

'That is disgusting. I hope you're not going to double dip!'

'Not at all,' he replied, rinsing the teaspoon under the tap. 'I suppose you either love Marmite or you hate it. C'mere, give me a kiss.'

'No way!' Gill pushed him away gently, but forcibly. 'I can't stand the smell of it, never mind the taste. I'll kiss you once you've got rid of the Marmite taste.'

Laughing, Liam said, 'You could be waiting some time.'

'Well,' said Gill wickedly, 'we'll just have to see who caves in first.'

They took their toasties and mugs of tea through to the living room, where they sat on the floor, side by side.

Liam flicked on the TV and said, 'What do you want to watch?'

'I don't mind – another film perhaps?'

'Let's see what we've got then.' He channel-hopped for a few minutes, before leaving it on a romcom.

After they had finished their tea and toasties, Liam

paused the film and fetched them some wine. They lay on the couch intertwined, laughing at some of the heroine's more hilarious escapades.

At eleven thirty, when the film was over, Gill said, 'I better go. Can you call me a taxi?'

Liam looked at her seriously, took her hand and said, 'Gill, I don't want you to go. I'd like you to stay.'

Gill hesitated. They still hadn't slept together and she wasn't sure she was mentally ready for that yet. As if reading her mind, Liam said hurriedly, 'We don't need to, you know. I just want you to sleep beside me and be there in the morning when I wake up.'

Gill was torn. She wanted to stay, but she didn't know if her willpower would hold out if Liam did try to make love to her. She liked him a lot, but she had been very hurt by both Anton and Charlie, and she was being ultra-cautious. Weighing everything up, she eventually said, 'OK, but no funny business.' She smacked him playfully on the arm.

'None whatsoever,' said Liam as he tackled her and they rolled on the floor, where they kissed and kissed and kissed.

Eventually Liam led her by the hand into his bedroom and, after an inordinate amount of kissing, touching and stroking each other, they fell asleep in each other's arms.

'Morning, sleepy.' Liam shook Gill gently.

Gill struggled to open her eyes. She'd had the best sleep in ages and not even in her own bed. Although they hadn't had sex, perhaps the overall feeling of well-being had made her go into a deep sleep. Gill often thought foreplay without sex could be just as stimulating, and in many cases better than the final act. Having to hold herself back, wanting to do more, but psychologically knowing she wasn't ready proved quite a turn-on. Sleepily, she raised herself up on one elbow until she drew level with Liam, sitting on the bed beside her.

'Hope you're hungry. I've made quite a spread.' He gestured to the breakfast tray on the bedside cabinet.

'You're not kidding!' Gill surveyed the contents which would have fed a family of five. She didn't like to tell him she didn't usually eat much first thing in the morning, preferring to wait until a few hours after waking. Her eyes fell upon the muesli with side order of fresh raspberries and blueberries. Hot buttered toast, pancakes, orange juice and freshly brewed coffee completed her sumptuous breakfast.

'And if you're still hungry after that, I can do you a full cooked.'

'I don't think that'll be necessary.' Gill looked at him in alarm. 'What are you having?'

'Well, I've had some toast, but I'm going to make myself a bacon roll in a minute. I just wanted to bring you breakfast in bed and steal one of your raspberries,' he said, nicking one before Gill's hand could swat him away.

'Paws off! People have died for less,' joked Gill.

'OK, lesson learned. Right, I'm off for a shower and then I'm making bacon rolls. Enjoy!'

Gill surveyed the laden tray in front of her. A tear formed in her eye. She couldn't remember the last time anyone had done something so nice for her. No one had ever brought her breakfast in bed. At thirty-seven, this was the first time someone had been kind enough to spoil her in this way. Wasn't that rather sad?

By the time Liam returned, barefoot and wearing only a pair of Levis, Gill had demolished a good portion of her breakfast.

Freshly shaved, his skin felt baby soft as he kissed her. Soon he removed the tray and climbed on the bed, reaching for her.

Retrieving his discarded Levis from the floor, Liam said, 'Bacon roll?'

'No, I'm good, thanks.'

'Well, how about I make two and you eat half of one? I always find one is never enough, but two is too much.'

Gill reflected upon this and then said, 'You've convinced me. I'm going to take a shower, if that's OK?'

'Yep, just don't be too long. Bacon roll will be on the table in ten minutes.'

As Gill stood under the jets of Liam's power shower, she realised she felt happy – very happy. When was the last time she had felt this happy? Unexpectedly her thoughts turned to Anton. She did not want to go there. She wouldn't let him spoil this moment. He was the main reason she still hadn't slept with Liam.

After brunch, Liam drove Gill home for a change of clothes. Then they headed back to the west end and the Botanic Gardens. Gill had never been and Liam said she absolutely had to go.

Liam was surprisingly knowledgeable about a lot of the flowers found in the Botanic Gardens and could even tell Gill a little of the gardens' history. Once they had examined the contents of the famous glasshouses, they walked alongside the nature trails which flanked the River Kelvin, chatting and laughing together. Onlookers smiled, noticing the couple, so clearly in love and enjoying their Saturday stroll. As they visited the arboretum on the return from their walk, Gill glanced over at Liam and couldn't believe how lucky she was.

Chapter Forty-four

November

'Do you want a Mai-Tai or a glass of wine?' Gill called through from the kitchen.

'Mai-Tai,' said Angela.

'Wine for me,' shouted Debbie.

'Mai-Tai for me,' Lisa yelled.

As Gill whisked up three Mai-Tais and poured a glass of wine for Debbie, she smiled and thought how great this was. Her life felt so right – balanced. Work was going really well. The conversion rate since Angus started had gone through the roof. He just seemed to have the Midas touch. Amanda was enjoying her new role; she and Janice got on famously and complemented each other well. Gill found herself with so much time to do things that she had wanted to do for years: plan for the future and revise her five-year business plan among other things. It wasn't beyond the realm of possibility that she would be able to take on another recruitment consultant in the spring, if business continued to go so well. But then she'd need to start thinking about getting larger premises.

It was Angela's birthday and they had arranged to have a girls' night in at Gill's house. They would go out at the weekend for dinner, but for now, they were having cocktails, wine, eighties music, a bit of chat and perhaps a romantic comedy.

'Thirty-eight, Angela, how does it feel?' asked Lisa.

'Er, exactly the same as thirty-seven.'

'But you're sooo much older now.' Lisa loved to wind Angela up. Just because it was Angela's birthday, it didn't mean Lisa would go easy on her. Angela, knowing her friend well, chose to ignore her. Instead she related to them the hilarious escapades at her school. The headmaster was besotted with a new teaching assistant in her early twenties, who had a gorgeous boyfriend, and who was completely unaware of her charms. Angela, herself, was apparently the object of a nerdy fourteen-year-old's crush, and it pained her to see the teenager go through the whole unrequited love process.

A once chubby girl had turned into a bit of a fox, in the space of a few months, and the very same boys who had been teasing her last term were now ogling her and angling for a date. To her credit, she was having none of it and politely, but firmly declined them all.

'That's what we need from our youth: more strong, independent women. Good for her,' said Lisa, munching on a breadstick. 'Gill, how long did you say this Chinese would be?'

'They said forty minutes.' Gill glanced at the clock. 'That was about twenty minutes ago. I have some olives if you've eaten all the breadsticks.' She gestured pointedly at the empty breadstick box.

'You didn't want any, did you, Debbie? Angela?' said Lisa, trying to justify her greediness.

'Well, we didn't get much of a chance. I think we should just call you The Bin,' said Debbie.

'Fine by me,' said Lisa sweetly, 'but I never put on any weight, so I can eat what I like.'

'And you do,' muttered Angela. 'And here was me wanting a birthday breadstick,' she joked.

'Ah, you know, once you hit forty it's so much more difficult to lose weight.'

'I'm thirty-eight,' Angela reminded Lisa through gritted teeth.

'Right, you two, ding ding.' Debbie rang an imaginary bell. 'Time out.'

Angela took the opportunity to change the subject. 'So, Gill, tell us more about Luscious Liam?'

Gill sat cross-legged, sipping her Mai-Tai, and told the girls what she and Liam had been up to, or most of what they had been up to, since she last saw them.

'So have you slept with him yet?' Lisa asked straight out.

'Lisa!' Debbie chastised her. 'That's up to Gill to tell us if she wants. You shouldn't ask.'

'We're all wondering. I'm just verbalising.'

'Something you should do less often,' said Angela under her breath.

'Ahem, I am here, you know.' Gill gave them both a look, which resulted in a 'Sorry,' from Debbie and a 'Well?' from Lisa.

'If you must know, no, I haven't slept with him yet. Or rather, I have slept with him, in his bed, several times, but we haven't had sex.'

Lisa snorted. 'How is that even possible?'

'It's called self-control,' said Gill, 'and self-preservation.'

'But you've been seeing him for how long now? A

month? A little more than that?' Lisa asked. 'And you've seen each other at least two or three times a week. Don't you want to?'

'Lisa, leave it,' snapped Debbie, uncharacteristically.

They waited for Gill to say something. Finally after a long pause, she said, 'I do want to make love to him, and to be honest, we already have, loads of foreplay, and it's all amazing, but something's holding me back from taking that final step.'

Lisa, realising she'd overstepped the mark, said a bit more diplomatically, 'And he's been OK about it? About you not…'

'He's been great. I think he may have had a rough time in the past, too.'

'When it's the right time, you'll know.' Debbie rubbed her friend's back and gave her a hug.

'I know. I'll feel it.'

Angela threw Lisa a warning glance, as she knew it was on the tip of her tongue to make a smutty remark.

The buzzer rang, indicating the arrival of their takeaway. The girls busied themselves arranging the food onto plates to be heated up in the microwave, and the subject was forgotten.

They had a fantastic evening: bitching about men, drooling over the lead in the romcom, and reliving all their yesterdays via the medium of music.

Around one, the girls left as they all had work in the morning. Just as she was going to bed, Gill noticed a light flashing on her phone, signalling a new text message. Liam. *Hope you had a great night with the girls. I missed you tonight and can't wait to see you tomorrow, Liam, x.*

Smiling, Gill prepared for bed, thinking of the question

Lisa had asked her. She felt the answer was *soon*. The right moment would be very soon.

The rest of the week flew by and soon Friday night arrived. Gill was due to meet Liam's friends properly for the first time. They were going for drinks in Merchant City. It was one of his friends' birthday and apparently they always celebrated in style. Gill deliberated at length over what to wear, even though Liam had told her not to fuss, she looked great in anything. But she could tell that he was secretly pleased at her extra effort.

The evening went well. The birthday drinks event was pretty raucous. They were a very sociable crowd and two of the girls, Kirstin and Petra, took Gill under their wing, keen that she shouldn't feel intimidated by some of the louder components in their party. Liam stayed by her side most of the evening, apart from when called upon to sing karaoke as a forfeit. The girls tried to quiz Gill on her feelings for Liam, but Gill shrugged non-committally, and just said things were going well. A look exchanged between the two made Gill think she was missing something, but she let it go. She was having too good a time to stop and analyse anything.

Liam and Gill had decided in advance that they would stay at Gill's that night. It would be the first time Liam had slept over at hers. But it made sense since they were out in the Merchant City and they planned to visit Pollok House, on the south side of the city, on Sunday morning. Then Gill would head up to Balloch for Sunday lunch with Christopher and Sarah.

They said their goodbyes to Liam's motley crew of friends, all in various states of drunkenness, and flagged down a taxi. They crossed the River Clyde around midnight and by quarter past were already back at Gill's flat.

'I've had enough to drink,' said Liam.

'Me too. I think I'm going to have a hot chocolate.'

'Hot chocolate! I haven't had that in years. Can I have some, too?' he asked, wrapping his arms around Gill's waist and laying his head on her shoulder. 'I feel quite tired, actually.'

'Me too. Your friends must have taken it out of us,' Gill smiled at him.

'They are a bit mad, but their hearts are in the right place.'

Gill handed Liam a steaming mug of hot chocolate and took a sip of hers.

'What do you fancy?' She was just about to say, film or music, when she saw the familiar gleam in his eye. 'OK, on second thoughts, why don't we just go through to the living room and see?'

Liam followed her and they sat on the sofa, mugs perched beside them. Something was brewing. Something irrevocable had changed – for Gill at least. She was ready. When Liam kissed her, she let him know something was out of the ordinary by responding even more ardently than usual. She untucked his shirt, her hands pressing against the firm contours of his chest and stomach, before sliding up his back. Suddenly their movements became more urgent. Gill knew, beyond doubt, that she wanted Liam, all of him, tonight. As they discarded layer after layer of clothing, Liam kissed Gill's throat, then her eyelids, then finally her lips. As they reached the point of no return, Gill gasped, 'Liam, I want you.'

'I want you, too,' Liam groaned.

'No, Liam, I want you inside me.'

Exhaling sharply, Liam scrabbled for his trousers, withdrew his wallet and took out a condom, which he deftly put on.

Kissing Gill gently on the lips, he asked, 'Are you sure?'

'Yeees.' Gill could barely contain herself. Needing no more invitation, as they were both already very aroused, Liam entered her and suddenly Gill wondered why she had waited so long.

They had to slow down a few times. Liam was afraid he might come, and he wanted Gill to enjoy the experience as much as he was.

They made love three times, before deciding they really did need some sleep.

As Gill lay in Liam's embrace, she felt content and glad that she had met this wonderful man who was starting to mean so much to her.

The following week

Gill's parents would be arriving any minute. They hadn't visited her for over a year. They hadn't exactly given her a great deal of notice either. Just the week before, her mother rang to say they were coming up to Scotland to spend a few days with Christopher and their grandchildren, and then on the return leg they would spend the weekend in Glasgow with Gill. Perhaps they could go to a show, have some dinner? Normally Gill would have been delighted to spend some time and go to the Kings' with her parents, but she was in the first flush of love, and eager to spend every minute with Liam. Even the girls had said they didn't mind, as long as they saw her in a few weeks' time. They all remembered how it felt, even if for some, it had been too long since they had last experienced it.

Plus Gill's parents didn't know about Liam. She hadn't met his brother yet and his parents were dead. She supposed she *had* met his friends, whereas he hadn't met hers. But it was still a bit of a stressful situation. It meant something – meeting your girlfriend's parents. Was that what she was – Liam's girlfriend? Did he view her as such? How did you know? Was there a deadline that you observed, after which you were termed as being exclusive to each other? Gill had debated for a few days whether to fob Liam off that weekend, but in the end, she decided to tell him about her parents' visit, invite him to dinner, and if he fancied going to see a show, then she'd get him a ticket, too.

Liam had been surprisingly relaxed about it all and said he would love to meet her parents. Gill definitely felt more nervous than he did. She'd spoken to Christopher to ensure he didn't fill his mother in on Gill's love life. He had agreed, as long as he and Sarah were next on the list to meet Liam. After all, Christopher pointed out, they did only live in Balloch.

'Mum, Dad.' Gill hugged and kissed her parents. 'Let me help you with your bags.'

As Gill brought in the bags, her mother walked alongside her. 'No, not that one, Gill. That's just dirty washing. That can stay in the car.

'You can use my machine, you know.'

'No, it's quite all right. It can wait until we get home. Robert, where did you put the wine we bought for Gill?' her mother asked.

'It's behind the passenger seat,' Gill's father called to his wife, from where he was busy trying to wedge open the outer door to Gill's flat.

'It's good to see you, Mum.'

'And you, darling. You do look well. You're positively glowing. Or maybe it's just the cold weather?'

Gill tried not to sigh. It was typical of her mother to give a compliment and just as quickly snatch it away. Carrying the remainder of the bags towards the flat, Gill took a deep breath and ascended the stairs.

'Tea or coffee?' Gill asked her parents, once they were suitably ensconced on her sofas. Her father was a little out of breath and she couldn't help feeling concerned for him. He seemed much frailer than last time she had seen him. She made a mental note to call them more often. Her mother, of course, was much more resilient. She'd probably outlive them all.

'Gill, there are some biscuits in that bag. No, not that one,' her mother scolded, 'the blue and white checked one. That's it – a luxury chocolate biscuit selection.'

'I do have biscuits, Mum.'

'I know, dear, but I know what we like.'

Gill bit her tongue. Her mother could be infuriating sometimes and she needed to keep the peace, since she was about to hit them with a major piece of news.

As they sat catching up on the gossip from her brother's and from her parents' neighbours, Gill waited for the right moment to bring up Liam, and the fact that he would be joining them for dinner and the theatre that evening.

Her opportunity soon appeared when her mother asked her what she had been up to, after, of course, reprimanding her for rarely calling them.

That works both ways, thought Gill.

First of all, she told them of the developments at the agency, and her new recruits. Her father nodded approvingly, delighted that the business was doing so well. Her mother tried to pry about facts and figures, but Gill remained vague, not wishing to be sidetracked from her purpose.

Then she talked about Debbie and how well Olivia was doing at school. Likewise when her mother asked after Angela, she told her she was doing well at the school where she taught, and that her son, Matthew, was also thriving. Gill's mother never missed an opportunity to comment on what a shame it was that Matthew's father didn't live with them.

Gill gritted her teeth and changed the subject. Finally, she talked about her trip to Barcelona and the bizarre circumstances which led to her meeting Liam.

'So, are you seeing this man, this Liam?' Her mother's forehead had scrunched up.

'Yes, we've been seeing each other for a few months now.' It was a little under two months, but her mother didn't need all the details.

After subjecting Gill to a thorough grilling on Liam, his prospects and his intentions towards her daughter, Gill's mother finally asked, 'So, are we getting to meet this one? We didn't meet the last one.'

Thank God for that, thought Gill.

'Well, actually, I've invited him to have dinner with us tonight, and he quite fancied going to see *Dirty Dancing,* too.'

'A man who wants to go and see a musical.' Her mother seemed torn between wondering if he was sent from heaven or gay. Meanwhile, Gill's father had perked up considerably at the news that another male would be present at the evening's proceedings.

As soon as she politely could, Gill slipped away to call Liam. 'Hey, how are you?'

'Good, you? Has the eagle landed?'

'Don't know about the eagle, but two pensioners, one very opinionated and who would give Hyacinth Bucket a run for her money, are here.'

Liam laughed. 'I'm sure she's not that bad.'

'Well, don't tell me I didn't warn you.'

'What time are we meeting at?'

'I thought we could meet at the restaurant at six thirty. The show starts at eight thirty. That gives us plenty time.'

'OK, I'm looking forward to it.'

Gill only wished she was.

She needn't have worried. Liam charmed her mother more than she would have imagined possible. At certain points, she was sure her jaw was hanging open, given how girlish her mother was around Liam, and how she would pat him on the hand and say 'Oh, you!'

Liam and her father had surprisingly a lot to talk about – not least when her father asked about the best way to regrout his bathroom tiles. Talk of hillwalking done in earlier years and golf also kept them occupied, and dinner passed all too quickly. Gill breathed a sigh of relief and crossed her fingers as they left the restaurant and headed for the theatre.

'What a wonderful performance!' said Gill's mother when the final curtain came down. Like the majority of the audience, she had given the cast of *Dirty Dancing* a standing ovation. Even Liam, who had come more for the sense of occasion than because he liked musicals, he'd admitted to Gill's dad, remarked on what a great job the cast had done.

They all tumbled into the taxi which Liam flagged down and soon they were heading over the river to the south side and back to Gill's flat.

Her mum was a little tipsy – a couple of glasses of wine, with her slight frame, and she was giggling like a schoolgirl. Gill stifled a laugh. It was hilarious watching her mum with Liam. Gill gave him the thumbs up as he regaled her parents with another tale from his repertoire, whilst she organised the drinks.

The four sat chatting happily together, Gill's father more animated than she'd seen him in years, whilst they drank their spirits and liqueurs. Whisky for Gill's father and Liam, Baileys for her mum, and Gill stuck to wine. Mixing her drinks gave her a hell of a hangover.

A few hours later, Gill's mum excused herself for yawning. Gill gave Liam a look. Liam said, 'Don't be silly, Mary. It's been a long day for you both. You've done well, quite frankly, to last the pace today. We'll let you get some rest.'

Gill's mum glanced at her daughter, as if to say *'What a sweet boy.'*

Gill brought bedding through to her parents and then said, 'Night, see you in the morning. Sleep well.'

'Night, love,' said her dad.

'Night, darling, lovely to meet you, Liam.' Her mother shook a bewildered Liam's hand.

As Gill and Liam closed the living room door behind them and entered Gill's bedroom, Liam said, 'I don't think they know I'm staying. Should I go?'

'No-o-o. Don't be silly. If they haven't worked it out,

that's their problem. I'm thirty-seven and it's my flat,' Gill said, then silenced his protestation with a kiss. Soon a pile of discarded clothes lay beside the bed, as Gill and Liam slid in between the sheets, covering each other's body with their own.

Fifteen minutes later, Liam stifled a moan as he whispered in Gill's ear, 'I'm coming, Gill, I'm coming,'

They collapsed together, exhausted.

Suddenly the door opened and the light went on, as Gill, horrified, heard her mother say, 'Gill, I can't get the sofa bed mechanism…aargh!'

'Mum, put the light off, please. I'll be through in a minute.'

For all his attempts to slide under the covers, Liam was still partially visible, on top of Gill. Gill was mortified, but Liam even more so.

'Oh my God, do you think your father will challenge me to a duel?' he said, trying to make light of it.

'I can't believe my mother walked in on us. Hasn't she heard of knocking?' Gill was outraged. 'I'm really sorry. Let me just go and deal with this sofa bed. I won't be a minute.'

Steeling herself, Gill slipped on her terry-towelling robe and left the room.

'Mum, what's the problem?'

Her parents fell silent as she entered. News obviously travelled fast, as they both turned to her guiltily. It was clear her mother had been divulging to her father that she had just interrupted Gill and Liam in bed.

She stared at them expectantly, daring them to take issue with her sleeping with her boyfriend, in her own home.

Her mother lowered her eyes first. 'I can't get the mechanism to release,' she finally said.

Relieved, sensing the moment had passed, Gill said, 'It's easy, look. You slip your fingers under here, push and voilà.' The bed sprang open and she helped her father unfold it to its full size.

'Thanks,' said her mother.

'Right, do you need anything else, or can I go back to bed?'

'No, we should be OK now, dear.' Her father smiled at her.

'Great, night then.'

Just as Gill was closing the door, her mother said, 'Oh, Gill?'

'Yes?'

'Will Liam want breakfast in the morning?'

Trying not to laugh, Gill turned to her mother and said, 'Full cooked, I should think. Night.'

As Liam and Gill lay in bed later, trying not to laugh at the sheer embarrassment of her mother walking in on them, Gill felt that things were finally working out for her.

Chapter Forty-five

December

The driving November rain had been replaced by the splendid, but deceptive December sunshine, which tricked you into thinking it was warm outside, when in reality it was bitterly cold. A scarf, hat and gloves were a prerequisite.

Gill shivered despite her warm coat, as she unlocked the main door to the building, before entering the agency. Even with the heaters on full, due to the old windows the rooms were not as toasty as she would have liked. She kept on her coat as she brewed the coffee.

When her team arrived, within five minutes of each other, Gill stopped working and came through to offer them tea and coffee.

'I want to talk to you about something.'

'Sounds ominous,' said Janice. Amanda seemed a little worried, whereas Angus merely appeared interested.

'Nothing to worry about, quite the opposite,' said Gill cheerfully, as she bustled around, preparing the drinks.

Gill finally placed the mugs on the table in front of her staff and said, 'I was thinking we should have a Christmas party. I know it's late and most places will be booked up, but I've done a little research and there are three places in town which still have some availability for the week before

Christmas. I just wanted to ask you all if you fancied it, before I book it.'

'Oh, we've never had a Christmas party,' said Janice, rubbing her hands together in glee. 'Not a real one, anyway, with it just being you and me,' she said to Gill.

'When would it be?' Angus asked. 'I have something on the Saturday before Christmas.'

'Well, I was thinking the Friday or the Saturday, the sixteenth or seventeenth, but if Angus is busy on the seventeenth, is everyone OK for the sixteenth?'

'It's fine for me,' said Amanda.

'And me,' said Janice.

'Don't see a problem,' Angus chipped in.

'Great, so now all we have to do is think about venue.'

Gill told them the three venues and the themed nights at each. She asked them to decide among themselves, and to let her know what they preferred by the end of the day, so she could book it.

As Gill sat doing the accounts, she could see the past few months had been good. She would have the full news from her accountant at their meeting in January, but already she had the gist of it, and the news appeared very positive.

Life was more balanced now. She'd even started exercising again and loved it. She and Debbie had found a Zumba class in Maryhill and had been twice already. Gill was determined to get fit and with the party season looming, the sooner the better.

With Christmas around the corner, and realising how stressful a time it could be, Gill had told her staff they could have a couple of long lunch hours to pop into town and do some shopping. Today it was her turn and she left the office, armed with her list, so she could hit the shops; a quick in and out. She needed to go to a specialist camera shop for the x2 converter she was going to buy for Liam. A hamper would do the trick for her mother, whereas anything wrestling related, plus pyjamas, covered her nephews; perfume for her sister-in-law; the list went on and on. She thought she had been pretty methodical about it. She wouldn't get everything today, but half would be a good start.

Ninety minutes later, as she walked back up Buchanan Street, laden down with shopping bags, Gill was full of Christmas spirit, listening to the street artists belting out Christmas carols instead of their usual fare.

Suddenly her legs gave way and she struggled to stay on her feet. About thirty metres in front of her, walking directly towards her, was Anton. She froze. She couldn't move. He hadn't noticed her yet. She had to get out of there. Too late. He glanced up, trying to pick out the shop he was looking for, and found himself staring directly at Gill. Confusion crossed his face and then his features broke out into a broad smile. Quickening his pace, he walked towards her. Gill didn't know what to do, so she turned and fled. Biting back tears, she turned onto St Vincent Street and tried to push past the lunchtime shoppers in an effort to get away.

'Gill,' she heard him call. 'Gill, wait.'

It was no use. He caught up to her. He didn't touch her, but instead stepped in front of her.

'Gill, I'm sorry. There's so much to explain. I barely know where to start.'

Gill was unable to get past him without creating a huge scene, so with her head bowed, she listened to him.

'Gill, there was a reason I couldn't contact you. I need to explain,' but Gill cut him off.

'That's nice, Anton, but I really don't need to hear it. Goodbye.' She pushed past him.

'Wait, Gill, please.' He caught up to her again and extracted a business card from his pocket. 'We have a lot to talk about – I don't want this to be the last time I see you. Please, take my card.' He thrust the card at her.

Realising he wasn't going to go away if she didn't take it, she took it from him, reluctantly, and popped it in her pocket.

'Goodbye, Anton.' She turned and walked quickly through the crowds, tears blurring her vision.

As she stood at the traffic lights, waiting for the green man to come on, she stifled a sob. What a shock! She hadn't been prepared for that. It was bad enough when she thought she would never see him again, but to see him, standing right in front of her; all the emotions had come flooding back, all the disappointment and feelings of rejection.

Trembling, she fished her phone out of her bag and called Debbie. She answered after four rings.

'Debbie, I need to see you urgently. Can you meet me after work?'

Her friend, startled by the tremor in Gill's voice, agreed to meet her at Chez Molinières at six thirty.

Gill wasn't sure how she made it through the rest of the day. When Janice told her that the three of them had decided that the Abba-themed Christmas party would be the most fun, Gill had tried a smile, but feared it came out as more of a grimace. She then asked Janice if she would mind calling to book, and Janice, seeing Gill's ashen face, said, 'Consider it done.'

As Gill was about to leave the office to meet Debbie, her phone rang.

'Hi, it's me. How's your day been?' Liam seemed particularly upbeat.

'So-so,' Gill replied evasively. She couldn't banter with him, not at the moment. She simply wasn't capable of it. Her mind felt overloaded, as if it would explode at any moment due to the pressure building up in it.

'How are you? How was your day?' she asked mechanically. This needed to be a short call. Thankfully she had the excuse of rushing out to meet Debbie, and Liam had called her on the landline.

She listened to him as he told her about his call from his brother in the US, and how he intended coming over for New Year. Liam sounded so excited.

'It's been too long,' he said.

Liam talked a little of their plans for the weekend, and then Gill, having difficulty keeping calm, interrupted him, 'Liam, I'm really sorry, but I'm going to have to run. I'm supposed to be meeting Debbie at Chez Molinières in ten minutes.'

'Oh, no problem. I'll see you tomorrow. Have a nice time.'

Gill dreaded the thought of the next evening. How could she see Liam tomorrow, with this maelstrom of emotions whirling around inside her? Any fool would be able to detect something was wrong, so her boyfriend would definitely guess.

With a heavy heart, she closed the storm doors to the building and set off to meet Debbie.

'A large glass of Pinot Grigio, please,' Gill said to the barman.

Debbie eyed her curiously.

'Gill, you look like shit. What's wrong?' Pausing, her mouth dropped open. 'You're not pregnant, are you?'

Wordlessly, Gill shook her head.

'No, you can't be, or you wouldn't be drinking,' Debbie thought out loud.

Running her hands through her hair, Gill sighed deeply and blurted out, 'I ran into Anton.'

Debbie's eyes widened and she was momentarily speechless. When she recovered, she said, 'Where?'

'In Buchanan Street.'

'What was he doing in Buchanan Street?'

'I don't know, Debbie. I didn't exactly ask him.' An edge of frustration crept into Gill's voice.

Realising how upset Gill was, Debbie didn't take her to task over snapping at her, she simply said, 'Tell me what happened.'

Gill relayed her brief encounter with Anton.

'So, what now?'

'I don't know,' said Gill. 'I feel sick. I can't concentrate. I don't know how I'm going to act normal around Liam tomorrow night. I'm furious,' she said, as tears threatened to fall. 'I thought it was just the shock of seeing him that made me feel like this, but that was five hours ago, and if anything I feel worse now.'

Debbie thought for a moment, then said, 'Why exactly are you upset? Are you upset because you saw him again, after he let you down? Or are you upset because you still have feelings for him?'

Gill debated this for a second, as much as she was able,

and then replied, 'Both, I guess, but I also want to know why. I've always wanted to know why. I thought he just shagged me and left me, once he got what he wanted. And now he turns up and tells me we have stuff to talk about.'

'What are you going to do?'

'What do you think I should do?'

Debbie shook her head, 'Gill, I can't tell you what to do. But you never did get any peace of mind with this. Are you thinking of meeting him, at least to get an explanation?'

Shaking her head and wringing her hands, Gill whispered, 'I don't know. I feel as if I don't know anything any more.'

'OK, well, how will you feel if you never see him again and never get to ask him why?'

Gill shook her head again, as if the concept of rational thought was currently beyond her.

'Do you want to see him again?' Debbie asked gently.

'I don't know,' Gill said. 'I'm so confused. I can't think straight. I keep wondering what he wants to tell me. What does he think he could possibly say that would make me want to listen to him?'

Debbie stayed silent, perhaps intuiting Gill wanted to say something more.

'It's just…he seemed so pleased to see me. The smile on his face, it was genuine. Even though he knew, he must have known, I wouldn't give him a warm welcome.'

'You don't need to make up your mind straightaway. You have his number. Wait and see how you feel over the next few days.'

Nodding, Gill agreed that's what she would do. Unable to eat anything, she ordered coffee and half an hour later, they left.

'Thanks for being there for me, Debbie. I really appreciate it. It has helped talking to you, even if I still don't know what I'm going to do,' Gill said ruefully.

'Don't mention it. Call me if you need anything, or if you just want to chat. I'm always here, OK?'

They hugged and then Gill headed for the bus home, her mind racing.

Next morning, after a fitful night, Gill had more pressing matters to contend with. Overnight, without warning, it had snowed heavily. Buses were unable to run on schedule and cars were abandoned everywhere as drivers struggled to find grip, particularly going uphill. The gritters had been out, but too late, so their efforts were ineffectual. Gill finally made it to work, an hour and a half late, only to find she was the only person in the office. There was a voicemail from Janice, saying she had had to turn back, as the weather was too bad and had caused the motorway to close. Both Amanda and Angus had left messages saying they were on their way in, but would be late.

Gill made a few calls to clients to arrange meetings for the following week, but after being told three times that the people she sought hadn't made it into work, she gave up. She was halfway through answering e-mails when Angus showed up, apologetic. Gill waved away his apology, saying it was hardly his fault and asked if he would like some tea. He looked frozen. The temperature was -10C, unusually cold for the central belt. In December, it often reached -2C, but rarely dipped below -4C. The departure from the norm could be felt and Gill turned the heating up as high as it would go. She only hoped the pipes wouldn't freeze and burst. Amanda arrived soon afterwards, out of breath and blue with cold. After fuelling her with coffee, Gill returned to her office and tried to rid herself of memories of Anton, by burying herself in her work.

It was no use. By lunchtime she had achieved little. Her thoughts kept straying to Anton and why he had seemed so pleased to see her. She kept asking herself the same questions over and over. She was driving herself mad. Before she could change her mind, Gill dug out his card and dialled his number. She hadn't even decided what she was going to say.

He answered on the third ring. 'Gill!' The joy in Anton's voice was clear. 'I'm so happy you called.'

'Anton, I don't know what this is about, but if you want one more chance to talk to me, meet me tomorrow.'

'Of course. Where? When?'

It was too painful to meet anywhere associated with their dates, so after thinking for a minute, Gill said, 'Meet me at the bar inside Central Station at seven o'clock.'

'OK...'

'I have to go.' She hung up, shaking and feeling physically sick. Finally she would find out why he had never called her again. Although angry at him, she also felt a sense of relief. At least she would finally have that oh-so-important closure.

Gill tried too hard that night with Liam. He had definitely noticed something was up. She had never refused intimacy with him, but she found it hard to act naturally around him. She felt as if she was being unfaithful, just by seeing Anton tomorrow.

Thankfully Liam was attending a meeting in London early the next morning, so Gill had the perfect excuse not to stay over. She wished him well on his trip and was relieved by the realisation that Liam wouldn't even be in the same country when she met Anton in Glasgow.

The snow was still a problem the following day and services continued to be disrupted. Gill went as far as to check that Liam's plane had managed to leave Glasgow. Again she felt relief that it had. She also felt guilty at feeling relieved. It wasn't as if she was planning for anything to happen with Anton, she just wanted to hear what he had to say and find out why. Then she could finally cut him out of her life and move on.

The day dragged. Whenever Gill hazarded a glance at the clock on her wall, barely five minutes had passed since the last time she checked. She couldn't settle to anything. She hadn't brought a change of clothes, she was going as she was, in her work clothes, to meet Anton. After all, it wasn't a date – on the contrary.

She turned up late intentionally, arriving at the bar at ten past seven. It was his turn to sweat. He was facing the door. When she came in, he held her gaze for a second then smiled weakly.

He stood up to kiss her hello and Gill held up her hand to stop him. 'Don't. You don't have that right.'

Embarrassed, Anton sat down again. 'What would you like to drink?'

'Sparkling mineral water.'

Gill noticed he had a glass of wine in front of him.

'You wouldn't prefer anything stronger?'

Actually she could have done with a brandy, but she wanted to be conscious of everything that was said, remember every nuance, without alcohol impairing her senses.

She managed to say, 'Water's fine.' Her voice rasped, as

if someone else had spoken.

Anton rose to go to the bar. He was limping. A few moments later he returned and set the glass on the table, then positioned himself opposite her once again. He gazed at her, as if drinking her in. Then he stared at his hands. He appeared to have difficulty starting the conversation, so Gill said, 'Anton, why did you want to see me?'

He took in every detail of her face, noting the angry set of her jaw, the stiffness in her posture, the vulnerability in her eyes, and sighed. Finally he spoke, 'Because I love you.'

Gill jumped as if she had been shot, then just as suddenly her body sagged. Could he be any crueller? He had discarded her and now here he was playing mind games.

'You have a funny way of showing it,' she hissed at him. 'I can't do this. Do you know why I'm here? Do you?' She was aware that she had raised her voice, but was powerless to stop herself. Anton tried to shush her, but that only served to incite her further. 'I'm here,' Gill spat, 'because I want to know why. That's all. Why?'

Gill hadn't realised she had stood up and was towering over him, until he guided her gently back into her seat.

'Gill, it's a long story.'

'Well, much as I'd like to use the old cliché, "I have all the time in the world", quite frankly I'm limiting how much more of my time I'm going to let you waste,' Gill seethed.

'OK. Here's the condensed version. I fell in love with you, we made love, I went to Minsk, had a road accident two days after I arrived, and got out of hospital last week.' Anton drew breath, looked at Gill to ensure she had taken in what he had said, and then took a sip of his wine.

Gill stared at him. She couldn't formulate any words.

Finally she managed, 'If this is your idea of a joke…?'

'No joke,' Anton interrupted her. 'If you don't believe it, I can get you proof: photos, documents, coverage in the local press.'

Gill didn't know what to say. She stared at the table, trying to work out what this meant. Anton hadn't intentionally abandoned her? Anton loved her? This had all been a twist of Fate?

Alarmed by a sharp sound, Gill started, then realised the noise was a hysterical half laugh, half sob which had burst from her throat.

Dozens of questions and scenarios flitted through her mind. Finally she simply said, 'What happened?'

'I was driving from the office back to my hotel, in very heavy rain, when the driver of a car coming from the opposite direction apparently lost control of the wheel, skidded and hit me head-on. He died. I survived, just. I was on the critical list to start with. They managed to stabilise me eventually, but my recovery has been long.'

'So what injuries did you have?'

'My pelvis was crushed, I needed surgery for my back, my leg was fractured and in plaster, and I had several cracked ribs. I suppose I was a bit like a broken rag doll,' he said sadly.

'But couldn't you have called me or e-mailed me?' The words were out before Gill could stop them. Of course he had more important things on his mind, like getting well. 'I mean, when you got back. What would have happened if I hadn't seen you that day in Buchanan Street?'

'I didn't think I could e-mail you after all this time. I wanted to see you. I looked up your agency. It wasn't so difficult to find you. Then on Monday I came to your office, but just as I was crossing the road and working out what to say to you, you came out, with a man. You looked–' it seemed to pain him to say this '–as if you were a couple.'

Liam.

The indirect question hung in the air unanswered.

He saw me with Liam and went away. Gill knew it was true. Monday was the only time Liam had come to her office. Her thoughts whirled around inside her head like clothes in a washing machine.

Suddenly she had problems breathing. Had the shock induced a panic attack? Anton, concerned, escorted her outside to get some fresh air, which she gulped in gratefully.

After a few minutes and after ascertaining she was OK, Anton gestured for them to go back inside and continue their conversation. Gill turned to Anton and tears coursed down her face. 'I can't. I wish things were different and I really wish you hadn't had that accident, but I thought you had abandoned me. I thought you didn't care. I-I-I'm with someone else now and I'm happy.'

Gill noticed the pain cross Anton's face, the sudden intake of breath, and the glance away from her to hide his feelings. When he turned back to her, he had regained his composure.

'Gill, we have been very unlucky. I love you, I probably always will, but if you love this man and he makes you happy, then I have to accept that is what's best for you. Because I love you and no matter how much I wish it were different, I wish you all the best.' He bent down and kissed her on the cheek and whispered, 'You can't know how much I wish things had been different. If you ever need me,

I will be there. You have my number.' He turned and walked away from her.

Gill stood for a few minutes, trying to gulp air back into her lungs. She had done it. She knew the reasons. She had closure, so why didn't she feel happy?

The next few weeks were a tortured time for Gill. Her thoughts strayed often to Anton and the conversation which had taken place with him. She remembered his limp; she didn't doubt the genuineness of his road accident, nor his reasons for not contacting her. She believed that he thought he loved her. It was all so unsettling. The cosy rapport she had enjoyed with Liam was shattered – the spectre of Anton coming between them.

When she made love to Liam, Anton and the night they had spent together came unbidden into her mind, and left her feeling guilty. Not even the Christmas party and having to dress up in an Abba costume – white satin blouse with a huge collar and puff sleeves, and spangly, flared bell-bottoms – lifted her spirits. Fortunately her staff had a good time and Gill put on as good an act as she could. She was glad that they had booked places at an event attended by lots of other companies. It made it easier for her to blend into the background, especially with the others constantly up on the dance floor, strutting their stuff to 'Waterloo' and 'Mamma Mia'.

Gill hadn't heard from Anton since that night. She didn't expect to. She wondered when she would be able to get him out of her head. It was so unfair. She had seen the hurt in his eyes when she told him she thought he had abandoned her. He had told her he loved her. That night and every night since, she had cried at the injustice of it all.

Christmas Eve rolled around. Gill was glad to be going to her brother's on Christmas Day. At least she wouldn't have to be alone with her thoughts then, or try to block them out as she tried to do when with Liam.

Gill felt nervous around Liam that evening, even more than usual since the meeting with Anton. There was something in the air. She couldn't quite identify it, but there was definitely an undercurrent. Did Liam suspect something? He was very jumpy.

They ate the special dinner which Liam had prepared: a traditional Italian Christmas Eve menu, from one of his many cookbooks. Apparently it was traditional in Southern Italy to have a fish-based banquet. He toned down the size of the banquet, but he had outdone himself on the content. Gill didn't like to tell him she didn't feel like eating a thing, but she ate as much as she could – a lot less than usual. The stuffed lobster was exquisite and Gill felt she didn't do the seafood risotto justice. It upset her that Liam had gone to so much trouble and she couldn't enjoy it properly. When he suggested dessert, she groaned and said she was too full.

'Maybe later then,' he said. He cleared away the plates, whilst Gill found them a film to watch. Gill wondered why the programmers put all the good films on over two weeks of the year, whilst the rest of the time they were awful.

When Liam entered the room, Gill smiled at him expectantly. She thought he was on the verge of saying something. He bent down in front of her and held out a small box. Only then did Gill realise he was down on bended knee. Shock, horror, disbelief and incredulity coursed through her.

This can't be happening.

A smiling Liam looked up at Gill from under his floppy fringe and opening the ring box said, 'Gill, will you marry me?'

Chapter Forty-six

Christmas and beyond

When Gill arrived at her brother's late on Christmas morning, her nephews barrelled into her.

'Aunt Gill, Aunt Gill, Santa's been. Look, I got a bike,' said George.

'I got a bike, too, and a wrestling ring, and a garage.' Harry pulled his aunt into the usually tidy living room, which now resembled a war zone.

'They're a bit hyper,' said Sarah. 'Where's Liam?'

'He's not coming. I'll tell you later.'

Christopher and Sarah exchanged a look, with Christopher throwing his wife a warning glance not to pry.

Her young nephews had soon roped Gill into playing at cars with them then gave her a blow-by-blow account of what was happening in the wrestling world, by way of a demonstration of who was the meanest wrestler. Interestingly, the boys could rattle off an entire biography of the wrestlers, including the fact that one was from Ayrshire and another hailed from Florida.

'Did you see John Cena when you went to Florida, Aunt Gill?'

Sarah rolled her eyes and handed Gill a glass of pink champagne.

'No, George, I didn't see him, but I don't know him, and Florida is a big place.' Gill sat on the arm of the sofa as her nephews continued to rat-a-tat questions and statements at her.

Gill surveyed all the presents they had received. Every so often she would hear her phone vibrating. She had put it on vibrate so it wouldn't disturb anyone, but she would know if it rang. It had been vibrating non-stop. She knew she'd have to talk to Liam sooner or later, but right now she couldn't. She tried to focus on what her nephews were telling her, but her mind kept shifting back to the night before, when Liam had asked her to marry him. She hadn't been able to answer him. She appeared to have lost all power of speech. Liam had given an uneasy laugh and said, 'Aren't you going to say anything? You're making me nervous.'

Finally she had uttered the two words that would change everything.

Christmas dinner was wonderful. She would have expected nothing less from Sarah. Christopher had taken her aside earlier to ask her why Liam wasn't with her and if she was OK, but she had waved him away and said, 'Once the kids are in bed. It's Christmas Day. Let's focus on them.'

So they had and they watched *Toy Story* on TV, although Gill was so distracted she couldn't have told you which *Toy Story*.

Gill was careful not to drink much, as she didn't want to cry and she wanted to be compos mentis enough to explain to Christopher and Sarah what had happened.

After dinner, she excused herself, went upstairs, and checked her phone. Forty-two missed calls. Twenty-two messages. Fifteen text messages. With a sinking heart, Gill went back downstairs and helped Sarah clear up. She'd read the texts and listen to the messages later, once she'd told Christopher and Sarah.

With the boys in bed, each settled with their favourite new toy, Sarah brought the three adults Irish coffees.

'I think we could use this. What a day! But I think the boys enjoyed it,' she said, offering a glass to Gill.

'Yes, well they certainly have enough toys and energy. I wish I'd seen them open their presents, though.'

'Gill, what's going on?' Christopher cut through the small talk.

Taking a deep breath, Gill said, 'Liam asked me to marry him.'

'Whaaat?' shrieked Sarah. 'I can't believe you haven't told us until now, you bitch!' She leapt up off the sofa to hug Gill, but her husband pulled her back.

'So why isn't he here with you?' Christopher, ever-logical, asked.

Playing with the zipper of her cardigan, Gill smiled sadly and said, 'I said no.'

Sarah's eyes almost popped out of her head. 'No? But why? You two are great together!'

'I know it's a bit soon to be talking about getting engaged, but I agree with Sarah. You two are great together. I haven't seen you this happy in ages,' Christopher said, then awaited his sister's response expectantly.

Gill sighed and ran her fingers through her hair, pulling at it a little, as she was wont to do when nervous.

'I ran into Anton,' she whispered.

'Anton!' Liam's tone was incredulous. 'After what he did?'

As Gill brought them up to speed, Sarah's eyes widened

in horror, whilst Christopher appeared thoughtful.

'So basically, Anton didn't do anything wrong,' said Christopher slowly.

'It seems not.'

'And now you're torn between how you feel about Anton and how you feel about Liam?'

'It's a bit more than that,' Gill admitted. 'As soon as I saw that Liam was about to propose, I felt horrified, not elated. I realised that whilst I was happy with him, that was in the knowledge that things could never be between Anton and me. And now everything's changed.'

'What did you say to Liam?' Christopher asked.

Remembering, Gill cringed. She wasn't exactly proud of how she had handled it.

'I told him I couldn't marry him. He looked shocked, then he said, "You're kidding, right?" but when I shook my head and started to cry, he realised I was serious. I tried to explain, but what could I say? He wouldn't let me comfort him, so eventually I said. "I think I should go. I'll call you tomorrow."'

'And have you called him today?' Sarah asked.

Gill shook her head. 'Not yet. I thought I would talk to you two first then return his many calls.'

'He's been calling you?' Christopher asked.

Gill delved in her bag and withdrew her mobile. When Christopher saw the number of missed calls and messages, he said, 'Shit!'

'So what are you going to do?' Sarah pressed her.

'I don't know. All I know is that I can't be with Liam when I still have feelings for Anton. I certainly can't marry him.'

'No, you're right. That wouldn't be fair, on anyone,'

replied Christopher as he got up to fetch them refills.

'What a mess!' Gill said.

'You don't need to decide right away,' Sarah advised her. 'Give yourself a few days.'

'That's what Debbie said, and that was before Liam proposed.'

They fell silent until Christopher returned with the alcohol-laced coffees.

'I'm going to take mine up to my room, if that's OK. I need to listen to Liam's messages and return his call.'

'*Good luck,*' mouthed Sarah as Gill closed the living room door.

Gill listened to and read the various messages:

Gill, I don't understand. What just happened? Please call me.

Gill, I love you, please don't do this. A tear rolled down her cheek.

Please don't throw away everything we have.

We don't have to get married. Things can just stay the way they were.

I didn't mean to frighten you off. I should have suggested living together first.

Gill, I'm at Michael and Petra's, please call me.

Say hi to your family. Wish them Merry Christmas for me, said without a trace of sarcasm, as he tried to remain upbeat. Her heart went out to him.

Don't you love me? I thought we felt the same way about each other.

What went wrong? We always have such a good time together.

The messages continued in the same vein. Mentally preparing herself, Gill dialled Liam's number.

'Gill!' The relief in his voice was palpable. 'Thanks for calling. Are you all right?'

'I'm fine. How are you?'

'I've been better – glad to hear from you.'

Gill didn't know what to say next. After a brief pause, she said, 'Can you meet me tomorrow? Kelvingrove Park, three o'clock.'

Liam jumped at this lifeline.

'I'll see you there, outside the art galleries?'

'Yes, see you then, Liam.'

This had to be done in person. It would be hard, but it was the only way.

Sarah and Christopher said goodbye to Gill at one thirty on Boxing Day, and wished her luck. They had given her strict instructions to call after her meeting with Liam. Gill hadn't even told any of her friends yet, not even about Liam's proposal. She hadn't wanted her screwed-up life to mar their happiness at Christmas.

She arrived at Kelvingrove Park early, so she took the opportunity to call Debbie. After wishing each other a Merry Christmas and listening to Debbie's news, Gill told her of the events of the past few days.

Debbie whistled. 'Gill, it's like a bad Latin American soap opera.'

'As I said to Lisa recently, no, this is just my shit life.'

'Liam will be devastated, but he *will* get over it.'

'I know. I'm just not looking forward to telling him. But I owe it to him, to tell him face to face. Do you think I'm doing the right thing by telling him why?'

Debbie mulled this over for a bit then said, 'Yes, I think so. It's not as if you've met someone since you started going out, or betrayed him with an ex. The circumstances here aren't exactly normal.'

You can say that again, thought Gill.

'OK, I'm going to go. I need time to think before I see him.'

'Good luck.'

Gill wandered through the park, enjoying the splendid isolation, as it gave her time to organise her thoughts. At five to three, she headed back to the art galleries. Liam was already standing outside, a hopeful look on his face. His eyes lit up as Gill approached and he moved towards her, ready to embrace her.

'Don't, Liam, please. This is hard enough.'

Stung, he recoiled and dug his hands in his pockets.

'Why don't we go for a walk so I can explain?'

As they walked through the park, Gill told Liam everything that had happened since that afternoon when she had bumped into Anton on Buchanan Street. She told him how she had felt about him before he went to Minsk and how, since seeing him again, her feelings had returned. As she held Liam's hands in hers and looked him in the eye, she told him how she did care deeply for him and hated that she was hurting him, but that she couldn't marry him, or even be with him any more, when she had such strong feelings for someone else.

Liam struggled to take it all in. It was clear he was only just holding it together. He inhaled deeply a few times, turned away and rubbed his face with one of his gloves.

'Do you need more time, is that it? More time to know what you want?'

Sadly Gill shook her head. 'Liam, when you asked me

to marry you, I should have been deliriously happy, but I wasn't. Who knows, if Anton hadn't reappeared, maybe things would have been different – although it *was* a bit soon to ask.'

'Are you going to start seeing each other again?'

'I don't know. I need time to get my head round things. All I know is I can't be with a lovely man who asks me to marry him, when I don't feel ecstatic that he has asked me.'

Reluctantly Liam said, 'I think I understand. I think. Gill, I love you. I wish I'd told you earlier. I wish I'd asked you to marry me earlier, but…' As if thinking out loud, he said, 'Maybe you would have just left me later.'

Gill rubbed his arm and said, 'Liam, I need you to know, I loved the time we spent together and I really never intended to hurt you, and it hurts me so much that I have to.'

Liam nodded weakly in comprehension.

She hugged him then, tears flowing openly down her face. She sobbed, 'I really want you to be happy. I hope you find someone who deserves you and who can love you as much as you love her.'

They clung to each other for a few moments, crying unashamedly. Finally, Gill broke away and said, 'Goodbye, Liam.' She turned and walked out of the park, digging in her coat pockets for a handkerchief, and hiccupping as she tried to stem another sob.

Apart from phone calls to Debbie and the girls, and to her brother, Gill lay low for the next few days. She did oodles of housework and watched crap TV to take her mind of things. She had barely left the house since Boxing Day, only venturing out to buy bread and milk. Her friends were worried about her, but she assured them she was fine; she just needed time to herself. She watched the entire period drama box set she'd been given for Christmas in two days.

On the thirtieth, Gill awoke to the birds singing. It was a brighter day. Wrapping up well, she walked through Queens Park. By the time she returned home, she had come to a decision. She knew what she was going to do.

'Hello?'

'Anton, it's Gill.'

'Gill, how are you? Merry Christmas.'

'Merry Christmas. I'm well. Anton, the reason I'm calling is because I'd like to meet you, tomorrow. I'll come through to Stirling. Can you meet me at the university, main entrance?'

'Yes, of course. At what time?'

'One o'clock.'

'I'll be waiting.'

'See you then.'

The next twenty-four hours passed as if in slow motion but finally the last day of the year arrived.

Gill parked her car and decided to take advantage of the free time and go for a walk. She'd never been to Stirling University before and was struck by the beautiful scenery and the backdrop of the Wallace Monument which towered above it. By the time she reached the main gate, it was five past one. At first she didn't see Anton, but then as she neared the gate, she saw him standing inside it, staring at the university buildings.

'Anton,' she said shyly.

'Gill.' He bent down and kissed her on both cheeks.

That she had let him do that, was a step in the right direction, she thought.

Now that she was here, she didn't know what to say. How to process all the thoughts that were tumbling through her mind and arrange them in a coherent fashion, so that someone else, he, Anton, could understand?

The university was closed, because it was outside term time, although some companies still worked between Christmas and New Year. But today was Saturday and it seemed no one was around.

Gill half-wished she had arranged to meet Anton in a café or a pub, somewhere where she would have something to do with her hands, somewhere where they would be facing each other and this would be easier.

They walked into the campus and after a short exchange of pleasantries, Gill blurted out, 'I'm no longer with my boyfriend.'

Anton looked taken aback, then hopeful. 'Why?' he asked.

Thinking carefully what to say next, Gill finally said, 'Because I realised that, whilst I care about him a lot, I love someone else.'

Assuming, correctly, that she was referring to him, Anton took her face in his hands and said, 'Gill, I will never let you down. I love you,' he said, then kissed her. With that kiss, all the worry about whether or not she was making the right decision evaporated, and when they drew apart, Gill smiled at him and said, 'I love you, too.'

They embraced again and when they pulled apart, Gill said, 'Here's to Caroline Morgan and Happy Ever After dating agency.'

'No,' Anton said, 'Here's to *our* happy ever after.'

Note From the Author

Did you get your FREE short stories yet?

TWO UNPUBLISHED EXCLUSIVE SHORT STORIES.

Interacting with my readers is one of the most fun parts of being a writer. I'll be sending out a monthly newsletter with new release information, competitions, special offers and basically a bit about what I've been up to, writing and otherwise.

You can get the previously unseen short stories, *Mixed Messages* and *Time Is of the Essence*, FREE when you sign up to my mailing list at www.susanbuchananauthor.com

Did you enjoy *The Dating Game*?

I'd really appreciate if you could leave a review on Amazon. It doesn't need to be much, just a couple of lines. I love reading customer reviews. Seeing what readers think of my books spurs me on to write more. Sometimes I've even written more about characters or created a series because of reader comments. Plus, reviews are SO important to authors. They help raise the profile of the author and make it more likely that the book will be visible on Amazon to more readers. Every author wants their book to be read by more people, and I am no exception! If you're happy to leave a review, please head over to Amazon.

Other books by Susan Buchanan

Have you read them all?

Sign of the Times

Sagittarius – Travel writer Holly heads to Tuscany to research her next book, but when she meets Dario, she knows she's in trouble. Can she resist temptation? And what do her mixed feelings mean for her future with her fiancé?

Gemini – Player Lucy likes to keep things interesting and has no qualms about being unfaithful to her long-term boyfriend. A cardiology conference to Switzerland changes Lucy, perhaps forever. Has she met her match, and is this feeling love?

Holly is the one who links the twelve signs. Are you ready to meet them all?

A tale of love, family, friendship and the lengths we go to in pursuit of our dreams.

The Christmas Spirit

Natalie Hope takes over the reins of the Sugar and Spice bakery and café with the intention of injecting some Christmas spirit. Something her regulars badly need.

Newly dumped Rebecca is stuck in a job with no prospects, has lost her home and is struggling to see a way forward.

Pensioner Stanley is dreading his first Christmas alone

without his beloved wife, who passed away earlier this year. How will he ever feel whole again?

Graduate Jacob is still out of work despite making hundreds of applications. Will he be forced to go against his instincts and ask his unsympathetic parents for help?

Spiky workaholic Meredith hates the jollity of family gatherings and would rather stay home with a box set and a posh ready meal. Will she finally realise what's important in life?

Natalie sprinkles a little magic to try to spread some festive cheer and restore Christmas spirit, but will she succeed?

Return of the Christmas Spirit

Christmas is just around the corner when the enigmatic Star begins working at Butterburn library, but not everyone is embracing the spirit of the season.

Arianna is anxious about her mock exams. With her father living abroad and her mother working three jobs to keep them afloat, she doesn't have much support at home.

The bank is threatening to repossess Evan's house, and he has no idea how he will get through Christmas with two children who are used to getting everything they want.

After 23 years of marriage, Patricia's husband announces he's moving out of the family home, and moving in with his secretary. Patricia puts a brave face on things, but inside she's devastated and lost.

Stressed-out Daniel is doing the work of three people in his sales job, plus looking after his kids and his sick wife. Pulled in too many different directions, he hasn't even had a chance to think about Christmas.

Can Star, the library's Good Samaritan, help set them

on the path to happiness this Christmas?

Just One Day – Winter

'Perfect for fans of *Why Mummy Drinks.*'

Thirty-eight-year-old Louisa has a loving husband, three perfect kids, a faithful dog, a supportive family and a gorgeous house near Glasgow. What more could she want?

TIME.

Louisa would like, just once, to get to the end of her never-ending to-do list. Every time she manages to tick something off, another three items pile on.

Husband Ronnie doesn't understand the magnitude of the problem and Louisa feels unappreciated and resentful. Will she be able to keep all the balls spinning but still find some valuable 'me time'?

A chance encounter puts Louisa's whole world in jeopardy. Will she stick with what she knows or leap into the unknown? And will she ever get to the end of her to-do list?

A feel-good, heart-warming story of family and friendship. Perfect for fans of Mhairi McFarlane and Fiona Gibson.

Coming 17 May 2022 – pre-order available now

Just One Day – Spring *(Book 2 in the Just One Day series)*

Mum-of-three Louisa thought she only had her never-ending to-do list to worry about, but the arrival of a ghost from the recent past puts her in an untenable position. Can she navigate the difficult situation she's in without their friendship becoming common knowledge or will it cause long-term damage to her marriage?

When her friend Nicky's new boyfriend becomes best

buddies with her husband, Louisa is delighted, until he begins to suspect there's more to her relationship with the new sous-chef than meets the eye.

Can Nicky convince her boyfriend that all is above aboard or does Louisa have to talk herself out of a jam?

A new addition to the family undoes the recent gains she has made in ticking things off her to-do list and finding balance in her life. With tensions running high between Louisa and her husband, will she manage to keep her family on track whilst her life spirals out of control?

Printed in Great Britain
by Amazon